The Things We Lose in the Dark

A novel

Sayword B. Eller

Published by At Fault Publishing, a publishing imprint for author Sayword B. Eller.

Paperback ISBN: 979-8-218-48072-1

Cover created using Canva. No AI images were used.

Interior formatting by Rippling Effects www.ripplingeffects.ca

For the survivors. You are not alone.

For April.

And for Shane. Je t'aime.

CONTENT WARNING

Child sexual abuse
Attempted suicide
Suicidal ideation
Drug and alcohol abuse
Domestic violence
Terminal illness

If you, or someone you love, has been a victim or needs assistance, help is out there.

Sexual abuse/assault helpline: 800.656.HOPE
Domestic violence helpline: 800.799.7233
Suicide and crisis lifeline: 988

ONE

I know three things for sure: life is hard, it gets harder, and people will take what they want whether you agree to it or not. This knowledge wasn't inherent. I wasn't born knowing these things. I learned them in the dark, in soft firelight, in the backs of cars, and in alleys and gas station bathrooms. If you let them take what they want things will be better for you in that moment. No one gives a shit how they'll be in five years, or ten. No one gives a shit about you at all. Sometimes the people who take the most are the ones you should be able to trust not to take anything at all.

That's how I ended up here, I think. In this room with beige walls and warped blinds. One night after years of bad ones I chose to take the easy way out. Just like everything else, I got that wrong too. Now I'm forced to talk to a stranger about what led me here. Encouraged to tell her the deepest darkest things I've never told anyone. *I can't help you if you don't want to be helped.* How often have I heard that in my life? It's hard to explain exactly how I'm plagued by my past. Something unwanted turned into something desired. Something harmful. Something wrong. But it didn't feel wrong, not in the end. How can I be expected to tell this woman what's wrong with me when I'm all jumbled and disjointed?

I just want the voices to stop, his voice. Some days they're louder than others, rising from a whisper to a shout. Reminding me that I like it when people treat me badly. I like it when they make me do things that most women wouldn't do. Humiliation fuels me, makes my blood pump and my insides empty. The pain is my fault because I seek it out, I attract it. I desire it. Other days the words are soft, audible only when the room grows silent. Those quiet words tell me exactly who I am. They know the very core of me and they're not afraid to use the secrets I keep as ammunition for more pain. That's why I did it. I just needed a little peace. Tired of rallying against the husky voice in the darkness demanding that I *just be a good girl*. After another failed relationship, another lackluster exit from my life, the last thing I wanted to hear was my past whispering to me. But how do I tell the shrink that? How do I tell my mother, whose arms wrapped so tight around me that I almost couldn't breathe? How do I tell them I swallowed a bottle of pills for a little peace and quiet without sounding like a fucking lunatic?

She came to the hospital twice, my mother. The sight of her eyes, red-rimmed and raw, full of questions and worry when I finally came back to this godforsaken world was enough to have me undone, make me wish I could have just one more go at getting the suicide thing right. But even I wouldn't have taken another shot at it. Not and risk that face again, fear and regret, and disappointment. That stupid look of sadness that made me want to claw her eyes out. How dare she feel sorry for me. *Me.* She made this mess. Helped anyway.

It crossed my mind when she came back this time that I might look like a deer in headlights. Maybe it's because the years of pills I've swallowed have finally evacuated my system and this godforsaken place is alcohol-free. Not that I enjoy the taste of it much, but even the burn of whiskey tearing its way down the back of the throat is helpful in a pinch.

Oh, but I must have been a sight; frozen, eyes rounded, bracing for impact. She didn't speak, didn't need to, but she did pull me into that crushing embrace that said more than words ever could and then led me to the car. It was the exact opposite of what was expected. The last time we saw one another—before I landed myself in this nifty resort for the unsound—there was a symphony of screams, mine and hers; her telling me she couldn't let me ruin my life and me telling her, *"It's my life, I'll do what the hell I want with it."*

I'm afraid to leave here now. Especially with her. She's been surprising in every way since her arrival—no outward judging, no lectures, nothing—I still wish Hattie had been able to come and get me. Sisters don't judge. Despite her good showing, I know my mom is. It's obvious in her posture; the puffed-out chest, her superior head angle, and the swagger in which she walks. Even the way she loaded my bags into the car was haughty. Meanwhile, I'm doing my best to keep from screaming at her in front of the staff. It was obvious then, just as it's obvious now that she's patting herself on the back for knowing how things would work out. She judges hard and she'll let it all out in no time, of that, I am sure. It's in her DNA.

Upon waking my only desire was to be released from this place, to be away from the watchful eyes of staff, and to get as far from the therapist as possible, but now that my mother has arrived and the release papers have been signed, I can't bring myself to move. What if I fuck this up again? *Take it one day at a time,* the doctor said. *That's all any of us can do.* She'd better be right.

———

"WANT SOME LUNCH?" My mother asks, shattering the silence that's filled the car for the better part of two hours.

I could answer her, but what's the point? I'm not hungry. I'm desperate. Now that the numbness of the initial shock has worn off, the realization that I failed at something as simple as taking my own life, I just want to escape this damn uncomfortable situation. What I wouldn't give for one of those perfect little pills that will mellow her voice and lull me to a place where she can't reach me. How do you say *I just want something to take the edge off of your presence* to your mother?

Not waiting for my response, she says, "Well I'm going to grab something," and pulls the car into the parking lot of a clown-happy burger joint that seems only vaguely familiar. At the drive-thru, she orders a combo, two drinks, and an apple turnover. I know the pie is for me. They've always been my favorite. It's impressive that she remembers.

She parks on the far side of the lot and unwraps her burger, "You sure you don't want something?" She asks, burger poised to take a bite. That's the southern part of her. People often get us wrong, thinking that we're all genuinely concerned about the well-being of others. I'm sure there are those truly interested in the feelings of others but most of us just want to offer so that we can't be made to look like the bad guys.

I shift again, turning away from her to look out the window. Outside, birds I can't identify hop from one tree to another in the line of Carolina Pines standing like sentinels along the railroad tracks that lead away from here. I wonder if they're as hot as I am, the birds. Do they feel things the way we do? Summer in the South sucks, both figuratively and literally. After her divorce, my mother considered moving up north to be closer to her sister. At the time I secretly hoped she would and that she would take me and Hattie far away from the soupy air and devil men of the south. But she didn't. I turn to observe her, disgust rolling over in my gut, churning like the old cement truck my father's father used to drive.

It's her fault. All of it.

I don't know why I'm still so angry with her. The therapist told me every action my mother took was for me. But it wasn't. Didn't she do it out of fear? I liked it. He told me I liked it. She had no right sticking her nose into my business. My relationship.

"What?" my mother asks, the remains of her burger poised for another bite.

I blink. It's odd how you don't always realize when you've checked out.

"You're staring at me." She brings her other hand to her chin. "Do I have something on my face?"

It would be easy to unload on her right now. Maybe then the anger would stop eating at me.

"Gracie, what is it?"

I hate her. Want to. The therapist says my anger is misplaced, that I'm loading it all on the one person who's tried to help me, who's been content playing the part of my punching bag. The therapist is my mother's biggest cheerleader.

When I turn my head away, she resumes pecking at the tasty burger. I know it's tasty because I can smell it. Hell, I can almost *taste* it. The smell is pressing in on me, the sound of her chewing gnawing at me.

I grab the door handle. "I need to go to the bathroom."

She puts her hand on my arm, eyes ablaze with panic. "Can't you wait?"

"No, I can't. We've still got an hour and I'm about to piss myself." She recoils, and satisfaction unfurls in me like a spring bloom.

"At least let me go with you," she says, packing the burger away.

"I can go on my own."

"But the doctor said you shouldn't be alone for too—"

"I don't need a fucking babysitter." That was a low blow. Even for me. Taking a deep breath I add, "Just finish your sandwich. I'll be right back."

The gravel is hard beneath the thin soles of my flip-flops, pointy edges poking into the foam far enough now and then to hurt. I don't mind the pain or the missteps. My whole life has been a wrong turn up to this point. Concentrating on the rocks, the sound of the gravel beneath my feet, and watching my step takes my mind away from here. From her.

A couple of weeks ago I thought my life was over. Another failed relationship, another man telling me that I'm too fucked up to love, me certain I couldn't take the pain anymore. How does one go from being the center of someone's desire and love to being something they can easily discard? How can they live their lives without the one thing they've said over and over they can't live without? That's how it was at the beginning of my first relationship with a man. It was wrong and I knew it in my bones, felt it every time he touched me, but he always said he couldn't make it without me in his life. I believed him. What little girl doesn't want to feel that important to someone?

Inside the confines of the brown and yellow bathroom, I find a mother and daughter washing up. The little girl, eleven or twelve, has her big doe eyes fixed on me, following my journey from the door to the sink bank. I fill my hands with cool water from the roaring tap, aware their eyes are still on me. I haven't even looked into the mirror yet, but I know I must look like hell. The water is cool against my cheeks that are burning from both the heat and the intense scrutiny of their stares. Apparently, neither of them has been taught not to stare.

I smile at the image of the little girl with bright blue eyes. "Sure is hot, ain't it?"

"Sure is," the mom says. Her tone my warning.

She's pretty; long brown hair piled in a loose bun on her head, bright blue eyes, and a heart-shaped mouth. Her yellow romper and gladiator sandals suit her golden skin and protective stance. My inadequacies begin whispering; hushed manic noises that fill my cranium, their pace and tone building into a howl before my legs begin to work again.

I smile and nod, averting my eyes from the fierce eyes of the mama bear. "Y'all have a good day," I say and rush to the closest stall.

There's no need to look back, I know their eyes are still on me.

I'm the story she'll use with the girl on those particularly bad days. *"Do you want to end up like that?"* I'm a cautionary tale for the ages.

It's no surprise to find my mother leaning against the sink when I emerge from the stall. I heard her come in. A ninja she is not. She's looking at me, her pity and guilt on full display. This is why I didn't want to call her, why she was the very last person on my in-case-of-emergency list. I don't need her judgments and I damn sure don't need her pity. She opens her mouth to speak, but I rush to the counter and turn the water on. The powerful stream distracts her.

Looking into the mirror, I jerk my head toward the stalls. "You'd better go too. You know how small your bladder is."

She nods and I can see her pack the words away for now. "Will you wait on me?"

I grab the door handle. "I don't want to listen to you pee. I'll be in the car." I'm an asshole. You don't have to think it, I already know I am. But I can't stop it. I can't swallow my anger. I want to spit it at her and watch her melt.

The mom and daughter are at the counter when I emerge from the bathroom, the gladiator queen placing their order. The girl's big eyes are on me again, their depths filled with terror but also—and I may be imagining this—intrigue. *Oh the things I could teach you, kid.* I wink at her and keep walking.

Carolina is boiling. I really think that. I guess that's why I ran away. After my relationship, as it were, crumbled and the proverbial cat was out of the bag. There was no other way for it to go, I suppose. The second I knocked on his door, the moment I threatened to pound the face of his new girlfriend into the pavement, the instant the neighbors called the police it was all over. Sixteen years old and sobbing on the doorstep of my uncle, what else was my mother to think when she showed up? After that, I felt a little too much like a chicken in a pot of boiling water, especially after the termination and talking to the police. If I had to trace it, and the therapist says I should, I guess that was the moment I started hating my mom. After all, if she hadn't been so goddamn smart everything would've been fine. After all that, I couldn't wait to split and that's just what I did on graduation night.

That's life, I guess. Fuck it.

Mom left the car unlocked, not surprising. After scanning the back seat (old habits), I open the door and dig the turnover from the bag, then lean against the outside of the car and begin to devour it. Maybe I can finish it before she comes back. No such luck. I'm still stuffing my face when she joins me, a pleased look on her face. Pleased she was right. It's always been pretty important to her to be right.

With my mouth full, because I know she hates that, I say, "What?"

She shakes her head. "Nothing. You ready to get back on the road?"

"In a minute."

She doesn't argue with me. Another shock. Without another word, she gets back into the car and peels open the crumpled bag, rummaging through to extract the remains of the burger. I keep my eyes fixed on this landscape. I've been here before. Of course, I remember now that I've been staring at its facade for the better part of ten minutes. It was after I was discarded. After I was told, at sixteen, I was too old. I might've handled it better if he'd told me he just wasn't that into me anymore. Or if he'd been honest, like Barry.

That's the memory the old brown and yellow building invokes. Me in the bed of a truck with Barry Overman on top of me grunting and panting. He called me Gracie. Everyone called me Gracie then. I guess that's what happens when you grow up with a name like Zedwynne. You prefer for people to call you by your middle name. After dating, if that's what you call humping in the back of his truck in various locations, for a few weeks Barry broke up with me right here at this place. Probably not far from this parking spot.

Rolling off of me, he huffed and puffed, and finally said, *"I don't think we should hang out anymore."*

Naive, I turned to face him and asked, *"Why?"*

His face was empty, his eyes dull. He shrugged. *"You're no fun."*

I laughed, but the sound caught in my throat. *"What?"*

"When we fuck, all you do is lay there. If I wanted to bang a board, I'd cut a hole in my wall."

If a man were to say that to me now, I would prove to him I am not a terrible lay, but that night I was stunned and silent. For years all I had to do was lay there and now it turns out I was doing it wrong. My teenage self was confused. *I'm supposed to do stuff?* I wasn't upset with Barry, though. Never be upset with them. Especially not when they give helpful insight as to how I'd lost my longtime lover. I rode in the back when he drove me home, bracing myself against the chill of early fall. How could I sit beside him in the confines of his truck cab after such a disclosure?

"Gracie, are you ready?" My mother asks, breaking into my thoughts. Always intruding. Tossing the remnants of my pie onto the ground, a feast for hard-working ants, I climb into the car and buckle up.

"It's Zed."

I can feel her looking at me. "Pardon?"

"Call me Zed. Not Gracie."

"Oh." She gets the car back out on the highway. "That'll take some getting used to."

"Well, I haven't gone by Gracie for years."

"I might know that if you came home to stay now and again." Her tone is non-confrontational. She's just stating a fact. Unlike some truths she puts out there this one is accurate. I don't come home unless I have to.

"I've been home. I was at your wedding."

Laughter sputters from her. Little puffs that remind me of the Tommygun sound in old movies. Ratta, tat, tat. "Six years ago." She straightens. "You didn't even come to your sister's wedding."

"I couldn't."

She nods. "I know."

She doesn't know anything. Never does. Just says she's aware so everyone will believe she's some fountain of knowledge. I'm sure if she knew the reason I couldn't come she'd judge me. I would deserve it. Who blows off their little sister's wedding for a guy? Me, that's who.

I turn away from her in the bucket seat and close my eyes. One more hour and I'll be back home. Except it won't be home. Not really. It will be Camille and Duke's home and I'll be an unwanted guest. Hattie won't even be there. All grown up and living with her husband, her room will be empty or maybe filled with exercise equipment. Isn't that what parents do when their kids leave home? Fill their bedrooms with hobbies they've always wanted to devote more time to, or fitness. I guess I'll never get it. Of course, I never have to worry about having kids. Not that I've given it much thought since the fruit of my womb was plucked out by force. My punishment for such a sinful relationship. Ironically, it wasn't as devastating as the look on my lover's face when I told him I'd lost our child. He was happy. I think the bastard even smiled. Is that irony?

<hr>

I MUST HAVE FALLEN ASLEEP. Two things clue me in, we're sitting in my mother's driveway, and I don't see an enormous, carnivorous worm anywhere in sight. It's funny. I haven't had that dream since childhood. Sitting up, I wipe the tiny dribble of drool from my chin and turn over in the bucket seat, not at all surprised to see my mom napping. She wouldn't leave me. Not now. A fact that causes me more than a little stress. She hasn't been there for so long, am I really prepared for her to be over me 24/7 until I get my shit together?

What if I'm never together?

It would be easy to get out of the car now and just walk away.

Never look back. But I can't move. I'm like the ancient mosquito found in amber, frozen in place. My mother is a lovely woman. Tired, but lovely. Her shoulder-length hair is peppered with gray, and her eyes are slightly bagged. For a moment my hand itches to reach out and touch her softened jaw, to trace the line of it, but when her lids flutter open, and I'm faced with her emerald eyes all desire to touch her is gone. I read once that only 3% of the population has green eyes. As a child, I thought that made my mom special.

She smiles. "Did you have a nice nap?"

Sinking back into my chair I shake my head. "Not really."

Her sigh is audible and almost shakes the car. "Honey, I know you're not happy. I'm sorry for that. I wish I could've been there for you."

I roll my eyes despite the sheet of rain currently covering them.

"But we're going to make it work this time. I'm going to make it work this time." She pulls the keys from the ignition. "If you will let me." Gathering the restaurant bag and her purse (Mom never leaves trash in the car), she taps my shoulder. "Let's get your bags and get you inside."

I want to refuse. Want to scream and kick and tell her how much I hate her for everything she's done to me. I think about punching the dash, but I've never been one of those brutes who demonstrates their anger by damaging other things. I grab the silver handle and push the heavy door open. I know the moment my foot touches the gravel below my life is no longer my own.

Maybe that's not such a bad thing.

Two

I called the therapist last night to report I've been home a whole three days and haven't slit my wrists yet. She didn't find it funny. Oddly enough it didn't stop her from bringing up the fact that my method of choice was pills. Did you know 36.2% of female suicides are death by poisoning? Yeah, me either until I met the therapist. She would chastise me for presenting it as though we'd met in a coffee shop and not in the nut ward. She claims I do this to deceive myself in order to continue living in an altered reality where what's happened to me isn't a violation, it's love. I say it's abandonment.

Camille is behind me in the still-dim kitchen. I guess that's what I get for coming out of my room for something to eat. She's shifting back and forth on her heels, the rubber soles of her slippers rubbing against the aging vinyl with every move. It's an unnerving sound, the constant swishing of the overly anxious. I close my eyes. *Please just make it stop.*

Her voice is soft, riddled with her anxiety. "What did she say?"

Despite knowing the answer already, I ask, "Who?"

"The therapist, when you called her."

I shrug. "Way to go."

Her slump in posture is almost audible in the silence of the house. "Come on, Gra—Zed, you're supposed to tell me. You promised."

I promised? It's always what I do for everyone else, what they can get from me. She wants honesty and openness, but there's no way she could handle it. Once I open up to her, *on* her, I don't think I'll be able to stop until my words have made her vanish. A long-needed vanquishing.

Balling my hands into tight fists, I turn. "She just wanted an update. The fact that I called her with one shows I'm alive. It's all good."

"When do you call her again?"

So thick. "I don't know."

She nods, her eyes shining in the dull light of the old doublewide. "Did she give you the name of the counselor you're supposed to see and when? It's a group, right? I need to know when the meetings are so I can make sure to get you to them."

"No."

Her eyes are pleading with me now, but I don't give a shit. I shouldn't have to tell her when the stupid group meets. It's none of her fucking business. None of this is.

She nods, averting her gaze. "Okay. Just let me know."

"I can get to the meetings myself."

"How? You don't have a car. I'm sorry but I can't let you take mine."

"It's fine. I'll figure something out."

She takes a deep breath, it's audible despite the fact that she's turned away from me. I guess I'm hard to look at. "Do you want some breakfast? We can talk a little before Duke wakes up."

I shake my head. "No." Turning, I begin toward my room, then add, "Thanks."

"Just let me know when you want something," she says behind me, but I don't respond.

Going into my room I close the door, but not before I hear her say, "Your sister will be here later."

Plopping down on the old twin bed that creaks if you look

at it, I wrap my arms around my body. At the hospital, all I could think about was my little sister, sure that she's all I would need to get out of this funk, but it's not the same. She's visited once since I've been home, and it wasn't the reunion I imagined. No open arms, no declarations of support; *You're okay, Zed. You're not broken.* Instead, we were quiet, muted by the years we've spent apart. Awkward silence that our mother tried to fill with chipper talk of how great it was to have us all back together again. I shouldn't have been surprised by our lack of connection. After all, we were children when I left. Now we're grown women from vastly different worlds; virtual strangers.

My little sister is pregnant. Twenty-two-years old, building a new human. I was pregnant once. Never as far along as this. Mine was stolen long before nature had the chance to stretch my skin or give me stretch marks.

I wish Hattie wouldn't come.

MOM IS MAKING QUITE a production of having both her daughters home. The good plates are out, and she's even made Duke put on a button-down shirt. It looks nice on him. The soft blue plaid brings out his eyes, or something. Anyway, his smile seems kind today. He's a tough guy, a real 1940s kind of man, but there are moments when I catch him looking at me with pity. How I despise pity. I'm sure she told him. My mother is just about the last person in the world you want to tell a secret like mine to. Not that I volunteered the information. No, Camille— Cami to her friends—is too smart for her own good.

Hattie is seated at the table, her body relaxed against the old wooden back. My mom's table set is from the early '90s. One of those deals with wooden and wicker backs, seat cushions, and legs that aren't really legs. I've seen many a hefty person bend chairs like these to the ground. Hattie's still pretty small though, save for the little beach ball on her abdomen. She smiles at me, and I look down. I don't deserve her smile.

"How're you feeling today, Gracie?" she asks.

Mom leans over to place a dish in the center of the table. She rests a hand on Hattie's shoulder. "She wants to be called Zed now, honey, remember?"

Hattie nods. "Sorry. I keep forgetting."

I shrug. "It's fine."

"How are you settling in?" she asks.

Another shrug from me. "Fine, I guess."

Duke's voice booms from the other end of the table. "Well, you look better."

I smile, bowing my head a bit as I do. I don't want praise from anyone, especially not him. He's a great guy, and he loves my mom, but I don't want him to notice me. Ever.

Cami settles in at the table. "Go ahead and dig in, y'all. I made your favorite."

Meatloaf is not my favorite. It's never been my favorite. Too much meat and grease. But I don't tell her that. What good will come of it? I cut a square in half and place it on my plate.

She's gone breathy. A true Southern mother. "Lord, no wonder you're so tiny!"

I look at her. She used to be small. Still is compared to many. But when I was a kid she was a size five. Now I'd put her at a twelve. It looks good on her. I wonder if putting on a few pounds will help me. I don't want to be like those people who say they built a wall of fat because they were *victimized*, though. I guess in order to do that I would have to think of myself as a victim. He told me I liked it and eventually I did.

Cami's looking at me, concern now masking her former good mood. "Are you okay?"

"Yeah." I grab the mashed potato spoon and slap a scoop of carby goodness on my plate, then slide the spoon over to Hattie. "I'm fine."

"You looked like you were a million miles away."

"She was, Mom," Hattie says, scooping a helping of fluffy potatoes onto her plate. "Let her alone and let's eat."

"Thank you," I mouth. If I say it out loud, I know it'll start another production of *what's going on with Zed.*

Hattie nods.

The meatloaf isn't how I remember it. It's better. Maybe the key is good company. Duke is regaling us with stories of his work and the people he comes across. He's an electrician. I watch his hands as he talks. They're large and calloused. I think about those rough hands doing manly work and then I think of him tenderly touching my mom's face when he thinks no one is watching. I don't remember my dad showing Mom little moments of tenderness like that. He wasn't a bad guy. He just wasn't present. Or aware. I blame his father.

I blame his father for a lot.

"Tell them about the time that woman met you at the door in her negligee, Duke." Cami's eyes are bright, her smile is wide.

"Now, honey, I don't think it'd be right to tell your girls how we met."

Hattie and Cami howl as if he's just made the funniest joke they've ever heard. Who knows, maybe it is. I hope not. I smile. I don't know if I'm capable of actual laughter at this point. While Duke's stories have been fun, I have to be honest with myself. I don't care. I don't want to be here. It is painful to sit here and pretend that I belong with them.

My voice is low. "May I be excused?"

Duke's jovial facade fades. "I didn't mean to upset you, Zed. I didn't really meet your mama that way."

I shake my head. "You didn't. I like your stories." I smile to be reassuring. "I do. I'd just like to be excused."

Mom shakes her head. "Of course. Leave your plate, I'll get it."

I hurry away from the table keenly aware they're all staring at me. I know they'll talk about me once my door closes. I wonder if they'll call me rude or if they'll be genuinely worried. Right now, I think they'll be worried. I haven't been home long enough for them to be sick of me just yet.

Once inside, I throw myself across the bed and take a few deep breaths. In the hospital, I was sure I could do this, come home and be surrounded by the past without falling apart, but the stretching across my chest, the clenching of my gut, and the crawling of my skin are all indicators that I've bitten off more than I can handle. Raising my arm, I trace my finger from the bottom of my palm midway up my forearm. I've never tried pulling a blade along this tender skin, but sometimes I think about what it would be like. Mostly when I'm sober and the whispers become too much. There's a reason pills were my go-to for ending this, though. I figure I'm in enough pain already, no need to add physical torture to the mix.

Hattie comes to my room after supper. "Can I come in?"

I sit up, throwing my legs over the side of the bed closest to the door. "Sure."

The gentle scent of honeysuckle fills my head as she settles in on the bed beside me. "How're you feeling?"

I shrug. "Fine. I guess. Sorry about out there."

"It's tough for you, huh?"

I look at her. "That's life, right?"

"Not for everyone." She reaches out, her hand gingerly tucking a stray strand behind my ear. "You know Mom is just trying to make you feel normal, right?"

Leaning forward, I rest my elbows on the edge of my knees and fix my gaze on the carpeting below. "She's failing."

She chuckles. "She usually does." Bending forward, she contorts her body until she can look me in the eyes. I don't expect it, so I jump back slightly, and she laughs again. "You're jumpy, big sister."

"I'm sorry."

Disappearing from my sight, she sighs. "What's happening in that big head of yours?"

I look up. She used to ask me that all the time when we were kids. I would be miles away, usually thinking of ways to stay away from my uncle. To keep him away from me. Until later when I was dreaming up ways to be with him more. She would sigh and ask where I was. I never told her. Probably never will.

She's leaning back, her belly open and welcoming. My fingers itch to spread out across the raised plain of it.

"You can touch it if you want," she says. Pressing around, she grabs my hand and presses it against the side. A tiny push makes me draw back. Mouth agape, my eyes meet hers. She's smiling. "Weird, right?"

"It's amazing." Heart pounding, I reach out and press my palm against the same spot, fingers splayed as far as they will go. *Come on, kid.* "What is it?"

"A baby."

My mouth jerks back in an involuntary smirk. "Boy or girl?"

"Girl." A soft smile plays on her lips as she looks at her abdomen. "We just found out today."

I wish it was a boy. Instead, she's cooking another one for the bad guys. Another sugar and spice-filled victim they can use for their own selfish and lascivious purposes.

She's looking at me again. "You okay?"

I nod. "Who's the father?"

"J.C. Leonard."

"Leonard?" The name is vaguely familiar.

She nods. "Yup." She seems so happy. Her face is practically shining, but I can't place him beyond his name.

"The youngest one? The one in my class?"

She shakes her head. "No, he was a few grades ahead of us. He's the oldest."

His face flashes before my mind's eye. "He's, like, thirty."

Laughing, she nods. "Thirty-three. It's only nine years. That's not a big deal."

I want to be repelled by her choice of partners, want to tell her she doesn't have to live with a man so much older than her, but I can't. After all, I believed I was in love with a man almost twenty years my senior not too long ago.

She lays back on the bed and I do the same. We're silent, both of us finding our own world in the popcorn ceiling. I push through the layers, past the crumbling exterior, into the thin drywall, and out into the beyond. Staring at ceilings, past them, is something I became very adept at as a child, getting lost in the layers to escape what was happening to me. Before he was right. Before I liked it.

"You know Cousin Angel is pregnant too, right?" Hattie says after the silence has almost lulled me to sleep.

"Oh?" I didn't expect to talk about Angel. Not that I didn't want to ask about her and her family, particularly her father, upon my mother's arrival at the hospital.

"Yeah. She's having a boy. Isn't it funny?"

"Funny how?"

"We're both pregnant and we're having the opposite of the other."

"Yeah." I look at her. "Who's the father?"

She shrugs. "No idea. She doesn't live around here anymore. I only know she's pregnant because we talk to each other on social media." Rolling to face me, she begins to twist the shortened strands of my hair around her fingers. I like it. Closing my eyes, I focus on the little tingles it creates, riding them like waves through my body. "What's your plan, Zeddie?"

"What do you mean?"

"Mom tells me you're here for a while. What's your plan?"

I open my eyes. I think I know what she's hinting to. Will I go back to *him*? By now the whole town must know I was in an incestuous relationship with my uncle. My face begins to burn.

She surprises me by asking, "Are you going to get a job? Or will you wallow in this tin can?"

Thank goodness. I shrug. "I haven't thought about it."

"Don't you think you should?"

She's right, of course. I should be out doing something with my life instead of hunkering down inside the thin sheetrock walls of the old Oakwood special, but I'm not ready.

I shake my head. "Maybe."

"To hell with your maybe." She sits up, the sudden movement jarring me from the trance she's lured me into. I follow her, nerves jangled by her actions, but also because her hands are on her abdomen. I stare at her, but don't speak.

She follows my eyes, smiling as if to reassure me. "It happens. Just twinges."

"Is it scary?"

"Nah. My doctor told me I would have them from time to time."

"Can I see it?" She lifts the light tunic, tucking its edge beneath her full breasts. It's difficult to believe my little sister will be nursing from them in such a short time. The skin of her belly flexes and retracts like an animal caught in a net. "What does it feel like?" I ask, my eyes following the movements.

"Like a butterfly in a net."

I smile. It's not surprising her description is akin to mine. We always had a strong psychic bond as kids. We're not having psychic visions or feelings, but we were certainly in tune a lot. "I was thinking a net."

She's looking at me and it feels a little sad, like she's disappointed by something I've said or done. "I'm glad you're home, Zeddie."

My mouth jerks back in an involuntary smile. "Thanks."

"Let me finish." Her hands are covering mine. They're soft and warm, uncomfortable. The urge to pull away is strong, but I remain still. "I'm glad you're home. But at the same time, I'm afraid. Mom's going out on a limb for you. Bringing you here, going to work, leaving you here alone while she's gone."

"What do you mean?"

Her shoulders fall. It's obvious she thinks I should be

following along. "You just... You have to do more than exist here." Her eyes meet mine. "Do you understand?"

"Yeah. No more being a loser. I get it." My body begins to jerk. Anger and hurt bubble in my gut, my insides turning and rolling with every passing instant. "Jesus, Hattie, you do realize I lived out there in the big bad world without Cami for ten years, right?" She looks down as I stand up and begin to stalk back and forth in front of her. "As crazy as it is to believe, Fuck-Up-Zed paid her way. I wasn't homeless." Rarely, anyway. "I had a job." Most of the time. "And I paid my own fucking way."

"I'm just trying to help, Zed," she says, her eyes meeting mine again. "You need a smooth transition, and you won't have one if you don't get back into a routine." She pats the bed. "Please, sit down. You're making me nervous."

I stop pacing, sit down as requested, leaning forward, head between my knees. If I stay like this long enough, I'll start to float.

After a lengthy silence, Hattie continues, "They don't have a lot of money and Duke is only patient to a point. If he feels like you're mooching he's going to lose it. He's real nice and he loves Mama to death, but he's also very old school." Her tone has turned timid, hesitant. She feels like she's flubbed this up.

Truth is, she has.

Sighing, she adds, "Just don't go too long without a job, okay?"

I nod.

"I have to go," she's saying when the ringing in my head subsides. The last great hoorah of unforgiving rage. "See you soon?"

Another nod.

I don't move until the latch on the door catches. Then, laying back, I fix my eyes on the popcorn above. It has no stories to tell, no accusations to make, and no misconceptions to rest on. It just is. Kind of like me. I'm not a woman. I'm not a girl. I am discarded. I am the one no one wanted.

I am the one no one wants.

This place has moved on without me. Mom and Duke, Hattie and J.C, Angel…It's like they've all rushed into the future and I'm still here. I'm still waiting for someone to notice I'm not there yet. But why do I want them to notice? Why should I even fucking care? I was gone for years and none of them, not one, tried to bring me home. Not that it would've worked. Good sense says I should call the therapist, but I'm not in the place for an hour of silence and quiet judgments.

I follow the valleys of the ceiling created by haphazard construction, wishing there were tiles. It's always better to count tiles; first forward then back, then side to side. There's a measure of peace in it. I try to focus on each dot. It's fruitless to attempt counting them, but I am the impossible girl, so why not have a go at the impossible task?

"Zeddie?" My mom's voice is soft in the heavy silence of the room.

I don't want to stop counting, but she's fucking it up again. "It's Zed."

"I—I'm sorry. I heard Hattie calling you Zeddie." There's a pause. "I like it."

I turn my head toward her. "Did you need something?"

Her shoulders fall. "Well, Duke and I have to work tomorrow, and…" She wrings her hands. "I don't know what to do. I've taken off all the time at work I can."

I sit up and turn my body toward her. "Will you feel better if I promise not to off myself while you're gone?"

Her eyes pop open like a sunburst. "Zed!"

"Relax. I'll still be taking up valuable space when you return."

"I wish you wouldn't say things like that."

I want to tell her I wish a lot of things but remain silent. After a moment she nods and departs. I wonder what the nod means. Is she giving up again? Will she nark again? This time to the therapist instead of to the cops. I wonder how much she's talked to the therapist and how much that hypocrite has told her. It's none of my mom's business what really happened to me. Her opportunity to find out vanished years ago.

THREE

It's nice waking up to a quiet house. Duke goes in around four in the morning and my mom has to be in by seven. Now, at eight-fifteen, the house is blissfully silent. Rolling out of bed, I don't bother to put pants on over my boyshort panties, and I damn sure won't bother with a bra. I'm a B cup. Not even full. I don't need the contraption for any purpose other than to hide elongated nipples from predators. When I developed breasts, I thought my nipples were like slopes because of the sucking. Like a baby fresh from the womb, he was always sucking. I didn't care for it. Not then. Now I don't mind. When I'm in the mood.

I'm dying for a cigarette. Odd because I've never really liked to smoke. Drink, yes. Swallow things that make me feel numb, absolutely. But smoking has never been my thing. I guess it will be a suitable replacement for drinking and popping pills. No, it won't, but I need something to occupy the spaces where alcohol and pills once lived. I'm lying to myself a lot lately.

I'm okay. I'm happy to be alive. I'm going to be happy and well-adjusted. I don't know why I'm buying into this bullshit. What good are therapists?

I stop in the middle of the living room and soak in the silence. This is what I want. No expectations. No questions. No memories. Just quiet. Dropping to the floor, I pull my legs close in the style that used to be called Indian and close my eyes.

It's impossible to think of the future when you're locked in the past. I'm living in my childhood home, sleeping in the same lumpy bed of my youth, fraying under the judgments of my mother. It was easier before that day on my uncle's doorstep, the one where I confronted him with his new girlfriend. Lacey was her name. When the police showed up, he claimed she was a family friend dropping by to pick up something for her mother, but she gave him away. I never would have. Never did until that day until my mom showed up and put all the dirty details together. They asked Cami if she wanted to press charges as if it was her virginity he'd stolen, her heart he'd broken. I never should have gone there.

The room is a kaleidoscope of colors when I open my eyes again. A look at the clock over the mantle tells me I've been sitting here, pondering, for more than twenty minutes. I guess meditation really is a thing. Won't the therapist be thrilled? My legs protest movement after so long in the same position, creaking and clinching as I work to untangle myself and stand. Moving slowly so as not to anger my tingling limbs, I go to the mantel, using the faux cherry wood ledge for support, making shapes in the dust of its surface as I wait for the pins and needles to subside. It's no surprise to find the top coated by weeks of dust. When does Cami have time to dust anyway? She works like a dog to take care of a loving husband and now a fuck up daughter.

Going to the kitchen, I grab the dust rag from the broom closet and go back to the fireplace, lifting each item to swipe underneath. It's not much, but this is the least I can do. What genius came up with the idea for a fireplace in a mobile home anyway? One ember could burn it down in a minute. The ambiance, I guess. A fireplace means a place is cozy and a cozy place is home, right? In theory, perhaps. Doesn't matter anyway. Cami feels the same way I do about fireplaces in cheaply built places. We only used it once in my youth, one year when the power went out after a big ice storm. It was nice, the three of us huddled around it, our faces warmed by the flames, but even then, I could see my mother was just as worried as I was about this place going up in flames. There were a lot of things to be angry at my dad about. I guess keeping the house was a small one. There's nothing wrong with this place. It's four walls and a roof, as my Gramps always said, and it was all my mom could afford after the divorce, even with their help.

At seventeen, when I decided I would leave home, get the hell away from my mother and this damn town, I thought briefly of running to my grandparents' house. My Gran would've taken me in, I know it. That's what she does. Never turn away a soul in need. But how could I face her after my uncle's arrest, after the allegations my mother hurled from the privacy of our home into the public sphere, after Cousin Angel's testimony, and after I stood before a judge and denied every last thing they said? They all knew the truth. Suspected it anyway. No matter how many times I shot down her accusations, no matter how many times I discredited my cousin Angel in public, it didn't matter. They all knew. I did it for him, of course. Foolishly thinking we could be together afterward. Didn't he always say we could? We'd just run off together and start over. Happily ever after. I wish I'd gone to my Gran's house now, though. Maybe I could have avoided the hard years. Maybe.

Leaving the mantel with its images of good times and precious little cherub knick-knacks, I go into the kitchen and sit down at the small vinyl-topped table, eyes fixing on the yellow phone hanging on the wall. It's been a while since I reached out to anyone. To my Gran. Years maybe. Probably. Going to the phone, I grab the receiver and hurriedly dial. Funny the numbers you remember. After a few moments, she picks up and my throat ignites, the heat of it clouding my eyes.

Swallowing against the flames, I croak, "Hi, Gran."

There's a long pause. "Who's this?" Time hasn't stopped with her. I hear it in her voice.

"It's Zedwynne, Gran."

There's a sharp intake of breath. I realize I'm now holding my own, waiting to see if she will hang up or worse. "Well, how do!"

I smile. Damn, I'm getting good at using these muscles. I swipe at the tears on my cheeks. "How are you?"

"I'm doing alright, I reckon."

My mom's mom is seventy. She was in her thirties when Cami was born. A surprise for the ages is what Gran has always said. I always thought that meant my mom was special. It wasn't until I grew into a teenager that I learned what it truly meant. My mother was a hellion as a teen, and she made my Gran and Gramps pay dearly for bringing her into the world. Guess she got her come-upping.

"You gave us quite the scare, young lady," she says almost half an hour into our conversation. She's always known when to broach a subject. "How are you settling in?"

"Fine, I guess."

"It'll take some time. Don't rush yourself."

I want to ask her what Cami told her, but she's too honest. First, she'll chide me for calling my mother Cami and then she'll fuss at me for trying to hurry God along. "I won't"

"Good. How's your sister? I haven't talked to her in a while."

"Pregnant."

She chuckles. "Hard to believe, ain't it?"

"Very."

After an hour of catch-up, I end our conversation with a promise to visit one day soon. "You be good, Zedwynne," she says. "And don't you go running off again."

"I won't, Gran. I promise."

"Good girl." She pauses and I think, for a moment, she's ended the call, then she adds in a softer voice, "I know life's hard, honey, but you're a fighter and I know you're gonna be fine. Just give yourself some time."

I nod, though I know she can't see me, but words are lost for a moment as the back of my throat begins to burn again and my eyes rebuild their walls of glass. No one has told me I'm strong, that I'm a fighter. In group, one of my fellow nuts said we're all weak. *That's why we tried to off ourselves. Can't handle life.* Even as he said it, I thought he was wrong. Hadn't we tried to do it to spare our families and friends the heartache of living with us? Isn't that something akin to selflessness? To strength.

"You there?"

I nod again, then add. "Yes, ma'am. Thank you for saying that."

"You come and see us soon, okay?"

I promise to and hang up the receiver. My legs are aching from standing so long. Why my mom still has a wall phone is beyond me. Allowing them to fold beneath me, I stretch out on the kitchen floor because the sofa is too far away. I'm not worried about how dirty the faded white linoleum is. I've slept on far worse. I think of Duke's boots on them after a long day of work, the germs and bacteria that have attached themselves to the soles of them. I think about cleaning up, being something more than a...*what did Hattie call it*...a mooch, but I don't. Instead, I turn my focus to the ceiling and begin to trace the lines in the texture.

HATTIE AND I ARE OUT. I'm still a little angry at the ambush. She'd come in while I was lying on the kitchen floor and began to freak out. It's insane to see her panic. Arms and hands flying everywhere, her voice raised to a pitch only dogs can hear, and that belly of hers. God, it looks huge when she's standing over you telling you to get your ass up.

I'm thankful for the loud humming of the Bronco as she tears down the road. She's still fuming.

I'm compelled to say, "I'm sorry, Hattie."

"Who the fuck lays on a kitchen floor like a fucking corpse?" She looks at me, tears streaming over her full cheeks, lips trembling, and my heart breaks.

"I was resting. My legs were hurting from standing up talking to Gran."

"Normal people don't rest on the floor, Zed. They go to the fucking couch!" Her voice squeaks in places as she chastises me. I've heard that women become a bit more emotional when they're pregnant. I don't know if Hattie has because I have nothing to measure this against. The girl I knew is gone, replaced by this woman who has little tolerance for me.

"I'm not normal." Is all I can manage.

She stops the car violently and shoves the gearshift into park. "You'd better *get* normal." Her body is turned toward me, one hand on the steering wheel and one on the side of my seat. "Don't do that to me and Mom."

"What?" I turn to meet her gaze. "Rest?"

She shakes her head, red-rimmed eyes boring into me. "Don't make us *find* you."

I'm stunned. What is a proper response to that? I turn to look out the front window, mute and stupid. Unlike others from group, I put very little thought into who would find me and how they would cope with the discovery of a dead body.

"Come on," she demands. Shoving her door open, she gets out and slams it. She's feisty. That's one thing unchanged, I suppose.

Following directions, I get out of the car and join her. I look up at the supermarket, the big blue kitty welcoming all who would cross its threshold. "What are we doing here?"

"We're getting a few things for you."

"Hattie—"

She puts up her hand. "And Mom. She doesn't have a lot of money and since you're back in the house she has even less."

"Way to make me feel like a burden."

Her face is stone when she responds, "You *are* a burden."

It stings. The truth. I am a burden. I'm an adult, but I'm contributing nothing to the house. I don't even want to. What I want is to find something that will make me forget about my mom, Duke, and even Hattie. I thought my little sister wouldn't judge me, but it seems like it's all she can do from way up on her high horse.

The only response I can muster is, "Thanks."

She takes a buggy, pushing it up to the wash station. Grabbing an antibacterial wipe, she scrubs the handle and then her hands. I can't remember when we became a country in need of antibacterial wipes and hand sanitizer. To me, it seems too clinical, like we're afraid to be connected to other people. I get it. We don't want diseases, people don't wash their hands, yada, yada, but it feels like we're distancing ourselves. Arming ourselves.

I don't realize she's holding the wipe out to me until the alcohol odor fills my nostrils. I shake my head. "No. Thanks."

Tossing the fabric into the tiny wastebasket, she sighs, posture softening. "I didn't mean to be so harsh. It's my damn hormones. I get mean when I get scared." She cocks her head to the side. "Maybe it's my mother instinct kicking in." This seems to make her happy. Did she think she wouldn't have that most basic intuition? "We're all burdens in one way or another, Zeddie."

"I know."

She talks while we walk around the supermarket. Not of important things, but of gossip and inconsequential matters that will keep us in a good mood. She tells me that Betsy Franklin, a rival of mine from high school, is working as a waitress at the local strip club. "Topless!"

I laugh, but it's more for my sister than anything. While she continues to talk, I think of Betsy and how she must feel walking around naked while men glare and sneer at her. Do they touch her? I'm sure they try. These men who, no doubt, are former teachers, mailmen, and checkers at local shops. It must be humiliating to know every day someone you will see outside, with your clothes on, will see you in such a vulnerable position. I think of my Gran calling me strong. I think she's wrong. I'm not strong. Women like Betsy are strong.

Hattie interrupts my reverie, waving a box of snack cakes in my line of sight. "You're miles away again."

"Sorry. I was thinking about Betsy."

"Isn't it sad?" She tosses the box in the cart. "Do you need anything else?"

I shake my head and we begin toward the front of the store.

"I always thought she was easy in high school," Hattie says.

"She wasn't."

"How do you know?"

I shrug. "She was a virgin."

My education of Betsy Franklin came in the bed of a truck. I couldn't tell my sister that Barry told me one night after he'd shoved himself into my mouth. He came and then began to laugh as I vomited over the side of the truck. After I stopped convulsing and leaned my head against the back of the cab, he thrust his hand between my legs and began to jab and run his clumsy fingers too hard over tender flesh. He thought this excited me. *You're way cooler than Betsy*, he'd said. *She's all talk. Fucking tease. That's why I don't waste my time with virgins. You're not a virgin, are you baby?* I shook my head, my teenage self feeling somewhat triumphant over Betsy. I pretended to come, and his inexperience led him to believe me. In an instant, I was on my back, and he was on top of me. Thus, the lesson concluded.

Hattie looks thoughtful for a moment. I think she wants to ask more questions, but she says, "I had no idea."

I remain mostly quiet as we drive back toward our mother's home. *My* home? I still can't think of it that way. Hattie is chatting away over the roar of the Bronco's engine. Outside Tiger

Lilies dot the landscape, peeks of oranges and blacks through the heavy weeded shoulders of the highway. I begin to search them out, to smile when I catch a glimpse of one. My own personal game. Always my own.

Hattie's tone becomes heavier, uneasy, bringing me out of my game. I hold my breath. "I told Dad you're home," she says.

I don't want to answer right away, but I can't help asking, "You talk to Dad?"

"Of course. Why wouldn't I talk to him?"

For a moment I want to strike her. How can she talk to our father? How can she talk to the man who believed his brother over everyone else and continued to parade his own daughters before him? Then again, why wouldn't she? As far as I know, Hattie doesn't know anything about the depths of our uncle's depravity, nor does she realize our father's role in it. I put my head between my legs and begin to rock back and forth.

"Zed? Zeddie, what's wrong?"

I want to answer, want to tell her I have no idea what's wrong, but I know. It's all wrong. Me, him, my dad. We should've been exterminated, wiped from the face of the planet. Bad seeds washed away by a torrential downpour of reckoning. I'm going to vomit all over her Bronco. "Pull over."

"What's—"

"Goddamn it, just pull over!" I don't wait for the wheels to still before I jump out and rush toward the patch of trees off the shoulder. The Tiger Lillies welcome me. Even in my desperate sprint to get as far away from the car as possible I find myself drawn to them, longing to lie down before them and let them be my marker. No one would be able to find me. Only in June.

I heave, remnants of the morning's breakfast meeting the earth below.

"Look out for snakes," Hattie is yelling over the roar of cars and trucks barreling by. I wave her back. Away. Just stay away. But she continues toward me. "Are you okay?" She's beside me now, her hand stroking my back. She'll be a good mother.

I nod. Falling back on my haunches I look up at her. I want to tell her not to tell Dad about me, but a small part of me, the poor little girl who refuses to die, wants her to tell him. If she tells our father, then he will tell my uncle.

"Zed?" Her voice is far away. "Zed!"

Her screech follows me into darkness.

FOUR

om and Duke are arguing. This is the third time they've argued since I returned home. I don't know what the first time was about, but I know the follow-up arguments have been about me. He's probably angry about the hospital bill. Hattie didn't know what to do when I passed out by the side of the road, so she called 9-1-1. Four hours, one bag of I.V. fluids, and one drug test later I was released. Now in the cool darkness of my room, I can hear how stressful my presence is for my mother. She's pleading with Duke. He isn't being overbearing, just stern. God, he's good at being the strong silent type.

I stand up, swaying just a bit at the sudden movement, and go to the door.

"They gave her a drug test, honey. She's clean. Doesn't that say something?" She's desperate. I wonder if he's wanted me out since day one. "She's doing remarkably well. Considering."

"She can't stay in the house all the time, Cami."

"I know."

There's silence and then, "I just don't want you to get run down. I know how it can be."

"I know."

I think of lying back down. Pretend I haven't heard any of their conversation, but they both know I can hear. Or they should. Turning the knob, I step out into their world. Mom is on Duke's lap, her head buried in his shoulder.

He nods at me, and I nod back. "Feeling better?"

"A little. Thanks." I'm suddenly dying for a cigarette. "Can I bum a smoke?"

Mom looks up. "Oh, honey, you're not starting that habit, are you?"

I open my mouth, the tiny razors on my tongue preparing to strike out, but close it and head out onto the front porch. The mosquitoes will eat me alive, but I can't say that I care very much right now.

It's typical early summer. Crickets and katydids competing in the dark. I prefer the rumbling of the cicada, such a sound created by a little booty shaking. Hattie and I used to watch them. Track them, really. Nothing much else to do around here as a child. Watch bugs. Maybe because we're so much like them. Especially as children. You can be squished just as easily.

Across the street, Lucinda has begun her nightly ritual. She's an odd woman. Late-forties with shocking white hair, small build, and the most perfect posture I've ever seen. My spine aches to see her walk. She never speaks. Merely regards with a nod before beginning to straighten up her property. Sometimes, late at night, I can hear her husband yelling. I wonder if he beats her.

Behind me the door opens, and Duke's footsteps fall heavy on the old wood of the porch. I don't look up from my place on the stairs. I'm too intent on watching Lucinda. She even knocks the pebbles out of her cemented driveway.

His gruff voice pierces the night. It doesn't belong out here. Not now. "Hey."

I look up at him, silent until he takes a place by me. "Hey."

His legs stretch out, the heels of his boots resting against the grass below us. *Man, he is tall.* He hands me a cigarette and creates a flame from the lighter nestled in his palm.

I take a long draw and then release the smoke. *God, that's good.* "Thanks."

He nods. "I don't want you getting the wrong idea, Zed."

"About what?"

He smirks. I can see why my mom finds him attractive. It's his smile. "Never try and kid a kidder. I know how thin these walls are."

I shrug.

"It's not that I don't want you here. I do. Truth be told, I think this is the best place for you."

I rest my chin on my arm, training my eyes on him. I want to be as direct as he is. I want him to know I'm capable of at least that. "But?"

He's uncomfortable. I know it by the way he looks over at Lucinda and then down to his feet; the way he picks at his jeans. "I want what's best for you."

I'd love to lean back, rest my elbows on the floor of the porch, but that would seem like a seduction. Hell, I think I've used that as a seduction once. Teenage boys are easy when they think the girl is. Best to stay as I am.

"And I want what's best for your mama. For all of us. Do you know what I mean?"

I nod. "Hattie told me I'm a burden."

He's shaking his head. "Now, that's not what I'm saying. Not at all."

"That we're all burdens sometimes." I turn my face back to Lucinda. She's standing still now, the final part of her ritual. "I think she's right. I didn't get it when she said it, but I do now. Even if we don't try to be we still are."

His voice softens. "Some burdens are easy to carry."

I think I love him a little for that. "I'll get a job, Duke."

"I don't want to rush you now. Your mama says you need time and I believe her."

I shrug. "My whole life has been nothing but time. Sounds

stupid to say since everybody's life is, but that's how I feel." I turn to him. "I'll get a job and I'll help as much as I can."

He smiles. "I think that'll work just fine." He pats my shoulder and stands. "You know how much she loves you, don't you?"

I nod.

"Alright then. Don't stay out here too long. Damn mosquitoes will eat you alive."

With that, he's gone and it's just me and Lucinda again. I wonder what goes through her mind as she stares into nothing. I know she doesn't see the little singlewide or the old truck parked over a square piece of cardboard that keeps leaking oil from touching the sand-colored concrete. I wonder if she's thinking of running. Of leaving all of her order behind for something different. Something more. Maybe one day I'll ask.

Probably not.

Finally, she breaks, her silent wanderings complete. He never comes to check on her when she's outside. She looks over at me and I see something I haven't seen before, longing. Does she want me to talk to her? Is she so starved for communication that she stands in her driveway every night wishing someone would just give her an excuse to talk? I want to tell her she's got the wrong girl, that she doesn't want the likes of me in her life, but something tells me she's just as broken as I am.

I smile and nod. She returns the gesture. Then, with head down, she returns to the confines of her home. Satisfied that my promise to Duke has ended the quarreling for the night, I snuff out the cigarette, tucking the rest in my shirt pocket for later, and head back into my own prison.

Of course, I know the structure itself is no prison. I've made my own. But I'm not ready to dwell on that just yet. The therapist might give me props for even this slight realization, so I suppose I will too.

My mom is seated in Duke's chair when I enter the house. She's got a mug of tea in one hand and a book spread out over her lap. I consider asking what the book's about, extend an olive branch, but don't. What's the point in beginning a conversation I'm not committed to? I grunt my goodnight and begin toward my room.

"Zed."

I stop.

"Duke told me what you said."

I turn to her. "Yeah?"

"Are you ready for that?"

I shrug. "I've had plenty of jobs before."

She closes the book and places her cup on the table beside her. "I know. It's just that you've only been out of the hospital for a little over a week. Are you ready for the stress that comes with a job?"

Unbelievable. "Considering I probably won't get anything too advantageous; I think I'll be fine."

"Zed." She stands and moves toward me. I take a step back and she puts her hands up as if to hold me there. "I just want to make sure you're okay to do this?"

"It beats laying around this tin can all day." I sigh, ready for the conversation to be over. "Look, I know I haven't acted like it lately, but I'm an adult. I can handle it."

She nods. "Okay. I have a friend who owns a place in town, Hank. I'm sure he'll hire you on there." Her hand is up again, only this time it seems to be in an effort to contain my dramatics. "I'll only call him if you want me to."

"What kind of place is it?"

"A diner. Jubilee's. Do you remember it?"

I shudder. I'll never forget it.

"Do you want me to call him?"

I nod. "Sure. Thanks." I start for my room again, but pause, turning back to her. "Aren't you afraid I'll see...you know...*him*?" It was the first time I'd dared allude to my former lover since being home.

She shakes her head, shifting her eyes slightly away. "No."

IT's funny how one word can keep you awake. Especially one as simple as 'no'. What did she mean? I certainly couldn't ask. It's not that I'm not allowed to ask, but the therapist says it would be in my best interest to stay focused on me and avoid all conversations directly involving the man who devastated my life. She used that term, *devastated*. I felt small when she said it as if I were ten years old again and had no control over what was happening to me.

The house is quiet. The silence thick, the darkness dense. My wonderings have my skin broken out in gooseflesh and my extremities shaking. I could pull my covers up, snuggle in and finally go to sleep, but all I hear is *no*. Why no? Is he dead? No, I would've heard something. Maybe. The last time I looked him up online he seemed to be alive, but people have a way of keeping pages and websites active as a way of memorializing a deceased loved one, though who would want to remember him is beyond me.

Resigned to the fact I won't be sleeping; I get out of bed and grab my hoodie. Pulling it over my head, I slide my flip-flops on and head outside. I love the sound and feel of the world at two a.m. Bugs I can't name making their night noises and a chill that can only be felt this time of night in summer. Moisture falling to the eager grass below and the occasional call of the night owl. This is the time of the nocturnal earth creatures. Humans aren't allowed. At least that's how it feels as I stretch out in the grass and fix my eyes above. How I long to see the Milky Way.

Once, several years ago, I hooked up with a guy who promised to take me out west to Montana or one of the Dakotas. He promised me night sights that would take my breath away. Every night of our month-long courtship I thought of that wide open sky and tracing every star in our galaxy. The knowledge I wouldn't be able to do it was the only reason to mourn when he decided he'd had enough of me. *You're too fucked up*, he'd said. To which I replied we're all fucked up in our own way. He was certainly no peach.

I wonder what he's doing now. Did he make it big as an artist? Did he make it to Montana? He never seemed the type to actually go for something. Just a talker. Maybe that's why he thought I was the fucked up one and not the doer that I am.

Who but a doer would go through with trying to off themselves? And who but a doer would consent to getting a job at the one public place in town where they'd seen their most humiliating moment? Red bricks rough against my face, dumpster smells crawling into my nose and mouth, and a grown man pushing himself into me, his hand full of my long, dark hair, jerking my head back with every thrust. Thank god he was quick. There were scratches on my cheek after that. Mom asked why, but I couldn't bear to tell her I'd been sold to the cook at Jubilee's and I'd happily gone along with it to please my lover. Her brother-in-law. How does a fifteen-year-old tell her mother something like that? *Hey, Mom, I'm a whore.* Besides, he told me not to tell, and he was so jealous afterward.

Footfalls on gravel break me away. It isn't ideal to come up against someone in the late-night hours, but it's better than remembering. At least for the moment. Sitting up I train my eyes in the direction of the sound half expecting to see the weird old guy from three trailers up. It's Lucinda. She's walking slowly, looking over her shoulder. I clear my throat and she almost comes out of her skin.

Her hand is on her chest. "Good lord you scared me."

Pulling my knees up to my chest, I wrap my arms around them. "Where are you off to?"

She shrugs. "I..." Her shoulders fall. "No place."

I pat the ground beside me. "Want to pull up a seat?"

She smiles but shakes her head. "No." She looks over at her home. "I should probably go back inside."

I look down at the small bag she's clutching and suddenly

understand I have interrupted an escape. "Don't let me stop you. I mean from wherever you're going. I won't tell a soul I saw you."

"Really?"

"Yeah." I stand. "I can walk with you for a few minutes, if you want."

"Oh. No." She shakes her head. "No."

It's funny how even strangers seem to know my worth. "No problem."

She seems to realize she's struck a chord with me. "It's not you," she offers. "If he..." Her eyes fall to the ground briefly before looking back up at me. "If he sees you with me, he'll kill us both."

I nod, not bothering to tell her courting death is what brought me here in the first place.

"He doesn't mean to be a bad man." Her gaze travels back to the trailer. "He just gets so mad."

"They never mean to, but they often are."

She appears stunned. I wonder if this is the face she gave the first time his hand met her tender flesh. I had one of those too. The first time my uncle pushed into me. The first time I was struck by a lover. I think all of the faces are the same. Mine: eyes empty, mouth slightly open. That's the way they like us best. Complacent. Quiet. Void.

"Who are you?"

I extend my hand. "Zed."

Her handshake is loose, non-committal. "Lucinda."

"I know."

She looks confused. "How?"

I motion toward my house. "My mom."

"Camille is your mom?"

I nod.

A light bulb seems to go off. "Ah. The wayward daughter. She was so sad when speaking of you." She smiles. "I'm glad you're back."

Again, not the best time to bring up suicide.

She looks back at her home. "I would like to talk. To get to know you. But..."

"You have to go." I nod. "No worries."

One more lingering look across the street. I wonder why she does it, but I already know. As much as you want to get away from something, or someone, there's a part that holds you back. Usually it's the one that says, *No one will want you now. You're spoiled goods.* At least that's what my voice says. Without another word, Lucinda turns and continues walking down the path that will lead her away from this place. She'll be back. I know it and I'm sure she does too.

FIVE

ank is nice. From the way he talks about my mom I suspect he'd do anything for her. I'm hired in record time, at least for me. Within ten minutes he's given me an apron and is introducing me to a few of the suckers I might be working with from time to time. Charles, the cook (*Who did not bang me against the brick wall out back*), Amy and Carol, the two front girls for today, and Kenny, primarily maintenance. It's odd that Hank has someone come in daily just to do the cleaning, but I like it. I hate to clean up after the public. We still do a soft clean while on shift, but Kenny handles the big stuff.

"There's a few more staff members not here this morning, but I imagine you'll meet all of them in time." He removes his Jubilee's visor and scratches the balding patch at the center of his crown. "We get pretty busy here at lunch and then pick back up again after the kids get out of school. How would you feel about working eleven thirty to six?"

I shrug. Makes no difference to me. "That sounds good."

"Great!" His smile is genuine. I wonder if he is one of those rare breeds of man. The ones who do favors and kindnesses without asking for anything in return. "You can start tomorrow."

"Thank you."

Hank leans in and lowers his voice. "Ah. It ain't nothing. Your mama told me you've been going through a rough patch. I know a little something about hard times. My door is always open. Work related or not."

I wait for him to wink, but he doesn't. He just smiles. I don't trust him.

"Thanks," I say. "See you tomorrow."

"Eleven thirty."

I nod and push the door open. Hattie is waiting in her Bronco, windows down and some pop song blaring. It's a little embarrassing. She's my chauffeur today. First the job interview and later group. I tried to get out of going to this counseling thing. It's bullshit. I don't need to go and air my past to a bunch of fucked up strangers. I just need to focus on getting my shit straight. But I promised and that means something, I guess. When I open the door to the old tin can, Hattie turns the volume down and gives me a huge smile. She's bigger now than she was a few days ago. I swear that kid must be huge.

Her eyes are bright, expectant. "How'd it go?"

I hold up the shirts and my very own Jubilee's visor. "Great."

She squeals, clapping her hands together. "We should go to Montrel's to celebrate!"

"It's ten o'clock in the morning, Hattie."

"And? You don't have group until this afternoon. We have plenty of time."

I laugh despite myself. "Don't you think it's a little early for ice cream?"

She points to her belly. "This kid doesn't think so. Come on."

Tossing the shirts in the back, I pull the visor over my disheveled hair and climb inside the truck. There's no sense arguing with a pregnant woman when she's got a craving. My friend, Amanda, taught me that. Three-thirty in the morning was a fine time to head out to the all-night Walmart to pick up a tomato. Who the fuck eats a tomato sandwich at four o'clock in the morning but a pregnant woman?

Montrel's is basically deserted, save for the older woman behind the counter. Her name is Emma and she's worked here since I was a child. She probably owns the place. I could ask now without being labeled a nosy kid, but I don't care enough. Hattie is practically bouncing off the fading black and white walls that look like they haven't been updated since before I was born.

"I don't know what I want. What do you want?"

I shrug. "I'm not really hungry for ice cream."

"Oh, come on!" She's pouting, batting her unnaturally long eyelashes at me. "I'm buying."

I want to ask her to buy me some Nyquil and cigarettes, but instead shrug. "Fine."

We step up to the counter and she eagerly orders a double chocolate deluxe fudge something. Then Emma looks to me. I'm frozen, much like the selection encased in glass before us. This is too normal. People like me don't go to the local ice cream shop at half past ten in the morning. People like me aren't even awake at half past ten in the morning unless we're unlucky enough to have a morning shift. We're still spread out across our beds, or someone else's, sleeping off the night, dreaming about the next party. *But I haven't been to a party in weeks.* And just like that, I realize I don't know who I am. Not anymore.

Emma is still staring at me, apparently none-the-wiser that I'm having an internal crisis. She doesn't look like the type who gives a shit anyway.

Hattie's voice has darkened a little, taken on a sense of dread. "Zeddie?"

I look at my little sister, but I don't see her. How can I see what shouldn't be there? *Why am I here? What am I doing? This isn't my life.*

She's beginning to panic. "Are you going to order?"

I smile, though I have no idea how I've managed to work those muscles. Not when every inch of me seems to be on fire. "Vanilla."

Hattie smiles and seems to relax a little, though I catch her eying me suspiciously as we wait.

We sit by the front windows, Hattie happily devouring her monster of a sundae and me stabbing at the glob of vanilla. *How did I get here?* I never planned to come back to this shit town. Yet here I am, watching ghosts through the window of the old ice cream shoppe.

Montrel's is on the fringes of downtown, which is why most of the high school kids like it. Or they did when I was in school. Far enough away from the prying eyes of adults, but close enough to be a nuisance, if one wishes to. Across the street is a small gas station, the only one in town still offering full service. I like that. The mid-20th century may not have been ideal for a lot of people, but it had its good points. In my opinion, full-service gas stations were one of those things.

"Are you nervous?"

I pull my focus back to her. "About what?"

"Group. You're still going today, right?"

"Yeah." I stab the vanilla glob in my paper takeaway cup. "I don't think I'm nervous."

"You seem nervous."

It's like she's ten again, making up her mind about something and doing her damnedest to make it a reality. "Hattie, I'm not."

She smiles. "Good." Taking another bite, she closes her eyes. I envy the smile. Happiness seems to come easy for her. I mean, it's ice cream for fuck's sake. Who gets happy eating fatty milk?

Looking back down at my own, I cut into it a couple of times with the spoon, not bothering to actually eat it, before shoving the bowl away. I'd rather have a smoke. "Can I borrow five bucks?"

She opens her eyes, suspicion settling where moments ago euphoria rested. "What for?" she asks, wiping the chocolate from her lips.

"Not drugs." *Stupid, stupid. Now she's going to think it's drugs.*

Her lips thin out. "You're acting weird. I don't feel

comfortable giving you any money unless you tell me what you're going to do with it."

"It's five dollars, Hattie. What's the big deal? I can't skip town with it." My hands begin to tremble. "What the fuck?"

She leans in. "Why won't you tell me? Is it drugs?"

"It's not drugs. I just said that."

"Then what is it? If it isn't drugs you shouldn't have a problem telling me what it is."

"Jesus Christ." I scrub my face with both hands. "It's fucking cigarettes, *okay*?"

She disapproves, as is evidenced by her scrunched-up nose and mouth, but there's something else. Relief? Grabbing her purse, she digs through and pulls out five one-dollar bills. Thrusting them at me, she says, "You're going to need to clean your language up before this baby gets here."

I know she's joking. Trying to lighten the mood. Trying to calm me down. But I don't want to be calmed. Snatching the cash, I stalk out of the building and cross the street. The gas station attendant, a young guy with a full, dark beard jumps when I enter, his elbow knocking the give-a-penny-take-a-penny into the floor behind the counter.

He scrambles, crouching down to gather the spilled change as I step up to the register. "C—Can I help you?" he asks placing the little red dish and its five pennies back in place.

"A pack of Pall Mall. Please. And a lighter."

He lays my selections on the counter, and I give him the five ones. "Keep the change," I say as I head out the door. Another few pennies for the dish.

Outside, I rip open the pack and light up, taking a long draw. The first one is always the best. Not because it tastes good but because in this moment, I am myself again.

"Feel better?" Hattie's on the bench by the door. No surprise there.

Taking another draw, I hold it in and release slowly before answering, "Oddly enough, I do."

She stands, tossing what remains of her ice cream in the garbage. I wonder if she tossed mine out before crossing the street, but it's obvious she must have. "Let's go," she says walking ahead of me. Then, over her shoulder, "You can't smoke in my truck."

She's different now; back straighter, easy smile gone. I want to ask. *Dammit.* But somehow, I suspect it's me. I have a way of bringing out the worst in people. A trait surely passed on to me by my uncle. He's certainly brought out the worst in me over the years.

The car ride is quiet, even stormy, despite the roaring of the wind coming through open windows. Hattie's looking straight ahead, stray strands of amber flying around her head and occasionally landing in her line of sight. She pushes them down, a constant battle she's sure to lose. I settle deeper into the old bucket seat, part of me glad she's stopped talking. This is what I want. No bouncing around with excitement, no pretending the last fourteen years of my life never happened. No more denying the fact that I tried to take my life. On purpose. Planned it out.

This is what I want.

Still, I turn to look at her. "What're you going to do with this monster when the kid's born?"

She shrugs. "Sell it."

I catch sight of The Wet Spot and think of Betsy Franklin. Is she in there now? Is she topless?

"You going to start hanging out there too?" Her tone is accusatory.

"I was just thinking of Betsy." I look back at my sister. "What do you think it's like for her?"

"Hard."

"Being a waitress?"

She shakes her head, tugging at another stray strand as she does so. "She's got a sick dad and a worthless husband. You remember Dalton Thompson?"

I nod.

"That's who she ended up marrying. He doesn't work, so

Betsy had to take a job at the club because it's the only thing she could get around here that would pay the bills."

She turns the Bronco onto a once-familiar road and I shift, an effort to suppress the bile rising in the back of my throat. "Where are we going?"

"I need to drop something by Dad's house. Can you hold it together long enough for me to do that?"

"Why couldn't you do that yesterday or the day before? I don't want to see him."

"It will take me less than ten minutes."

"I don't want to see him, Hattie. Turn around. Turn around!" The last words come out as a shriek with me clawing at the door like I'm going to actually jump out of a moving car onto gravel.

She grabs at me, her manicured nails scraping across my skin. "What is your problem, Zed? Stop it." She slams on the brakes, making the Bronco slide across the gravel and sending me into the windshield, but she doesn't fully stop. I guess she's afraid I'll jump out and hightail it. "What is wrong with you?"

I sit back, pressing my hand against the spot on my forehead that connected with the glass. "I told you I don't want to see him. I can't see him."

"I understand you don't want to spend time with him for whatever reason, but everything I do can't be about you." Ouch. "I took you to your job interview and I'm taking you to group, the least you can do is be grateful."

"I am."

She stops the truck, turning the ignition off and jerking the keys out. "You could act like it, you know?"

"I'm sorry."

Pushing the door open, she grabs her bag and slides out. "Wait here. I'll be back in a few minutes."

Waiting for her to disappear into the interior of our childhood home, I push my door open and exit the truck. I haven't been here for years. It was the perfect place for two little girls to grow up. Plenty of room to roam and neighbors far enough away to lend an element of privacy, but what was our playground also became his.

After the divorce my uncle moved into my father's house. On weekends when Hattie and I would stay with our dad we'd often be left alone with Dan, especially when he was made to work weekends. This isn't where the abuse started, but that man was happy that fortune had smiled upon him and delivered me twice a month.

Rounding the house, I'm not entirely surprised to find our old play set still standing, barely. It's stood the test of time as well as I have.

"Zed!" Hattie's panicked voice rounds the corner. "Zedwynne!"

Rushing to the corner of the house, I stop as my sister and father come into view. She's panicked, standing by the Bronco, hands cupped over her mouth screaming my name. My body is urging me forward, pushing me toward them in order to keep my pregnant sister from worrying, but apprehension is holding me back. My dad is unchanged in appearance. Still lanky and skinny, still wearing the same AC/DC shirt he'd worn when I was a child.

"Zedwynne!"

"Calm down, Sweetie," I hear him tell Hattie, his hand going protectively to her shoulder. "All this stress isn't good for the baby."

She looks at him, her eyes red and glistening. "I yelled at her, Dad. She isn't in the place to be yelled at. What if she took off? I couldn't live with myself."

My chest tightens at the sight of her, and I step forward. "Hattie," I say, my voice as tight as my chest. "I'm here."

She rushes across the divide, throwing her arms around me. "Oh god. Thank goodness. I was so scared." She's sobbing now. "I thought you were upset with me." She pulls back, holding me at arm's length. "I'm sorry for yelling at you."

I cup her face. "It's okay. It's okay. I'm not upset. I deserved it." Just stop crying. Please stop crying. "I was an asshole."

She releases me, wiping her cheeks with the hem of her tunic. "I told you to stay in the car."

"Since when do I listen to anyone?" I'm trying to make her laugh, but the presence of our father ruins the moment.

"Never," he says. Hattie falls in beside me and we both face him. "Hey, kiddo." He moves to hug me, but I hold my hand up. "Another time."

I nod.

"You girls want something to drink?"

"No thanks, Dad," Hattie says, grabbing my hand. "Zed's got an appointment we need to get to." She's leading me across the yard, releasing me only when we've reached the truck. "Maybe me and J.C. can come over this weekend for supper." I climb into the truck and look out at them, my eyes meeting his. "We haven't been over for a while."

He smiles. "That would be nice." Then, to me, he says, "You coming with them?"

"She has to work," Hattie says quickly, giving him one of her patented *would I lie to you* smiles.

"Oh yeah?"

"Yeah. Hank gave her a job at the diner."

I'm melting under his gaze. "Good old Hank. Well, maybe we can have lunch sometime soon."

"Maybe," I say, but it's all false. He knows I want nothing to do with him. He's known it for years. I could've called my grandparents all those years ago, but I didn't. Instead, I called him, but he was too angry about the trial and the accusations against his brother. How're you feeling now, motherfucker? "But I doubt it."

Hattie climbs quickly into the cab and closes the door. "See you this weekend, Daddy," she says as she fires up the engine and begins to back up. "Let me know if I need to bring anything." We were back at the main road before she spoke again. "I had no idea things were that bad between the two of you."

"Yeah," I say, turning my attentions out the window. Pointing at the upcoming service station, I add, "Let's go get slushies. I need something cold."

HATTIE WANTS to go to the park after we get our drinks. I don't mind. We've still got a couple of hours before my appointment. Exiting the vehicle, we cross the gravel parking lot to the refurbished rubber-clad playground. Several mothers are there with their little ones. I keep my eyes on them as Hattie leads the way to the swings toddlers can't use. I wonder what they're thinking, but the hardness of their glares and their change of formation says it all. I am a threat, and they will do what it takes to keep their little ones safe.

"I'm sorry for being hard on you," she says when we sit down. The set is the same one from our youth, but the rubber seat isn't nearly as comfortable as I remember. "You just got so upset in town because you thought you couldn't get cigarettes and then you lost your shit about going to Dad's." She looks at me and then down to the ground. "I'm worried about you."

I fish the pack out of my pocket and light a cigarette, taking a puff and holding it in. After a moment I release smoke into the air. "I'm worried about me too. And I want to go to this fucking group thing about as much as I wanted to go to Dad's."

"Do you want to talk about it?"

I look at her. She's glowing from pregnancy and her eyes are bright. It must be over ninety already, but she's cool as a cucumber. Strangely, I do want to talk about it. I ache to talk about it. To tell someone else every little thing. Just not a roomful of strangers and not my little sister.

I shrug. "Not really."

She sighs. "When you're ready, I'm here."

I smile. Some half-smirked effort. "Thanks."

I watch the mom group as I nurse the watermelon big slush. They're observing us, a pack of wolves eying their prey. Hattie's hand falls softly on my arm, pulling my attention from their carnivorous stares. I look down and follow her finger as it glides over my skin, tracing the vine tattoo I ended up with at eighteen. I have no recollection of getting it, but I think it was a dare and I was wasted.

Her voice is far off, like she's present but absent all at the same time. "You have a lot of them," she says.

Placing my cup on the ground, I say, "Yeah," like that one half-assed word is enough for this moment.

She turns my hand palm up and finds the first one. "A firefly?" She traces its image. First the body and then the wings sending little trills up my arm, across my shoulders, and throughout my body. "It's beautiful."

I'm itching to pull my hand away, to retract within myself from her touch. From her need. I want to tell her I'm not in a place to handle what she needs, but her hand is so soft on my skin, and she found the firefly. *Our firefly.*

She slides her hand into mine and faces forward. "It's hard to believe how much everything has changed."

I'm trying to keep in sync with her swinging rhythm. It's suddenly the most important thing in the world.

Her voice is softer, far away again. "Some days I want to get out of here. Just like you did. I don't want to think about anything or anyone. Just pack my shit and get out." She touches her rounded belly. "But then I think about this one." She drops my hand. "How did you do it, Zeddie? How did you leave all of us behind?"

It's a fair question. One no one has bothered to ask before. Probably because Cami already knew the answer and Hattie was too afraid to know. We used to share everything until my uncle told me not to tell.

Tossing my cigarette on the ground, I collect my cup and stand. "I just couldn't stay anymore."

She's up too, following me as I make my exit. This is what I do, and I do it quite well. One of the moms is coming toward me, her face contorted with anger. We're on a collision course and she seems hellbent on our coming together.

"Hey," she says. "Hey!" She's pretty. Maybe a few years older than me with chestnut hair piled into a bun atop her head. She's got heart lips that are currently trembling and bright eyes. I don't know why I think of those Big Eyes kids, but I do. She's wearing jean capris and a white top. I like the eyelets. "You can't leave that over there."

I look back. *Hattie?* "What?"

She grabs my arm (*why is everyone touching me today?*) and pulls me back over to the swings. Hattie is watching, her eyes equally big. The woman bends down, her elegant finger pointing to the butt I left moments ago. "That. You can't leave *that* on a playground."

Too stunned to do anything more, I pick the offensive item up and shove it into my back pocket. "Sorry."

"You would have been sorry if one of those toddlers had gotten ahold of that and ate it. How can you be so careless? It's *poison!*"

Hattie is standing beside me now. She looks defiant, as if she will attack this woman whose only concern is the babies running around without a care in the world. "She said she's sorry, lady."

"What good will sorry do next time?" The woman is furious, which now seems a bit dramatic considering the butt is in my pocket. I know why. It really has very little to do with my offense and more to do with my existence. "And how can *you* defend her?"

I put my hand on Hattie's shoulder. "Let's go."

"Oh yeah," the woman says. "Better get to another park so you can poison more children."

Here we are, three women, one heavily pregnant, one despicable, and one in full Mama Bear mode, in an unnecessary standoff. This woman should know I won't disappear no matter how much she longs to see it happen. I wonder if she has a broken person wreaking havoc in her own life, so she wants to eradicate it from everyone else's. I'd like to let her know that death didn't want me so this world will just have to deal, but my little sister is steadily encroaching upon her. Is she going to hit her?

I put my hand on her shoulder, "Hattie, it's fine. Let's go." But she holds her position. Staring at the woman who is, likely, almost ten years her senior. She draws her mouth up, her brow knitting together, her cheeks the healthy cherry color of rage.

Hattie opens her mouth and part of me expects her to spit all her rage into the woman's face, but to my surprise, she says matter-of-factly, "I hope your kid eats poop!"

The woman's pursed lips relax—it's clear she was expecting the same thing I was—and her mouth hangs open. I can feel mine is doing the same. *What the fuck just happened?*

"Come on, Zeddie," Hattie says, grabbing my hand. "You don't need her bullshit."

I'm aware of their eyes on me as we walk, our spines straight, to the car. She's trembling. Such anger can't be good for someone in her condition, right? It isn't until we're in the car that I allow myself to speak. We're looking at one another, Hattie's eyes bright with the fire of victory.

I smile, "Poop?" She nods, her full lips pulling back in an I-can't-believe-I-just-said-that smile. "Why poop?"

"Seemed fitting." Her laughter was voracious, filling the car like an invisible raft that's cord has been activated. Soon we're both roaring. *"Poop!"*

Surely any passersby will think we're crazy, but I don't care. "I can't believe you said that to her!" Adding, "You have to tell me. Why poop?"

"I don't know!" She's howling. "It's worse than tobacco, I think." She lays her head back. "Did you see her face! Oh my god. So priceless."

Our laughter peters out and I lay my head back against the headrest. "I feel kind of bad, though."

She's confused. "Why?"

"Because I could have hurt one of those kids."

She turns toward me as best she can. "Listen to me. You have enough to torment yourself with. Don't add this to the list. You picked it up. No one is getting sick from your cigarette." She grabs my hand. "Let it go. I mean it."

I nod.

Letting go, she starts the Bronco and we leave the park. We're quiet for a few minutes. I guess neither of us wants to deal with what happened back there, but we feel unfinished. Like a book I read once written by someone in a Jewish prison camp during World War II. I don't know why I started it. Probably bored. Besides, I've always had an interest in history, and at that time I was sleeping with a history major. The book leaves off mid-thought because the author was interrupted by his own execution. I don't want the scene in the park to be how I leave things with my little sister. Not that I am in danger of execution. Most of the time it just feels like it.

"Hattie."

"Yeah?"

"Can you pull over?"

She begins to slow. "Are you okay?"

I nod. When the car is in park, I turn to her. "I don't want to leave things the way we did."

She shakes her head. "It's fine. We don't need to talk about it."

"But we do. I don't think you know why I left."

"Mom said bad things happened to you and you needed time."

The urge to tell her about my relationship with our uncle dissipates. I can't find the words to tell her that he raped me over and over again until I thought I liked it. "Oh."

"Is that it? Is that right?"

I nod. "Yeah." This lie is okay. It's better she believe this than know what actually went on.

She sighs. "You can trust me, Zeddie. I'm your sister."

"I know."

"I don't think you do. Not yet." She turns toward the steering wheel. "But I hope one day you will."

Me too, little sister.

WE'RE MEETING in the basement of a Methodist church. I wonder how my father's father would feel about this. The man had a vendetta against any church other than Baptist. I always found it very unchristian to be so unkind to someone simply because their church practiced the same religion in a different way than he did, but he was a bitter man filled with hate. I guess it shouldn't have been surprising. Hattie pulls into the lower parking lot, and we find that the door to the fellowship hall is open with a sign announcing the group meeting dangling from the doorknob by a fraying string.

She turns to me. "Are you going to be okay? Should I come inside with you?"

I shake my head. "I don't think they'd like an audience." I pat her hand. "Thank you, though. I appreciate the thought." I take a deep breath, releasing it slowly. "What will you do while I'm inside?"

"I saw a bookstore on the way in. Maybe I'll go and see what they have in their parenting section."

"Okay then. See you in an hour." I jump out of the truck, giving her a wave as I head inside the building. The toot of the Bronco's horn is her way of wishing me luck.

A rush of cool air greets me upon entrance into the old building. This church has been standing since the early twentieth century, but the fellowship hall wasn't built until the '70s or '80s, a fact evidenced by the white speckled linoleum floor covering the vast space. In the center of the room is a clearing, odd looking among the rows of tables laid out for the next fellowship meal. A circle has been made with chairs and I am not the first to arrive.

Sitting huddled together is a woman and a kid who must be almost ten years younger than me. She looks up as I take a seat, tipping her head back in greeting. I do the same.

Moments later an aging woman wearing a summer sweater and brown slacks joins us, placing a metal bottle beside her chair.

Eyes zeroing in on me, her rose-colored lips pull back into a smile and she says, "Good afternoon. I'm Rebecca."

"Zedwynne."

The woman and boy a few chairs over from me snap their heads around and I see the boy mouth my name to his friend from my peripheral.

Rebecca smiles. "Welcome. I'm glad you're here. We'll begin soon." I nod and she exits the circle, disappearing into the back hall.

I glance at the boy and woman, both still have their gazes fixed on me. I nod.

"Sorry," the boy says.

"No problem," I say despite the fact that it is a major fucking problem. This is why I didn't want to come to this place.

"I'm Claiborne," he says. "They call me Clay."

I nod. "Zedwynne."

"This is Deidre." He points to the woman beside him.

"Hey," I say, and she nods, her dark eyes suspicious. Fuck, this is awkward.

The kid leans forward, hands on knobby knees. He can't be twenty yet. His skin still holds the angry red puffs of pubescence, highlighted by numerous piercings; two in his lips, two in his eyebrows, and one in his nose. No tattoos, though. Well, none that I can see. Maybe they're under the long-sleeved hoodie he's wearing. Who knows. His dark hair is plastered to his head, a sure sign it hasn't been washed in a few days. Deidre, on the other hand, is wearing a short-sleeved shirt, buttoned to the neck, the yellow making the soft brown hues of her skin pop, and jeans. Her hair is natural and the only piercings visible are those in her ears. I avert my eyes, sure that the amount of time I've stared at them is unacceptable.

"What're you in for?" Clay asks.

"Being a fuck up like the rest of us," Deidre says, giving him a nudge. "Lay off."

I don't get to respond, not that I'm looking to, because the room begins to fill up. All eyes are on me, prompting me to wonder how often they get new people in this particular corner of hell.

"Welcome, everyone," Rebecca says, taking her place in the circle. "If you find yourself in need of a break during session, you may visit our refreshments table along the front wall." She giggles and lifts her shoulders at the mention of the goodies. *Kill me now.*

HATTIE IS all smiles when I climb into the Bronco. "How'd it go?"

"I don't want to talk about it."

She frowns, all excitement visibly draining from her. Turning the key, she backs out of the space and points us in the direction of the road.

"Are you going to keep going?" Her voice is small, fearful.

I shrug. "I don't know."

My first thought as Eddie, some over-forty loser with a drug and alcohol problem, started talking was to bolt, but there was something about him that kept me in place. Something about the way he let it all out in front of everyone. Ten people sat in that circle, at least one of which he'd never seen before, and he just let it all hang out. I don't think I'll ever get to that point, but it's admirable, I guess. In a way.

"What are you going to tell Mom?"

I sigh, shifting in the seat. "I don't want to talk about it, Hattie, okay?" I look over at her.

She nods. I'm not putting any money down on her being

quiet for the rest of the ride, but if we can go a few miles in silence maybe I can get my head together. Maybe.

Six

Jubilee's is busy at lunch. I wasn't ready for this. Body after body filing in to eat at the greasiest spoon in town. Hank isn't here, but he's left me in the very capable hands of Oliver, his shift lead for the day. He looks to be a couple of years older than me, but I don't care to ask if I'm right. Overhearing some of the morning's conversations it seems he may also be a hostage in this charming little town. I imagine his captivity is a bit more metaphorical than my own, though. Unless he has a mother and sister watching his every move. Not likely. Probably.

"How's your first day?" He asks me as the next person in line surveys the menu.

I smile. Trying to be as pleasing as possible is more work than the actual job. "Good," I say, keeping my focus on the woman before me.

"Cool. Just keeping a check on our new girl for the boss man." He winks and takes off again; a chihuahua on speed.

"Oh dear, are you new?" the woman asks, finally finished with her exhaustive review of the menu.

I nod.

"Are you okay with special orders?"

She's older. Maybe late-fifties. I can humor her. "Yes, ma'am. The computer does it all for me." *Thank god.*

AFTER LUNCH HOUR is over and the dining room becomes something of a wasteland, I begin to tidy up. I'm not surprised to turn and find Oliver approaching. Amy told me to watch out for him. Turns out he's got something of a reputation with the women of Jubilee's.

His smile is crooked. Cute. "How was your first lunch rush, new girl?"

I look at him, willing myself to remain unimpressed with his dancing blue eyes and unkempt dark hair. His lips, full and wide, aren't tempting at all. *Not at all.* "It's Zed and it was fine."

He feigns a wound, placing his hand over his chest in an exaggerated way. "Ouch." He looks around. "Did you wipe down all the tables?"

"Yes."

"And you swept the floor?"

"Yes."

He looks at me, a question in his blue gaze. "Break time?"

I shrug. "Sure."

We go through the kitchen and out the back door. He leaves it open and tells the cook to yell if Jessica, my partner on the front since Amy's shift ended, needs help. I look over at the dumpster. Feel the rough brick against my cheek.

"You okay?" he asks. He's looking at me.

Bristling, I respond, "Yeah. Why wouldn't I be?"

He shrugs. "You just look a little, I don't know. You just have a weird look on your face."

How observant. "I'm fine."

He pulls a pack of Marlboros out of his pocket and extends it to me. I gladly take one and he lights both. "So, what's your story?" he asks after his first drag.

"I don't have a story."

He smiles, tilting his head slightly, and my treacherous mind imagines what those pillows he calls lips feel like. "Everybody has a story."

I shake my head. "Not me. I'm just a girl."

"You don't look like a girl."

I want to ask what I look like. A puppet? I've certainly played the part many times. Broken? Can't deny that. I turn toward the patch of woods behind the building and nurse my Marlboro.

"Hank likes to hire people with a story."

I look at him. "Oh yeah? What's yours?"

His smile is nice. So is the way he tilts his head to the side. "I asked you first."

I shrug. "And I told you I don't have one. I just moved back to town. Hank is letting me work here until I get my feet on the ground."

"Sounds like a partial story to me."

He's beginning to annoy me. Who exactly does he think he is? I rub out the tip of my cigarette on the brick, making sure not to crush it. No need to waste it. "I'd better get back."

"Wait." He extends his hand as if he might touch me and I recoil. Nodding, he shoves it in his pockets. "I'm sorry. I didn't mean to startle you."

"You didn't."

"I just wanted to tell you that I'm here. If you need anything."

I nod. "Thanks." Without another word I rush back into the building, eager to get away from Oliver and his full lips and his mountain of questions.

Jessica is leaning against the counter when I return, elbow resting on the orange countertop. She turns, her head looking as though it will snap off her neck as she does.

"Did I miss anything?" I ask.

She expels a puff of air that lifts her wispy bangs. "Hardly. I hate this time of day." Straightening, she leans her body against the counter. "So, what did you and Ollie talk about?"

"Ollie? Sounds weird."

"I only call him that to piss him off." She sputters out a laugh. "He hates it."

"I don't blame him."

"So, what's your story?"

Leaning against the wall, I cross my arms. "Why do people keep asking me that?"

She laughs. "Because Hank don't hire anybody who's not down on their luck." She tugs her sleeves up to reveal puffy scars running down the length of her forearms. "We've all got a story."

I've never cut before. I've thought about it. A lot. Turns out I like to hurt myself in other ways, especially when I'm letting someone else do the hurting.

I drop my arms. "I'm sorry."

"Don't be sorry for me." She tugs her sleeves back down. "I'm handling my shit. Looks like you're just getting started."

"Yeah. Maybe."

She picks up a rag and tosses it at me. "Why don't you go wipe down some tables." She looks out over the empty dining room. "I'm going to clean the windows."

I've already wiped them down, but the task seems an appropriate way to end an awkward moment.

MOM PICKS me up from work. She's smiling the way she used to when she would pick us up from grade school. So proud, though I don't know what she has to be proud of. She's looking better today. Not quite as tired. Oliver is standing outside the building. He raises his hand to me, and I manage a small wave.

"Who's that?" she asks. I don't look at her, but I can tell by her tone that she's smiling.

"Shift lead, Oliver."

"He seems nice." She's always been a sucker for men. Especially if they're moderately attractive.

"Actually, he kind of seems like a douche."

She laughs. "Well, he's a cute douche."

I look at him. She's not wrong, but I wish like hell she was. I don't like him staring at me as if I should be on the Jubilee's menu.

My mom's voice breaks into my thoughts. "You're looking well today."

"Am I?"

"Yes. I think work suits you."

I laugh. "It was my first day." I slide the cigarette from my pocket and plop it in my mouth. "There's still plenty of opportunities for me to fuck it up."

"Don't light that."

I look at her, my lighter poised to meet the stub hanging from my lips. She's serious. I think about doing it anyway, let her see how it feels when someone insists on doing something you don't want them to do, but even I'm not that petty? I slide both items into my shirt pocket and face forward.

After a mile of silence, she says, "Your doctor called today."

I don't move, certain she's trying to gauge my reaction. "What did she want?"

"To see how you're getting on, I suppose. I wasn't home. I only heard her message."

"Great."

"Have you called her this week like you're supposed to? I'm sure she'd like to know how group went." I remain quiet and she takes it as her cue to add, "You know she's expecting to hear from you."

"I know." My voice is sharp in the small confines of the car.

After a moment of quiet she says, "Well?"

"Please stop talking to me."

"Don't act like a child, Zed."

Fury bubbles up from the depths of me like lava, its angry flames licking my face. "Maybe I'm making up for lost time." Direct hit. Her face falls.

Her grip tightens on the steering wheel. "You can't keep doing this whenever I ask questions, Zed." She's waiting for a response, but I refuse to give her what she wants. "You agreed to do certain things—"

My tone is clipped. "I'm aware of what I agreed to."

"Then do it."

"I am." I draw my hand into a fist, release, repeat. "I went to that fucking group just like she asked. I sat in there with those assholes and listened to their sob stories—"

"Do you always have to be so vulgar?"

"Yes, I do. If you don't like it, stop talking to me."

"Zed, you're being unreasonable."

"Am I? I'm trying to mind my own fucking business, what're you doing?"

"I'm trying to make sure you're okay!" It isn't often that she gets this exasperated, high-pitched tone, the one that lets everyone around her know she's on edge. Maybe if she'd keep her nose out of my business she wouldn't have to have it now. She flexes her hands around the steering wheel, and I immediately stop moving my own. No way I'm like her at all. In a more defeated tone, she adds, "Just call your therapist, okay? And stop shutting me out. It's time for you to start giving."

A sputter escapes me, and I look at her. She's trying to meet my gaze and still keep her eyes on the road, but she's failing. Always failing. "All I've done for my entire life is *give*. You know it as well as I do."

"You allowed people to take. There's a difference."

Allowed? My eyes are burning, and fire is erupting at the back of my throat. "Pull over and let me out."

Her hands are in a flurry and she keeps looking from the road to me and back again. "I didn't mean it like that. You didn't allow Dan to do—"

The air in the sedan is growing too thin. I can't breathe. "Pull over," I choke.

"But we're miles from home."

I grab for the wheel. I can't stop. Not now. My voice pierces the interior. "Let me out! Let me out!"

"Zed, please calm down." Her eyes are wild, her arms trying desperately to block me from the wheel. I'm going to kill us.

I pull away and press my body against the door. "It's all your fault."

"Please don't." Her voice is calm, crawling over me in an attempt to infiltrate my defenses. I won't let her win.

I grasp the handle and look at her. "I'm out either way."

The car begins to slow and merge onto the shoulder. "I didn't mean to upset you," she's saying, but I can hardly make out the words. "Can we please talk about this?"

I push the door open. "We have *nothing* to talk about." Slamming the door is satisfying. Cami hates the slamming of doors. Not just car doors.

I walk up the shoulder away from her, but she waits there until I'm almost out of sight. I imagine she believed I would come back. Shows how much she knows. When she finally pulls away, I plop down on the ground, only somewhat concerned a copperhead will venture out to bite me. Total truth? I don't know why I lost it back there. Maybe it was the mention of *his* name. I don't like to verbalize it. Not anymore. When I was a child I whispered it in my nightly prayers, asking God to make my uncle stop hurting me, then as a teenager, I whispered it with love as he pushed into me. He liked to hear his name, to know that I was his. Then, after his abandonment, I whispered it into the night because the darkness is the only one who listens.

Sadly, this isn't my first time being abandoned on the side of the road. I know my mom didn't really abandon me, but Doug did. Left me right out in the middle of nowhere all because I dared to ask who he was sleeping with other than me. None of my business, he'd said. When I continued to press, he pulled the car over and chucked me out. Just like that. I must have waited for hours for him to return, for him to care enough about me to check on my wellbeing at least. When I made it back to his place the few belongings I had were outside his door. I knocked and another woman answered. That was enough.

Oliver is still standing outside when I arrive back at Jubilee's, sweat rolling down my face. It doesn't seem like he's gone inside at all. He smiles as I approach. *What big teeth you have.* "Hey. Did you guys break down or something?"

"Or something."

He looks concerned. "Is everything okay?"

I consider telling him nothing is okay. Everything is shit. Suddenly he is the one person in the world I want to unload on. Maybe it's because I don't like him. Maybe it's because I do. Whatever the reason, my desire to share my load has me paralyzed, eyes leaking and lips quivering.

He tosses the remains of his cigarette onto the ground. "Hey." His voice is soothing. Before I realize it, his arm is around my shoulders and he's guiding me away from the front of the building. I freeze when we stop, when he stands me up against the building. *Rough brick.* I expect the worst, but he asks, "What's going on?"

I swipe at my tears, angry they decided to go on parade. "Nothing." I look down. "I'm sorry."

"You two had a fight?"

How perceptive. I nod.

"Did she kick you out of the fucking car?"

"No." I shake my head. "No."

"Then where the hell is she?" He backs up, looking out to the parking lot. "Why the hell hasn't she come back for you?"

"I told her to leave me there."

He's stunned.

I feel the need to explain to him. To make him understand this is just how things are right now, but I can't. "She pissed me off and I told her to pull over." I look at him. His blue eyes have darkened. Guilt tightens my gut at the sight. "I'm in a bad place right now. I overreacted when she asked me a question." Jerking what's left of the Marlboro out of my pocket, I grip it between my lips. He grabs it, tossing it to the ground before supplying me with another. "Thanks." I light it and pull in deeply.

"What did she ask? Don't tell me she wanted to know about your day."

I expel a puff of laughter chased by smoke. I don't want to tell him about the therapist. "Something mundane. I don't even know why I got so mad." I take another draw. "I guess I'm just angry."

"We're all angry, Zed." He leans against the building beside me. "I'm pissed off about damn near everything. This town." He shakes his head. "This fucking town is bullshit."

I laugh.

"My ex." He lights his own replacement and takes a long, drawn-out drag. Seconds later he releases it and adds, "She's a fucking headcase and she makes me one."

"Wife?"

He looks at me and I can tell he likes that I'm interested. "Yeah."

"What's that like? Marriage, I mean."

He holds his hand up. "I ain't married no more, what does that tell you?"

I lean my head back and close my eyes. "Why does everything have to be so fucking complicated?"

"You've got me."

As we stand in silence I settle into the brick. It's cool against my skin, still damp from my walk back. The cicadas in the distance sound like maracas in the late day, their pitch building and building only to fade away. As a child, I thought their sound was the earth sizzling. I asked my uncle once, in the late afternoon. His big hand covered my thigh, the weight of it making my skin crawl. In an effort to distract him from his explorations, I asked him why the earth made such a sound. His laughter was deep and spilled out in hot puffs against my neck, *"Gracie, honey, you know those are bugs, right?"* I told him I did. Of course, I did. I was only playing. When his chin rested on my shoulder I stilled. *"It's their mating call."* His words were quiet, meant only for us. I didn't know what mating meant—not then—but he would teach me. I like to listen to them now. Not as a memory of what once was. It's oddly comforting to know I'm not the only creature rattled.

I open my eyes. Oliver is staring into the distance, his mouth set firm. That ex of his has him all mixed up. It's written all over his face. I snuff out my cigarette and consider covering his mouth with my own. I haven't felt the touch of a man, not sexually, in a while. His hands look nice: Long fingers, wide palms. I want to know what kind of lover he is.

He turns to me. I think he'll be annoyed, but he smiles. "What?"

I turn my face away to hide the color burning my cheeks. "Nothing."

There's ninety-degree coloring and there's I-was-picturing-you-naked coloring. Despite what you may think, they are not the same.

"What were you thinking?" He tosses his cigarette to the ground, grinding the toe of his Van sneaker into it to snuff it out.

Turning, I head toward the front of the building, tossing a response over my shoulder, "I have to call my sister."

He's scrambling to catch up with me. "Wait." I stop just short of the corner and turn to him. He slows up. "For what?"

"A ride."

"I'm off. I'll take you home."

I want to say no, tell him I would prefer my sister pick me up. It's safer that way, but I nod. That's what I do. When faced with a circumstance I know I should run from my voice leaves me and all I can do is nod, mouth agape, like a dumb, mute girl.

THE RIDE IS QUIET, but my skin is ablaze. I'll have to call the therapist now. She'll tell me that beginning any kind of romantic relationship at this stage could interrupt my healing. I know she'll say this because she already has. In our last face-to-face session. I didn't listen then because it didn't occur to me I would crave a man's touch again. It seemed absolutely ridiculous to even consider I would feel *anything* again. But here I am, feeling.

I know it's a leap, to think that he might be attracted to me in the same way that I'm attracted to him. But you never know. Sure, I look like shit, some beat-up old addict—who's not really an addict—with big dumb eyes and a scrawny body. Stranger things have happened, though. I mean, I dated a guy once who thought the best look for women was heroin chic. It didn't last long.

Oliver clears his throat, an indication that he's going to say something. I brace myself, expecting that this is the moment he'll make a move. Why else talk to me all day? Why take an interest enough to drive me home? More importantly than all that, how will I react? The old me would tell him to pull the car over, hardly waiting before pouncing on him.

"So, where do you live? I mean, I know you said to go this way, but I need a destination." He's grinning. "It's kind of important."

My cheeks warm. "Hastings Road."

"The—"

"Yes, the trailer park. My mom couldn't afford anything else after the divorce."

His hands go up. "Easy. I was going to say mobile home community. I've got a buddy who lives over there."

"Oh."

"You live with your mom and sister?"

"Just my mom. And her husband." The cloth seat of the old Ford is becoming uncomfortable. Too hot or too stiff, but I don't know which. I shift, turning my attention out the window in an effort to stop communication.

"I think I'd like to live with my mom again," he's saying. "She's a widow. Never remarried." He laughs. "She asked me to move back in after the divorce. My divorce. But I don't want to go back there. Instead, I live with four other guys." I grunt my response, hoping this will serve as a better indicator, but he continues. "She hates it, though. Says it isn't natural for so many men to be living together without women. Oldtimer."

"How old is she?"

"Fifty-four."

"Doesn't sound old to me."

He looks over, holding my gaze a little too long considering he's the one driving, then chuckles. "I just meant her thinking. You know how her generation can be."

I nod, but I don't know at all.

"Anyway," he continues, "she keeps pressuring me to move back home with her, but I don't want to go back to that town. There's just nothing for me up there, you know?"

"No, I don't." I try to sound gracious, but I've never been very good at it.

His gaze shifts to me once or twice more during the ride. I wonder if he's trying to figure out what the hell is wrong with me. I want to tell him it's not worth it to find out, but the therapist tells me I shouldn't assume I know what's going on in the minds of others. The thing is, though, people aren't that hard to read. I knew how to do it when I was ten and my uncle started looking at me like a woman, and I know how to do it now with Oliver looking at me the same way. Like a woman. A crazy, nut job woman. I wonder if he wants to fuck me too.

"What's *your* story?"

I shift. "I told you I don't have one."

"And I told you Hank only hires people with a story."

"I've heard." I look at him, catching his eye as he glances over. It's dangerous to hold the stare of the person who's supposed to be watching for oncoming traffic, but I can't help myself. I don't like for anyone to pry and that's exactly what he's doing. I'll tell my story if, and when, I decide. He's not special just because his lips are full and lush and inviting. "What's yours?"

"Ladies first."

I smile. My best I'll-out-bitch-you face. "I insist."

I've seen exchanges like this a million times in those regency movies I've become weirdly fond of over the last several years. I've never read Jane Austen but I'm a sucker for her movies.

He smiles. "Okay." Turning back to the road, he shrugs. "There isn't much to tell. My wife left me, divorced me, and, practically, ran me out of town."

The silence presses between us. It's our wills fighting against one another, his pressing into mine, demanding I inquire, that I ask more. Mine pushing back, just give me peace. Ultimately, his wins.

"What'd you do?" I ask, and the pressure eases.

"She won't tell me?"

"And you have no idea."

"No."

A sputter escapes my lips.

"What?"

I shake my head. "Nothing. Is that it, your whole story?"

"No. When I came down here, I hooked up with some people and started partying pretty hard. I mean, I took to it like a fish takes to water. Or so they tell me." He shifts in the seat, his relaxed wrist on the wheel seeming to be the only thing keeping us on the road. "I went into Jubilee's one day and started talking to Hank. I was broke, jobless, homeless, high...I was in a pretty bad way. He hired me on the spot."

"And now your life is perfect?"

His laughter fills the cab. "Sure." He looks over at me after a moment of silence. "Your turn."

I see my mother's house come into view and point. "That's me." I jump out of the vehicle as soon as it stops in the patch of gravel that serves as our driveway. Turning to him, I offer my best smile. "Thanks for the ride."

"Anytime." Then, before I can get away, he asks, "Do you want to hang out?"

"Tonight?"

He smiles. "Sometime."

I look at the house to see if anyone is witnessing this man

dropping me off, stomach dropping when I see Duke there. The last thing I need is Cami reminding me I shouldn't be getting involved with anyone romantically. *The therapist said*!

Looking back at Oliver, I give him a fleeting smile. "Probably not the best idea."

"If you change your mind." He leans across the seat, extending his hand. There, between his first two fingers is a piece of cardboard with a number scribbled across it. "You still owe me your story."

I accept the paper and nod. "Thanks again. See you around."

DUKE IS on the front porch nursing a long neck. It's a little embarrassing that he witnessed Oliver passing his number off to me, but also worrisome. There are no secrets between the lovebirds. He's older than my mom by almost a decade. I wonder if that's why she got with him. Something about the security of an older man. My dad was her age, and he hadn't been able to protect his family. Hadn't believed there was a reason to. What she needs to know is the age of a man doesn't matter. It's all about what he's made of.

He lifts his bottle in salutation, and I nod. "Care to sit a minute?" he asks, motioning to the other chair. They're the old metal ones from decades ago. All metal, no comfort. I take a seat. "How was *your* day?"

Cut the shit, man. "Fine. What's up?"

He leans forward. "Why don't you tell me why your mama's been crying since she got home. Without you."

I shrug, unable to meet his gaze. "We had a disagreement in the car on the way home."

"I gathered that. What was said disagreement about?"

Another shrug. No way I'm going to tell him his wife is too damn nosy. Especially not when he's allowing me to stay in their home.

"Zed." He flexes his hand, and I can't help wondering if he

wants to hit me. Most people do, I guess. "I'm trying real hard to stay out of whatever's going on between you and your mama. She's asked me to, and I want to be a good husband and respect her wishes. But I'll be damned if I'm going to watch her come in here most days after talking to you and cry. I'm just not going to do it."

"I don't know why—"

"You don't need to speak."

"She's crying." I talk at the same time he's speaking, but don't fail to hear that he's shutting me down. That's what men do when a woman is a threat. Shut us down. But I'm tired of being shut down. I'm tired of men thinking they make my decisions or that I'm nothing more than a walking piece of meat. "Duke, look."

"No, you look."

"No," I say, standing. "You look." I've never been good at sticking up for myself. My voice gets shaky, and my knees begin to feel like rubber. Sometimes I dream of confrontation and when I try to speak it's all garbled, like I've got a mouth filled with cotton. "I appreciate you letting me stay here. I appreciate your patience while I'm trying to get my shit together. But you don't know us. Me and *her*."

"I know more than you think."

"You know her story. You don't know shit about mine." I hold my hand up, a gesture used more to calm me than him. "I don't mean any disrespect, Duke. But you can't fix me and her. It's too broken. If you want me out just let me know."

I don't wait for his reply. Truth is, I don't want to hear it. I have no fucking clue where I'll go if he kicks me out.

SEVEN

The therapist tells me I'm making progress. Even when I tell her about the fight with my mother and my demand that she drop me off on the side of the road, she tells me I'm doing much better. She has a point, I suppose. Before my stint in the hospital, I would've taken something afterward, something to dull the pain. Funny thing is, I know it should hurt now but I'm empty; numb. No point in getting lost in pharmaceutical land. I know where they are, though, where Camille keeps her little stash. Now and then I sneak into her room, fish out her little box, and swipe a couple. Just in case. I may be a perpetual void at the moment, but there are no guarantees this voodoo will last. Like a good head doctor, the therapist praises me for obtaining gainful employment, though I'd hardly call $8.00 an hour gainful, and she doesn't even freak out when I tell her about my attraction to Oliver. Instead, she reminds me to stay on track. Relationships will come later. Now is the time to focus on me. Keep going to group. *Blah, blah, blah.* I don't bother to tell her I don't plan to build relationships with anyone.

It's never really been my thing.

Hanging up, I go to the kitchen. My mom is there tidying up

from dinner. I'm starved, but the thought of asking her for anything turns my stomach. "I called the therapist," I say, keeping my distance.

Her body tenses and as a result her height increases just slightly. Looks like her feelings are still hurt from yesterday's fight. Good.

"That's great news," she says, though she doesn't turn to look at me.

I know should broach the next topic carefully, but I've never been known for subtlety and I don't have time to wait. My next shift is tomorrow and the thought of being trapped inside a car with her, no matter the distance, is more than I can stand to think about at the moment.

Taking a deep breath, I say, "I need a car."

She turns slowly, a look on her face I can't quite describe, though I saw this pivot enough in my childhood to know exactly what it means. "And?" Her hands work with the towel in her hands. "Am I supposed to get you one?"

I shrug. It's insolent to respond in such a way, but I can't help saying, "You assumed responsibility for me when you picked me up."

It isn't fair for me to ask. I know this. But what do I do? Fight with her every single car ride home, ignore her, or keep accepting rides from Oliver that will end in us in the bed of his truck humping?

"Incredible." She tosses the towel on the counter and turns back to me. "Let me get this straight. You can speak to me however you like, curse at me, and treat me like garbage, and I'm supposed to just let it roll off my back and get you a car?"

I remember this mom. This is the one who stared at me with cold eyes and told me she would rip the one important thing from my life because it was *the right thing to do*. I don't like this mom.

"Forget it."

"Why?" She's almost in full dramatics now. *Lovely.* "I mean, you need a car, right? Let me just go into my purse and pull out the money to make that happen for you."

We're both in standoff mode. She's shining with indignation, and I with contempt. I knew this wouldn't work. The moment she pulled around the circle drive at the hospital I knew.

Suddenly Duke is at the door. "Everything okay, Cami?"

I cross my arms over my chest and look between them. I didn't have to worry about Cami having backup when I was a kid. Dad was rarely around and when he was, he was never really there. But Duke is always here. Always watching. Always judging.

She breaks away from me and looks at him. Her body is rigid, but I can see the pleading in her eyes. *Please help.* She's always relied on a knight in shining armor. That's why she left my dad. He's no one's hero.

"Zed needs a car." Her voice is clipped. This may be the moment she's realizing what she's done by bringing me back here. Maybe she thought there was hope for us when I was looking at her through a fog in the hospital, but now she seems painfully aware that we are broken. It's in the cut of her eyes and the curl of her lip.

Duke looks at me, his face taking on a look that is half disbelief, half annoyance. My mouth is poised to tell him to forget it, but I'm halted, unable to make the words actually form.

He shakes his head. "We can't help you with a car, Zed." He pulls my mother into his strong arms. They look strong. Just now I wish I had a pair to rely on.

I won't win this. Not that I care too. Maybe this is why it's so easy to leave them standing in the kitchen, Duke glaring at me and my mom clinging to him as though he is a buoy in rough waters. Always the victim. I'm being an asshole. I know my mother doesn't have the money to buy me a car. She's never had the money. I guess I thought she might let me use her car or Duke's old truck. He rarely uses it from what I can tell. Again, I've fucked up, though, approached her in the wrong way. Throwing myself across the bed, I close my eyes forcing my ears to shut out their hushed tones. No doubt he's telling her she can't give me everything I want when I can't give even an inch. He has no idea how much I have given, how much his precious Cami has stolen. But even as the insolent, bratty part of me wants to throw a huge tantrum and tell both of them to fuck off, the part of me that's been in their position was aware well before my ill-fated conversation with Cami that it was a long shot. Not only is there little incentive to give my crabby ass a car, they just can't afford it. Fuuuuuck.

———

IT's full-dark when Hattie's hand falls rough against my shoulder. Torn from sleep, I struggle against her, shielding myself from the blows my fuzzy mind feels certain are coming.

Her voice is low. "Get up."

Throwing my legs over the edge of the bed, I sit up, shielding my eyes against the harsh light of the bedside lamp she's turned on. I look up at her through one eye. "What time is it? What are you doing here?"

"After nine. Come on." Her quiet tone hints that the rest of the house is sleeping. Not unusual since both our Cami and Duke have to get up at ungodly hours to go to work. "I want to show you something."

The night air has taken on a sticky chill, the kind you get on the occasional night in the South when summer hasn't fully committed to showing up. Odd it would happen in late July. If only the days could feel like this. Unfortunately, we'll be sweltering until mid-October. Hattie is quiet as we climb into her old SUV. I don't mind it. I'm not ready to talk just yet anyway. Across the street, I see the light in Lucinda's trailer is on. Two forms are visible in the window against the shade, one cowering. *I know how it is to be trapped, Luce.*

Hattie's voice is clipped, annoyed. "I talked to Mom."

There it is. Her reason for dragging me out of rambling sleep.

Always Cami. I keep my eyes trained on the headlights bumping over dirt and rocks. "Yeah?"

"She said you were pretty nasty to her."

I drop my head back and close my eyes.

"Well?"

I look at her. She's tired, the dark circles lining her eyes visible in the soft light from the dash. This kid is draining her life force. "Are you feeling okay?"

She stops the car at the edge of the asphalt that leads two places: into town and away from here. "Don't try to change the subject. What the hell were you thinking?"

The weight of her stare is heavy, punishing, accusing. Outside my window is freedom. Roads leading into darkness, away from the judgments and oppressive regime that is my mother and sister. They're never going to see me any other way. I'm just the fuck up. It would be easy to pull the handle. It feels good in my hand, cool. She'll follow me, I'm sure, but for how long? I just need some peace and quiet, some time away from their incessant nagging and prodding.

"Zeddie, I need you to talk to me."

Goddammit! "She accused me of not following the doctor's orders."

A big guffaw filled the car, pushing me closer to the door. "So you made her put you out on the side of the road!"

We're moving again. Headlights bumping over asphalt, bouncing off of greenery on the side of the road; remnants of tiger lilies left from June and a ravenous groundhog. I don't want to talk about this. Any of it. Isn't it enough I speak to the therapist? "I thought that was better than getting into another argument. It seems like that's all we do."

"And why is that?"

My eyes are on her again, but she doesn't look away from the road. Of course, she would blame me. She's just like Cami now.

She jerks the tin can into the gravel parking lot of the local park. This one's for the poor kids. The proof is in the outdated, rusty equipment and the grass it sits on. Kids don't play on grass anymore; they play on recycled rubber or that squishy cork stuff. I'm glad my childhood came before that shit. Not that I remember using the swing set or jungle gym. The main use of this place when I was a kid was hooking up. Warm summer nights and the anxious hands of a teenage boy.

"What're you thinking about?"

I turn to find her staring at me. My dear baby sister hasn't learned how to hold onto the anger and think about other things yet. I'm happy she hasn't had to. She's still in battle mode, still ready to make me understand what I did wrong. I push the door open and jump out, heading over to the merry-go-round.

She's standing by the ancient contraption sooner than expected, hands on her hips, belly sticking out at me like an accusation. "Well?"

I shrug. "Robert Sinclair." Her eyebrows raise and her eyes twinkle in the light of the nearby streetlamp. "He brought me here a couple of times to make out."

She sits down, hands instinctively grabbing the bars flanking her. "I didn't know you dated him."

"We didn't date. Not really. He just called me when Annie wouldn't *open up* for him."

"And he thought you would."

My laugh is husky, an old box opened. "*Knew* I would." She lays back and I follow. Above the sky is black, littered with dying lights. "There's a lot you don't know about me, little sister."

Her hand finds mine. "But I want to. I want to know everything."

"I know, but I'm not ready to share. Not yet."

She turns her head toward me, and I do the same. "I can wait, Zed. Mom can wait. But you are going to have to give too."

I nod.

"I mean it. You can't keep doing this shit. I've got Mom crying to me on the phone almost daily, and Duke...He's a nice guy but you're pushing it with him. He loves Mama more than anything else in this world."

"He hates me, doesn't he?"

She squeezes my hand. "Duke doesn't hate anybody. Just try. He's the kind of guy that effort will go a long way with."

Hattie doesn't know what happened. At least I don't think she does. Gut tells me she would hate our mother too if she'd been forced to do what I was. Being ill-used by my uncle was one thing, but being betrayed by my own mother is something I may never get over.

"Will you try?" Her voice lacks the anger from moments ago.

My eyes meet hers. Wouldn't it be nice if trying were that easy? Someone asks you and you make the promise to try. I guess trying is a lot harder than making a promise. I nod and this is good enough for her. We've always been the kind of family to take things at face value to avoid dealing with the bigger issues.

"I'll do my best," I say.

The shift of her eyes and gnawing of her lip is a clue that she isn't entirely pleased with the answer, but she doesn't say anything. She rolls onto her back to look at the sky above. I do the same. Her grip has loosened on my hand, but she's still holding on. Always holding on. I guess I should be appreciative that she's never let go all these years. Always trying to stay in touch, call, send letters. Maybe it was annoying because I wanted her to give up on me like everyone else had.

"Zeddie," her voice is quiet.

"Yeah."

"Can I ask you something?"

Fear settles as a lump in the back of my throat. *Please don't ask about Uncle Dan.* "Okay," I croak.

"Why didn't you come to my wedding?"

An equally devastating question. "Um." I pull my hand from hers and sit up.

She struggles to sit upright, so I lend a hand. "I'm not mad at you," she says. "And I'm not asking to give you some guilt trip. I just...why didn't you come?"

"Hattie."

"You didn't receive the invitation, right?"

Shaking my head, I lean over. "I was in Nashville." Homeless. "And didn't have a way back home."

"Why didn't you call?"

I straighten, scrubbing my hands over my cheeks. "I—um. I guess it's because I didn't want to ask for help." Didn't want you to know how big a loser your big sis was. Is. "I'm sorry I missed your wedding."

Wrapping an arm around my shoulders, she pulls me into as good of an embrace as the bars of the merry-go-round will allow. "I'm sorry you didn't call."

"Me too."

She releases me, leaning against the rusting red bar that countless children have, no doubt, clung to in fear and excitement. "It's okay to ask for help, Zed."

"I know."

"Do you?"

I meet her eyes. "I'm learning to."

"That's what they call progress," she says with a smile and a wink. "Now, tell me about Robert Sinclair and don't you leave out a thing."

It's after one when we pull back into our mother's driveway. The lights are off at Lucinda's. I wonder if he made her suffer for leaving in the middle of the night like she did, already knowing he absolutely did. It's in their DNA to make us suffer.

Hattie is staring at me. "What's going on in that head of yours?"

My shoulders rise and fall. "Nothing. Just worried about the neighbor."

"Lucinda?"

"Yeah." She smiles prompting me to ask, "What?"

"I think it's good that you're worried about her."

"Yeah. Maybe." I pull the handle to get out and she grabs my hand. "Mom told me about the car."

"I guess she told you how I treated her horribly and then came at her demanding transportation like an ingrate."

"No. God, you're so negative about her. She just said you need a car."

"Oh."

She inhales, her hand going to her swollen abdomen. I want to ask if she's okay, but I remain silent. After a moment the twinge passes, and she looks back at me. "J.C. wants me to get a new car. He doesn't like me driving this. Especially not with the baby. When she comes." She's quiet a moment. "Anyway, I'd like to give it to you, but I'm afraid to."

I know the answer but play along. "Why?"

Her eyes are shining in the dim illumination of the dome light. "I'm scared you'll run away."

"You're afraid you won't be able to keep me under thumb."

"That's not fair, Zed."

I'm standing outside the vehicle now, turned in to face her. My legs shaking, though I'm not furious. Why should she trust me? Why should anyone trust that I won't run off in the middle of the night? Maybe Lucinda and I will get in my sister's old Bronco and head for the horizon, never look back at those who've hurt us. But we need them. As much as I hate to admit needing anyone, I need my sister and Cami.

I lean against the door. Defeated. "I'm not running away, Hattie. Not this time."

She nods. "I'll pick you up after work and you can drop me off at home."

"Thank you."

Her head is moving up and down again, lips pressed tight together, and eyes shining in the dark. I've done this to her. *We* have done this to her; me, our mother, and my uncle. "Just don't make me regret it."

EIGHT

I t's been quiet since the night we spent at the park. Cami is keeping her distance and Duke is keeping an eye out, but it hasn't been particularly unbearable. If this is what normal is, people living their own lives independently of one another and keeping their mouths shut about everyone else's business, then I'm down for living the normal life.

"Hey!" Oliver's voice is too chipper, too loud in the small space behind the counter.

I turn away from the Jubilee's dining room ready to tear into him, but something stops me. Maybe it's the dark circles under his eyes, or the way that his shoulders are hunched ever-so-slightly. Whatever the reason, I can't bring myself to devastate him. Not when he looks like he's been run over already.

I toss my head in greeting. "What's up?"

He shrugs, stepping up beside me to lean on the counter. His eyes scan the dining room as he talks. "Nothing much."

Never one for tact, I say, "You look like hell."

A half-laugh sputters out of him. "Thanks."

"Sorry."

"No need to apologize. You're right." He leans forward. "Hey, Becs." My counterpart at the front counter turns around from where she's refilling the condiments. "Can you watch the front for a few?"

"Whatever," she says with a roll of her eyes. I've been the recipient of that roll at least four times in the two hours we've been working together. One day someone is going to smack her, and they'll stay that way. One can only hope.

"Thanks," he says. Then, turning to me, he smiles. "Care for a smoke?"

This is becoming a thing with us, I'm noticing, always going out for a smoke. I wonder if the rest of the staff is noticing too. Do they think I'm fucking him? I could. He's not bad on the eyes and sex isn't a big deal. But I won't. Even though I kind of want to. He lights a cigarette for me and hands it my way.

Lighting his, he leans against the building, head against the bricks and eyes diverted to the cloudless sky above. "Do you ever want a do-over?"

"I've wanted a do-over since I was ten years old." I take a long drag off the cigarette, holding it in briefly, allowing enough time to fill my lungs, then release it slowly. "But life doesn't work any way we want it to." He's looking at me as if I have egg streaming down my face. "What?"

"Damn!"

I shift, angling my body away from his. "What?"

"Nothing. I think that those are the most words you've ever said to me at one time."

It's my turn to shrug. "You asked a question, I answered." We fall into silence, but the quiet is too much. I falter. "What's up...with you?"

He sighs and a billow of smoke chases it into the heavens. "Do you seriously want to know?"

I push away from the wall. "Oliver, I've got things to do. You invited me out here, I thought to talk, so get to it or I'm going back in."

He smiles, which does nothing to improve his looks. Now instead of looking like a junkie he resembles an over-the-top villain. "That's why I like you, Zed. Not afraid to call someone out on their bullshit."

I fall back against the brick. "Then, what is it? Why do you look like shit?"

He laughs, then takes another drag. "I look like shit because I haven't slept. I was out all night."

"Spare me the details."

Another laugh. "Nothing like that. Just a party. Sometimes you just need to lose your mind, you know?" Often would have been a more accurate word.

"But?"

"But there are repercussions."

This is beginning to feel like pulling teeth. "Like?"

"I called my ex-wife."

"Oh."

"Yup."

I look at him. He's forlorn, genuinely upset. "What happened?"

"I learned two things. One, never, under any circumstances, call *anyone* when you're high and/or drunk. It never turns out well." He smiles as he says this, which makes me wonder how many times he's had this particular epiphany. "And, two, she hates me. Like, seriously hates me."

I want to offer him something, anything, but words won't form. I know rule one already. I've broken it more times than I care to admit, or even think about. The second rule is never show up on someone's doorstep drunk and/or high, but that story is for another day.

He tosses his cigarette onto the gravel, grinding it with the sole of his shoe. The sound reminds me of another day. "I guess I thought one day we would, you know, get back together. But she told me that will never happen."

"What made it end?" I want to offer a hug, to allow him my shoulder to lean on, but I put more distance between us.

He shrugs. "At the time she said she needed space. I thought the divorce was something her mom talked her into." His head drops. "But she wanted it all along. Said I'm not going anywhere. I'm a loser."

"That's rough."

A ragged laugh escapes him. "Yeah." Leaning back against the wall, he swipes at his eyes. "Harsh as hell, right?"

"Yeah." I look at the kitchen door, legs itching to start walking. Ex-marital discord suffered by my co-worker is not an ideal way to spend time away from the counter. Then again, this is kind of what we do. He pulls me out to smoke and unloads all his shit on me. Sometimes I give him the tiniest bit of mine. "Where was the party?"

"No idea. A friend of my roommate." He looks at me. "Want to go next time?"

"No. It's not my scene."

"I get it." He blows a plume of smoke out and I follow it across the gravel toward the tree line.

"Do you think you'll get past the ex thing?" When he looks at me, I straighten. Not sure why. Probably something I'm making up, but I've seen that look before. It's a beginning look. One that's considering other options. "I'd better get back inside. I bet Becca is ready to go on a break." I don't wait for a response, just turn and leave him standing by the dumpster.

OLIVER HAS KEPT his distance since my abandoning him out back. It bothers me that I care as much as I do, that my stomach lurches every time he looks away from me. Caring what any man thinks will forever be my downfall. The lunch rush is a whirlwind with lines stretching around the building outside and almost to the door inside. Becca says it's the result of two factories nearby that actually give hour lunches. I haven't known anyone by name, but some faces are familiar. I wonder if I went to high school with them and they're just as unsettled by my presence as I am by theirs.

Last in line is a face I do recall. It's the smile. Cocky and sardonic all at the same time. I think sardonic means god-like. That's what I mean. And he was a god. At least to sixteen-year-old me.

His smile widens and I know he recognizes me too. "Well, if it isn't Grace Skinner. How are ya, darlin'?"

I don't return his smile. In fact, what I'd like to do is melt into the old orange linoleum. Maybe Becca will throw some cold water on me. "It's Zed."

His eyebrows raise. "Huh?"

"My name. I don't go by Grace anymore. It's Zed."

He nods. "All right then." He's smiling and I'm suddenly reminded of Matthew McConaughey in that movie where he's always hitting on high school girls despite having graduated years before. "Do you remember me?"

"Yeah. Davis, right?"

"You know it." He leans forward making himself comfortable against the counter. "When did you get back?"

"A while ago."

Another nod. "You looking to party? If I remember correctly, you sure did enjoy my parties."

"I was a kid. I enjoyed all kinds of things I shouldn't have." Behind him, another customer is waiting. I see the man shift from one side to the other. "What can I get for you?" His eyes trail down my body, what he can see of it. "From the menu," I add, swallowing back the bile his leer has conjured.

He smiles and I can see the years of smoking shining back at me. "Say you'll go out with me, and I'll order."

"I can't." My eyes shift to the man behind Davis. He's visibly angry. I look to Becca, and she nods, drawing the man away from my line to hers. "I'm out of the game, Davis."

"Married? Shit."

My head is shaking. My whole fucking body is shaking. "No. I'm out of the partying game."

"Then why don't we just get together? We'll have a lot of fun. Like we used to."

I'm looking at him, this man who used to be so attractive to me. I want him to leave. To get away from me and never come back, but I'm stuck. "I really can't. What can I get for you from the menu?"

He's affronted, but persistent. "I'll take a number 6. Coke to drink." I collect his money and deliver his receipt. "You got a pen?" I give it to him and watch as he scribbles his name and phone number across the back. He hands them both to me, his smile never wavering. "When you're ready give me a call."

I don't shove the paper in my pocket until he walks away. I'll toss it later. Maybe I'll burn it. Fire cleanses things, right?

Oliver is beside me. "Everything okay?"

I look at him. Angry that he's been so wrapped up in his own shit that he left me standing there like that, with Davis all but crawling over the counter to eat me up. Would he have eventually come out? Does he allow female employees to be harassed by overzealous customers often?

"No thanks to you." I look at Becca. "I'm going on break. You got this?" She nods and I take that as my cue to exit.

Oliver is behind me, following closer than I care to acknowledge. "Wait. Zed, wait."

But I can't wait. I'm feeling too much. My stomach is rolling and dropping like a stone, like shoes in a dryer. I can't get away from any of it. My past is all right here in this town, and I volunteered to come back. Who the fuck does that?

"Zed!" He grabs my arm as I step out the back door, turning me around. "What the fuck?"

I jerk away, stumbling back against the dumpster. "What the fuck!"

He backs away, hands up in the air. "I'm sorry." I'm cowering, bending over trying to catch my breath. He's silent a moment and then, in a voice smaller than I've ever heard, asks, "Are you okay?"

He's wringing his hands, staring down at me as if he should be doing something more than he is.

I take a deep breath and straighten up, leaning back against the cold metal of the dumpster. "I'm fine."

"What happened out there? Everything looked fine and then it didn't." His hands are in his pockets, his brow furrowed. I want to crush my mouth to his, shove my tongue down his throat, and lose myself in him. But isn't that exactly the behavior that brought on Davis's proposition?

Eyes averted; I cross my arms over my chest. "I used to know that guy."

"Yeah. I gathered."

"We used to..." I don't want to say *fuck* out loud. Not to him. Not about this. "Hook up."

"Yeah." He doesn't get it. I can tell by the puzzled look on his face.

I shake my head. "I just need—"

"To get out of here?"

I look at him, my posture and arms relaxing slightly. "A minute. I just need a minute."

"If you want to cut out early, I'll cover the rest of your shift."

Is this what it feels like when someone gets it? When they understand my erratic behavior? "Really?"

He shrugs. "I've got nothing else to do. Nobody's waiting on me at home, remember?"

My laughter, if you can call the sputter of sound a laugh, is inappropriate, but unstoppable. "I'm sorry."

"I know, I'm a loser."

"For being on your own? Nah." I'm feeling a bit steadier, so I push away from the dumpster. "I'm good now."

"So, to make you feel better all I have to do is remind you of my life?"

I smile. It's strange how it happens that one day you can feel so unsure about someone and the next you can smile easily with them, but it's happening. Maybe it's the softness of his smile or the worry creasing his forehead. Maybe it's because he seems to get me. Whatever it is, I like him.

I DON'T LIKE this church. It's old with the faintest odor of must and hypocrisy. This group is shit. Just a bunch of people sitting around talking about their problems. I mean, I get that it's all part of the process, but does it have to be so damn tedious? Leaning against the back wall of the fellowship hall, I survey them, this group of unfortunates. I don't belong here. They all come here because they think it's going to help to talk about their troubles. That isn't me. Nothing is going to make me better and no amount of coffee or camaraderie is going to change that. I'm not judging them. My story isn't worse than anyone's here. It's just different.

"The last group I was in didn't have coffee." It's Deidre. Her lips are blood red, giving her a furious look. It's obvious she's been through some shit, but those lips and the strength of her posture say she couldn't give a fuck less about any of this. Well, except for Clay. "I guess it's up to the leader if there's food and drink."

I nod, cup still pressed to my lips as though I'm nursing it. There's no need to engage with these people. I won't be back.

She grabs four sugar packets and empties the contents into her cup. "What about you?" I meet her eyes. "What was your last group like?"

I straighten, lowering the cup. "I didn't have one."

Her eyebrows raise. "Oh."

"Yeah." I fidget, tugging at the bottom of my t-shirt. Montana's band shirt.

She turns to face the group. Everyone has stood from their chairs and is chatting in different little pockets. Eddie, the forty-year-old loser guy from last time, is the only one not talking with another group member. He's currently involved in what looks like a heated discussion with Rebecca.

I gesture toward him. "What's going on there?"

Deidre looks from me to Eddie and Rebecca. "Don't know. Not my business." She looks at me. "Not yours either."

My eyes meet hers, but only briefly. Why is she so goddamn intimidating? "Right."

"Hey, gals," Clay says, bouncing up beside Deidre. "What 'cha talking about?"

"Nothing," she answers.

He looks from her to me and then sighs. "Don't let her get inside your head, Zed." He smiles. "Oh, that rhymes." Then, as if remembering himself. "Sorry." I like his smile. "We're getting out of here. Me and D. Oh!" He claps his hands together and it's evident he's delighted by his additional rhyme. "Want to join us?"

I shake my head, but Deidre beats me with her very stern, "No." Then, looking at me, she adds, "No offense, Zed, but I don't trust you."

My hackles are up. "It's mutual," I say, tossing my cup in the bin by the table. "Thanks for the invite, Clay." I head for the door, ignoring Rebecca's request for me to wait. Despite what she may think, not everyone wants to stand around chatting with her, and not all of us give a damn what she thinks of our progress. Increasing my pace, I head to the Bronco with no intention of ever looking back. Fuck this place.

NINE

The aftermath of a storm is something I've always enjoyed. Maybe it's because my life has seemed like a storm for so long. Or perhaps I keep it chaotic because I enjoy what comes after. I like to see the cleanup, the efforts to put everything right again. Tonight, the sky grew dark, and the heavens opened, pouring the rage of the gods over the land. Driving home in the Bronco during the downpour made me realize why Hattie's hubby is keen to keep his kid out of it. It's a death trap. Every connection with pooled water becomes a lesson in how not to become roadkill. But cheating death on occasion is a small price to pay for freedom.

Sitting out on the grass, the blades and soil still clinging to the remnants of the evening's deluge, I hug my knees tight, nursing a cigarette as I stare into the inky sky. I don't have to work at Jubilee's tomorrow, so the night is my friend. The stars are misleading, as is the clearness of night. If this were fall, I would be chilled to the bone, but the sticky air clings to my skin like a drowning man desperate to stay afloat.

The day's events keep making a loop in my head: Oliver's vulnerability and Deidre's mistrust. How can one person trust me after having known me such a short time, having no idea what a mess I really am, while another, who has only the slightest idea of how truly fucked I am, can't even fathom it? I suppose it's all about interactions. I haven't shared in group yet. Instead of talking, I watch each of them pouring their insides out for the rest of us to sort through. It's stupid. Why do we need to share all those broken pieces? Why can't we just mend them on our own?

"Hi." Lucinda's voice startles me. I look up at her, it's doubtful she can see how frazzled her sudden appearance has made me, but I can see her clearly in the remnants of light stretching out from a nearby streetlight. Her lip is swollen and split down the middle. My stomach turns, but I don't say anything. I make room for her on the expanse of grass and hold out my pack of Marlboros. She takes one and settles in beside me, lighting hers with the butt of mine. "I guess you knew I'd be back, huh?" Her voice is small. Ashamed.

"I hoped you wouldn't be." I take a long drag off my cigarette and turn to look at her. She's broken. Aren't we all? The half-moon around her eye is high yellow. Backhanded, for sure. I remember those days. Why is it that some men think it's okay to take out their own insecurities on the people who love them?

I turn my head slightly to blow out the smoke, never taking my eyes off her. "What made you come back?"

She shrugs. "I love him, I guess."

"Yeah." I lay back on my elbows, cigarette dangling from between my lips, water from the grass soaking up the back of my tee. "Love'll do that to you."

She's looking at me as if I haven't got a clue. "Why are you still here? I see you have a car now. Fast getaway."

I shrug. "I promised my sister I wouldn't run away."

"You're thinking about it, though."

I smirk. "Always."

"Yeah." She takes a long drag, holds it in, and then releases it into the night air. The wisp of it is swallowed immediately by the humidity. "I guess."

We're quiet, each of us staring into oblivion. I wonder what she's searching for. I stopped trying to find anything a long time ago.

"What's your story, Luce?"

Her eyebrows raise as she looks at me. After a few seconds, she shrugs. "I don't have one. I'm from Arizona. My sister is still out there. She's always asking me to move in with her. Promises I can stay in her guest house."

"Fancy."

She smiles, her hand instantly raising to her cracked lip. "She's done well for herself."

"How does your dearest feel about your sister asking you to come live with her all the time?"

"Oh. He doesn't know." Her posture is perfect even sitting on damp grass. My spine straightens like a reflex but gives up when a muscle tightens. "He wouldn't understand."

"Probably wouldn't let you talk to her anymore."

"Yeah."

The smoke I release drifts up into the darkness. "How long have you been with that asshole?"

"Ten years." Her sigh sounds more like exhaustion than reminiscence. "Rex is my second husband. My first found someone new fifteen years in. It was a great anniversary gift."

My smoke comes out in sputters. "Shit. He told you on your anniversary?"

"Yeah." She looks at her cigarette as if it holds the key to all of life's mysteries.

"Did you guys have kids?"

"No. Maybe that's why it was easy for him to find someone new." She shrugs. "I stayed single for a few years and then one night I met Rex." She drops her head, waits a beat, and then looks back out into the darkness. "That's the night my life changed completely. My first husband was a jerk, but he never..." She presses the palms of her hands to her eyes. "Oh God, I don't even know why I'm telling you all this."

"Sometimes we just need someone to talk to." *Shit.*

Her eyes are on me. They're dark, dull. "Who do you talk to?"

"Myself. Well, I used to. That didn't work out." I take a long drag, holding it in until my chest burns. "Now I talk to my shrink once or twice a week. You know, depending on how needy I'm feeling. And a fucking group." My head aches from the force of my eyes rolling.

"Oh."

"Yeah." There's no need to tell her I haven't started sharing in group just yet.

"I tried to go to counseling once a few years ago. Rex said I didn't need it." She looks back at me, her eyes shining in the light from the nearby streetlight. "He said I just need to learn to listen."

That's a good girl.

Gut clinched; I sit up. "I bet he says a lot of things."

"Yeah." She's looking at me. Those eyes are too much, they need too much. Dark orbs full of desperation. I wonder if this is what people saw when they looked at me. Is it what they still see?

She shrugs, jabbing the remains of her smoke into the grass, her long, graceful fingers grinding it in harder than necessary. "One day I'll get away, one way or another."

I straighten against the cold chill snaking its way up my spine. After a few minutes of silence, she stands, staring down at me. She has no idea how to get away from him, not in any way that allows them both to get out alive. I consider telling her not to use pills but stay quiet.

She shifts. "I think about killing myself sometimes."

I'm stunned. Silent. No way am I opening my mouth right now.

She shifts again, looking over her shoulder. "Just to get away, you know? From the humiliation and the hurt." She sucks in a shallow breath, releasing it in puffs of sad laughter. "But I stay."

"It's hard to leave," I offer, though common sense tells me I shouldn't have said anything.

Her posture goes rigid as she turns fully toward her house. I follow her gaze and see Rex charging across the yard wearing nothing but a pair of old gym shorts. Not the new kind with length. No, these are straight out of the early 1980s.

"Where the fuck you been?" His voice is rough, not fully exorcised of sleep.

"I'm just talking to Zed." She motions toward me, but his hardened eyes stay on her.

"I woke up and you were just gone. Do you know how that made me feel?" He grabs her arm, jerking her toward him. His possession.

"Hey!" I scramble to my feet. "Chill out, man."

He looks at me, emerald eyes sliding from my face to my feet and back up. His lips turn up and he releases Lucinda's arm. "So, you're Cami's girl. I've heard about you." He slides his hand over his belly, the motion of someone hungry who's trying to decide on a meal. My eyes flash to Lucinda. "Oh, she ain't said nothing. Sides, she don't need to. I know all I need to know from looking at you." He steps closer, the smell of beer and cigarettes engulfing me. I lower my eyes, trying desperately to keep from meeting his, and see the front of his sunflower yellow shorts bulging.

I snap my eyes back up, meeting his gaze. "Back up."

His smile widens. "Do I make you nervous, sweetie?"

"Rex, honey, come on," Lucinda says, reaching out to him without conviction.

"You need to leave," I say through gritted teeth. My insides are molten lava over unsteady ground, but he doesn't need to know that.

"I know what I need, sweetheart." He grins, tipping his head back like he's the fucking alpha. "Are you going to give it to me?"

I screw my mouth up, ready to expel the surplus of saliva that's built up but abort the motion when another voice booms in the night.

"What can I do for you, Rex?" In unison, we all turn to find Duke standing mere feet away, shotgun in hand.

With his hands up in surrender, Rex backs away from me, but his smile never waivers. "Hey there, Duke. It's been a while."

"It has," Duke answers. "Is there something you need from my stepdaughter at this hour?"

Rex cuts his eyes at me. He's been thwarted, but men like him are never put off for too long. "Nah. I just came over to get Lucinda. I was worried about her."

Sure thing, asshole.

"Looks like you've got her." Duke steps closer and Rex takes a step back. "Y'all have a good night now."

"You too," Rex says, and I hear Lucinda say the same. Then, he turns his eyes back on me, his lips pulled back into a hungry sneer. "I'll be seeing you."

Incapable of movement, I keep my eyes on them as they cross the yard, Rex jerking Lucinda with every step.

"You okay?" Duke asks, his voice now filled with softness.

I nod. "Yeah."

We stand in silence, watching as the couple walks across the road and into their home.

After a moment, Duke's arm snakes around my shoulders. I flinch as he pulls me close to his side. He's probably as sure as I am that Rex is staring out the window. My body softens as my brain catches up to what's actually going on here. Duke is showing Rex that I have someone. He doesn't release me until we're inside with the door closed.

Placing the shotgun in the hall closet, Duke turns to me, "Be careful who you associate with around here. Most people are just hardworking folks like me and your mama, but a few are scumbags that never do nothing but harm."

"Thanks, Duke."

With a nod, he's gone, and I'm left standing in the emptiness of night.

WHEN I WAS a little girl one of my favorite things was the smell of pancakes in the morning. Especially if it was accompanied by bacon. That smell is what lured me into the light today. Soft fluffy circles of goodness with the promise of a salty chaser. Camille is standing in front of the stove when I enter, her back to the door. She's humming softly, a sound that instantly transports me to weekend mornings before Angel ruined everything by telling the world her daddy was trying to touch her inappropriately. I never believed her. Especially when he told me not to. *Why would I touch her?*

Cami's voice pulls me back to the present. "Morning, sleepyhead."

I nod. "Morning. Is there coffee?"

She jerks her head toward the coffeemaker. "You want a stack?"

"Please." I grab a mug from the cabinet and fill it. She makes good coffee. "Is there bacon?"

Her smug smile answers me even before the plate is placed before me. "How'd you sleep?"

"Fine." I look behind me into the den. "Where's Duke?"

She settles in across from me, tugging the opening of her robe closed. "Sleeping in."

Something's up. "He's not working on a Friday?"

"It's a holiday." She points to my plate. "Eat up."

I don't trust her. "What's going on?"

"What do you mean?"

"You only ever made pancakes when you were going to break bad news."

"That's not true." She can't even convince herself.

I eat my pancakes. I'm not giving them up for anything and it only makes sense to finish them before the bad news drops. She watches me eat, nursing her cup of coffee. I wonder if she has anything extra in it like she did after the divorce from my dad.

"Duke told me what happened last night. Are you okay?"

I look up from my plate and nod. "Yeah. Rex is just an asshole."

"Oh, I know." She laughs, some private joke with herself.

"Thinks he's God's gift or something." She takes a sip of her coffee. "Are you and Lucinda hanging out now?"

"We've talked a couple of times." I take another bite of pancake, then a quick sip of coffee. My dad's voice enters briefly, *Swallow your food first, Gracie. It ain't ladylike to eat like a horse.*

"I feel bad for her. She's in a bad spot."

I shrug. No need for her to know I agree. We're not going to bond just because she's made me pancakes.

"I wish I knew her family. I'd let them know just what she's going through over there." She takes another sip of coffee. "That Rex is brutal."

I look up at her and she averts her eyes. "Did you—" I don't want to know the answer to this. "You and Rex?"

She nods. "I'm not proud of it, but we were both single and he's not a bad looking guy."

"He's a dick."

Another nod. "You're not wrong about that." Leaning forward, she grabs my hand. "Stay away from him, honey. Okay?"

Jerking my hand away, I stab the last pancake on my plate. "I don't want anything to do with him. And I didn't invite him over last night."

"I know." Her voice has diminished, and she's retracting back into herself, hands wrapped around her mug as if it's the only thing keeping her here. "Duke told me what happened."

"Why was he even out there?"

"He can't sleep sometimes. Said he saw Rex coming across the street and figured there would be a scene if he didn't stop it. He said you looked like a deer in headlights." She takes a sip from her mug. "Said he was worried about you."

"He doesn't need to be. None of you do."

"That's not quite true, is it?"

I look at her, anger licking up at me. I know she's right. Everyone should worry about me. Hell, I should worry about me. But some things aren't worth worrying about.

"I'm glad he couldn't sleep," I say, wishing I could add that

I'm also glad he was worried about me. I am, but if I tell her, it's just going to encourage her to stay in my business.

After taking the last bite I try to stand up, but she holds her hand up to stop me. "Zed, honey." *Here we go.* "Will you stay here just a minute? I want to talk to you." I sit down. There is no excuse to give. She knows I don't work today. "Are you enjoying the Bronco?"

Steady. "I like having a way around that doesn't inconvenience you or Duke. Or Hattie."

"It gives you a sense of independence, doesn't it?"

Now we're getting to it. "I already promised Hattie I won't take off."

She shakes her head. "I'm happy to hear you say that, but I didn't think you were going to run away."

"Yeah?"

She laughs. "I'm not dumb. If you wanted to take off not having a car wouldn't have stopped you." She's not wrong. "It didn't last time." Her last words are soaked in regret.

"What is this then?"

She sighs. "I just want to talk to you." I want to tell her we're not there yet, but I stay silent. "And I want to give you something."

My hands begin to sweat. What does she want from me? "W —what?"

She reaches into the chair closest to her and lifts a small bag. I take it and look inside and then back to her, anger closing its vice grip around me. *What the fuck?*

———

HATTIE IS SITTING on her sofa. I think I've woken her up, but I don't care. I've been seeing red since Cami handed me her ingenious gift.

"Calm down, Zeddie."

I turn on her. "A fucking phone, Hattie? Did you know about this?"

"No, I didn't know she had it already, but she mentioned getting you one."

I'm wearing a hole in the dark walnut of her living room floor. "Because she thinks I'm going to run away."

"Because she's worried about you."

I thrust it at her. "I want to know if there is a GPS on here. Can you tell me?"

"What did Mom say?"

"The usual. It's for my own good. *No, we don't think you're going to run off.*" I plop down on the sofa beside her. "Is there a GPS on it?"

She nods. "It's a smart phone, of course it has GPS."

"I mean one of those app things, the ones that overbearing parents use to keep tabs on their kids."

Another nod.

"What the fuck, Hattie? Why didn't you give me a heads up?"

"Zed, calm down." She puts the phone on the table, her hand grasping her abdomen as she does. "It's just a phone. You're not running away or hanging out at drug houses, so it shouldn't matter."

It's now that I truly see her; pale and exhausted, with dark rims around her eyes and a messy bun on top of her head. "Are you okay? When's the last time you showered?"

Her eyebrows arch in surprise. "I'm fine. I've been too exhausted to shower."

"Where's J.C.?"

"Work."

I lay my head back on the sofa and look at her. "You look like hell."

She laughs, smacking me halfheartedly. "Thanks."

We're quiet a moment, our eyes fixed on one another. I want to tell her that I am scared, that my old habits are beginning to whisper in my ear, but I can't. She doesn't need my shit. Not now. "Thanks for letting me use the Bronco."

"Just don't make me regret it."

"You know I'm bound to, right? Statistically speaking."

She looks at me. There's a smile on her dry lips, but we both know there's a grain of truth in my joke. "Do your best, okay?"

I nod, then turn to look at the television. She's got our favorite old movie paused. "Strait-Jacket."

"Yeah. I like to watch it when I'm feeling crummy."

It's almost to the part where Joan Crawford's character gets too fresh with her daughter's fiancé. I look at Hattie. "Want to finish it?"

A sparkle comes into her eyes, and she smiles. "Do you have time?"

"I've got all the time in the world."

Settling deeper into the sofa, she hits play and the room is filled with the blaring sound of fast music and the jangling charms of Crawford's bracelets. Hattie is focused on the screen, the lights dancing in her eyes. I've often wondered what I left her to; a mom that was falling apart, a dad who would rather look the other way than realize his daughters were in danger, the memory of a sister so consumed by her own shit she didn't have time to consider what her little sister might be going through.

My voice is almost a whisper when I say, "I'm sorry, you know."

She looks over at me. "For what?"

I avert my eyes to Joan, her manic dancing and flitting giving me a particular kind of comfort. "Abandoning you."

There's a lengthy pause before she quietly says, "It was like you died."

I'm struck. "Hattie—"

She shrugs, her hands clutching the blanket covering her lap. "Mom was...well, she wasn't good."

"And you?"

Another shrug. "I was angry. You abandoned me. Us." She

lays her head on the back of the sofa. "Mostly me." Reaching out, she cups my face, her palm clammy against the warmth of my cheek. "I think I actually hated you for a while."

Her visage has become glassy, and my bottom lip is quaking. I'm afraid to speak, afraid the emotion will spill forth; terrified that I'll be unable to form words that will make sense coming out of my sputtering mouth. Still, I manage to choke out, "I'm sorry."

"You did what you had to, Zeddie." She pulls her hand back, burying it in the blanket. "When she told me you tried to kill yourself—"

"It was an accident."

"Was it?"

I look away, furiously swiping at the tears sliding down my cheeks. "Yes." *Liar.*

"When Mom told me you tried to kill yourself, I didn't know how to feel. We hadn't spoken in forever, not since Mom's wedding to Duke, and you didn't come to my wedding. I guess I was angry that you would put us through all that hurt again. That loss. And then I was sad because you didn't think about us at all." She grabs my hand, giving it a gentle squeeze. "But I understand. It's tough dealing with emotional trauma." She sounds like my therapist. "So, I took all that blankness and anger and sadness and turned it into something else. Determination maybe."

"Determination?"

She shrugs. "I guess." Her sigh is long, heavy. "I don't know how to explain it. Mom told me you were coming back here. I was determined not to let my anger show up when you did." She's looking at me, but I can't meet her gaze. My eyes go again to Joan. Her therapist is interrogating her, and she's close to breaking. I'm close to breaking. "I knew I had to be there for you this time. No matter how difficult you make it."

My voice cracks as I speak. "You...*hated* me."

Her hand is on mine, and I can't help looking at her. My little sister, so round, so tired. "For a while, yes." She forces my head to turn, and her eyes bore into mine. "I hated the hole that you left when you went away." Her eyes are sparkling in the dimming light. "But how could I keep hating you after what you went through?"

What does she mean? What does she *mean*? Does she know everything that happened?

My reflex sends me away from her. Suddenly the arm of the sofa is centered in my back. Her hands are outstretched to me, but I can't return the gesture.

"Wh—H—Wha—" My speech is infantile, my brain unable to formulate the questions I need to ask. How can she know?

"Mom told me."

Of course.

"Don't be mad at her. I made her tell me."

Language rediscovered, I almost shout, "It's a lie."

"Zeddie."

My head is shaking back and forth. *How is this happening?* "She doesn't know. She's never known." I'm standing, pacing back and forth. How could she have told Hattie?

Hattie is standing, her hands sticking to me as if she were some human squid trying to devour me. I push away. "Zed, stop!"

I look at her.

"My god, you're like an animal." Her hand is grasping her abdomen. "After you freaked out about Dad, I asked her. She didn't want to tell me. Said she made a promise she would leave that up to you, but when I thought Dad did something terrible to you, she told me."

"W—what did she tell you?" I swear, it's like I've only learned to speak this minute.

She lowered her hands. "That you were molested." A sputter escapes my quaking lips. "That's all. I swear." She's trying to steady me with her gaze, but I can see that something has changed within it. Recognition lies there, shining out at me as if I have somehow given away the truth of what happened to me. "*Is that all?*"

Do I lie? Tell the truth? I've never been good at honesty, but

I'm damn good at keeping secrets. I consider honesty. After all, who cares now? I haven't seen or heard from my uncle in years. But I've been keeping this secret for so long I'm not sure I could verbalize it now if I wanted to.

I need to distract her, and the shaking of her hand provides me the opportunity. "Are you okay?"

She emits a sound I can't quite describe. Something akin to a sigh but strangled. "I don't know."

Crossing the divide, I wrap my arm around her shoulder. "What do you need?"

"I need to lie down."

"What about the hospital? Shouldn't I take you?"

Her head is moving back and forth. "No, just help me to my room."

"Hattie—"

"Zed." She places a clammy hand on my cheek. "I'm okay. Just help me to bed."

The room is cool and dark. I'm not sure where to go. Hattie reaches beside us and flips a switch illuminating the room she shares with her husband. Centered on the exterior wall is a four-post bed turned down for the night's sleep.

I help her in and pull the duvet up. "Snug as a bug."

She smiles. "Will you lay with me for a little while?" Without hesitation, I round the bed and crawl in beside her. She rests her head against my chest and grabs my hand. "Do you remember when we were little kids? When we would lay out across the grass and stare up at the fireflies?"

"Of course I do. I told you I was afraid to catch them."

She smiles. "Because you would steal their light."

"Yeah." Those summer nights, long after the sun had settled for the night and the heat of the day began to drip to the earth below, we would be still, watching the fireflies dance above us, their tiny bodies creating an orchestra of light. "I haven't thought about that for a long time."

Her voice is a whisper. "I think about it all the time. I wish we could go back to then, one of those moments. When you were happy."

Before he stole my light.

"I'll be happy again. I hope."

"It feels weird to hear you say that now." She lifts her head, her eyes meeting mine. "I thought your anger would eat you alive right in front of us."

"It still might."

Her head moves swiftly back and forth with a force that makes her eyes flutter. "Not a chance."

I stroke her hair as she drifts into sleep. I hope she's right. I really, really do.

TEN

The therapist wants me to see someone locally. She's worried I am on the...*what did she call it...* precipice of making a bad decision. Her tone signaled that she didn't appreciate my pointing out that life to this point has been a series of bad decisions made by yours truly. I wonder if she thinks I'll try to do it again. Off myself, that is. I'm sure she does. They all do.

Her voice was soft when she suggested that I transfer my treatment to someone closer, the patented tone shrinks put on when they're dealing with a live wire. Though she couldn't see it, I stood in my mother's kitchen shaking my head furiously. My answer was simple. No. All my life it seems people have been waiting for me to screw up. Why should she be any different?

It's yesterday's conversation with the shrink that has me sitting once again in the basement of the Methodist church, drinking in the sad stories of those around me as I sip on the sparkling punch Rebecca has provided today. *It's like a Mimosa,* she'd exclaimed. *Without the alcohol.* God, she's insufferable.

Deidre and Clay are sitting next to me for whatever reason. Deidre's lips are hot pink today. Her shirt reminds me of lemonade. Why Rebecca didn't think to bring that as a refreshment I'll never fucking know.

"I didn't expect to see you again," Deidre says, and I shrug.

Rebecca closes the outside door and rushes to our circle. She's out of breath from her mad dash to and from the other side of the vast room. It occurs to me that the woman may be on speed or something else. Wouldn't that be a gas, the woman responsible for helping us stay off drugs is eating them herself.

No, I guess it wouldn't be.

"Hello, everyone!" Her eyes narrow in on me. "I'm grateful to see you all again." I smirk. There is little doubt that she's spoken to the therapist, or someone else associated with my file. "Let's get started."

Eddie begins. He always begins. He's been having dark thoughts since his ex-wife told him he can't see the kids anymore. She thinks he's still using, but he claims he isn't. His mannerisms tell a story that supports the ex. We listen, no one speaking until he's finished talking. The dynamic here is weird. People talk, some listen while others are contemplating what parts of themselves they will share, and then there's an afterward. That person becomes the focus of the entire group and we're responsible for making them feel better about their pathetic life. No one is going to make me feel better about mine.

Instead of allowing the rest of the group to chime in, Rebecca places her hand on Eddie's shoulder and says, "Let's take a few moments to talk before you leave today, okay?" He nods, and she turns a smile on everyone else. "Clay, why don't you tell us about your week? Did you speak to your father? I know you were thinking of doing that last week."

Clay leans forward, his sapphire blue head bowing slightly. "Can I go last today?"

Deidre puts her hand on his knee, and he covers it with his own. "I'll go," she says, looking up at Rebecca. "I broke up with my girlfriend last week." There is a collective expression of sadness. "We weren't together long. Only a couple of months." She sits back. "I can't seem to get it together with them."

"Who?" Rebecca asks. Sometimes she chimes in. It's annoying.

"Women. We start out great. Happy. And then it all goes to shit." She sits back, hand in her lap. I watch as her thumbs run along each fingertip, first the cuticle, then the nail. She finds what she's looking for and her thumb steadily pushes at the cuticle while she speaks. "I think I'm doing everything wrong, and it makes me feel worthless, and then I start telling myself I'm worthless, and then it spirals from there. She says I'm too negative. She can't be around toxic people. *Toxic*." She looks into the faces of every group member, stopping on me. "It's stupid, I know."

"No," Cathy, a quiet blonde, chimes in. "It isn't stupid at all. My mom always tells me I'm negative." She lowers her head, her voice lowering. "We can't be sunshine and roses all the time." She's a slight woman with long hair and a beak nose. She looks beaten down, but it's no surprise given her statement.

Rebecca is all business. "Why do you think you're drawn to these women who, inevitably, end the relationship on these terms?"

Deidre shrugs. "Because they've got what I don't, I guess. Happiness."

There is another collective show of emotion, something akin to a sigh and acknowledgment.

"You want to siphon it from them?" The question is out before I can stop it.

She looks at me, her pink lips pulling back in a smirk. "Maybe."

I'm aware of the tugging back of my lips, much like being aware of another's lingering gaze.

Possibly suspecting our back and forth won't end well, Rebecca cuts in, "Who'd like to go next? Zedwynne?"

I straighten in my chair. This is the moment I talked about with my therapist. *I encourage you to share in group*, she'd said. *It will help with your recovery*. I don't want to share. There's nothing about me I want these people to know, but I also don't want to find myself back in the hospital, or worse. The doctor was kind enough to remind me that I'm not out of the woods. One false step and I could be back to square one. Or dead. I don't want either.

"Zedwynne?" Rebecca's voice is shrill against the throbbing in my head.

I nod. "Okay."

ODDLY ENOUGH I didn't hate sharing with the group. Everyone listened attentively, savoring every word of my recent drama. Trying to kill myself over another failed relationship and returning home after more than a decade, though I didn't go into details about my long absence. There was no need to. My current events were enough to quench their thirst. It was also enough to get me an invitation to Deidre and Clay's after-party. At least that's what they call it.

Now the three of us are seated in a back booth of some retro diner in the disappointing downtown area not far from the church. It looks like they're trying with this place. It ticks most of the boxes required to make a quaint little town, hair salon, diner, bookstore, and hardware store. I guess I spent too much time in the bustling metropolis of Asheville to appreciate it. Clay and Deidre are staring at me over their respective baskets of burgers and fries as if I've grown another head. I take a long, slow sip of the strawberry shake I ordered to compliment my turnover and fries, my gaze meeting theirs.

Clay is the first to break the silence settled over us. "Shit, man, I never thought you would share." Deidre nudges him under the table, evident by the way his body sways toward the outside of the booth. "What?" He's laughing as if he's dropped something in the short drive from there to here. I wonder if he'll share. He picks up a fry and points it at me. "But I know you didn't tell us everything."

I touch the tip of my nose to indicate he's right on.

"What made you do it today?" He shoves the fry in his mouth. "We had a bet you wouldn't even be back."

"Clay!" Deidre's tone is sharp, shutting him down.

"Sorry."

I shrug. "It's cool. I wasn't planning to come back, but I was *encouraged* to."

"Ah." Deidre's eyebrows raise. "The kind of encouragement that comes with consequences if you don't embrace it?"

"Maybe." I shove a fry into my mouth. "I didn't want to take any chances by not coming back."

"Sounds like you needed to," Clay says, his voice quiet. "You've got a lot of shit going on."

"Don't we all," Deidre says. Picking up her giant cup, she takes a long drink.

I raise my milkshake in salute. "Amen."

"We're going to the skate park after this. Wanna go?" Clay's eyes are bright and he's swaying back and forth. I look at Deidre and she holds her hands out to surrender. I guess the kid gets what he wants.

I look at my watch. Mom and Duke would be getting home from work soon and I don't have a shift at Jubilee's today to keep us distanced from one another. Things have been good with Duke since the night with Rex, but I don't want to chance being alone with Cami too long and getting into an argument. He may have come to my aid but that doesn't mean he'll have my back over hers. I'm not foolish enough to believe that at all.

"Come on. D gets so bored there. It's mostly kids and guys."

I look to Deidre, who nods. "It may be nice to have someone to talk to while he's doing his thing."

"Okay," I say. "Sure."

THE SKATE PARK is broken into indoor sections and outdoor. There's even a playground for younger kids. They seem to have thought of everything. Clay jumps out, board clutched to his chest, and hurries away, leaving Deidre and I on our own. She leads the way to a nearby tree, making herself comfortable on the bench. I drop the remains of my milkshake in the nearby bin and join her.

"This place is interesting," I say, leaning forward to rest my elbows on my knees.

"It's shit. I only come here on group days with Clay." She stretches her legs out, relaxing against the curved metal back with her eyes closed against the midday sun. "I hate this fucking place. It's loud and the kids are atrocious."

"Why come?" I can't keep the amusement from my voice. "If you hate it that much."

She shrugs. "I guess so Clay won't be alone."

I lean back as well, stretching my legs out beside hers. "What's the deal with you two?"

"What do you mean?"

"You..." I look over at her. "Don't seem to have a lot in common."

She opens one eye and trains it on me. "Because I'm black?"

I laugh when she smiles. "Because he's a kid and you're not."

"We came to group at the same time, and I guess we just gravitated to one another."

"Because you're both gay?"

She sits up and I follow. "No, not because we're both gay." She shakes her head. "Do you have a problem with gay people?"

I will not squirm under her glare. "No reason to."

She shakes her head again. "He came out to his parents, and they disowned him. It was his father's decision and his mom backed him. I guess I saw a little of me in him."

"So, your parents..."

"My mom. Yes."

"I'm sorry."

She shrugs, relaxing again. "I'm over it."

"No disrespect, Deidre, but none of us are over our shit. If we were we wouldn't need to go to this lame-ass group."

She laughs. "I guess you're right." We settle into watching Clay skate with a group of kids nearby. After a few moments, she says, "I know who told me I was worthless, I know who told him." She motions toward Clay. "But who told you?"

I consider her question. "No one told me, but everyone showed me."

"Even your mom and that sister of yours?"

I look out over the park, my focus shifting from Deidre and her fucked up question to the kids sliding down the ramps and through the air. The answer is no, I know this, but I can't form the words to confirm the truth. What happens then?

She sits back, folding her arms across her chest. Oh yeah, she's smug. "Rebecca would call that a home run question."

I let out a scoff. "Fuck Rebecca."

"I wouldn't mind it." I look at her and we both laugh. "What? I bet she's...interesting in bed."

"Maybe."

We fall into silence again, but Deidre isn't one who likes too much silence. It doesn't take long to figure out that much about a person. I can go for hours without speaking, but some people are afraid of the silence, scared of what they might think about when it settles over them.

"So, what's up with your hair?"

My hand moves to my head. "What do you mean?"

"It's all Shane McCutcheon season two."

"Season two of what?"

A hefty laughter fills the space between us. "Another time."

<hr>

IT's after eight when I pull into the driveway of my mother's home. The house is in full shine, every light blaring in every single window that faces the road. It's unusual, but also possible that Cami has decided to stop living in the dark. Climbing out of the Bronco, I force myself forward. A trickle of sweat is sliding slowly down the valley between my shoulder blades, a lover's touch, and my hair is clinging to my sweaty brow. Hoping this wasn't an indication of what is awaiting me inside, I twist the knob and push the door forward, preparing for the worst.

Duke is seated in his recliner, newspaper open in front of him. I didn't know people still read the actual newspaper. I thought it was all done on smartphones. It's refreshing to see that not everyone has taken to digital reading. Cami is in the kitchen, evident only by the cacophony of noise from pots and pans banging together.

"Hey," I say.

Duke lowers his paper and nods. "Find the band and you'll find your mom."

"Is she mad about something?"

He turns his wrist, surveys the face of his watch, and then looks up at me with an eyebrow crooked.

Goddammit. "I didn't call."

"Bingo." He raises the paper back up to resume reading and I move toward the door. "Don't be too harsh with her, Zed," he says. I pause, thinking I might reply that he should tell Cami the same, but decide against it and continue.

The kitchen smells like nutmeg and cinnamon and it's hot as blazes. "Damn, it's hot in here. How long have you had the oven on?"

She whirls around, possibly startled by my entrance. I'm sure it was difficult to hear over the clanging of her vintage Stoneware. I should apologize for scaring her, but I can't bring myself to do it. I cross my arms and lean against the edge of the counter separating the kitchen from the eating area. Why have an eat-in kitchen and a dining room?

"You startled me," she says, tossing the hand towel on her shoulder.

"I gathered that."

She turns back to the sink, immersing her hands in the water. "We already ate."

I'm hesitant to tell her I've already eaten, too. "Okay."

"I'm baking a pie. Should be ready in a bit." Her clipped tone is more suited for a teenager coming home after curfew, not a grown-ass woman coming home too late for dinner. But in the interest of going easy on her, I don't mention how annoyingly passive-aggressive she's being. Nor do I remind her I'm the insolent one here, not her.

I push away from the counter and turn the oven light on, bending over to peek inside. "What kind of pie?"

She whirls around and I bolt upright. I don't think I've ever seen her move so quickly. "Where have you been?" She's a full inch shorter than me but right now she looks taller, like her anger has boosted her standing.

"I went to group. You know it's an hour away."

"They met at eleven this morning, Zed. Where have you been since then? It's nearly nine."

I take a step back and straighten. She doesn't need to think even for a moment that she's got the upper hand. "First off, it's eight fifteen. Second, I went out with a couple of people from group afterward."

Her mouth slacks open. "You what?"

"Yeah."

Recovering, she asks, "Where did you go?"

This dynamic sucks. She never cared where I was when I was a child, but now that I'm almost thirty she needs to know my every fucking move? It's ridiculous. People try and fail to kill themselves every single day and they're left alone, why am I the one subjected to this type of scrutiny?

"Why does it matter where we went?"

She slaps the towel she's holding on the counter. "I couldn't find you."

"On the GPS thing?" I ask, trying not to let the little ember of rage over her tracking me ignite again. She nods. "I forgot my phone in the room. It's on the bed."

"Yes, I know where it is, Zed. I found it this afternoon when I hadn't heard from you."

"I don't understand what's going on here." It's the wrong thing to say, but it's all I've got. "What does it matter?"

She looks at me hard, her eyes shining with so many different things, anger, humiliation, guilt. "How can you ask that? After what happened." She picks the towel up, tosses it on the counter again. "I'm trying, Zed. All I want to do is keep you safe...and alive. Why won't you let me do that?"

The ember has grown into a living thing, slithering through my veins like a greedy snake, seeking to fill every part of me. I should leave the room. Turn around and get as far away from her as possible, but it's too late.

"Maybe because you never cared to do it before," I say, happy when she falls back against the sink with her hands over her face. I should feel compassion here, I know I should, but it's difficult to feel anything other than contempt and disgust. Why now? Why not then? "I don't need your protection, Cami. I don't need it and I damn sure don't want it."

She lowers her hand and straightens, her posture conveying that she's done. "You may not want it, but you've got it." Her jaw tightens. "You can't leave your phone at home anymore, Zedwynne. You are to take it with you at all times. You promised to follow my rules if I let you live in *my* house."

"Do you want me to leave?"

She scoffs. "Where will you go? Across the street?"

Ignoring the tightening in my throat, I say, "I'll figure it out."

"Well, until you do, you're stuck here." She knows she's got me right where she wants me, but I don't see any enjoyment in her features. I turn to leave, but she catches me. "There's a package for you on your bed. Beside your phone."

I glance back at her with a nod before exiting. That didn't go at all the way I thought it would.

ELEVEN

Oliver is leaning over the counter, his eyes trained on the empty dining room. This is the quiet before the rush. We should be prepping for the lunch crowd, but he's sulking instead. I nudge him and he straightens up, looking down at me with feigned hurt.

"Break time?" he asks.

I look at Becca who rolls her eyes. That's good enough for me. "Sure."

Out back, he lights a cigarette for me, and I take it without the slightest hesitation. "What's up?" I ask, blowing my first long plume into the clear blue sky.

He shrugs, leaning against the old, chipped brick.

"It must be something. Becca could've used your lip to sweep the dining room."

A chuckle escapes from his lips causing the puffs of smoke to putter, long then interrupted. Like the trains I used to watch as a child. "How very astute."

"Astute? Wow. Nice word."

His hand is soft against my shoulder as he gives me a shove. "Shut the fuck up, man."

I laugh. It doesn't escape me that this is too easy. My laughter, our banter. "Alright," I say, settling against the wall. "What is it?"

"My ex."

I'm dumbstruck for absolutely no reason. "You called her." *Of course, he called her.*

He nods.

I open my mouth to ask him when he's going to stop letting her string him along but clamp down over my words. I already know the answer to my question. Oliver and I are very similar when it comes to relationships. We're in it until we can feel like we're worth it, knowing that we never will.

"I know I shouldn't have. But the last time we talked she..." He throws his hands up. "One minute she wants me and the next she just wants me to leave her the fuck alone." He looks at me. "She said that. *Leave me the fuck alone, Oliver. Stop making it hard for me.*" He takes a long drag and looks at me as he exhales. "For her."

"Maybe it is tough for her."

"She left me, Zed. I'm the one who's had his fucking heart ripped out and stomped on."

"I'm not saying you're not." I take a drag and focus on the line of Carolina pines that separates Jubilee's from the junkyard behind. "I'm just saying maybe she's going through her own shit."

"Then why keep calling?"

I think of me sleeping outside my ex's apartment, of me sobbing and banging on the door begging him not to shut me out. I didn't want to be with him, but being with him was better than being alone.

I shrug.

"She calls to check on me. Tells me she loves me before we get off the phone." He's jabbing the cigarette in the air as if ticking off items on an imaginary list. "She asks me to dinner for chrissake." He's looking at me, but I don't know what to say. I'm not the person to give advice on matters of the heart. "What am I supposed to think about that? Are those the actions of a woman who wants to be left alone?"

Again, I shrug. "How long were you married?"

"Five years."

"That's a long time."

"Yeah."

"Maybe..." I close my mouth. Why am I commenting on this? What gives me the right?

"Maybe what?"

"Maybe she *is* worried about you. I mean, she has to care about you, right?"

"But saying she loves me? And dinner?"

I look at him. "Why would she be concerned, Oliver? Is there a behavior you're exhibiting that would make her worry?" *Is there a therapist in the room?* "Do you call her every time you're drunk or high out of your mind?" I take a drag and blow out quickly. "I mean, you're always hungover lately when you come to work. Maybe she just wants you to know she still cares enough to be there for you."

His head snaps toward me. "What the fuck, Zed? Are you on her fucking side?"

I straighten. Then, tone sharpened by hurt, say, "Never claimed to be," and move away from him. "I was just trying to find possible answers to your questions."

"Well don't." He tosses his smoke on the ground and snubs it out. "Mind your fucking business." He pushes past me.

"Don't make it my business then." But he doesn't hear me. I don't have the nerve to say something so harsh to his face.

He doesn't meet my eyes through the lunch rush. Not even when I address him directly over an order. I'm not trying to be his friend or give him advice; I just need to know if the fucking order is up. Still, he avoids me. When the rush is over, he disappears in the back, and I don't follow him. Choosing to keep myself occupied with chores for the front, collecting trays, cleaning them, wiping tables, cleaning up spills. I don't need his shit. Not now, not ever. I've got enough to worry about.

As if on cue, Hattie waddles through the door. I'm standing by the condiments stand, wiping up the spilled ketchups and sweet tea.

"Hey," I say, slapping the disgusting rag down on the tray propped on my hip. "What're you doing here?"

She smiles, nose crinkling, but I can see a hint of something else. "I was craving one of Hank's greasy delicacies." Stepping up to the counter, she says a very cheery hello to Becca before ordering.

I round the counter, tossing the rag in an awaiting bin and adding the tray to the stack waiting to be cleaned. That's the last chore of the day. Specifically saved for the last hour of my shift. It keeps me busy, and a busy mind doesn't watch the clock.

Hattie looks up at me as she slides her card to pay. "Why're you looking at me funny?"

"I..." *Don't like my worlds colliding.* "I just didn't expect to see you here."

She places a hand on her belly, fingers splayed out, as if this would explain her appearance. "I woke up this morning craving one of these burgers. They're so good and so, so bad. One won't hurt me, though. I hope." She winks at Becca, who's extending the largest cup we have to her.

Becca smiles, and I realize I've never seen that many of her teeth at once. "When are you due?"

"Ten months ago." Hattie laughs, then cradles her belly again. "Not long now. How's your baby doing?"

"Not a baby anymore." Becca's smile doesn't look half bad on her. "She's starting pre-school soon."

"Oh my goodness! I can't believe it. Well, you give her a big hug from me." Becca nods. "And don't you go getting too friendly with any other hairdressers, lady. Those locks are mine." She winks. How the hell is she this person?

Becca turns to me when Hattie ambles away to get a large cup of soda. "How do you know Hattie?"

I grab a tray and the nearby rag and begin to scrub. "She's my little sister."

Her eyes say more than she knows. *How?* I could tell her that when two people love one another very much they make babies, but that seems too harsh. Why wouldn't she be surprised that Hattie, apparent queen of the nice people, and me, overlord of the damned, are sisters? I glance at the clock as Dante places Hattie's order in the window.

"Order up," he shouts.

I reach for the tray, but Becca grabs it first. "I'll take it," she says. "You look like you could use a minute."

Hattie isn't buying what I'm selling. She should, though, considering every word of it is true, but Cami has already planted the seed of doubt. *She wouldn't tell me where she was. Left her phone at home. What is she doing that she doesn't want us to know about?* I don't know if those are her exact words, but I'd be willing to bet they're close enough.

I look out over the river selecting my words carefully before asking, "Is that the real reason for your craving this morning?" I can't help the tone of my voice. This is bullshit.

"No, I really wanted the sandwich. I don't think you understand how powerful these cravings are." A pain shoots through my chest. She leans forward. "Some women eat dirt. Can you imagine?"

Shaking my head, I turn away from her. I don't want to imagine. Don't want to remember that I was on the path to knowing what the cravings of pregnant women entailed, but my journey to motherhood was cut short, my fruit ripped from me. It was for the best; I know that now. The memory of Dan's face when I told him about the baby. The disgust. *I don't know whose kid it is, but it ain't mine.* How could he say that? Then, to see the glee in his eyes upon learning his little problem was gone. That was the most heartbreaking thing of all. So many years of being his girl, his Gracie, only for it to be gone with one look.

"Zed?" Her hand is waving in front of me, fuzzy at first, then sharp and far too close.

I lean back. "Sorry."

"Where were you? I'm going on and on about the trials and tribulations of pregnancy and look over to find you a million miles away."

"Sorry. What were you saying?"

She leans back, resting her shoulder against the wooden bench that's seen better days. "The river's low today," she says, her eyes focused on the large boulders protruding from shallow waters. She's not wrong. Usually only the very top of the same rocks are visible. "If we don't get some more rain soon it's going to dry up."

I laugh. "A river can't dry up, Hattie."

"Sure, it can. Everything dries up eventually."

I think of my uncle's affections, how they shriveled instantly when I became old enough to drive. *You're too old for this.* Funny enough, I thought I was finally the perfect age for it. My notebooks were filled with plans for us, scribbled wishes that we would run away and be together forever.

"You're gone again."

I look at her. "Sorry." My stomach flops and I cover my mouth, afraid I might retch on her.

"You okay?"

I nod. "I think I ate something that didn't agree with me." *Remembered something.* I close my eyes, willing a breeze to cut through the thick summer air. "I didn't know Becca is a client of yours?"

"Yeah. I've been seeing her for a few years. Poor girl. She's had it rough."

"She seems okay."

Hattie laughs. "You still don't get it, do you?"

Turning to her, I ask, "What don't I get?"

"Everyone who works for Hank has a story. Some are recovering drug addicts, some are trying to get on their feet after toxic relationships, some have tried to kill themselves."

"Okay. Which one is Becca?"

"A little of everything, I guess. She got with the wrong guy her junior year of high school, got hooked on pills, got pregnant, went to jail." She sighs, shifting on the bench. "Told me she didn't start getting her shit together until her boyfriend OD'd in the bathroom at some restaurant a few towns over."

"Shit."

"Yeah. Now she's working at Hank's, trying to get her life together so she can get custody of her daughter again." She turns to me. "Everyone at Jubilee's has a story. They're not better than you, they're not worse. They're just people with shit going on. Don't tell Becca I told you anything, okay? I don't want to lose her as a client."

I pull an invisible zipper across my closed lips.

She laughs. "Thanks. Now, will you tell me what happened yesterday? Mom is super worried."

A long groan escapes my parted lips, startling a woman and her dog who happen to be passing by. Hattie thought we'd have more privacy at the end of the trail, but she didn't account for the health nuts that follow it all the way out and back.

"She doesn't need to be worried. Nothing happened. I went to group, shared a little, and was invited out by a couple of people."

"You shared in group?" Her eyes are dancing. "I'm so proud!"

"Don't be."

She feigns annoyance. "Who invited you out? Where did you go?"

"A woman, Deidre. And Clay, whose actual name is Claiborne. He's a kid."

"Is he Deidre's kid?"

"Nope. Just some kid whose parents disowned him." I'm

instantly regretting this description of him. It doesn't seem like enough, so I add, "He loves skateboarding."

She's smiling. "You like him?"

"He's hard not to like, I guess." I tug at the fabric of my jeans, straightening the legs to give me something to do. "We grabbed some lunch and then went to the skatepark."

"Does she skateboard too?"

"Deidre?" I chuckle. "No. She goes there for Clay."

"It seems like they're good friends."

I nod. "She worries about him. It's sweet to see them together. She's like a big sister."

She grabs my hand, lacing her fingers with mine. "Big sisters are the best."

I know she's not trying to put pressure on me. Maybe she means it, though how she can I have no idea. I've been a shit big sister. Abandoning her when my uncle took me over and again as teenagers when I got the hell out of this place.

"I'm glad you went out with them, Zeddie," she says, her voice only slightly higher than the water flowing over the exposed rocks across from us. "You need friends. Real friends."

"Yeah, but should they be as fucked up as I am?"

She considers the question, then, "Yes, I think so." She turns her eyes on me and I'm exposed. "No one will understand what you're going through better than people with similar struggles. That's why these are the best friends for you and Jubilee's is the best workplace for you." She squeezes my hand. "I'm so proud of you."

"Don't be too proud. There's still plenty of time for me to fuck this up."

Her arms are around me. "Time is what I'm counting on."

TWELVE

Hank has me on the night shift today. I don't know if it's his idea or Oliver's. I haven't been able to get Mr. Shift Lead to talk to me in two days. He's usually on break or busying himself with some "important" business in the office, only appearing when the rush becomes overwhelming and Dante screams for help. Why we only have four people working during lunch hour is beyond me, but I guess Hank is doing what he can. If the number of faces I see every workday counts for anything, it's working. Since I don't have to go to work for several hours yet, I've decided to take some time to myself, but I'm doing it outside despite the weather. I wish I could say it isn't like me to hold a grudge, but the truth is, I hold them quite well. Especially when it comes to my mother. That's why I'm sitting outside in the blistering heat instead of inside the air-conditioned house. The air out here may feel like a pillow pressed tight against my face, but that's better than being trapped inside of four walls with her.

Laid out before me, resting on the soft pink sheet I discovered in my closet, are the journals from my childhood. I started keeping them when I turned eleven, just after my mom and dad split and my whole world felt like it was coming down around my ears. That's the year Hattie and I discovered Joan Crawford and it's the year I learned how to reciprocate oral sex. You won't find that last part spelled out in these pages, though. I burned those, one version going up in smoke and the other burning like hot coals in the near corners of my mind.

Turning the pages is like opening up a new door in my mind. Every picture in this first journal tells a story. Nothing happy, nothing that should be in any child's journal. To think, all I had to do was leave it out on my bed one day. Cami would've found it and maybe she would've been able to see the secrets in the hastily drawn illustrations, the deep chasms of darkness stretching out behind the little girl staring out at the world. But I squirreled them away, tucking them behind a loose piece of drywall in my closet. *He told me I liked it.*

"Going down memory lane?" Lucinda's voice washes over me and I shiver.

Slapping the cover closed, I look up at her. "Sort of."

"Oh." She motions to the edge of the sheet. "Mind if I sit?"

"Knock yourself out." The fresh bruises on her neck indicate this isn't the best turn of phrase to use with her, but I'm still a bit annoyed by the shit her husband pulled the last time we spoke. She sits on her hip, legs drawn up at her side like a mermaid. A straight-backed mermaid. I pull the journals toward the base of the tree. "What's up?"

"I've wanted to come over for a few days." She picks a blade of grass and begins sliding it through her fingers, starting when the fine blade slices through her skin. Pressing the injured finger to her mouth, she adds, "To say I'm sorry. About what Rex did."

I crook an eyebrow. "Took you look enough."

"He…uh…he didn't want me to."

"And you do everything he wants you to, right?" Pathetic. Remembering that I'm not above that sort of obedience, I add, "Sorry."

"It's fine. You're right."

I glance past her toward her trailer. "Is he over there?" She nods. "What made him change his mind about you coming over?"

"He encouraged me to."

As if conjured, Rex steps out onto the front porch of their home, his eyes trained on the two of us sitting under the tree. He's always there now since the incident so many days ago. Always watching me, hand running up and down his abdomen as if he's the predator and I'm the prey. *Not anymore buddy.*

I look at Lucinda. "He doesn't seem the type to apologize."

"Not usually." She won't meet my gaze. Instead, her fingers are tugging at the grass by her feet.

I tried to shake off the bad feeling settling like a boulder in my gut. "What's this about, Lucinda?"

She looks at me. "What do you mean?"

"He wants you to ask me something, right? Why else would he be standing over there wearing that shit-eating grin of his? What is it?"

She shakes her head. "I don't want to say."

"Well, I don't have all fucking day. What is it?"

Her eyes go to Rex, then to me, and finally to her lap. "He wants you to be...with us," she says, her voice a whisper. At first, I'm not sure I've heard her right, but she can't look at me. Another humiliation courtesy of Rex.

Trying not to take her head off, I ask, "Is that what this was about?" She nods, though the movement is barely visible. I stand and walk past her, my eyes meeting his. He's smiling. That goddamn motherfucker is enjoying this. When I turn around, she's standing behind me, tears shining in her eyes and lips trembling. "Lucinda—"

"He said he's going to...show you how a real man *fucks.*" Her tears should touch me, should make me feel for her, but the fact that she's saying these things when it's clear she doesn't want to, when it's obvious it's killing her, makes me want to grab her by the back of the head and introduce her face to the tree.

Seething, I say, "No."

"He said…"

"I don't give a fuck what he said, Lucinda!"

"He'll pay you."

I look across the street at Rex and then back to her. "You know he doesn't love you, right? How can he when he gets so fucking hard pushing you around?" I rake my fingers through the ragged mop on my head. "I don't fucking believe this."

Her cheeks are drenched. "I'm sorry."

Finally, sympathy kicks in; my shoulders relax, and I move closer to her. "There's nothing for you to be embarrassed about. This is what assholes like Rex do." I wish looks could kill because right now I think mine holds the power of a Mac truck going full speed. I grab her arms, preparing to stick my tongue down her fucking throat, but I shake my head. He'd like that too much. "My answer is no."

She nods. Then, without another word, turns and heads across the yard and the gravel drive. Maybe I should be pissed at Lucinda for buddying up with me, for getting me to lower my guard before dropping such a bomb, but it isn't her fault. We're not born knowing how to manipulate, we're taught, and Rex has spent years working on her. I guess I'm stupid for believing I could get away from all of this. You can't run from nature. I was born with something inside of me that allows them to sniff me out. Maybe it's a magnet that attracts people like my uncle and Davis and Rex, something only men like them can recognize. I guess Lucinda has one too.

"Lucinda, wait!" I jog across the yard to her, yanking her around to face me. "He's not going to hit you because I said no, is he?" It hasn't escaped me that Rex has now moved to the edge of their yard, thumbs hooked through the loops of his jeans. She shrugs. "Goddamn it." Why do I feel so fucking responsible for her?

Her hand is covering mine, applying the slightest pressure. "It's okay," she says. "I don't want to do it anyway."

Rex looks as though he might cross over to us but stops when the storm door to my mother's home slaps shut. I look back and find Duke standing, shotgun resting against his shoulder. Halfway between the porch and us I see Cami, eyes wide, posture poised to strike. I release Lucinda and she crosses to her husband. Rex puckers his lips, then grabs his wife's arm and drags her into the house.

I turn, almost colliding with Cami. "What the fuck?"

She reaches for me, pulling back just before contact. "Are you okay?"

"I'm fine." I look up to where Duke is still standing on the porch, then turn back to my mother. "Were you watching me?"

She steps back. "Um. No. I just...I looked out the window and saw you heading for the road, then I saw Lucinda and Rex."

"That's a lot to glance out a fucking window."

"Please stop using that language with me."

"Then be straight with me. Were you watching me?"

"Not until I glanced out the window and saw Lucinda." She's fiddling with the hem of her jean shorts. Cut offs, of course. "After the last time, I just wanted to make sure everything was okay."

"I don't need you watching after me." I turn and stalk back to the tree, snatching my journals and the bed sheet up from the ground. She's right beside me. Sniveling. Disgusting. "I lived with men like Rex for a long time, Cami. I know how to handle them."

"Don't call me Cami," she says, breathless from trying to keep my pace.

"Whatever. I've got work."

She's following behind me, a ball at the end of a chain that must be attached to me. "Don't walk away, Zed. Let's talk about this. I was just trying to help."

I whirl around on her, the suddenness of it making her stumble. "I don't like your kind of help," I say, the force of it sending sprays of spit through the air between us. "You think helping is tracking me with my phone. You think helping me is filling Hattie's head with the same lies about me that you tell yourself. What did you tell her I did after group the other day?"

Stunned, she says, "I told her I didn't know."

"The last thing she needs is to hear doubt in your voice when it comes to me." I'm done now, anger spent. These are the moments that follow me and there's nothing I can do about it. "Stop trying to help me. All you do is make things worse."

Duke watches as I climb the stairs to the front porch. If he planned to say anything he's changed his mind now. The gun is gone. I hope to never see it again. But I'm glad it was here. Men like Rex don't stop unless their mortality is threatened. That's what makes them dangerous.

I HATE THE NIGHT SHIFT. Nothing to do except watch teenagers scroll through their phones while hanging out. I'm not even thirty yet, but that is definitely not how the kids I went to school with hung out. Whatever happened to raising hell and making out? Maybe it's a good thing those days are gone.

"It's a real thrill working the night shift, right?" Ada drops her towel on the counter, leaning over the top on her elbows. "I hate this job."

"Why have it then?"

"Gets me out of the house, I guess," she says, though her angsty tone says otherwise. "I'd rather work in the daytime. You guys have all the fun."

"Oh yeah." I laugh. "Serving the assholes who hate their jobs more than we do within the limited window they have to eat. Yeah, it's a thrill ride."

She shifts around, her back now pressed up against the aging counter. "I don't mean that. You get to work with all the cool people. Dante, Becca...Oliver." She says his name as if she's just divulged a secret. "Loads of smoke breaks, I hear."

I grab the rag she's discarded and begin wiping the stainless-steel top of the food window, trying to act as though what she's said has no bearing on me whatsoever, but inside I'm rattled. I'd rather there be a rumor going around about me and Hank. At least then I could laugh it off with glib certainty. Oliver is a different story. He says we're friends, but I don't think you're supposed to think about your friends the way I think about him in the dark when I'm alone.

"So, is it true?" She's looking at me in a way I can't quite describe. It's like she's desperate for the news but can't wait to claw my eyes out.

"Is what true?"

"You and Oliver!" Her hand shoots out and it doesn't look entirely playful.

"That we talk while on break, yes."

"And?"

I toss the rag on the counter. "And what, Ada?"

"Are you guys fucking?"

The directness of her question has me stumbling, especially considering her age. She's still in high school. Probably the only person at Jubilee's who doesn't meet the criteria of having a story.

"No," I say. "No, we're not."

She smiles, turning as the kid who has appeared on the other side of the counter clears his throat. "Welcome to Jubilee's, how may I help you?" I take this moment to slip away from her, telling Charles, the shift cook, I'm going on break. I'm sure the two of them can have a laugh about me being on my own.

Outside crickets and frogs are talking back and forth, their voices raising up to mingle with the intermittent flashes of fireflies in the field behind Jubilee's. I read online that they're disappearing. It's odd because I've known for a while something was missing from the night but didn't guess it was the flying bugs we used to chase around as children. Now, though, I can remember many summers in the past few years where I didn't see any at all. Like the honeybee. Maybe we're all disappearing.

Digging my phone out of my pocket, I open messages and type one to Oliver:

> I hate working the late shift.

We exchanged numbers after he got over himself and decided I wasn't totally a shit friend. I don't wait for a response. Chances are he's heading to a party or he's already there. He won't see my text until three in the morning, if he sees it then. I want to send him another message informing him that we are the talk of Jubilee's, but I don't. What good will it do? As I crush my cigarette against the dumpster, my phone pings.

> LOL. Me too. Maybe this will be the only one.
> You do have friends in high places you know.
> ;-)

Shoving the cell back into my pocket, I return to the front of the store. "I'm going to clean the dining room," I say, grabbing the broom and dustpan.

"What're you smiling about?" she asks.

Sobering, I look at her. How do I answer a question I don't have an explanation for? "It's almost time to close." She doesn't believe me, but that's okay. I don't need a seventeen-year-old's approval. "Yell if you need me."

CAMI IS AWAKE, seated in her recliner with a mug in one hand and a book in the other when I get home from my shift. I wonder if I'll ever be someone who can sit calmly in a chair reading while sipping some relaxing brew, if I'll ever stop thinking my world is about to be upended. I don't think so. Maybe I'm more like my dad's mom, a woman who was constantly bustling around the house looking for something to do as if her life depended on it.

She died not long after that summer in Virginia. Heart disease. Something I can't name that she didn't know about.

My mother stretches as I close the door and lock it. "How was work?"

"Fine."

She stands, grabbing the mug as she does. "I was just about to go to bed."

"Goodnight."

I turn to go into my bedroom, but she stops me. "Do you want anything before bed?"

"I ate during my shift."

"Zed, I really want us—"

I hold my hand up. "Please stop. We don't need to talk. I just want a bath."

"This late?"

My hands curl into themselves, ragged nails pressing against the soft skin of my palm. "Yes," I say through clenched teeth. "It's been a long day and I smell like grease."

She waves a hand. "Of course. Sorry. Goodnight then."

If there were some magic potion I could take to erase it all, go back to the time before my uncle made me a woman too young, I would. It's harmful to the soul to dislike one's mother as much as I do. A psychic told me once that my darkness is going to swallow me up. If that's going to happen, I wish it would sooner rather than later. I can't keep carrying Cami's shit and mine too.

Thirteen

When my uncle began his treatments of me...when he began raping me (the therapist suggests I call a spade a spade) I would take long baths afterward. Sliding beneath the water with only my nose, and mouth uncovered, I would try to drown the memory of him on me even as my little girl parts, so ill-used, throbbed with the recollection. My method never worked to erase what was happening, but the quiet meditation allowed me to better process it, I guess. Tonight is no different. Above the tub the popcorn ceiling is cracking in places, humidity from hot showers taking its toll. My eyes follow the lines created; the black speckles visible in some places a reminder that life isn't all that different from the ceiling of an old trailer. It's cracked, warped, and it has bad things hiding beneath the surface.

Through my thoughts and beyond the water is a commotion. Dull at first, distant. I open my eyes, waiting to see if it happens again or if the sound is part of meditation. Another muted series of thuds reaches through the water, propelling me upward. I stand, water dripping off of me in one big *whoosh*, but not even that can cover the sound of the thudding in my chest. I should speak. Maybe I should yell. Either way, I'm mute. Dumb. My legs are ready for flight, the fear sliding down along my limbs to awaken them, readying them to run if necessary. The fact that there's nowhere to go except through that door is only minutely important at this time. Grabbing a towel from the rail, I wrap it around me and step out of the tub, legs quivering. Taking a step forward, I reach out to turn the knob, recoiling immediately when the door explodes inward.

Suddenly Duke is standing inside the room, eyes wide and hair disheveled. He's looking around frantically until he registers my presence. I'm too stunned to speak. *What the hell is going on?* He grabs my arms, jerking each of my wrists face up, then drops them.

"Duke, wha—"

He puts his hand up. This is it. He's reached the end of his patience.

My mother is suddenly behind him. "Is she okay?"

That's it then. I zero in on her hoping that she can feel the death rays that are my eyes. My chest is heaving, my legs, still electrified, are becoming unstable. My lips twitch, begging to open so the wrath I'm holding inside can spill out. *Why the fuck can't you trust me!* Why do I expect she will? Every action she's made has been to show me how little faith and trust she actually has in me. I did this.

Duke's voice is level, but the cracks are there just like the popcorn above the tub. "I want both of you in the living room." I open my mouth to protest, prompting him to add with a bit more demand, "Now."

He is unhappy. I suppose this was inevitable. Men like Duke have no idea how to handle women like me and my mother. Well, as a pair anyway. Sitting in his recliner, he is leaning forward, elbows resting on his knees, head bowed as if praying. Maybe he is. I want to say something, to defend myself against whatever Cami may have told him, but even I have a bit of good sense left. I look at where she's sitting, her frame tiny in the overstuffed chair. She isn't looking at me. Probably for the best.

Duke pulls in a deep breath and looks up. His mouth is turned down creating deep frown lines on either side of it and his brow is furrowed. "There's got to be some changes around here." He looks at me. "This can't happen anymore."

I know I shouldn't speak, but anger is still wicking up inside me. "Baths?"

Cami's voice is small. "Zed!"

Now my eyes are on her. "What? Why is it my fault that I can't even take a bath without you thinking I'm going to slit my fucking wrists?"

"I knocked. You didn't answer." Her cheeks are gleaming from the rivers flowing from her eyes. "I was scared. You've been so stressed—"

"Because of you, Cami! It was a fucking bath!"

Duke stands. "Respect your mother, Zedwynne."

I stand as well, my fury flooding into the room with my movement. Why is it always my fault? Why do I have to carry the goddamn burden? "Sure thing, Duke. I'll respect her the way she's always respected me."

"She is the only person who has been there for you."

"Oh yes!" I'm on fire now, consumed by my own bitterness. "She's an angel. Always there for her daughters, right?" I glare at her. "Ready with great advice, ready to tear fruit from their wombs and call the police to action. A real fucking Mary Teresa!"

Mary?

He's towering over me, his frown lines gone and his eyes blazing. "Young lady, if you're going to stay in this house, you'd better start listening to what I have to say. I've been quietly watching your mama try to handle you, but I'm done. You need to get your life together and stop acting like a damn kid."

I took a bath. Looking between the two of them, I consider voicing this again, consider asking when I will be able to do normal human things without someone suspecting I'm trying to finish what I started, but I remain silent. There is no use.

Turning, I go to my room and lock the door. They're having a heated discussion now. I imagine she's trying to get him to calm down. I couldn't care less. Grabbing an old bag from my closet, I stuff as many items of clothing as I can inside and sling it on the bed. Throwing on a band shirt and jeans, I toss the cell phone on the comforter and climb out the window. It's not the first time I've used this avenue for leaving, but it is damn sure the last.

Lucinda is standing in the driveway, her nightly ritual returned, I suppose. She looks over as I toss my things into the Bronco. Crossing the street, I go to her and grab her shoulders, boring my eyes into hers. "You need to figure out what's best for you, Luce."

Her eyes are saucers, and her eyebrows are raised. Beyond her, Rex is on the front porch, arms stretched above his head, fingers hooked into the metal lattice that frames the dipping roof. Lucinda looks at him and then back at me.

"Get the fuck off my property," he says.

I nod, releasing his wife, then cross back over to the awaiting Bronco and get inside. As I back out of the driveway the front door to my mom's trailer opens and she rushes out, her eyes wide and almost wild. I want to scream at her, to curse her for everything she's ever done to me, for not being there, but when I stop in the center of the road, my eyes locked on hers, I can't utter a sound. After a moment her shoulders slump and I know this is her letting go. She knows no other way to handle me.

I throw the old tank into drive and bolt down the road. She'll be on the phone with Hattie soon to recant the whole thing. I'll have to call her later just so she won't worry. Stopping at the stop sign on the main road, I put my head down on the steering wheel. Leaving always seems like a good idea when I'm doing it. Maybe one day I'll actually know where the hell I'm heading.

***

I spent last night on the side of the road one town over. I could've stayed in a motel, probably should have, but Cami has probably been calling every hotel and motel in a two-hundred-mile radius since this morning to see if I'm checked in. Let her worry. I hope her nails are bitten to the quick and she hasn't had a moment of sleep. Serves her right.

The sun has finally said its goodbyes, the last rays scarcely visible on the horizon. Already the air is cooler, the light breeze rustling through nearby trees like a child playing hide and seek. My eyes are closed, left arm dangling out of the Bronco's opened window, a feast for the mosquitoes, though they've never been very attracted to me. On the radio, Neil Young is singing about a harvest moon and I can't keep my head from swaying. Outside, the crickets have begun their nightly gab session with frogs. Maybe they're asking the old croaks to leave them be. *Why can't we be friends?* Guess no one has told them predators don't give a damn how much you beg. They kind of like it.

I crack an eyelid when the door across the way opens and music from inside the old brick structure spills out into the night. It's something sexy. I guess it has to be in a place like this. The old steel door slaps shut, and I squint to see if I know the woman standing beneath the light. No use, I'm too far.

I'm not sure how or why I've ended up outside the The Wet Spot Gentleman's Club. As if a gentleman would be caught dead in this joint. Set back from the road, the aging facade looks tired even in the darkening landscape, the old neon sign standing proud before it depicting a pair of long, fishnet stocking legs with the words The Wet Spot spelled out in the gush of waters from between them. So, this is where Betsy Franklin ended up? Could be worse.

Using the old crank, I roll the window up and get out of the truck, crossing across the dusty expanse toward the building.

"Hey." A voice from the side of the building stops me.

I turn toward her but don't speak. She's older than me, dull, blond hair and too much makeup. *We're all used up.*

She points to the building, leaning forward a bit as she speaks. "They ain't gonna let you watch no girls in there. It's a *gentleman's* club." She cackles, then takes a drag from her cigarette, her next statement soft as if she's only talking to herself. "Gentlemen. Yeah, right."

"I just need the phone."

"Don't you got a cell phone?"

I shrug. "Lost it."

The woman waves her cigarette through the air. "Well hell, I'll let you use mine. Ain't no need to go in there if you ain't got to."

She has a point. "I'd rather use the pay phone. Does this place still have one?"

"Sure, sure. Not every man that comes in here has the money for a cell phone. He's got the dough to look at tits and ass, but not enough to stay connected. Priorities, I guess."

I nod. "Reckon they'll let me use it?"

"How the fuck am I supposed to know? Just go on and ask them. Josh is working the door."

"Thanks." I don't wait for her to say anything else. Turning, I head for the entrance, almost colliding with the door guy as I step up to pull the handle.

The man I presume to be Josh is big, tall, with arms the size of my waist. He's currently indisposed with the *gentleman* he's got gripped by the collar. I move to the side as he passes. "Excuse me, lady." *Manners. Nice.* Shoving the inebriated guy toward the unpaved lot, he points at him. "You can't touch the girls, Tim. You know it. Now go on home and sleep it off."

"Fuck you, man," Tim slurs, his hands flying around him like a swarm of gnats on a summer day before shoving them into his pockets. He looks at the bouncer. "Where the fuck's my keys, Josh?"

"I've got a car coming for you."

Points for Josh. A bouncer with a heart. I think they made a movie about one of those.

"Give me my goddamn keys, man. I ain't too drunk to drive." His hands have turned into flying insects again countering his claim.

Josh's hands are up, and I can't tear my eyes away from his arms. "Look, man, you can wait here for the car, or I can call Helen. What's it going to be?"

Without another word, Tim plops onto the ground, a defiant toddler who knows he's defeated.

Josh looks at me. "Sorry about that."

I put my hand up. "Not my first time."

He smiles and my pulse quickens. He's not bad looking with his huge arms, tapered midsection, and chiseled jawline.

"Are you new?"

I shake my head. "I just need to use the phone."

His brow furrows and his dark eyes narrow. "You don't have a cell phone?"

I shrug. "Lost it."

He reaches in his back pocket and presents his own phone. "Want to use mine?"

"I'd rather use the pay phone."

He shrugs. "Suit yourself. It's just inside the lobby." He pulls the door open, but steps in front of me. "You can't go into the theater, though."

I smile. "Is that what they call it here?" He nods. "Fancy."

"I'm serious."

"Not that I want to, but what if I did?" I lean forward, my voice taking on a teasing quality that disgusts even me. "What if I like looking at naked women?"

He shrugs. "Not my rules."

"Well, someone needs to change them."

"Do you like looking at naked women?" He looks serious.

At this point, I kind of wish I did. "No. I just need to use the phone."

He moves out of my way. "Stay out of the theater."

My hand is up in a faux scout promise. "You have my word."

Inside, I grab the receiver, scraping it across my leg to wipe off any cooties associated with the last user. If Hattie offered me a sanitizing wipe right now, I would gladly accept it.

The phone rings twice before I hear my little sister's panicked voice on the other end of the line. "Zeddie?"

"Yeah."

"Oh my gosh, where have you been? We've been so worried!"

Regret settles heavy in my stomach. "I'm sorry I didn't call sooner."

Her voice levels out a bit, less scared and more annoyed now. "What the hell happened last night?"

"I can't stay there anymore."

She sighs and even I can feel the weight of it. "You know that was a condition of your release. You have to stay with Mom."

"It was voluntary, Hattie." I pick at the peeling paint of the encasement. "I can't live with her anymore."

"Where will you stay tonight?"

I look at Josh as he steps through the door. I wonder if he's got anyone to go home to. Staying the night with him would sure beat sleeping in the Bronco again.

"I'll figure it out," I tell her. "I just can't go back there."

"I'd let you stay here, but I don't think you and J.C. would get along."

"Don't worry about it, little sister. I'll let you know where I end up."

"How? You didn't even take your phone and this number showed up as The Wet Spot. Why are you even there?"

"I just needed a phone." I shift away from Josh's scrutiny and add, "I just wanted to let you know I'm okay. Don't worry. I'll call you when I find a place to stay."

"Call me in the morning. I'm going to ask a few friends if you can stay with them."

Embarrassment tightens my voice. "No!"

"You have to stay somewhere, Zed."

"I'll figure it out." Taking a deep breath, I add, "Please, just let me figure it out."

She's silent for a few seconds before saying, "Okay."

I place the receiver back in its cradle and turn to Josh. "Thanks."

"No problem." He pushes the door open. "If you need a place to stay, I could use some company."

Stopping at the threshold, I turn to him. A few months ago, I would've taken him up on it, especially given his physique. He's definitely a step up from my usual preference.

I give him a quick smile. "Thanks, but I'll have to pass."

Yeah, sometimes I even surprise myself.

FOURTEEN

In the summers of my childhood, when my sister and the other children would catch fireflies and lock them inside their glass vaults, I would sit and stare at the insects for ages, watching how they would climb the sides of the jar, their lights seeming to fade a bit. I thought then that they were saddened by their capture. That somehow it was causing their lights to fade. I would tap the glass with my jagged nails. *Tap, tap, tap.*

As I grew older and was trapped in a glass jar of my own, I would tap the glass in an attempt to let them know I understood their fear, that I, Zedwynne Grace Skinner, knew what it was like to be caught in a jar unable to escape, light fading. *Tap, tap, tap.* My own form of Morse code.

I can hear it, my little girl nails rapping against glass. Why didn't I let them out? What's the worst that would have happened? The other kids would have been mad. So what? So what if they wouldn't let me play with them anymore? Why didn't I just save one jarful of them? Open the lid and let them out, shake their clingy little bodies onto the damp grass. Why didn't someone open my jar?

Sitting up too quickly, I almost bang my head against the steering wheel of the Bronco. A dream. Thank god. I was a little girl firefly stuck in a glass prison, my uncle's big, green eye staring inside at me. Peering inside. I shudder, wrapping myself in a tight hug. *It's okay, Zeddie. It was only a dream.*

Three raps against the driver's window almost send me into the passenger seat. I look over, stunned to see Hank's face pressed against the glass. I crank it down quickly.

He smiles, but I can see something else there. Worry? "Morning, Zed." I nod, still unable to speak. "I don't have you set to open today." He looks at his watch. "And we don't open for a couple of hours yet."

"I—" How am I supposed to explain this to my boss? *Well, you see, Hank, I hate my mom and we had a huge fight and...well...I ran away from home.* It's laughable.

His smile remains, but his brow furrows. "Why don't you come inside? I'll make some coffee and we'll have a chat."

Great. I nod, though there is no real thrill about being locked inside a closed restaurant with a man triple my size who I hardly know, and get out of the Bronco, following this lumbering giant into the quiet of Jubilee's.

THE COFFEE IS thick and black, motor oil run too long in an engine. Our regulars like it that way. I don't. I sip slowly as Hank pours the contents of a number of sugar packets into his cup. I guess he's no fan either.

He stirs slowly, maybe trying to figure out what in the world to say to me. I don't blame him. I don't even know what to say to me. "What's going on, young lady?"

I take a sip of my coffee, wincing as the bitterness hits my tongue. "What do you mean?"

He shoves the sugar packets toward me. "Well, I don't normally find my employees sleeping outside the restaurant. I can only assume that either you love this place so much you can't wait to get to work, or your home life isn't the best."

Understatement of the century. "I guess I love it that much."

He chuckles. "Nobody loves this place that much. Not even me."

I shrug. "There's a first time for everything."

"Cut the crap, kid." He pats my hand reassuringly. "I talked to your mom. I know you two don't get along so well."

My mouth will remain closed.

"She's been a bit strained since you came back."

"It's not my fault."

He takes a gulp of his still steaming brew and I wonder how on earth his tongue isn't sizzling. "Yes, it is." I move to stand up, but he puts his hand up. "But it isn't entirely your fault."

My body relaxes.

"I don't know a lot about your situation, but I've gotten to know you a bit since you started here. You're not a bad element, Zed. You just need a little time."

"I never said I was. A bad element."

His eyes are soft, kind. Brown pools of sincerity that I have to look away from. "You don't have to say it."

This is too much. I want to leave. I have two options; I can flee through the kitchen and out the back door or I can just run right out the front.

"I want to offer you something, but I don't want you to be offended or suspicious."

Too late. "What?"

"I have a trailer out behind my house. It's nothing spectacular. One bedroom, one bathroom, and old as hell, but it's a roof over your head. A place you can take your time."

"Why?"

"Pardon?"

"Why would you do that? Why would you do any of this?"

He tips his cup, staring into the deep brown liquid. "I just like helping people, Zed."

Still not buying what he's selling, I ask, "What do you want in return?"

Wincing, he says, "I guess I could charge you rent, but I don't see the need. My wife used it as her studio before she died. My daughter's been hounding me to do something with it. I can't think of anything better than helping out a wandering soul."

My gut twists. "Okay."

He slides a piece of paper across the table. "This is my address. Go get your things from your mom's house and I'll get Hanna, my daughter, to get the space cleaned up for you."

"You don't need to do that."

"Nonsense. Hanna will be thrilled."

A 'pfft' escapes my lips. "How old is she?"

"Fourteen."

"Oh yeah. She'll be thrilled."

He smiles. "Is that a yes?"

I nod, then voice my agreement. It's a gamble, taking an offer like this from a man I hardly know, a man who signs my paychecks, but right now even the potential drawbacks of his offer are a better option than returning to my mother's house.

"Give it a couple of hours and you should be ready to go."

Stuffing the napkin in my back pocket, I nod again. "Thanks, Hank."

MY MOTHER'S house stands silent against the gray morning. I think it expects me. Maybe that's why the sky looks as though it will explode with fury at any moment. Everything is waiting on the final showdown. This is the quiet before the storm.

I slide out of the Bronco and walk slowly to the house. Duke's truck is gone. Thank god for small favors, I guess. Fishing the key out of my bag, I turn the lock and walk into the quiet interior. Everything looks different. The same, but inherently different. This is a house with missing pieces. Or maybe just the inhabitants are incomplete.

Going to my room, I gather the rest of my sparse belongings and shove them into the bag I used for gym a thousand years ago when I attended the local high school. After zipping the bag, I move to the desk in the corner, plopping down on the wicker chair. Too many more plops and it will fall to pieces. I've left it twice before, this room that saw some of my scariest moments; the rejection, the good news, the ultimatum, the spiral, but I've never been as hesitant to leave as I am now. Maybe this is what it's like to actually consider an action before you make it. Any memory of me doing so before now is gone, but it's most likely that I have never stopped even for a moment to consider what my actions might be. Do I seize this offer to live on my own again? At the diner, I took it because it's an easy way to avoid Cami, but now that I'm sitting here in this room, at this corner desk where my history is somewhat written out in the *Lisa Frank* notebooks it holds—happiness on the outside and consuming rage on the inside—I wonder if I should leave. What good will it do me to be on my own if I'm not ready? I can't end up in the same place again. Death will surely win next time.

"Your therapist called."

I jerk at the sound of Cami's voice, the drawer meeting my knee with a bang. "Shit." I look at her, rubbing the spot to dull the pain. "You scared the shit out of me."

She leans against the door frame, arms crossed loosely over her abdomen. "Sorry. I just wanted to let you know she called."

"And?"

"I told her you weren't in."

"You didn't tell her about the other night?"

Shaking her head, she answers, "No."

"Why?"

Her voice waivers and I say a little prayer to the universe that she won't start crying. "Because I don't want them to take you away."

"They won't."

"If you're a danger to yourself I think they can."

"I'm not."

She takes a deep breath, closing her eyes. "I know."

"Do you?"

"Yes." Her eyes are open again, meeting mine. "If you think for a minute I wouldn't have called them when you left if I thought you were, you're wrong." Her arms fall to her sides. "I've done everything wrong, Zed. I wanted to keep you safe, but I can't. I've never been able to."

I want to tell her it isn't all her fault, but something keeps me quiet. Maybe I like knowing that she feels so guilty about her actions. Someone should have to live with it like I have.

"Hank offered me a place to stay."

She nods. "I know."

"It's a trailer behind his house."

"And you're going to do it?"

I nod.

She closes her eyes again, but only for a fleeting moment. "That's good."

"Yeah?"

"Yeah." She walks toward me, holding her hand out. "Please keep this with you. Just in case you need me, or we need you." I lift the smartphone from her hand. "I'm sorry, Zed," she says, her resolve finally crumbling.

I don't move as she cries. When I was a kid, I would sit still as things were done to me, paralyzed by the awkwardness of the situation and how wrong it all felt. Suddenly I'm there again. Surely, I should be compelled to go to her, to wrap my arms around her. Hattie would. I avert my eyes, stare out the window into the summer morning until she pulls herself together.

Sniffling, she says, "Take care of yourself, okay?"

"What about the therapist?"

"Just call her like you're supposed to."

I nod.

"I'll leave you to it." She stops at the door and turns back to me. "I hope one day you'll forgive me."

She stares at me. I know she's waiting for me to respond, but I can't speak, not now. The words will just be all jumbled, part rage and part desperation. I don't want to be this way, don't want to be the girl who can't love her mother, but I'm stuck in a place where soft feelings toward her are just out of my grasp. After a long moment passes, she taps the frame of the door and turns away, disappearing into the depths of the double wide. Opening the drawer, I grab my journals and shove them into the bag, then hurry out of the house before she comes back to try again.

FIFTEEN

Hanna is still cleaning up my new living quarters when I arrive. At least I assume the statuesque girl with waist-length, blond hair and a sour disposition is Hanna. Hank's place was easy enough to find. Right off the main highway about a quarter mile back. I always wonder about people with really long driveways. What are they trying to hide from the world?

"Hi." My voice is small as I speak for the first time to this girl who already seems to dislike me. Guess I can't blame her. I wouldn't be happy about cleaning up for some stray either.

She looks up, her brown eyes tinged with annoyance. "Hey."

"I'm Zedwynne."

Her shoulders lift and fall. Unimpressed, that's what she is. "Hanna."

"Your dad told me."

"Great." She continues sweeping the porch barely big enough for the small table and Adirondack chair that reside there.

"Can I help?"

"Nah. I'm done now." She props the broom with its fraying skirt against the aluminum of the old trailer. "Want the tour?"

I nod and climb the three stairs to meet her.

Inside she stands in the middle of the main room. "This is your front room, that's your kitchen, and beyond that is your bedroom and bathroom. Tour complete."

"Thanks."

She turns on me then, her amber hair swinging around with grace. "My dad doesn't need any trouble."

"What do you mean?"

Her voice is tight, "I mean he doesn't need a hanger on. He's not looking for a lady friend."

I nod, doing my best not to grin. Hank must be a great dad. "Understood."

When she's gone, I bring my paltry belongings inside and begin to set up house. The living room is decorated with an old yellow sofa, the seams frayed from use, and a small coffee table. In the corner is a tiny television, not that I intend to use it. It's never been my medium of choice. I guess when you're living life going from one party to another there isn't much time left for the tube. The kitchen has a working sink, stove, and a buzzing refrigerator. Beyond that, the bedroom is big enough for the double bed and a small chest of drawers, and the bathroom is scarcely big enough to turn around in. Yet I am smiling. It isn't something I'm aware of at first, but a glimpse in the mirror above the old green sink exposes me.

Going back to the living room, I dig the phone out of my purse and dial Hattie.

"Zeddie!"

"Hey."

"Mom told me you stopped by the house."

I lean against the counter, free hand tucked under my arm. "God, does she ever stop?"

"She knew I was worried."

"I called you last night."

"From a strip club. I was terrified you would end up dancing beside poor old Betsy Franklin."

I close my eyes against the dull pounding at the back of my head. "What makes you think she has it so rough?"

There is a *guffaw* at the other end of the line. "She's a topless dancer! Duh!"

"Waitress. Besides, I bet she makes great money. If I remember correctly, she had one hell of a rack in high school."

She laughs. "Still does."

"I bet she kills it."

Hattie is quiet for a moment. "Yeah. Maybe." Another moment of silence. "But how do you think she feels walking around town? It must be weird."

"Maybe." I don't want to talk about Betsy and how she may or may not feel. "I have a new place."

"Mom told me. I'm glad you're bunking out back of Hank's place. Nobody in the world I would trust more than him."

"Who is this guy, Jesus?"

Hattie laughs. "Just a very good guy. You should know by now. Haven't you been working with him long enough?"

I shrug. "I mostly work with Oliver."

There's a pause and I know I've stepped in it. "Is he the cute one? He's not why you moved out, is he?"

"Hattie, please don't."

"Seriously, Zed, is he? Because you don't need to lose focus. You're just now beginning to get your own life together. You don't need some loser—"

"Hattie." My tone is harsher than I intend, but her sudden silence is golden. "Oliver is not a loser. He's just some guy I work with." *And want to fuck.* "Nothing more."

"Promise."

I cross my fingers. "Promise."

She doesn't believe me. I can tell that even through the miracles of modern communication. "Okay then. I'm fixing to go in for my doctor's appointment."

"Let me know what they say?"

"Of course." There's another pause. "I'll talk to you later," she says before the line goes dead.

It hurts that Hattie doesn't have more faith in me. The therapist says I need to focus less on others having faith in me and more on me having it in myself. Maybe she's right. Who the hell knows nowadays?

I'VE JUST BEGUN to entertain the thought of my first supper out from under thumb when I hear two quick taps against the metal of the old front door. Muscles tensing, I round the counter from the kitchen and peer through the diamond window, not entirely surprised to find Hank standing outside, a broad smile on his aging face, and a bottle of wine in hand.

Opening the door just wide enough for my body to fit in the opening, I say, "H—hi. What's up?"

"Just thought I would welcome you to the neighborhood." He holds up the bottle. "Welcome."

"I can't drink."

He looks at the bottle, then back at me with that toothy smile. "It's non-alcoholic." His bulky body is too close for comfort, a tactic I realize for him to get inside. I step back, granting him entrance. His eyes scan the interior. "Looks like you're getting settled."

"Yeah." I'm only vaguely aware of my arms crossing my chest like a shield.

"What do you think? Is it everything I promised?" He's going into the kitchen, rummaging through the cabinets to pull out two juice glasses.

"It's great." I close the storm door but leave the interior open. Maybe if he knows his daughter can walk in at any moment he won't try anything.

As if he's read my mind he looks up, mid-pour, his eyes darkening. "How're you doing? Okay?"

"Ummm. Yeah. I was just thinking about supper."

He straightens. "Oh. I can leave. If you want."

There it is. They always give you that moment, the one where you can back out. *It's your choice, kid.* I always choose wrong. Always.

"No," I say, despite the screaming in my head. "I'm just—"

"Thinking I want something from you?"

I nod.

He lifts the glasses and crosses the room to me, holding mine out. His eyes have brightened, and he looks almost amused.

"Do you? Want something?"

"Yes."

There it goes, the other shoe dropping. I recall Hattie's words, that Hank is the one person she would trust. Always naive.

"What?"

He motions to the old yellow sofa. "Why don't we sit down for a bit?"

"Hank."

I'm too late. His bulk is situated on the sofa and he's patting the old, faded place beside him. I sit at the other end, prim and proper like my grandmother taught us.

"Do you think you'll like it here?"

"Here? Or in town?"

He shrugs. "Both. Here and *here*."

"I think this town sucks. I'm not sure about this place yet."

He takes a long gulp of the fancy grape juice he's brought over and sits the empty cup on the coffee table. "I think you're adjusting to being back pretty well."

Not sure of what he's playing at, I nod and take a small sip of my own drink.

"You're doing really well at the diner. Oliver can't stop talking about how great of a job you do."

My face warms at the mention of him.

Hank wrestles with his bulk to turn more toward me. "I think you're doing well too."

What do you want from the good girl?

His eyes are searching my face for something. My skin is crawling, trying desperately to get away from me before this begins. I wonder if my epidermis has rational thought. Does it think we are cursed, me by birth and it by association?

"More juice?"

Should I mention that this technique only really works if there is alcohol involved?

I shake my head. "I'm fine."

"I think I'll have some." He stands and ambles back over to the counter. The jagged stubs of my fingernails dig into the tender flesh of my thigh. Filling the glass, he looks up at me. "Do you think you'll stay?"

"I don't know." Again, I'm not sure if he's talking about the trailer or if he's talking about town. I'm not sure about either. I shrug. "Maybe."

The sofa depresses a bit under his weight as he resumes his position. "I could use another full-timer at the diner."

"Oh yeah?" My heartbeat is drowning him out a bit. Is this how I have lived my life for more than a decade? Yes, it is.

His hand is resting on the cushion between us. "Yeah. You like working at Jubilee's, right?"

I swallow. "I appreciate the job." We could stay like this, him asking me vague questions while seeming to inch closer, or I could just face him head-on. Taking a deep breath, I level my gaze on him and ask, "What do you want, Hank?"

His face is dumb, slack jawed and eyes wide. "Just to talk," he says, jerking his hand back.

I place my cup on the table. "In my experience when a man wants to talk, he's looking for something in return. Something I'm not thrilled to give in most cases."

Before I can understand what's happening, Hank is standing, his stout form crossing to the front door. "Lord no." He steps forward long enough to put his cup on the coffee table. "No." His eyes are slanted in an odd way. I've never seen this look on a man's face before. Desire, rage, disgust, but never this. What is it?

I stand, the feeling that I've misjudged the situation pushing me up. "Hank—"

His hands are outstretched. Like a shield. "Stay there."

"I'm sorry." *Why am I apologizing?*

"No, I'm sorry. I didn't mean to make you think..." His hand presses against the top of his balding head. "Oh man. I've done this all wrong." He straightens. "I'm sorry, Zedwynne, I shouldn't have come over unannounced and I certainly shouldn't have..." He looks at the bottle sitting on the counter like an accusation. "Damn." He looks at me. "I don't want anything from you. I just want you to feel safe. Your mama told me you haven't felt safe for a long time."

Knock me over with a feather. Please.

"If you need anything just give a call to the house." He opens the storm door. "I'm sorry."

I plop down on the sofa upon his anxious retreat. Even its spongy cushion isn't enough to comfort me. What have I done?

God, this group is a fucking joke. All tears and sighs and hopes. I want to punch most of them square in the jaw. How does one go through life thinking that everything is going to work out fine? Bad things happen one right after the other and yet these assholes think there's hope for all of us. I blame Rebecca. Her smug smile and kind eyes. Bitch.

"Zedwynne, you look as though you have something to share." Rebecca is smiling at me. "Would you like to talk to the group?"

"Not really." Insolence is my best defense. "But I've had a shitty week, so, okay." I chance a glance at Deidre and Clay. They've chosen to sit a few chairs away from me today. Some new guy joined. I suspect they've assigned themselves the welcome party for all new recruits. I shouldn't be too surprised. In fact, I shouldn't care at all.

"When you're ready," Rebecca says. This is her way to hurry up the speaker. She's smiling, but I can see the *hurry the fuck up* in her eyes.

I lean forward, elbows resting on my knees and eyes averted to the floor. "My neighbor's husband propositioned me recently. Well, he had his wife proposition me." I hear a sound from my right and figure it's Deidre thinking how fucking ridiculous I am. Whatever. "He wants a threesome because he thinks I need breaking, and he wants to be the one to do it." The last part came out in a choke. "It caused an uproar at my house and my mom and I fought. Again." I lean back, narrowing my eyes on Rebecca. She's not stunned, not even surprised by the look of her. In fact, a slow survey of the circle shows that no one is that affected by what I've said at all. Maybe I am an idiot.

She shifts in her chair, tugging at the long skirt she's chosen to wear today. "Group, does anyone have anything to say to Zedwynne?"

Eddie is the first to speak, "That's tough, man." His gray eyes meet mine. "Some people want to steal from us. They see us as a threat because we're open to feeling. That's why we're fucked up, because we *feel* everything. It scares them, I think, so they try to take it and hide it away so we're just as miserable as they are. But the joke's on them, isn't it?"

I nod because I can't do anything else. He's absolutely right.

"Eddie," Rebecca's voice is soft. "You're making them the enemy." He bows his head, turning his body away from the group. My lips itch to open to release my frustration with her. She's silenced the only person in the room that seems to get what's been happening to me my entire life. Her eyes meet mine again and my anger quells. "Anyone else?"

Excusing myself from the circle, I head over to the

refreshments table. No coffee today. Maybe Rebecca is aware that people prefer cold drinks on days when hellfire is burning on earth. I've heard bits and pieces about the circles of hell. The temperature outside says we're firmly in the ninth circle, but since we're all attempted suicides in here, I guess we fall closer to the seventh. That is, if Montana knew his shit. Something tells me, he did. Grabbing a paper cup, I fill it with cold water from a sweating pitcher.

"That's fucked up," Clay says, walking past me to the table. "What you said."

I look over the rim of my cup at him.

"I had a married man offer me money to have sex with him, but he never mentioned bringing his hubs into it."

"That's prostitution," I say, lowering my cup.

He shrugs. "I guess." Grabbing a piece of lemon cake, he takes a big bite. "She makes these, you know."

"Who?"

"Rebecca." He laughs, crumbs spurting from his mouth. "What a snooty name. Re-becc-ah."

I shift away from the group, keeping my voice low. "Are you fucking high?"

His bright green eyes shift to me, finger touching the tip of his nose.

"We're not supposed to be using."

He laughs, a huge guffaw that pulls Deidre from her seat to us. "What the hell, man?" She pushes him around to face away from the group. "I told you to be quiet."

"I was!" His pout is made comical by the crumbs that coat his lips.

Deidre is surveying me with suspicion. It doesn't take a genius to dissect her thoughts. She thinks I'm going to narc, that I'm going to run right over to Rebecca and tell her that our dear boy Clay is high as a kite.

Placing my cup on the table, I lean over to Clay, making sure to keep my eyes on Deidre and say, "Don't worry, kid. Your secret's safe with me," before going back to join the others in the circle.

She doesn't say another word to me until we're packing up to go. It's the group's responsibility to put the chairs and tables back the way they go. I guess we do it at the end since Rebecca does it before we arrive. Deidre appears beside me as I put the last chair in place. Today she's wearing a band shirt and palazzo pants. Her hair is up in a sort of mohawk, sleek on the sides and loose curls on top. This look can't be effortless, but she doesn't seem the type to spend a lot of time on vanity.

"Hey," she says. "We're heading to the diner after this. Want to come?"

"Who's we?"

"Me, Clay, and Eddie." I suppose she senses my confusion because she adds, "He comes sometimes."

"Sure," I say with a nod. Then, leaning closer to her I add, "You don't have to worry about me ratting him out, you know. But, Jesus, what the fuck was he thinking, getting high before group?"

We're both looking at Clay. She shakes her head. "Beats the hell out of me."

At the diner we're quiet as we chew on the best damn french fries I've ever eaten. I swear, if Jubilee's were to find out this recipe it would up our game. I shake the thought out, not sure where it came from or why. This place isn't as lame as I thought before. Set up like a pop shop with red retro tables and chairs in the center of the black and white tiled floor and teal and white booths lining the windowed wall. Like last time, we're in a booth; me and Eddie on one side and Deidre and Clay on the other. The kid is coming down, it's obvious by the way he's slouched over his plate, eyes closed as he munches on his fries.

"What was it?" Deidre asks. When he doesn't answer, she nudges him hard with her shoulder.

"Ow!"

"Answer me, goddammit. What was it?"

"Nothing." She nudges him again and he shoves her. My hand halts in mid-air as she turns to him.

"Boy, don't you ever do that shit to me." He's cowering and I don't blame him. She's already tall, broad-shouldered, but now she's pissed and even I'm scared.

"Come on, Deidre," Eddie says. "Leave him alone. He'll tell you when he's ready."

The turning of her head is so sharp it hurts my neck. "You think so? Because the last time he pulled this shit he didn't tell me. Two days later what happened?" She nudges Clay again. "Go on, tell them."

"Just stop, D," he says, his hand covering his face as he turns toward the window.

Deidre levels her eyes with Eddie. "I got a call from him in the hospital. He didn't have nobody else. Begged me to come and get him. *Swore* he'd never do that shit again." She turns back to him. "Now look at him. Not even six months later and he's high out of his goddamn mind again."

I want to speak, can feel the desire tightening in my throat. A lump of words that wants to fly out at her, strike her, remind her that we're all fucked up, but I remain quiet. I have no dog in this fight. I don't even know why I'm here.

"Was it that motherfucking Preston again?"

"Don't call him a motherfucker." Clay's voice is soft, defeated.

Deidre's hands come down hard on the table and my body goes rigid. She looks at Clay, then me and Eddie. Her eyes are shining, but it isn't indignation or rage. My limbs relax as I understand that she's terrified.

She stands. "I'm going to get some air. Watch him," she says to both of us, but my legs are ushering me out of the booth to follow her out into the scorching afternoon. "I told you to watch him."

"Eddie's with him." I motion to the window where Clay and Eddie are still visible. "Besides, I don't take orders very well these days."

She makes a 'humph' sound and settles against the bricks, her top half folding over slightly.

"Are you good?" I ask.

Her head raises and her wet eyes meet mine. "Do I *look* okay, Zedwynne?"

"It's just Zed."

She shrugs. "Okay?"

I fish the fresh pack of smokes from my back pocket and offer her one.

"Hell no. Those things'll kill you."

I drop my head to the side. "I think cigarettes are the least of our worries, don't you?"

She sputters a laugh. "Fair point, I guess, but I still don't want your cancer stick. If I have to be here, I prefer to be healthy."

I nod my understanding. "What's going on in there?" If Hattie could see me now. Making friends. Asking questions. Engaging.

Deidre stands, leaning back against the cool brick. "He's got an ex, Preston, comes around once or twice a year to leech off of Clay for a while." Her gaze is heavy on me. "He's the reason Clay tried to kill himself last time."

"I thought it was an overdose?"

"Intentional."

"Ah." Looks like Clay and I have a bit in common.

She looks toward the window. "I just don't know what to do for him. I'm not his mama, but he's got nobody else." Her eyes are back on me. "Tell me something, how can a mama turn her back on a person she brought into the world? I get a dad, but a mom?"

"I wish I knew." I don't elaborate, not knowing how Deidre

will react if I tell her I have the opposite problem. My mother is too interested in my well-being. "What're you going to do?"

Her eyes go back to the window, and she sighs. "I'm going to go back in there before he bolts, that's what." She opens the door and looks back at me. "You coming?"

"In a minute."

I could leave them, stick them with my bill, and take off. I don't live in this town. I'd never have to see them again. But my legs won't move in the opposite direction. They are the last thing I want, this merry band of losers, but I think they're everything I need.

Instead of cutting out, I smash out my cigarette and deposit it in the nearby pot before going back inside to join them. By the time I reach the table Deidre is holding a sobbing Clay tight against her and Eddie looks like he's ready to bolt.

"Is everything okay?"

Eddie looks at me, shrugs.

"He's fine," Deidre says. "Just coming down hard." She strokes his hair, keeping her arm around him.

I ease back into the booth as Eddie slides over to give me room. I look at him, unsure what to say next. My brain seems to know, though, because without hesitation I say, "Thanks for what you said today. In group." I smile. "It helped."

"Rebecca didn't think so."

"Y'all leave her alone." Deidre's voice is strangled a bit, but still firm. "She's got a tough job keeping us crackpots in line. Especially those of us with the tendency to fall apart on a weekly basis."

Eddie laughs. "Point taken."

Clay separates from Deidre and begins nursing the chocolate milkshake that's now more milk than shake.

Deidre sits back, eyes on me. "What's up with this neighbor anyway?"

"He's an asshole. Beats on his wife. I guess he wants to beat on me too."

She shakes her head, those deep brown pools lingering on me. "No, honey, I think he just wants to fuck you."

I shrug. This conversation is not one I'd like to have with people I hardly know.

She grabs a fry and bites it in half. "What'd you tell him?"

"No. What did you think I told him?"

"What I think doesn't matter, does it?" She pops the other half in her mouth looking smug as hell.

I scoff. "Why the fuck am I here if you think I'm a whore who rats on people?"

"Don't think you know what's in my head."

"But isn't that what you were thinking? I must fuck everything that moves, so I must have said yes."

Deidre sits back, arms crossed over her chest. "You want to know what I think?"

"Lay off, D," Clay says, flopping back in the booth.

"No, I won't *lay off*. She wants to know what I think, I'm going to tell her." Leaning forward, she rests her elbows on the table. "I think you've got secrets just like the rest of us, secrets that make you think you don't deserve better. I think you shove good people away to avoid dealing with the messy stuff of somebody actually caring about you, and you migrate to the ones that couldn't give less of a shit. It keeps you from accepting responsibility."

I've never hit anyone before, but she's just close enough that my fisted hand could give her a good knock.

"Not responsibility for whatever hurt you, which you still haven't shared, by the way, but responsibility for who you are now. It takes a lot of courage to move past what causes pain and I think you just ain't ready for that yet." She sits back, arms crossed over her chest. "That's what I think of you."

What can I say to that? It takes a moment to register all eyes on me, each of them staring as though I should now open up and pour out my insides. Instead, I dig a ten-dollar bill out of my pocket and place it on the table. Too much speaking now will only crack open the burning knot at the back of my throat.

"See you guys next week," I say, my voice almost too low for my own ears to detect. I look at Clay. "Take care." He nods and I take my exit. Who the fuck does she think she is opening my life up like that in front of everyone? *This is why I build the walls, Deidre. To keep people like you out.*

Sixteen

It's difficult now to go out alone. I guess I'm so used to my mother or Hattie being around that the mere act of going to the grocery store alone seems foreign and, somehow, not quite right. Maybe this is what will take the most getting used to, not that I no longer have a house full of people to keep me from screwing up, but that I am now fully—and completely—responsible for my own actions. What's more terrifying than that? Maybe I should call Deidre. I'm sure she would have something provocative to say about these feelings. Bitch.

The big blue lion greets me from its perch as if to say *don't fuck this up. I'm watching.* Maybe it's Hattie's suspicion following me around, or my mother's. That I can't do this. That I'm not ready. Showing him my little birdie, I head inside, comforted by the frigid air that greets me through the second set of double doors.

I pause at the entrance, unable to remember what a shopper does next. How in the hell did I make it a decade on my own?

After a moment my legs begin to move, no longer frozen in place, and I begin the path most familiar. First, the deli; a whole cooked chicken means I don't have to wow myself in the kitchen —and some Brie to celebrate my new life. It is mine, isn't it? Then to Produce for something to go with the cheese. In the old days, I might choose a nice wine cooler or hard seltzer, but for now, I think I'll choose something a little less likely to lead me astray.

Satisfied with my apple and grape selections, I head straight to aisle four—coffee—halting when Betsy Franklin, girl-with-the-bad-rep from high school comes into view. False bad rep, I guess I should add. At first, it seems as though she hasn't recognized me but then she does a double-take and, with the appearance of a smile on her big red lips, approaches. She hasn't changed much. Still a little full around the hips with boobs that put my little rack to shame. Her hair hangs around her shoulders in soft, ginger waves giving her the look of one of those boss babes, false eyelashes and all, her big-frame sunglasses perched like a crown on her head.

"As I live and breathe," she says, a gold-adorned hand going to her chest. "Grace Skinner? I heard you were back in town but didn't quite believe it."

I nod. "Betsy Franklin."

"Oh, I'm Betsy Thompson now, but I bet that sister of yours has already filled you in."

Only that you've been circumscribed to a life of serving creepy ass men with your tits out is on the tip of my tongue.

Instead, I say, "I didn't know you and Hattie knew one another."

She shifts her weight to one full hip with a chuckle. "This town ain't that big, Grace. Come on, now." She hooks the shopping basket over her wrist, sending the array of gold bangles hanging from her arm into a brief symphony of jangles.

I smile, shifting my gaze a little. "Truth is, I keep forgetting we're not in high school anymore." I know I shouldn't feel inferior to her but the confidence she's got has me seeking a safe space.

"I wish!" she says, free hand darting out as if to touch me, pulling back just short of actual contact. "It'd be nice to change some things."

"Yeah."

Her eyes are on me, but they also seem to be elsewhere. Maybe back in time to a place where she was too afraid to say yes, and I was helpless to say no.

"Well." Her voice is tight, clipped. "Best not think of some things, I guess. So, what're you up to now? You living back with your mama?"

"Was. Now I've got my own place."

Her face lights up, surprise looks good on her. "Damn, girl, how long you been back?"

I shrug. "A little while."

Her catty grin is back. "You got somebody?"

She means do I have a sugar daddy or someone who's taking care of me in exchange for a little something sweet. I shake my head. She doesn't need to know I've never had that type of relationship.

I look down at my chicken and then back at her. "I gotta go, Betsy. It's been nice seeing you."

Not waiting for her goodbye, I hustle past her, grabbing my preferred roast on my way off the aisle. My escape skills clearly need work, though, because she's already waiting for me on aisle five, in full smirk.

"You know," she begins. "I'm having some people over tonight. I'd love for you to come."

"People?"

She juts her head forward as if to say *duh*.

The aisle is closing in. "I—I—"

"I'm not inviting you to the electric chair, Grace. It's just a party."

Hearing my old name quiets the racing of my heart. This is something I can control. "Zed."

Her eyelids flutter as if she's trying to compute. "Pardon?"

"I don't go by Grace anymore. Call me Zed."

"I'll call you whatever you want as long as you come to my

party." Thrusting a folded piece of paper into my basket, she adds, "See you later, *Zed.*"

I watch her walk away, saunter in her step and long, ginger hair swaying with her stride. She isn't the same virginal Betsy from high school, though why I thought she would be is beyond me. The one truth in our conversation is that I do sometimes forget I'm no longer in high school. Maybe I want the last few years to be a dream...a nightmare, or maybe I just want a do-over. I damn sure deserve one.

I DON'T KNOW why I chose to come. There was no impulse, no invisible rope pulling me along. I'd just known from the moment I touched the paper Betsy had thrust into my basket that I would end up here. It's different than I imagined. Different than the image Hattie burned into my brain. I expected a run-down trailer, junked-out cars in the yard, and mangy dogs tied up outside. The stereotype. I'm facing a brick ranch-style home, a manicured lawn, and the most vivid teal door I've ever seen in my life. This is far better than my own rotting Adirondack chair or my mother's dying Hydrangeas.

I press the doorbell and listen to the drawn-out chimes inside. Moments later Betsy is at the door, her hair up in a loose bun that exposes her graceful neck, the line of her party dress low enough to expose bountiful cleavage.

"Grace!"

"Zed."

She smiles. "Sorry. Zed! You came!"

I shove the frozen coconut cake at her and enter when she moves to the side. "Great house," I say, taking in the entryway as she closes the door.

"Awww, thanks. This was Dalton's parents' home, but they gave it to him when they decided to run off to Florida." Is she lying? I'm sure Hattie told me his father was ill and that's why

Betsy has to work at the strip club. "All the renovations were paid for by yours truly. More specifically Kate and Ally." She turns toward me long enough to jiggle each of her breasts, then enters the kitchen just off the entrance. Tossing the cake on the granite countertop without breaking her stride, she motions for me to follow. "Come on, everybody's in the party room."

She's not being grandiose, there really is a party room and it's massive. Her arm is around my shoulder as we move through what must have previously been the door leading into a garage. Inside, the room is dark, illuminated only by low-wattage sconces on the walls and fairy lights.

"Isn't it gorgeous!" she says over the pounding speakers just inside the door. "We just finished it a month or so ago and I've been *dying* to do this."

We're standing in the center of the room now and she's moving me around to point out where the bathroom is, where the booze is, and where the dope is. I put my hand up to let her know I'm not interested in any.

"That's not the Grace I remember. You were always up for anything."

The truth of her words stings. I suspect it's more because the Grace she remembers is exactly who I was up until the night I swallowed a bottle of pills.

"Zed."

She leans forward. "Huh?"

"My name is Zed."

She pulls back. "Of course." Fanning her hands about she tells me to enjoy the party before disappearing into the crowd. I'm suddenly exposed, and the music is too loud and there's a smell I can't quite place.

Standing in the center of the makeshift dance floor is a bad idea. There are bodies banging into me, shoving and pulling, hands sliding over my hips. I used to love this. A few months ago, I would have closed my eyes and molded into these strangers; probably would've ended up in the bed of one of them before the end of the night. As they toss me around, push me, knead me like my grandmother's bread, I can't help questioning my decision to give all this up. The invisibility and total exposure. You can be anyone in a place like this. The Cure is playing. I'm sure it's them. They're crawling out of the speakers, slinking through the crowd, wrapping themselves around the bodies like ivy in summertime, before finally crawling all over me. What's wrong with all this?

I close my eyes, lean back, extend my arms. I'm consumed. Dinner for a man named Spider.

It's a curious thing, how music can both heal and harm. Pounding drums and heavy riffs can transport, make your brain forget for the moment how absolutely broken you are. How lost. But this...I've been devoured. Over and over he devoured me and all that's left are the remnants. Not enough pieces to put back together, but Hattie thinks there are. My mother thinks there are. I want to believe them, but I know too well what's left.

I am released, held now by some thumping song I'm not familiar with, but I'm still in the shadow of their voices and those of my past; transported to dark nights when the same voices guided his hands over my body. Despite my best efforts to remain in the present, to get away from those hands and his soft whispers, I'm stuck, going down. I can't go there again, can't let him pull me under; can't submerge myself. *Be a good girl. That's right.*

All around the music is thudding, clawing its way into my head, swelling my brain to the point of it pulsing against my skull. *Hey, baby, want a hit?* I shake my head and push past. Through the haze everyone looks ghastly, all pawing at one another, reenacting my darkest nights. *That's right.*

Betsy is by the door, her body pressed firmly against a man I don't recognize. She smiles when she sees me, her glassy, half-lidded eyes sparkling in the pulsing light of the strobe. She steps forward, attempting to pull me into an embrace.

"Hey, Gracie," she says, pushing her fingers through my hair. "Wanna get wasted? You used to like that, right?"

I could tell her my name again, but something tells me it

doesn't matter. Not to her. This invitation was for her own twisted fun. Maybe she wanted to get back at me for Barry. Why she would, I have no idea. If she wanted him, she should've married him.

Shaking my head, I try to push past her, but she grabs me. "Come on. I've got some good stuff." Her fingers are raking through my hair, her hands cupping the back of my head to pull me forward, and then her mouth is crushing into mine, lips parting to allow her tongue room to explore.

I push against her, and she falls into the unknown man, stunned. "What the fuck, Grace?" Her voice is shrill against the booming music, her eyes wide open. That's a good thing.

Leaning close to her, I say, "My name is Zed," then straighten and push through the crowd to the breezeway between the party room and the house.

"Whoa!" A body says as I collide with them.

"I'm s—" My apology dies as I meet the glassy eyes of Oliver. Stepping back to put some distance between us, I say, "H—hi."

"Hey." His lips spread into a pleasant smile, though I don't know if it's me or the drugs doing it. "What're you doing here? I thought this wasn't your scene."

"It isn't. I'm leaving. Sorry for running into you."

"No worries." Moving past him, I stop when he asks, "You want to go someplace and talk?"

I could use a friend. "Sure."

"We can go to the other side of the house. I'm sure Betsy won't mind."

The memory of her tongue sliding between my lips and her reaction when I rejected her had me shaking my head. "Um. No. I think she will."

He's curious, I can tell by the way his eyebrow is slightly crooked.

I hold my keys up. "We can sit in my car. If you want."

"Sure."

Exiting the party is no easy feat considering how many people are still coming through the door. Oliver takes the lead and pushes through until we've made it out into the soupy air of the night.

"I think it was cooler in there," I say as we walk toward the Bronco.

It isn't even evident he's heard me until he nods and responds, "Gotta love late summer in North Carolina, right?"

We cross the driveway to where my Bronco is packed tightly between two sedans.

"I guess I'm not going anywhere anytime soon, huh?"

He laughs. "More time to talk." Opening the door, I motion for him to get inside, but he surprises me by bypassing it and climbing on the hood. "Too hot in there."

Closing the door, I climb up beside him. "It's too hot anywhere."

We're both settled on our backs. It's the first time I've lain with a man in more than two months and probably the first time in my adult life it's been a fully clothed platonic situation. As the moments pass, we fall into a quiet contemplation. Well, his is likely whatever he's got in his system. It's nice here, though. The metal of the hood is cool against the warmth of my back and a light breeze touches us now and then.

"So, what happened in there?" Oliver asks. "It looked like you were running for your life."

I look over at him; his face is forward, eyes closed. "Nothing really. I wanted to leave, and Betsy wanted me to get high."

"You seriously don't do this party shit, huh?" I'm waiting for him to look at me, but his eyes remain closed. "It's probably for the best." We fall into silence again, and again I'm looking at him instead of the inky sky above. He peeks out of the side of his eye and smiles. "What?"

Snapping my face upward, I try to focus on the stars above. I learned the difference between a star and a planet once. If it twinkles it's a star, but if the light is constant, you're looking at a planet. Simple enough, I guess.

"Seriously," he says, propping himself up on his elbow. "What?"

I turn away so he won't see the tug at the corners of my mouth. Why do I always smile when I'm nervous?

He's smiling now, I can hear it in his voice; light and playful. "That's not nice."

Looking back at him, I laugh. "It was nothing."

"It was something. Tell me."

My mind is racing, trying to find the most appropriate lie. I certainly can't tell him I was looking for the sake of looking. "I was going to ask how things are going with your ex."

He shrugs and lays back, all playfulness vanished. "Over."

"Obviously," I say.

He sits up, drawing his knees back in a relaxed way I envy, and smiles. "Yeah, yeah. I was a fool for her. But that's over. Door closed. Finito. Time for me to move on."

"With Becca?"

Laughing, he shoves me. "Fuck off."

Our laughter is easy and welcome. I don't laugh enough. Never have. Even as a child, I was too busy staring wide-eyed at everyone, thinking more about their reactions to me than just letting go. I look over at Betsy's house, watch it pulse from the music and the bodies and the drugs inside, a small part of me longing to go back in there. But something has changed in me that I can't quite peg. Forgetting is easy. I don't know if I want to take the easy way anymore.

Oliver lights a cigarette and offers it to me. I take it, pull in a long drag before handing it back. "I miss her, though." He takes a drag, holds it for a moment, and pushes the plume out into the night. "Maybe I just miss us." He holds the cigarette out to me, and I take it, pulling in as much as I can before releasing it. "We were good at first."

"Everybody's good at first," I say.

"Yeah. Last time she seemed different. Like she wanted to tell me something. Maybe she's having second thoughts."

"That's dangerous."

"Why?"

"Because people don't usually have second thoughts after almost a year. Didn't you say it's been almost a year?"

"Yeah." He looks at me for a long moment, then nods. "Yeah. Maybe. I don't know. I mean, I know I'm over her." He swipes at his pant leg. "She's definitely over me."

No need to keep going down this path after what happened last time. Not if we want to stay friends. "You'll figure it out." I lean forward, eying the vehicles surrounding my car.

He chuckles. "You're kind of stuck here, you know?"

"Looks that way."

"What're you going to do, then?"

I shrug. "Wait it out?

He lays back, resting his head on a crooked arm. "You and me both."

I lay back beside him, determined to keep my eyes from his face. "Are you going to call her?"

"Who?"

"Your ex."

His shrug is audible. "Maybe."

"I don't think you should."

Looking over at me, he chuckles. "I know I shouldn't." He rolls onto his side, his finger tracing the fading paint patch with his finger, before looking up at me to say, "You'll learn that I have a history of doing things I know I shouldn't do."

"You and me both."

"Is that what landed you back here?" He stops tracing the patch, his undivided attention now on me.

"Kind of, I guess."

He smiles, looking down to release something of a chuckle.

I draw my legs against me, wrapping my arms around them. "What?"

"We've known one another for a while now, right?"

"Yeah."

"You know just about everything there is to know about me, but I still have no idea who you are."

Resting my head against my knees, I say, "There's nothing worth knowing."

"I don't think that's true." He sits up, one fluid motion that has him sitting close enough for me to smell the musky scent he's wearing. "This is your hometown, right?"

"Yeah."

"When did you leave?"

Innocent enough. "Graduation night."

"Where did you go?"

"Hickory."

"What made you choose Hickory?"

I shrug. "Not enough money to get to Asheville."

He cocks his head to the side. "Seriously?"

Lowering my head, I laugh. "No. I knew some people staying there."

His eyes are sparkling. "Now we're getting somewhere." Rubbing his hands together like a magician, he presses on. "How long were you there?"

"I don't remember."

He tosses his arms out. "Fuck that!" Before I know what's happening, he's facing me, his knees touching mine, eyes shining with amusement. Maybe determination?

Another laugh sputters out, and I avert my gaze. "What? It was a long time ago."

"Okay then, what made you leave?"

"Hickory?"

"Here."

A stone settles in my stomach. "A lot of things."

"Like?"

I release my knees, stretching my legs out long. "Just a lot of things." Then, to stop his questions, I ask, "Did you party like this before your ex split?"

"Not fair, Zed."

I smile, giving my best impression of innocence. "I'm not judging. I'm just curious. How hard did you party before your split?"

Sober he wouldn't be able to be dissuaded, but tonight he's out of his mind. Truth is, I probably could've told him everything and he wouldn't remember it tomorrow, but I can't take that chance. The last thing I need is all of Jubilee's knowing about my shit.

"Not often. I didn't start to party until after we broke up. I was trying so fucking hard to be straight for her." He looks down at his black high-top Converse, reaching out to brush something away. "She hated how much time I spent with my friends."

"That's harsh."

"I guess. I think she was just tired of it all. We'd been together since high school, and nothing was changing. It didn't help that she had her mom in her ear." He slides back around beside me and lays back, rolling onto his side. I follow, the hard metal of the hood uncomfortable against my hip. His eyes find mine. "Do you think I'm a loser?"

My voice is quiet. "No."

"Then why do I feel like one?"

I wish I could answer him, speak some magical phrase that will make him understand he's better than what he thinks, but all I can say is, "You're just stuck is all."

"You think?"

I nod, trying to steady the quiver in my throat before saying, "We all get stuck sometimes." Some of us stay that way. His eyes are soft, half closed, and his mouth is relaxed. My fingers itch to touch him, to run along the line of his jaw and the surface of his lips. Would it be scandalous for me to straddle him now, to crush my mouth to his and see where this goes? It's doubtful anyone inside would even notice.

"What're you thinking about?" He asks, his voice soft. He's alert now, looking at me as though he's seen the images playing inside my treacherous head.

I shift away, sitting up. "Nothing."

He sits up, eyes fixed on me, and my body stills. The air grows calm and the crickets quiet as time slows. Anticipation whispers in my ear, preparing me for the feel of his arms pulling me into an embrace, his lips against mine, and I'm eager to experience the reality of those promises.

He clears his throat. "Um. I should probably go."

From the haze of dissipating expectations, I respond. "O...k."

Jumping down from the hood, he turns. "Thanks for the talk. I'll see you tomorrow."

I could stop him. It might only take one word; *stay.* I don't, though. He's high and drunk. Bad decisions will abound, just not with me.

<hr>

THE JOSTLING of the Bronco wakes me at some point in the night. I open my eyes slowly, peeking at the intruder, hoping it isn't a partygoer looking to take advantage of a vulnerable woman. Thankfully, I find Duke peering in through the open window. Sitting up, I shove the sweat-soaked fringe from my forehead.

"Duke? What're you doing here?"

"Your mama's been trying to call you. When you didn't answer she used the tracking on that thing and asked me to come and check on you."

Figures.

"What're you doing sleeping out here?"

I look around, ready to tell him that I was waiting for the party to clear out, but the cars once blocking me in have disappeared. It isn't surprising no one woke me, though I am amazed I slept so soundly.

"I was blocked in." He looks around. I look at my phone, surprised to find it's nearly three in the morning. "Shit, Duke." His eyes are back on me. "I'm sorry she made you come out this late. I was just waiting for the cars to clear. I guess I fell asleep."

"It looks like it." He motions to my hair. "You look like one of the Little Rascals."

I shift in my chair, doing my best to ignore the prickles rising at the back of my neck. I don't want to fight. Not here. "If I knew what that was, I might be able to say something back."

He looks at me, a side-eye I never quite expected to see face-to-face. I'm sure he's done this a number of times during one of our major meltdowns, but I never saw those. His lips tug back in a smile and the knot in my stomach releases a bit.

"Why don't we have a chat, Zed."

"Here? Now?"

He shrugs. "Seems as good a time as any." Before I can decline, he pats the hood, then climbs up into the spot Oliver occupied only hours before, though not as easily.

Slowly, I descend from the car, legs shaking. I'm not entirely sure this quaking is due to the chill that only three a.m. brings. Grabbing my cigarettes, I close the door and join him on the hood. I extend the pack to him first and he accepts, then I get my own.

Duke takes a long draw, letting the smoke sit in his lungs for almost a full minute before expelling it into the night. He knows how to make a tense situation last.

"What do you want to talk about?" I ask, unable to stand another moment of his silence. The night sky is not that fucking interesting.

He looks over at me as if he's forgotten I'm there. "We didn't leave off in a good place. I don't like that."

I nod. "Okay."

"Do you like your new place?"

"I do."

"This it?"

"No. This is Betsy Franklin...ummm...Thompson's house. She had a party here tonight and invited me." He keeps his eyes forward, his hands resting on his crossed knees. "But you already figured that, didn't you?"

"I knew this wasn't your place. I've seen Hank's house and this ain't it. Didn't know about the party, but I figured there was something. Why else would Cami send me out at such an ungodly hour?"

I shrug. "She shouldn't worry about me. I'm an adult."

Duke takes another drag, letting it sit a shorter time before letting it and his words out into the dark. "Young lady, do you remember why you're back here in this town?"

"Yes."

"I know you don't understand it now, and I know you and your mama have a lot of broken pieces but getting a call like that...that one of your babies has tried to kill themselves, it's a tough thing."

My cigarette is lit but I've yet to take a single drag. How can I when his purpose is choking the life out of me. I nod but remain quiet.

"Hattie told me you're mad about the GPS, but I hope some part of you can understand why Cami needs it."

"She told me she turned it off." I'm sulking. Not very adult-like, I know. "Can we talk about lying?"

"She had it off but turned it back on when she couldn't get you on the phone. Your mama ain't no liar, Zed. She's just worried."

I nod. "I get it. But she shouldn't worry. I'm doing good. Really, really good."

His eyes catch mine. "You came to a party tonight. Looks like plenty of drinking. I imagine they had their share of drugs too. Dalton Thompson ain't likely to have changed much in the last few years." I turn to him, and he gives a wink. I should've known he knew whose house this is.

"Yes, they had all that. But I didn't touch any of it." *Thought about it. Maybe wanted to* "I tried to leave hours ago but I was blocked in. Duke, I swear to you, I—"

"I believe you, kid. Cami will too." Tossing his spent filter to the ground, he shifts toward me. Every inch of my body is fighting to jump back, but I remain still. "She's a good woman, your mom."

"Yeah."

"And she loves you and your sister more than anything."

"I know."

"Then why can't you give her a chance?" He settles back against the windshield and my body relaxes. "She don't expect things will be peachy keen between the two of you, but she wants some kind of relationship with you that doesn't involve screaming and ripping each other apart."

I know all these things. Why Duke feels the need to tell me, I'm not sure. Maybe he thinks I'm that clueless. Maybe he's right. "I don't want to fight all the time," I manage. "I just can't forgive her for some things that happened."

"I can't imagine my mama doing anything that would've made me hate her."

"We're all different." Looking down, I flick the end of the cigarette and take my first drag.

"Maybe." His face is upturned, his eyes focused on the heavens above. "I reckon you'll understand more about decisions your parents made when you're a parent yourself."

"I almost was...a parent." The words are out before I can stop them, and Duke's eyes are back on me. "When I was sixteen. It's part of the reason why I left."

"You lost it?"

I can't look at him. "Sort of."

"That don't mean you won't have one someday."

"I don't want to have children. Not anymore." Why I'm telling him this is beyond me. I didn't even know until this very moment. Why bring a child into this fucked up world? People like Hattie might be strong enough for it, but I'm not. No way.

His eyes are on me again, but I can't look away. This is what adults do, right? They look one another in the eyes, force themselves to face uncomfortable situations; tell the truth.

My voice is quiet when I ask, "Did anyone ever steal something from you that you can't get back?"

His shoulders lift in a shrug. "In a way, I guess."

"But not, like, when you were a kid and couldn't stop it, right?"

"No." He lowers his head. "No, I never had nothing like that happen. Not when I was a kid."

"It confuses you, makes you think you've done something bad, that there's something wrong with you. That you were born wrong." I toss the cigarette to the ground. "And then that thing stops, and other people make decisions for you, force you to do other things you don't want to. It's this cycle. A fucked up cycle."

"Sometimes cycles are reset, Zed. The ones that are uneven or wrong. It ain't easy starting over, but maybe this is your chance to set things right." He's so genuine. It's in the softness of his mouth and the shimmer in his eyes. He has hope. It's sweet.

I shrug. "Maybe." It's a way to end our conversation. I don't believe what he's selling, but I want to. Without another word, he jumps down from the truck, rounds the hood, and holds his hand out to help me down.

"You going to be okay driving home?"

"Yeah. I got a good few hours of sleep."

He looks at the Bronco. "I don't know how you can sleep in that thing."

I smile. "I've slept in worse places."

"All right then. Be safe." He starts toward Cami's sedan, head still upturned to the sky.

"Duke."

He turns, his eyes questioning.

"Tell her I'm okay. I promise."

Nodding, he throws his hand up and walks away. I know he'll tell her. Whether or not she believes him is another thing altogether.

Seventeen

It's raining. Hallelujah. I remember staying with my father's parents for a summer in southwestern Virginia when I was very young. The rain there was soft, falling like a breeze from above. Hattie and I would sit on the expansive porch and watch as it poured down from the heavens, covering everything with its scent. Coolness followed, sometimes making it necessary to grab a shawl from inside. North Carolina isn't like that. Not at all. The rain falls heavy and fierce, and the air still keeps its chokehold well after the shower has ended.

"What's up?" Oliver asks from behind me.

I've been standing at the back door, eyes closed, and face turned to the sky. Maybe if I wish hard enough, I'll find myself back on that big front porch, Hattie by my side without a care in the world. I turn to him, eyes adjusting to the harsh lighting of the back room. He's looking well today, almost like he didn't attend another party last night. Of course, I know he did because he texted me a picture of him blowing smoke rings. I guess he didn't realize it wouldn't translate visibly if he was unable to make actual rings.

His smile fades a bit as his face clouds with worry. "You good?"

"Yeah. Just wishing I was somewhere else."

"Aren't we all?"

Grinding my cigarette against the blackened door frame, I toss the butt into the open dumpster and turn inward. "Hank's going to be pissed they left the dumpster open again."

Oliver leans to look out the door, his chin grazing my shoulder. "Dammit, Dante."

"Maybe it wasn't him." I take a step back, putting some distance between us, willing the flitting in my stomach to subside. "Didn't Josh work the closing shift last night?"

"Goddammit." He puts his hands on his hips as he looks back outside. "Why can't they just do what the fuck they're supposed to?"

I move toward the kitchen. "You know it's not that big of a deal. Hank will be annoyed, but he won't scream at anyone. And the dumpster will drain." Why am I making excuses for these assholes?

He touches my arm, halting me. "Can you just stop for a minute?"

I shift away from him and push my fingers through my hair, so he doesn't think I'm avoiding him. "I don't know why I'm making excuses for these assholes." I shake my head. "They fucked up. Yell all you want."

"It isn't that. Can I talk to you for a minute?"

I cross my arms, rubbing my hands along the gooseflesh that's risen on them. "About what?"

"I could just use a friend right now. You're my friend, right?"

It's on my lips to protest, to tell him we aren't friends, that I don't know what the hell we are, but I know my body shouldn't react to his closeness the way it does if that's all we are, but I keep the words in. Truth is, I don't know what having a friend is. I didn't have any in middle or high school. My uncle encouraged me not to, said I was too grown up for those girls. I guess that was another way for him to keep me to himself. Going from party to party with the same group of people doesn't make you friends. Not at all.

I shake my head, unable to answer him, but he smiles as if I've confirmed we are, in fact, friends.

Huddled in the back room, Oliver lights a cigarette and extends his pack to me. I decline, keeping my arms crossed as a shield. I'm entering new territory here and I don't know what the hell I'm doing.

"What's up?" I ask after too many excruciating moments of silence.

"I called her again."

"Your ex?"

He nods.

For fuck's sake. "Okay."

"Not because I wanted to get back together." He takes a drag and blows it out quickly. "I don't know why the hell I called her." He slumps against the door frame and exhales slowly. "She's getting married."

"Oh."

"Yeah." He takes a drag, holding it briefly before releasing it with something akin to a laugh. "All this time I thought she loved me and wanted to get back together. I'm such a dick."

"I don't think so." Not entirely.

"Then what am I?" His frown undoes me.

"A guy who wanted his marriage to work out," I say with a shrug. "Why do you need to be anything else?"

"Why do I feel like such a fucking chump?"

"I don't know. That's just what our emotions do to us." It might be nice for him to hear how I sat outside my lover's door while he had sex with another woman, eyes bleeding salt and my wails getting the attention of every neighbor in the building. It would probably help him to know he isn't the only pathetic human being on the planet, but that's my story and I'm not in a sharing mood. Instead, I add, "Give yourself some time." *And don't take an entire bottle of pills, no matter what.*

"Do you want to know the worst part?"

No.

His eyes meet mine. "The whole time I was on the phone with her I was thinking of someone else. Asking myself why the hell I'd even called her. I mean, I don't even want to cry about it. What does that mean?"

"I don't know, Oliver." I look toward the kitchen. Three nights ago he was still hoping she loved him, still missing what they used to be, and now he doesn't care enough to even cry over her upcoming marriage, over the finalization of their own? It makes no sense. I can't make it work in my head and I can't say that I want to. "I've got to get back now. You good?"

He nods, but his focus has turned to the outside. I don't wait for him to say anything else, simply turn and leave him standing with his thoughts.

Inside Jessica is still prepping the front. She rolls her eyes when I round the corner. "Mind helping?"

"Only if you lose the tone." I grab the closest rag and begin wiping the trays down.

She straightens from her place by the extra napkins and straws. "Maybe I wouldn't have a tone if you weren't constantly chasing after Oliver."

"One, who I'm interested in, or not, is none of your business, two, I'm not chasing anyone, three, I can take breaks." *Four, fuck off.*

"Always at the same time as Oliver?"

It would be easy to smack her with the tray I'm holding. In fact, I'm fairly confident that Dante, the cook, would applaud it. He hasn't liked her since he went down on her and she didn't return the favor. Some things just can't be unlearned.

I look at the clock. "We've got lunch rush starting in half an hour. I suggest you lose the tone or you'll be working this shit on your own."

"He's unavailable, you know."

What the hell?

I turn on her and she shrugs, wringing the rag in her hand absently. "I just think you should know. You know, so you don't get hurt."

"What's your problem, Jessica?"

"We're all tired of seeing you throw yourself at him." Her pretty lips turn down in an exaggerated frown. "It's sad."

"Fuck off." Turning away from her, I try to focus on the task at hand, but my attempt is thwarted when my eyes meet Oliver's staring out from the kitchen. My face warms at the notion that he may have heard this conversation, but he doesn't seem to be aware that Jessica is standing behind me. His eyes, dark blue and full of something I can't name, are only on me. Slamming the tray onto the stack, I grab the broom and head to the dining room. No way I'm letting him get to me. No way I'm letting anyone in this town get to me.

It's after seven when I get home from work. Hank's truck is in the drive, but if he's actually home, I don't know. Hanna is seated on the expansive front porch, her eyes focused on the phone in her hands.

Going inside, I drop everything by the door and plop down on the sofa. This is probably why it groans when body meets cushion. Years of people plopping down tends to take its toll. Grabbing my phone, I dial Hattie's number, surprised when she answers it after half a ring.

She's breathless. "Oh my god, I was just about to call you!"

I'm sitting at attention, every muscle tensing. "Is everything okay? Do I need to come over?"

"Huh? Everything's fine. Doctor says that I am progressing fine, but I have to take it easy."

I don't believe her. "What is it then? You sound out of breath."

"I had to dash to get the phone. Dad just left."

"Your house?"

"Yeah." There's a pause. "He wants to see you."

"I told you I don't want to see him. I thought it was clear the day you ambushed me with his house."

Her tone is sharp when she says, "I didn't ambush you. I had to drop something off at his house."

I shake my head. "Okay, whatever. My answer is still the same."

"Zed, I wish you would just see reason."

"No. No, I can't." I stand, unable to remain still with the energy that's building inside of me.

"But it's Dad. He misses you."

The laminate flooring feels different as I pace back and forth, softer. Is it going to swallow me? Part of me hopes so.

"I'm not ready, Hattie." I'll never be ready.

"Mom thinks it would be a good idea."

"What the hell do I care what she thinks?" Taking a deep breath, I try to steady myself. "I'm sorry. I didn't mean to snap at you." She sniffles and my heart drops. "I just can't. Not now. Maybe in time. I just need you to stop pushing me on this."

"Why do you hate them?" The edge to her tone feels like an accusation.

I swipe furiously at the tears beginning to cut a path over my cheeks. "I don't hate them." But I do. I do. God help me, I hate them. "I have to go."

"Zed."

"I'll talk to you later." Hitting end on an undesirable conversation should be more satisfying than this.

Going to the bedroom, I open the top drawer of the '70s-style dresser and shove the phone inside, covering it with t-shirts. I grab one, my favorite Creedence shirt snagged from the dick who promised me the stars and return to the kitchen, shedding my work pants, shirt, and bra as I do. Pulling CCR over my head, I open the fridge to see what I have that might be appetizing to a girl who just wants to be left alone.

THE PIZZA DELIVERY boy appreciates my appearance in the glow of the porch light. It's obvious by the way his gaze keeps slipping to my bare thighs, only to linger on my tits before looking back at my face with a smile. I grab the box and shove a twenty at him.

"You want your change?" he asks.

"Keep it." I shut the door in his face, not bothering to wait for the inevitable line. Guys like Pizza Boy can't help it. They have to try. I'm not opposed to it, as long as they don't try too hard.

Dropping the box on the coffee table, I flip the top back and grab a piece, settling in to enjoy the carb-filled cheesy extravaganza. I'd kill for a beer. I've been thinking about this. I wasn't a drunk before. I didn't sit around thinking about when I would be able to have my next drink. It was more an overall longing, one for forgetting. I could probably handle a beer now and again, right? I guess the aftermath is what I should be considering. Or maybe just a distraction. Leaning over, I pick up the remote and turn on the tiny television, nursing my pizza as I flip through the channels available. He's got cable out here. Surprising. How many losers has he helped? Settling on a show about women killers, I'm halfway through my second piece when two knocks fall hard against the door.

Muting the television, I stand and cross to the door, pulling back the battered bandanna covering the small diamond window, surprised to find that it isn't the horny pizza boy standing on the other side. It's Oliver.

I grasp the knob, ready to pull it open and allow him entrance, but stop when I realize I'm in no condition to meet company. Looking back through the window, I raise a finger to let him know it'll be a minute, then rush to my room. I grab the old pj pants off my bed and pull them up over my Wonder Woman novelty panties (*what grown woman wears novelty panties?*), then return to the front door.

"What're you doing here?" I ask, backing up to allow him room to enter.

He looks around the room, shifting nervously. "I'm sorry for coming over this late."

"It's okay." I close the door. "I was just eating. Want some pizza?"

His eyes are on me and I'm suddenly naked to him. Vulnerable. I wrap arms across my chest, again a shield, not at all surprised to find that my body is responding to his being near. When exactly it began waking up again, I don't know, but for weeks I have needed relief and it is always provided by him, though he has no idea. My cheeks color a bit at this thought and I have to look away.

With a tremor in my voice, I ask, "What's up?"

His slouch is endearing. I wonder if he's as nervous as he looks. "I'm sorry about earlier today."

I keep my voice soft and put a few more inches of distance between us. "It's okay. You were upset."

"It's not okay, though." He shakes his head. "I mean, I know it's okay that I was upset, but it's not okay that I was such a dick. Not to you."

"I shouldn't have...I should've kept my mouth shut. I have a problem with that sometimes."

He laughs, a nervous putter, and shoves his hands in his pockets. "The thing is, you were right. I've been drinking and partying a lot. I guess maybe I always have. I've never really thought about it."

"It happens." I go over to the sofa and drop down, nudging the box toward him. "Hungry?"

He smiles. Something is different about us together right now. It's the tone of his smile, the color of his eyes, the way he keeps rubbing his hands on the legs of his jeans. Grabbing a slice, he settles in.

"How are you like that?"

I pull my legs to my chest. "Like what?"

"I was a total dick to you and you're all, *it happens*. Anybody else would've told me to fuck off when I showed up at their door."

"You're dealing with a lot of shit. Everybody is." I shrug. "It spills over." I motion to our surroundings. "Why else do you think I'm living in this tin can instead of my mom's?"

"Yeah. I guess that's life." Leaning toward the box, he drops his unfinished piece in the lid and turns back to me. "We've been friends for a while now, right?"

"I guess." It's certainly the longest I've ever associated with a man without being intimate.

"Do you ever think of me? I mean, like, as more than a friend?"

Yes. Absolutely, yes.

I widen my eyes. An attempt to look innocent. Like I haven't been thinking of him several nights a week since the first time he drove me home. "What do you mean?" What a stupid fucking question.

"I don't want to make you uncomfortable."

"You're not," I answer too quickly.

"I just...I've been thinking about a lot of things lately; what I want, who I want. It always comes back to you."

I shift.

"And I think you think about it too. Trust me, I wouldn't fucking be here if I didn't think so."

"Oliver."

Holding his hand up, he continues, "I know you've got shit going on. We all do." He looks down, takes a breath, and then looks back at me with the most genuine look I've ever seen. "Tell me I'm wrong and I'll leave. We can forget I ever came over here."

Nerves on end, I place my own unfinished piece in the box and stand up. A very bad idea, now that I think about it. At least on the sofa I could use my legs as a shield.

He stands and I put my hand out. "Oliver, maybe..." He steps closer and my heart begins to beat faster, pushing all the longing inside throughout my body. I step back and round the table. If I can get to the front door and open it, maybe he'll abandon this fool's errand.

"I have to get to bed." *Oh jeez.* "I—I've got an early day tomorrow."

There's a twitch at the corner of his mouth. "We're on the same shift."

He closes the gap again and I realize I'm stuck, backed against the wall. I know it was on purpose. This is what I do to myself. Make sure there's no escape.

His hand is touching my hair, my face, my lips. "Do you? Think about me?"

I should push him back, create some distance. "Oliver, I..." *Tell him to stop. Tell him we can't do this. I don't want to.*

"I think about you." His eyes are holding mine. His, dark and confident, filled with want, and mine, panicked and twitching. "Almost since the moment we met." His voice is soft, his breath warm. "I can't think of anything else. Not since that night at the party."

"Your ex—"

"Is ancient history."

I shouldn't be doing this, shouldn't be entertaining the thought of giving into this, but I am. He's so close, so warm, and so present. I've never had anyone look at me the way he's looking at me right now. Lust is there, heavy and pressing against both of us, but there's something else too.

My voice is barely audible when I ask, "What do you want from me, Oliver?"

"Everything." What the hell does that mean? I grab his face and he tries to pull back, startled. "What the—"

"Tell me."

"What?" Our bodies are close enough, I can smell the mixture of sweat and sex that must burn in his blood.

"Tell me what it is? What makes you want me?"

His eyes narrow, focusing only on mine. Lust has gone, replaced by something I can't name. The soft cushion of his lips presses against my own and I close my eyes. I don't want to be distracted. Not now, not when the answer may be right here. What do they see that makes them pursue me?

I pull away. "Is it because I'm broken?"

He looks at me, his large hands pressing gently against my jaws. "You're not afraid."

I'm fucking terrified!

His lips are against mine again, his body pressing against me, his want pressing hard between us. I want to crawl all over him, probe him, and explore the depths of him, and I want him to do the same to me. My hands snake over his shoulders and meet at the back of his neck as desire rushes out of me, dampening my briefs and fueling the heat in my belly. He lifts me and I wrap my legs around his waist. Our bodies are screaming to remove the barriers keeping us apart.

I pull away, looking down into his face.

Through lips red and swollen, breath coming out in puffs, he asks, "What? Are you okay?"

No. No, I'm not.

"We have to stop."

Confusion clouds where desire once raged. "Seriously?" He moves his hips, and his erection presses against me.

"Yes." I peel my eager body away from his. We're panting. I swear to god, we're panting. Two dogs in heat, my grandma would say. Placing my hand on his chest, I push him gently back. "We can't."

"Why?"

"Because I'm tired of being *that* girl."

We're both struck. I know I am, but his eyes tell me he also is. I'm tired of being the girl who gets fucked. His retreat tells me he gets that too.

He goes to the couch and drops into the seat, head in his hands. "I shouldn't have come."

"Don't say that." I sit down beside him, pull his hands from his face, and force him to look at me. "I want this, whatever *this* is, but we've both got a lot of shit to deal with. I just don't want to move too fast." I lay against the cushion, staring at him, wishing like hell I could quiet the voice of this new part of me. "Give yourself time to get over your ex."

"And you?"

"I've been trying to get over mine for years."

He leans back, face once again inches from mine. "What happened?"

I consider telling him (*is that progress?*), but I'm not ready to lose him, and I certainly don't want him to spread the word about Zed. The last thing I need is for anyone else to find out.

"It's not worth talking about. Just one of those things that shouldn't have happened."

His chuckle startles me.

"What?"

"I just realized I don't have anyone to talk to about this."

"No buds?"

"Nope." He grabs my hand, lacing his fingers through mine. "Who am I supposed to talk to about the girl I can't get out of my head?"

My smile stretches from my lips to my toes. "I guess you'll just have to keep her a secret."

He leans over, brushing his lips against mine before pressing them to the nape of my neck. "I guess I'll whisper it into the night." Standing, he pulls me up and covers my mouth with his. "Let's not move too slow, okay? I don't know how long I can wait to do that again."

EIGHTEEN

Hattie is animated today. I don't know how she can have this much energy as pregnant as she is, but she has yet to stop talking. There is a distant part of me, the sullen and crabby bitch part that ran away from home eight years ago, that wants to tell her to shut up. Her voice is too high, and I am still riding the wave of giddy new-like, reliving Oliver's visit over and over in my mind. I don't want to share it with her. Not until she stops thinking of me as a fuck-up.

"Zeddie, are you listening to me?"

She's looking at me, expecting me to give back to this conversation, but I'm too caught up in recent events to contribute. Even the sweet cream ice cream she's treated me to this afternoon is no help. The guy behind the counter keeps staring at me as if he knows what I've done even though he looks to be about twelve. His experience with almost-sex is likely limited to bumping up against the girl he likes in the hallway at school.

"Zed?"

I blink. "Yeah?"

"Have you heard a word I said?"

My head is shaking, and apologies are spilling from my mouth. "My mind was a million miles away."

She lowers her spoon, resting it on the mound of gummy bears that she thought, for some ungodly reason, would be a good addition to her brownie sundae.

"What's going on?"

"Nothing."

She huffs, her hand going absently to her abdomen. I wonder what it's like to be as pregnant as she is. I never got to feel the flutter of life before it was ripped away by the miracles of modern-day medicine.

She levels her gaze at me, dark pools of brown that mean to see all of my secrets revealed. "Don't mess with me, Zed. What's going on?"

"Nothing." I stab my ice cream. Looking back up at her, I decide to take the defensive approach for whatever reason. Who the hell knows why I do half the shit I do. I certainly don't. "What?"

"You can't keep secrets. Didn't your doctor tell you that?"

"She told me I shouldn't take handfuls of pills." *And don't drink and don't, under any circumstances, become romantically involved with anyone. Especially not the emotionally fucked guy at work.*

"Zed."

"*Hattie.*" I smile to let her know I'm in no way being serious.

She's looking at me with an odd expression. I consider asking what it's all about, but something tells me I don't want to know. She's always up to something lately. Always scheming to get me closer to Mom or Dad. Why the hell I would want to be closer to the two people who contributed to the destruction of my life is beyond me, and why she would want me to is an even bigger mystery. Maybe I should tell her exactly what our dear uncle did, exactly what I did. I liked it. He told me I liked it, and I believed him. With all my heart I believed him.

Leaning forward, she grabs my hand. It's still such a shock when anyone touches me. Except when Oliver did. My stomach is still electrified after almost a week. That says something, doesn't it? Maybe that it's right this time.

"I don't want to stress you out, okay?"

I nod.

"I just want to help."

"I know." I'm stiff and wondering if she can feel how uncomfortable I am under her touch.

"Is everything okay?"

I nod again, hoping this will get her to remove her hand. "It's just work stuff."

She seems pleased I've shared this much. Removing her hand, she resumes eating her ice cream. "Tell me about it."

"Nothing to tell. The entire crew thinks I'm trying to mack on this guy I work with."

Her smile is genuine. I kind of like it. "Are you?"

It's infectious and I find that my own mouth is mimicking hers. "No."

"Do you want to?"

Yes. "I'm not allowed, remember?" My poor ice cream receives another stab as I scoop out another bite.

She shrugs. "Well yeah, but can they stop you from getting it on if you want to?"

Ice cream spews toward her. She bats at it as if it is an incoming missile set to destroy.

"Gross! Chew it, don't spew it!"

I'm laughing despite the voice in my head telling me to stop. "What are you, ten?" I'm trying desperately to clean up the globs from the vinyl tabletop with the tiny squares masquerading as napkins.

"Is everything alright over here, ladies?" the counter boy says appearing beside us. He's a pre-pubescent ninja.

"Yes, Ronnie," Hattie says through her laughter. "My sister just thought I should have a sweet cream bath."

I shoot him a guilty glance. He's older than I thought. Much older if the wrinkles at the corners of his accusing eyes are any indication. Hattie's reassurance that all's well seems to satisfy him, and he retreats behind the counter as a group of teens enter in a rush of giggles and whispers. I wish I knew what it was like to be them.

"You look different today," Hattie says breaking into my thoughts.

I sit back, tugging at the old t-shirt I slept in.

"What's up?"

I shake my head. "Nothing." The teens are staring at us from their place at the counter and my good humor has suddenly evaporated. "Can we go?"

Hattie follows my gaze to the group of girls, then looks back to me. "Sure."

Outside it's boiling. Carolina in late summer is no place to be if you're sane. Over-eager mosquitoes anxious to cover unprotected flesh in kisses, and humidity that seeks to choke the life out of anyone breathing. I shove my aviator shades on and smack at one of the little bloodsuckers as Hattie and I begin walking toward her new Toyota.

"I like the car," I say.

"Me too. I thought I would miss the Bronco, but this baby has air that is on point."

I laugh, though I know she's only distracting me in an effort to get more information.

She puts her fifties-inspired cat glasses on, the silver lenses glinting in the oppressive sunlight. "So, this work thing."

"Yeah?"

"Who's the guy?"

"I don't want to tell you."

She smiles. "Does that mean I know him?"

"You know everyone, little sister."

"True." She nods. "The only one I can see you giving the time of day to up there is, maybe Dante."

"Seriously?" It's an insult. "He's slimy."

"I thought that was your type." She giggles and pokes her elbow gently into my side. "I'm kidding."

I don't quite buy it, but I smile. "No, he isn't my type and no, it isn't Dante. Everyone thinks I have a thing for Oliver, the shift lead."

"Yeah?" We stop at her car. "Do you?"

Yes. "We're friends. He's going through a lot right now."

She presses the button on her fob and the car starts. "Everybody who works at Jubilee's is going through a lot right now, Zed. I keep telling you, that's what Hank specializes in. That place is his very own foster home. Plus side is, you get money instead of potentially no good foster parents."

"I can see it."

"You're settled into your new place then?"

"I guess."

"And you like it?"

I nod, ignoring the pooling in my belly. "It's nice. Not the place but being on my own." I shrug. "The place is cool too."

She smiles. "No, it isn't. But it's a place to stay." Opening the car door, she turns back to me. "Thanks for coming out with me today."

"Anytime." I mean it, I truly do. Now that the mouthy bitch in my head has stopped nagging me, I can appreciate today for what it is.

"J.C. will be calling soon to make sure I'm taking it easy." She rubs her stomach. "I hope this isn't a preview of what life will be like with this little thing." Leaning toward me, she presses her lips to my cheek. "See you later, big sister."

I wave as she pulls away, then dig my keys and cigarettes from the frayed reusable bag that serves as my purse, and head for the Bronco.

"Grace Skinner?" A voice, unfamiliar but strangely known, stops me in my tracks. "Is that you?"

I turn, keys in hand and cigarette perched to light. I haven't seen her for years, but I recognize her immediately. "Angel?"

She smiles. "Yeah."

We embrace briefly. Strange how distant family members are compelled to hug on sight. Like, we haven't seen one another for a decade, let's get personal.

"Wow." I move closer to her, though all I want to do is run. "How are you?"

She doesn't need to, but she turns to the side to provide a better view of the basketball currently serving as her abdomen. "Miserable!"

I laugh. That's the proper thing to do, right? Laugh at all the pregnant woman's jokes.

"How are you?"

I shrug, shoving the cigarette behind my ear. "Fine."

"Mom told me you were in the hospital. I hope it was nothing serious."

Leave it to Aunt Darla to spread the word. "Nothing too serious," I say.

She presses a hand to her forehead. "Can we go somewhere cool? I want to catch up. Do you have time?"

No. "We can go to the corral. It's just over there."

I lead the way, trying not to outpace her. Some people are natural amblers and Angel, as I recall, was always taking her time. Well, except when it came to tearing families apart. But I guess I shouldn't blame her for that. It was always him.

Inside the interior of the old retail space made to look like a Western tavern, we grab a booth in the bar area. Probably not the best idea for someone who isn't allowed to drink, but I don't plan to be here long.

Angel smiles. "You look different, but strangely the same. Does that make sense?"

"Yeah. You too."

We order two waters and an appetizer sampler. I hope she doesn't expect me to pay, but at this point nothing will be surprising. The universe is having a great laugh right now at my expense and paying for lunch will only serve as icing on top of the proverbial cake.

"How's Aunt Darla?" I ask as our server delivers our drinks.

"Good. Remarried now. Finally!"

"Nice guy?"

"The nicest. But I guess I would find anyone an improvement over my father." The mention of him makes me choke on my water. "What have you been up to? Are you married? Any kids?"

"No on both counts." I take a careful sip of water. "I'm just trying to get my shit together."

"I know the feeling. Devon, my husband, is worried about me traveling while I'm this pregnant, but I told him I have to get this over with, put my demons to rest before it's too late, you know?"

I shake my head. "No. What demons do you have to put to rest? You seem happy."

Her face is dumb. Like I've just delivered a riddle she has no idea how to solve. "Are you serious?"

I shrug. "Yeah."

"Um." She runs her fingers through her bobbed hair. "They didn't tell you?"

Now I'm the dumb one. Pushing my hands into my lap, I wrap them up in the hem of my shirt. "Tell me what?"

"I'm here to see my father."

"Okay."

"He's dying, Grace."

The world is spinning. "What?"

"Cancer." She takes a sip of her water, the liquid sloshing from side to side. Is she shaking? "They don't expect him to make it much longer."

My head feels fuzzy, like massive swabs of cotton have been shoved inside to fill the void. "What?" Her eyes are on me, and her mouth is moving but it's impossible to hear all the words she's saying. They come out scrambled, broken pieces seeking one another but never quite making the connection. I shake my head. "What?"

"I figured Aunt Cami would've told you." She places her hands, one on top of the other, on the tabletop. There's a glow around them, or maybe it's the table. No, it's me. The whole world is electrified, buzzing and amplified.

My eyes meet hers. There's a sick satisfaction in them. She's happy. "I—I don't understand. He's dying?"

"Yup. Serves the bastard right."

Maybe it's the shock of talking about him. Everyone else avoids the topic altogether but here we are talking about him as if he's real and not just some monster I dreamed up. I close my eyes, lean forward, and take several deep breaths. He's dying and no one told me. Cami was just going to let him die without telling me. Fucking bitch. Another protective decision made to save Zed. I don't fucking need saving!

"Are you okay?"

I look up to find that she's looking from me to the kitchen and back again, eyes wide and brows knitted. Am I overreacting? Straightening, I take a slow sip of water, trying to calm my buzzing insides. I'm itching to lash out, but logic is whispering in my ear, *It isn't her fault.*

"I'm fine," I say. "Just...We haven't talked about him since I got back. I didn't know."

"Would it have made a difference if you had?"

She's a shit. Always has been. "Maybe."

Her fingers are working with the straw in her glass, moving it around slowly in the water. Ice clangs against the sides. "Would you have gone to him?"

It's a good question. None of her damn business, but still a very good question. What would I have done? "I don't know."

The waiter arrives with our sampler, placing it on the table with a stack of napkins. "Are you ladies ready to order?" he asks, his slender frame leaning slightly forward.

"No," Angel says. "I think this is going to do us. Don't you?"

"Hmm? Oh. Yeah."

He cuts his eyes at each of us, surely annoyed that we would dare take up valuable table space without ordering. I had a friend in food service once and she hated that shit. *Just order something, fuckers,* she would shout. The server departs and we fall into silence.

For years I've longed for this chance, an opportunity to corner her and ask what it was she thought her father did to her. He told me over and over again that she was a liar. Just some little asshole that was jealous he was giving his attention to me. But now I wonder. She seems happy, not at all like me. She's polished and bubbly and confident, and here I am sullen with wrecked hair and a too-skinny body semi-fresh off a suicide attempt. We were favorites to the same man, yet she seems unscathed.

I take a deep breath. "Can I ask you something?"

She stops chewing, placing her niblet on the plate, and nods while I attempt to swallow my trepidation. You don't talk directly about these things. Probably because they always say to be quiet. *Be a good girl.*

"What did he do to you?" My stomach tightens in anticipation of the details. I used to think it was jealousy. Maybe at one time it was.

She waves a hand in the air. "You *know* what he did. It's all over you."

I'm struck but she doesn't give me time to react. Before I can pull away, her hands shoot out and she's captured mine, pulling me forward slightly. I don't fight, though my entire body is pulsing with the flight instinct. It never engages, this impulse to get away from trouble.

"Listen to me, Grace," she says, her gaze locked on mine. "Don't you dare let that son of a bitch get out of this life without seeing what he's done to you."

We're suspended, not even time dares to move. Why did I think she would give me anything? She's never been honest about what she claims he did to her. Now she's going to gloat over me, tell me I'm a mess while she's got the perfect husband and family?

Fuck that. She's the same self-entitled cunt she's always been. Homewrecker, life ruiner.

I jerk my hands away. "It's Zed," I say.

"What?"

"He called me Grace. Nobody calls me that anymore." I stand up, looking down at her, rage filling me up as if my tank had actually emptied. "You don't know anything, Angel. None of you do. He touched you? Tried to." I laugh, a bitter and dry sound that makes her flinch. "He stole everything from me." I slap the stupid tears away and stick my pointer finger against the top of the table. "*Everything.*"

"Gra-um-Zed...I'm sorry, but you have no idea what he did to me. The humiliation. Maybe he didn't do the same thing to both of us, but that doesn't change what he is, what he did, or how his actions affected us. I've been in therapy for a long time trying to accept and deal with the pain he caused." She reaches out, capturing my hand again. "It isn't your fault. It never was."

She's encased in water, a pitying prisoner of my fury. Jerking my hand away, I point a shaking finger at her. "Don't you dare."

"Zed, I—"

"You can save your sorries, Angel. I don't need them, and I damn sure don't want them." I leave her sitting there, not at all sorry she'll be stuck with the bill. Shielding eyes raw with rage and sorrow with my shades, I step out into the heat of the day welcoming its hands around my throat.

Nineteen

om's driveway is empty. She's still working. I'm grateful for the stretch of time I'll have to calm down. Uncle Dan is dying, and they kept it from me. I want to call Hattie, to scream at her for lecturing me about keeping secrets when she was holding onto this one, but such confrontation won't do her any good, not in her condition.

Getting out of the Bronco, I stumble over to the old pecan tree at the other end of the trailer and plop down against it. I don't know how to deal with this anger. I could call my therapist. Probably should. This is something she needs to know, right? Or maybe the group. They're meeting tomorrow. It could help, couldn't it? But I don't want to share him with her or them. Especially not Deidre. She's still unforgiven for that all too accurate accounting of who I am.

Tossing the smartphone across yard, I lay back against the trunk of the old tree and begin to sob. Large, heaving cries escape and I can't be bothered to shove them back in. He's dying. Karma is about to take him out and, as far as I can tell, it's well earned. What am I supposed to do with that?

I sit up, tears subsiding, and crush my fists into raw eye sockets to scrub them out. I swore I wouldn't cry for him again.

The day he stared at me with disgust while he held tight to his new girlfriend, I swore I would never cry for him again. Yet here I am, a puddle of mush because he's not going to be in this world much longer.

"Are you all right?"

I look up at Lucinda. Her hair is freshly trimmed into its signature pageboy style. I wonder if that's something her asshole husband stipulates. Maybe on some level he likes little boys.

She's timid, as always. "I saw you pull up but didn't want to bother you. Then I saw you..." Her eyes avert from me. "I just wanted to make sure you're alright."

"Yeah. I'm good." I grab my bag and dig for the cigarettes within. I offer her one, but she declines.

"Rex doesn't like it when I smoke."

"I'm sure you don't like it when he knocks the shit out of you, but that doesn't seem to stop him."

She looks down at the ground, shifting her weight from one leg to the other.

I'm such an asshole. "Sorry. I shouldn't have said that."

Sitting down beside me, she says, "You're right." She hands me my phone and I shove it in my bag. "I spend all this time doing what he wants me to do, trying to be perfect for him, but it's never good enough." Her shoulders slump. "I don't know what to do."

Pulling my knees against my chest, I lay my head on them. "Leave?"

She looks at me. "I've thought about that a lot since the last time I saw you, but where will I go? I don't have a mom who loves me. My mom's been dead for years. And my dad is a bastard."

"Aren't they all?"

She grabs my smoke, taking a long drag before handing it back to me. "I could go to my sister's, but I've left and come back so many times. Rex is the only one who will take care of me."

"Until he kills you."

Her shoulders rise and fall in a defeated shrug. "Maybe." She leans back. "Where've you been? I haven't seen you for a while."

"I moved out."

"Good for you, kid." I hand her the smoke and she takes another drag. "You got a fella?"

"Nah. Just lucked up and found a place I could afford."

She's staring into the distance. After a long pause, she asks, "What do you think it's like to drown?"

I stretch my legs out. "When I was a kid, like eight, my parents took me and my sister to the beach. It was the first time I'd ever been." I take a drag and hand it to her for her turn. "I was in the ocean, finally brave enough to go in up to my waist. A wave came in and pulled me under. I kept grabbing for the sand, but it slid right through my fingers. I was swallowing water, and my heart was beating so fast." I look at her. "I thought I was going to drown. My chest burned and I couldn't catch my breath. I thought, this is the end of me."

"What happened?"

I shrug. "I don't know. But I'll tell you this." She's leaning in, waiting for me to impart wisdom I don't have. "I never went in waist deep again."

"Well." She looks down, sputtering out a smoke-fueled laugh. "That wasn't very helpful."

I laugh. "I didn't promise it would be. If you're looking for wisdom you've come to the wrong place. I don't know what the fuck I'm doing."

She takes another drag and hands me the remains. "I have a designated escape bag. Keep it at the back of the closet. Every day I wait for him to leave and I dig it out, pack my things, and decide I'm leaving. I even write a note telling him why I've finally left him. Then, a couple of hours before he gets home, I unpack it and put everything back in its place." Her laughter is filled with sorrow. "It's fucking stupid."

"What if he comes home early?"

She sobers. "Huh?"

"What if he comes home early and finds them, the bag and the note?"

"I..." She shifts to sit on her knees, as if she's about to pray. "I guess I've never thought about it."

We settle into silence, both staring out into a world that couldn't possibly get us. She's reckless in a totally different way from me. I seek destruction, latch myself onto it, and try to ride it out, but she stays just below the rumble of it, trying to go unnoticed until she gets up the gumption to take a chance, to shake things up. I bet she secretly hopes he'll come home.

"Go get it," I say, turning to her.

She looks at me. "What?"

"Go get your bag. Let today be the day you don't unpack it."

"Where will I go?"

"I have room. I live on my own. You can stay with me until you get on your feet."

"I don't have a job, Zed. You can't get on your feet without a job. It's not that easy."

"It's never easy to do something for yourself."

She's quiet a moment, and then, "You're wrong, you know."

"About what?"

She stands up. "I'd better get back. Take care of yourself."

I stand, dusting the back of my leggings off. "You do the same. Let me know if you change your mind."

She smiles. "Sure thing. See you later."

MOM IS surprised to see me. She approaches the front porch slowly, her old white bag positioned in front of her for protection, a timid smile on her face. "Hey, baby," she says, her voice filled with the questions she won't ask.

I stand in greeting but make no move to embrace her. It hasn't been long enough. "Can I come in?"

"Of course." She's fumbling with her keys. "Why didn't you just go inside? You have a key."

"I didn't feel like I should."

The interior of the house is cool and quiet. She drops her keys and purse on the sofa by the door and walks toward the kitchen. "Do you want some sweet tea? I'm just about to thirst to death."

"Sure."

In the kitchen, she busies herself with preparing a glass of sweet tea for each of us. I take a seat at the table doing my best to keep the anger that's wicking back up in check. Maybe she doesn't know.

"I got a call from your Aunt Darla," she's saying. "Angel told her that she ran into you today."

"Yeah, she did."

She places a glass in front of me and sits down at the table. "I guess she's pretty far along now, huh?"

"Not as far as Hattie." This game of hers has always been annoying, but I'm determined to follow it through. She should be the one to tell me about my uncle.

"Yeah. Your Aunt Darla said Angel told her you got a little upset when she mentioned your Uncle Dan."

I run sweating palms over my thighs. "How do you mean?"

"I guess she told you about..." Her hand makes an odd motion in the air before she adds, "his condition."

My fist balls, pulling the soft stretchy fabric with it. "Just say it, for fuck's sake."

Her shoulders fall and she looks at me, her eyes full of remorse. "I'm sorry I didn't tell you.'"

Through clenched teeth, I ask, "About what?"

"I didn't want to upset your progress by bringing him into the conversation. You've done so well since you came back."

Rage pushes me out of my chair and I'm standing over her, unable to hold it in any longer. "Just say it! Stop beating around the fucking bush and say it!"

Her eyes spill and tears begin to fall like heavy rain from them. "He has cancer, Zed. He's dying." She stands, arms crossed over her chest. "I didn't want to wreck your progress."

I swat her back. "You and Hattie talk about not keeping secrets." My eyes are burning into her, at least I hope they are. I want her to feel how badly I despise her. "Turns out, the only person not allowed to keep them is me!"

I turn to leave, and she grabs me. "Please don't go, Zed. Let's talk about this."

The newspaper publishes stories sometimes about matricide and everyone looks at the kid as though they're some kind of monster. What if it's the mom that's the monster?

"You stay away from me, *Cami*. I never want to speak to you again."

"Zed, please!"

Standing in the center of her kitchen, hands wringing the hem of her blouse, eyes and cheeks wet, mouth open and trembling, she reminds me of who I was before. Begging for someone to love me, anyone. Don't mistreat me, just love me for who I am. It's disgusting and pathetic.

"I'm sorry," she says. "I'm so sorry."

Swatting at my own tears, I hold her gaze, "How could you?" She's Medusa and my heart is heavy stone. Maybe real heartbreak isn't a break at all.

CLIMBING into the Bronco I turn the key in the ignition and jerk it into reverse, pausing only long enough to look at Lucinda's house, remembering my offer to her even now, then slam it into drive and push the accelerator to the floor. Take me from here, away from this place and this woman who should have torn me from her womb when she had the chance.

My heart rate has only begun to return to normal when a voice comes from the back. "That didn't go well then, huh?"

"Jesus Christ!" I jerk the car over to the shoulder and slam it into park, turning to meet the now panicked eyes of Lucinda. "What the fuck!"

"Sorry. I shouldn't have just popped up." She raises a small brown suitcase, and my heart slows. "I decided to take you up on your offer."

I stare at her for a long moment, my breathing finally slowing down and my heart finding its rhythm once more. "You could've texted. You know, given me a heads up."

"Do you even check that thing?"

I expel a puff of laughter. "Nah." I pat the front seat. "Shotgun?"

She shakes her head, eyes darting outside. "I should probably lay low back here. At least until we get away from the neighborhood."

I nod. "Sure thing." Pulling the car back onto the road, I try to keep the voice in my head quiet, the one that's telling me I've made a mistake. I always screw up, it's what I do, but sometimes my screw-ups turn out to be the best thing for someone else. I'm not going to let my inner bitch talk me out of being human. Not anymore.

TWENTY

We've met at the halfway point between our towns, some little coffee shop off the beaten path that smells of chocolate and dark roast. Deidre is wearing a yellow sundress today and her skin is glowing. It's been my experience that a glow like that only comes from between the sheets. She gives a half smile when she sees me, raising her iced drink in greeting. I stop by the counter, order something they're calling a refresher, and head over to her.

"Thanks for meeting me," I say, dropping into the chair across from her.

She nods, straw inches from her rose-colored lips. "I was surprised to hear from you after last time. Didn't expect to ever see you again, actually."

"Truth?" Her eyebrow raises as she takes a slow sip from her cup. "I never expected to see you again either. You pissed me off with that assessment of me and my character."

Chuckling, she says, "I tend to call them like I see them."

The girl behind the counter calls my name. I hurry to collect my glass and return to our table. Deidre is surveying me as I settle into the odd-shaped chair once more.

"How's Clay?"

She shrugs. "As well as can be expected. Claims he hasn't used since last week. He probably has, but he's been smart enough to stay clear of me when he does."

I nod, sipping my drink and averting my eyes. I don't know how to do this.

"What's this about, Zed?"

Swallowing the pomegranate concoction, I brace myself. "I don't know how to do this."

"Do what?"

"Talk to someone."

Her smile calms my ignited nerves. "I sensed that." She leans forward, elbows resting on the faux wooden surface of the table. "Go for it."

"I didn't know who to talk to about this. I have my sister, but things are still fucked up with us. She doesn't fully trust me. I don't blame her." I take a hurried gulp of my drink, doing my best to still anxious legs before they bang the underside of the table. "And I don't want to talk to my mother."

Eyebrow crooked, she says, "So you called me? I'm touched."

"You've been coming to group for a while, right? Been seeing a therapist for some time?"

"Yeah."

"And you're like me."

"I'm not, but I see where you're going." She leans back, crossing her arms across her chest. I wonder if they're her armor as mine often are for me. "We have enough in common that you think I can help you."

"Or just listen. Fuck, I don't know."

"Okay, okay, tell me what's going on and I'll try to help. No promises."

Taking a deep breath, I close my eyes and tell her how I've taken Lucinda into my home, the woman whose husband wanted a threesome. Then I tell her about Oliver, how I know I shouldn't want to see him romantically, but he's all I can think about, especially since the night in my living room when the only thing that saved us from making a huge mistake was the thin fabric of my pants. She considers what I've said, nursing the remains of her drink.

After an eternity, she places her empty cup on the table and sits up. "Let's talk about this guy—"

"Oliver."

She nods. "Let's talk about Oliver in a minute. First, I want to know what the hell you were thinking taking that woman to your house. Don't you have enough shit going on without inviting more trouble into your life?"

"It was an impulse. I'd just learned my uncle was dying of cancer and I was pissed at my mom and then Lucinda came over to check on me and she had bruises on her wrists and neck. I just wanted to help someone. *Anyone*. Especially since I can't seem to help myself."

"I'm sorry about your uncle." The compassion in her eyes is too much.

I shake my head. "Don't feel sorry for that bastard. He's getting what he deserves."

"Ah."

Anger flashing, I ask, "What's *ah*?"

She holds her hands up. "Nothing. Don't go getting mad at me. I just figure he's the one who hurt you." She makes a motion with her hand. "Given that you want him to die and all."

I sit back, winded by her observation. "I do." My eyes meet hers. "Want him to die, I mean. All this time I thought I felt one way about him, but now I'm just angry he's still allowed to breathe when I can't seem to."

"But not for much longer?"

"No."

"And that hurts too?" Her compassion softens her features and, quite frankly, makes me want to bolt, but what good will that do me?

I shake my head, averting my eyes so she won't see the tears building there. "What should I do about Lucinda?"

"I don't know, Zed. See it through, I guess. Don't be surprised if she goes back to him or he shows up at your house. Those situations are tricky. Sometimes women are ready to leave, but most of the time they're not."

"Is that healthy?" I ask. "Seeing it through."

She tosses her hands up, gold bangles clanging as she does. "Hell if I know. As far as I can tell we're all feeling our way through this."

Nodding, my eyes meet hers once more. "What about Oliver?"

"I can't give you relationship advice. I mean, we're not *really* friends, are we?"

"I don't know," I say with a shrug. "I've never had an actual friend before."

She stares at me a long moment, seeming to be considering something. Is she wondering whether or not I'm worth it? I can assure her, I'm not.

"What will it hurt to see what this is between you?" she asks. "Tell me the worst that can happen."

"I'll have my heart broken."

"And what's the best?"

Time is stretching out before us, long and slow. What is the best that will happen? That Oliver will rescue me from the darkness that's always at my back, that he'll love and cherish me, that he'll protect me?

I look at her. "I don't know."

She leans forward, smile returning. "I guess the question you need to ask is, do you want to find out?"

ABUSED WOMEN ARE HIGHLY UNPREDICTABLE, Deidre is right about this. Some of them are ready for the break and they don't call the man who's been making their life hell. But some of them do. Lucinda could go either way at this point. I mean, she's left him at least once that I know of, and she's told me about two other times. I knew better than to stick my nose in, to leave her to whatever bed she's made for herself, but here she is, seated on the old sofa in my living room, hands wrapped around the mug of coffee I've provided. Like Deidre said, I just have to ride it out now.

Taking a seat beside her, I pull my knees tight to my chest. "You okay?"

She shrugs. "I think so." Her eyes are focused on the front door. "I keep looking at the clock on your phone. I left my cell. I didn't want to take any chances." Probably a good thing. She looks at me. "What if I go back?"

"Then you go back." I don't know what else to say. Right now, it's hard to do anything more than focus on the rock in my gut.

"My sister." She looks at me. "I have a sister."

I nod.

"She told me that he would kill me in the end. She even said goodbye to me the last time, like I was already dead or something." A sputtering sound escapes from her mouth. "Who does that?"

"Someone who knows they have to let you do it your way?"

She places her mug on the table and leans back. "Maybe."

"I'm sorry."

Her eyebrows raise. "Yeah? Why?"

I shrug. "I'm always sorry, I guess. Even when it isn't my fault."

"Well, you shouldn't be. Never apologize for trying to help someone, Zed."

Standing, I look down at her. "I have to work for a few hours. Will you be okay?"

"Yeah. I usually last a few days before I run back."

I'm smiling, but the fact that she isn't kidding only adds another stone to my lead-laden belly. It's the cycle of abuse. We don't want to be abused. We just feel like we don't deserve anything better. "Hank and his daughter Hanna are next door."

"Cute."

"What?"

She's chuckling. "Hank and Hanna. Two H's. What's Mom's name?"

I grab my keys and bag, slinging it over my shoulder. "Umm, I don't know. She's dead."

Sober now, she nods. "Oh."

"I'll be back later." I go to the door, stopping before turning the knob. "Don't tell anybody you're here, okay? Except Hank or Hanna, I mean." She nods, but I don't trust her. Like I said, you never know what an abused woman is going to do. They want to be away but have been programmed to believe they *can't* be away. They get scared, maybe life *will* be better, and they don't deserve it, or maybe he *can't* live without them, is he really that bad anyway, and they make a phone call. One simple phone call is all he needs. It's all they ever need to know you're still vulnerable enough for them to get you back.

Jubilee's is slower than usual. Hank scheduled me for tonight because he was sure it would be hopping, but we're all standing around staring at the small family who chose to eat greasy burgers for supper just hoping they'll need assistance. Oliver is keeping his distance, but I catch him staring now and then. I wish he wouldn't. Every single time I catch him flames erupt in my belly.

"What's going on with him?" Ada asks jerking her teeny bopper head toward the back.

I shrug. It seems everyone thinks I have insider information on him, but I don't. Until our incident, I had no idea that he even thought about me in any way other than the grumpy girl at work he could confide in.

She lifts her ponytail from her shoulder to inspect her ends. "He's been gloomy all week," she says as she tosses it back and leans her hip against the counter.

"Oh yeah? I didn't know you two were on shift together all week."

She scoffs. "I talk to people outside of work too."

I grab a tray and rag. Anything to make myself busy. "Oh. I thought your mom didn't let you."

Her bottom lip protrudes as she crosses her arms over her sporty bosom. "She doesn't know everything I do." She looks back at Oliver and smiles. I bet she was embarrassed that her crush saw her being dropped off by her mom again. "Anyway, he's been mooning all week."

I laugh despite myself. "*Mooning*?"

She shrugs. "My mom says it when she's talking about someone pouting." Grabbing a fry from the prep station, she leans against the counter. "I think it's his ex-wife again. She's jerking him around."

"Oh yeah?"

"Yeah. He told me about it the other night."

She has my full attention. "The other night when?"

Shrugging, she says, "I don't remember. It was a few days ago." Blushing, she adds, "We hung out after my shift. Said he's all messed up."

I jerk my head around and catch his eye. "Where did you guys hang out?" I'm trying to keep my tone cool, but he's looking guilty and I'm beginning to fume.

Oblivious, Ada toys with the string on her apron as she replies, "The park. He was so worked up." She looks up as I turn, and I see the color rush to her cheeks.

Moving closer to her, I whisper, "Did you guys hook up?" I'm smiling, but every inch of me is humming with jealousy.

Her head dips. "God no. He's wanted to hook up for a while, but he knows I can't until I'm eighteen. My mom would have him locked up like that." She snaps her finger as she looks back at him.

I follow her gaze, hoping he'll be able to see the fury I'm barely containing, but he's gone. She sighs. "Besides, he had one of his roomies with him. Brad or something."

The towel I've been holding is wrapped tight around my fingers. I drop it, flexing my tingling digits. "I'm going to take a break, Ada. You got this?"

She looks at the empty dining room and expels a putter of laughter. "I think I can manage."

As suspected, Oliver is outside, his cigarette holding up well in the sprinkles falling from the darkening sky. He looks over when I step out onto the stoop, averting his eyes as I descend to the gravel below.

"Hey," he says, shifting against the wall. Guilty.

I jerk my head back in greeting, then light my own cigarette and take a drag, exhaling the smoke almost immediately. A waste. "Ada said you met her at the park the other night."

His expression is one of disbelief. "We ran into each other."

"That's not how she's spinning it. Apparently, you wanted to *hook up,* but you know she's too young."

He chuckles.

"What?" My tone is sharper than intended. I've never been the jealous type, but that girl and her blush have my insides twisted up.

"I wanted to hook up." He looks at me and my insides loosen, allowing the goo of my want to puddle. "With you."

"Then why meet her? I'm assuming it was after you left my house."

"I told you; I ran into her."

"After you called her. That's not running into someone, Oliver. That's meeting them."

He's smiling. Does he think this is funny?

"Did you fuck her?"

His smile fades. "She told you we didn't." Pushing away from the building, he takes a step forward. "Even so, how is it any of your business who I fuck?"

"Because that night you tried to shove your cock through my sweats and then you went to meet with another girl when I didn't give you what you wanted. A *girl*." My hands are flying around me. "She's not even eighteen, Oliver!"

He throws the remnants of his cigarette onto the ground, grinding his foot into it, then crosses to me. I'm held in place, heart beating so wildly it may just burst out of my chest.

"I didn't fuck her, Zed. I don't *want* to fuck her."

I meet his eyes, determined to be strong and unbending even in this moment when I want to wrap myself around him. "That's not what she thinks."

His mouth is covering mine before I can react, his hands cupped under my chin to hold me in place. This shouldn't be happening and, yet, I want it to happen more than I've wanted anything in a long time.

He pulls back, his hands falling to his sides. "I don't want Ada. I don't want Jessica. I don't want anyone else. I just want you, Zed. Only you."

Looking down at the gravel, I say, "We both need to get our lives straight."

"Why wait?" His flapping hands pulls my eyes back up from the ground. "I'm never going to be straight enough to take plunges like this logically. This," he taps his chest, "doesn't work with logic."

"So, what, you're in love with me now?"

His eyes avert to the door, and I turn to find Dante leaning against the frame his movements mimicking someone eating popcorn.

Oliver looks at me, his eyes a wall of glass in the fading light. "I have to go."

I don't stop him when he pushes past. How can I? I'm too winded by his actions, his words.

Dante is still in the doorway, a smug smile pasted on his semi-attractive face.

"What?" I snip.

"Ada needs help in the dining room." I climb the few stairs and he moves back to allow me entrance. "If you need to blow off some steam I've got you, girl." He grabs the bulge between his legs.

I look down and then back up to meet his hungry eyes. I want to say something witty and devastating, but with an ego as massive as Dante's there's no point. Anything I say can and will be used to pump him up. Oddly enough, I used to find that attractive. Without another word, I turn from him and go to the dining room, wishing I could melt into a puddle to be consumed by the earth.

Dante was right. I jump behind a register and type my code in. I glance at Ada. "Where did all these people come from?" She looks at me with red-rimmed, accusing eyes and I turn away, eyes forward. "I can take the next person in line."

It's after eleven when I pull to a stop in front of my trailer. The soft glow of the living room light signals that Lucinda must still be inside. I grab my bag and push the car door open, knocking it into Oliver. He backs away as I get out, shoving his hands into the pockets of his faded jeans.

My voice is a whisper. "What're you doing here?"

"I needed to see you."

Mere habit makes me turn to see if anyone from Hank's house has spotted him here. The structure is dark. Not that it matters.

I brush past him and head for the front door. "You need to leave."

"Zed, please just talk to me."

Whirling too quickly, I have to take a moment to right myself before poking a finger out at him. "How could you do that? There? How could you? I can't do this."

"Do what? What can't you do?"

"You kissed me there. At Jubilee's."

He smiles. "I know."

"This is not funny, Oliver. Dante saw and Ada knows and now Jessica will know." I point to Hank's house, my fury puttering out. "And *Hank* will know."

"And?"

"I can't do this, Oliver. I'm not supposed to."

He scratches his head. "Says who?"

"Says my therapist." I'm exhausted. I just need him to go so I can sleep. If I'm asleep I won't think about the pain pills my mom keeps in the shoe box under her bed. I won't think about the nausea pills Hattie has in her medicine cabinet. "I tried to kill myself." Leaning against the stair railing, I close my eyes. "Three months ago I took a shitload of pills because..." I throw my hands up. "I don't know. Because I was just too tired of living. Of being the victim. Of being the girl that's only good enough to fuck."

"Zed—"

"Just leave, Oliver, please." My hand is up, motioning for him to go. Autopilot for the emotionally drained.

His arms are around me, crushing me against his Jubilee's work shirt. Oddly enough, the lingering grease smell is comforting. Struggling only serves to tighten his hold on me and after a moment I realize I don't want to get away. I'm tired of fighting.

I look up at him. "I'm just so fucking tired."

"Then let me help you."

"You'll break my heart. They always break me."

"I won't." His eyes linger on mine as he brings me back upright, making sure I'm standing on my own two feet before releasing me. "I promise."

"You shouldn't make promises you can't keep. Didn't your mom ever tell you that?" Reaching out, my fingers trail his tightened jaw, trace his lips. I should push him away, forget about our kisses, and how much I just want someone to love me, but I've always been a sucker for the promises men make. He's still as I lean forward, grazing his lips with my own. "Just promise you won't hurt me on purpose."

"I swear." His hands cup my face, and his mouth covers mine, soft at first and then more urgently. I wonder if the salt of my tears bothers him, but as our kiss deepens it's difficult to care.

Inside, Lucinda is asleep on the sofa, her body facing the wall. I lead Oliver into my bedroom and close the door. His arms circle my waist, and his forehead presses against mine. Is this how romance is supposed to be? Two fucked up people clinging to one another to keep from drowning? I'm sure to take him with me if he doesn't let go. *Never let go.* I lift my head and close my eyes. His lips cover mine and I am swept away.

Twenty-One

Lucinda is talking but I don't hear her. Can't. I'm too tied up in knots. Able to do nothing more than think of Oliver; his arms around me, his hand stroking my hair, and the quiet way he accepted my admission that I was sexually abused, omitting the details of how long it went on and who the offender was. So what if he thinks it was some random guy at one of the millions of parties I used to go to? Now Lucinda is trying to talk to me, trying to tell me what she hopes to do, and all I can think about is going to him, finding solace and refuge in his arms.

She's looking at me, a soft smile tugging the corners of her mouth. "You're not listening to me, are you?"

Embarrassed, I lower my head. "I'm sorry, Luce."

"Don't call me that." The smile is gone and she's looking straight ahead. "That's what Rex calls me."

I cover her hand with my own. "Understood."

I can't tell her that I understand more than she knows, can't bring myself to tell her that for my youth everyone called me Grace or Gracie because my parents had burdened me with such an ugly name as Zedwynne. I can't tell her that I stopped using that name years ago when the man I loved, the man who ushered me into womanhood against my will, discarded me for aging out.

I won't tell her that he would whisper to me in dark, *You're my Grace. No one else's,* while stroking my budding breasts. No, I won't tell her that, to me, Grace is a sham, a scared shitless little girl that I killed the day I left this shit town.

She's looking at me again. "My sister calls me Cinda."

Nodding, I remove my hand, tucking it into the nook created by my crisscrossed legs. "Got it."

"She wants me to come and stay with her."

"Your sister?"

"Yeah. I know you told me not to call anyone, but I called her." She looks at the table again. "She's living in Santa Fe now."

"Will you do it?"

She looks back at me, eyes shining. "She already bought my ticket."

"That's great news. When do you leave?" My smile is wide and genuine, radiating from the depths of me. Isn't it funny how you can actually feel where a smile begins?

"Four hours."

Stunned, I respond the only way I can. "Wow."

"Yeah." She's running her hands along the tops of her thighs. "We both think it's best that I go now. Less chance of going back to him."

"What do *you* think? Are you ready?"

She's quiet. This is a delicate time in the cycle of abuse. This is the time that she will choose to leave for good, for herself, or go back to him. If she's unsure about this move, she'll never stay away.

Looking at me, she says, "I want to go." Uncertainty is back, though the smile is still present. "I'm scared, though. I've been with Rex for a long time, and I love him. I do." Tears have begun to trace the smooth surface of her face. "But he's never going to change." She turns her entire body to face me, her own legs going crisscross-applesauce. "I don't deserve to be abused. Do I? I mean, he tells me that it's my fault, that if I hadn't seasoned the food wrong or hadn't taken so long to get him off, he wouldn't have to hit me. If I were in the mood more."

I grab her hands, wishing I had the words in me that she needs to hear.

Her eyes are on mine. "I think he hates me as much as he loves me."

"Not you," I manage. "It's not your fault. It was never your fault."

She nods. "I think I've always known that." Her lip is quivering. "I can't help him, can I?" I shake my head. She inhales, the breath hobbling through the small opening of her lips, and exhales slowly. "If I can't help him, I have to help myself." Her posture straightens. "I'm going to Santa Fe. Today. And I'm never looking back." She holds up a sealed envelope. "I'm mailing this to him with directions for sending me my things. I think he'll rip it up, but I need to tell him goodbye, and this is the best way I can think to do that."

"It's a good idea. Where are you telling him to ship them?"

"My uncle's house in Des Moines. If they make it there, I'll figure out how to get them."

I smile. "I'm proud of you."

"Me too." She laughs, a small sound that's still a bit unsure of itself. "Who knew the weird girl across the street would give me the strength to leave?"

"This is all you."

"But you gave me the opportunity. I couldn't have done it without you." Her shining eyes meet mine. "Thank you for taking me in and not judging me. I'm sorry for putting you in this position."

Taking her face in my hands, I hold her gaze. "You didn't put me anywhere I didn't agree to be." She nods and I release her. "Do you have everything ready? We need to get moving if you're going to catch that flight."

Hank is working in the yard when I return from seeing Lucinda off. Despite our little town being far removed from the airport I couldn't help looking over my shoulder until she was safely past security, though there's no way Rex could know she was leaving out today. It still seems as though I'm caught in a bit of a whirlwind. Difficult to believe that I'll be alone in the house again, though Lucinda was scarcely here longer than a moment in the grand scheme of things. Hank is wearing shorts cut just long enough to remain decent, and a wife beater. I wish we could find a better name for that style shirt. Tank top must sound far too feminine for the manliest of men.

He straightens when I approach, wiping the back of his yellow glove across his glistening forehead. "Hey there, stranger. Where's your friend? I saw y'all head out earlier."

I smile. "She's going to stay with family. Thanks for being cool about her staying here."

"You know me," he says with a smile.

Motioning toward his plants I say, "I didn't know you garden."

"It helps me think." He takes the gloves off and throws them on the ground. "I'm glad you came over. I've been wanting to talk to you. About that first day."

"Not necessary."

"I think it is. Your mom told me that you've had a rough time of it and that you don't trust men. Sometimes I forget that I'm this big, intimidating guy."

"Hank, it isn't necessary for you to apologize." Confusion settles over his face. "I came to apologize to you."

His voice has an air of caution. "Okay."

"I overreacted that day and I'm sorry I made you feel like I didn't trust you." His shoulders visibly relax. Score one for Zeddie. "The truth is, I didn't. She's right. My mother. I've had a lot of trouble with guys in the past and I let that affect how I treated you that day. And I'm sorry it's taken this long for me to say it. Sometimes I'm slow to act." I look down, surveying the damage the toe of my Converse has done to the crabgrass, then back up at him. "Anyway, that's all."

"Thank you." His smile lights up his words. "It's unnecessary but appreciated." Motioning to the porch, he adds, "Do you have a minute? Shop talk."

I follow him under the canopy and take a seat in the old '70s garden chair, the cool metal kind like the ones my Gamma had in my childhood.

"I've been talking to Oliver about you." My cheeks flame. "And he says you're doing a great job." He hands me a glass of sweet tea, the outside already sweating from the mixture of heat and humidity. "Have you decided what you're going to do?"

"What do you mean?"

"Are you going to stay or go?"

I pause, mid-sip. I haven't thought about whether I will take off during the night or settle down in this godforsaken town for weeks. I shrug.

"Well, let me know when you decide. I'm looking for another shift lead and I think you'd be a great fit."

I nod, unable to do anything else. Jubilee's is the first job I've managed to hold down for more than a couple of weeks and I just figured it was because I can't screw it up, not when Hank seems to owe my mother something.

"There's no rush," he's saying. "I know you're not looking to make a career out of it, but," he lifts his arms as if to say *why not,* "it's a good place to start."

"I'll let you know." Standing, I place the glass on the metal table. "Thanks, Hank."

"I haven't done anything."

"Well, I appreciate everything."

Stepping off the porch, I head across the yard. From the moment I watched Lucinda walking toward her new life, I realized there is something different about me. For the first time, I know where I'm supposed to be. It isn't something that has dawned on me, rather something I am finally acknowledging. I've been running from belonging for so long, and why? Because a man who is now being devoured by cancer stole my peace of mind? As I close the door against Hank's fatherly stare, I think of my uncle and say a silent prayer to any god who may be listening, "Please let him suffer."

I've been sitting at the small coffee shop I met Deidre in ages ago sipping on an iced latte for a quarter hour. She was supposed to meet me here with Clay, but they're late and that isn't like her. She is prompt if she's nothing else. I take a look at the face of my phone, opening my text messages to make sure she hasn't tried to get in touch that way, but there's nothing. The shop is quiet today, most likely because it's late afternoon and most people are either leaving work for home or they're already there. I've never been much of a people watcher, choosing instead to ignore and avoid, but with nothing else to do I find myself looking over the few occupants of the cafe, wondering what their lives are like. Are they meeting potential friends for a coffee and a chat, are they writers, are they stalkers? The guy at the table in the corner looks like he could be a potential creeper.

Adjusting, I place my cup on the small table beside me and gaze through the big windows that look out over the parking lot. This place is great with its heavy wood theme and old-world charm, but it's shit for privacy. I think I've spotted Deidre's car when someone steps into view. I look up, surprised to find Betsy Thompson staring down at me, her ginger hair loose and flowing over the bodice of the boho maxi dress she's wearing.

Her glistening lips pull back in a smile. "Howdy, Zed. Long time no see."

"Yeah," I say. "How's it going?"

She sits in the chair across from me, crossing her legs and leaning forward, elbow resting on her knee in a way that still allows her to drink. She's all grace and trendsetter.

"I can't complain, I reckon. How've you been? I haven't seen you since you threw me down at my own house party." She's challenging me. It's obvious now from her posture and the snarky look on her face. She wants an apology.

"Do you mean the night you stuck your tongue down my throat?"

She strokes her hair, nodding slightly as she averts her eyes and sips her drink.

"I thought so." Picking up my cup, I take a sip.

"What're you doing all the way out here?" she asks, recovering nicely.

"I'm meeting some people."

Her eyes sparkle. "To party?"

"It's five o'clock, Betsy. Who parties this early?"

"Plenty of people. You used to."

"Not anymore." I lean forward, raising my hand to signal Deidre who's just walked through the door.

Betsy looks around, her eyes falling on Deidre. "Wow. Who's that?"

"The person I'm meeting."

Her head jerks around. "Yes, but who is she?"

"She is Deidre," she says, joining us. Her eyes lock with Betsy's for a moment. "Who are you?"

Betsy stands, extending her hand. "I'm Betsy. I went to school with Zed."

"Oh. Was she as big of a pain in the ass back then?" She winks at me.

Laughing, Betsy replies, "The biggest!" Then, digging in her bag, she pulls out a business card and presents it to Deidre. "I've got to run, but I'd love to chat. Give me a call and we'll get together."

Taking the card, Deidre smiles, though her face is drawn in confusion. "Sure thing."

"It was a pleasure to meet you," Betsy says to Deidre, then glances back at me. "See you around, Zed," she adds before sauntering away.

"Not if I can help it," I say before pulling a long sip of latte up through my straw.

Deidre dashes away to order a drink, settling into the chair Betsy occupied upon her return. She holds the business card up, her eyes roaming over the information on the front. "She's something else, huh?"

"That's one way to describe her."

"Why does she want to chat with me?"

Shrugging, I say, "I don't know. She's a topless server at The Wet Spot. Maybe she thinks you'd like to get in on the gig."

Deidre raises an eyebrow before tossing the card down on the table. "No, thank you." Taking a sip of her latte, she adds, "Sorry I was late. Traffic was a damn nightmare."

"Where's Clay?"

She looks down at her drink. "Rehab."

"What?"

"Yeah. Showed up to his therapy appointment high as a kite. They admitted him last night."

"Poor kid."

"Maybe he'll sober up this time," she says, but we both know that isn't likely. "You didn't make it to group this morning. Everything okay?"

"I had to take my neighbor...former neighbor to the airport."

"*The* neighbor?"

"One and the same. She's going to stay with her sister."

"One more battered woman saved," she says, lifting her cup in celebration.

"Here, here."

She leans forward in her chair. Attempting to keep her voice low, she asks, "And what about the guy, Mr. Hot Stuff?" I laugh, lowering my head to keep her from seeing the color I can feel heating up my face. "What happened with that?"

"We kissed and he stayed the night." She makes a whooping

sound, keeping it low enough that she doesn't draw too much attention. "It wasn't like that. We just talked."

"And kissed."

"Yes."

Composed now, she asks, "What did you talk about?"

"I told him a little about myself. Not all of it. I didn't want to scare him."

"You know what Rebecca would say about that."

"I do. I also know what my therapist would say, but I don't care. Why do we have to give everything up to someone we're not sure about? That's too much. It's too dangerous."

"I'm not arguing with that." She raises her cup again in a show of solidarity.

I look at her, how radiant she still is, how confident. I want to get there. "What about you? Are you trying it with anyone?"

"Not at the moment." She takes another sip of her latte. "I'm trying this on-my-own thing to see how it feels. I like it. There's no pressure."

"No pressure is good."

She leans back. "You want to talk about anything else?"

I shake my head. "No."

She's impressed. "No shit?"

"No shit." I laugh. "I guess I just missed your crabby ass."

Her smile is genuine. "You know if you keep this up, we might be friends."

I dip my head. Maybe that won't be such a bad thing.

OLIVER IS WAITING on my porch when I finally pull to a stop in the drive just after eight. Grabbing my bag, I take a deep breath and step out of the car. I've been thinking of him nonstop all day and now he's here on my porch and I'm petrified. What do we do now?

"Hey," I say, joining him on the porch. "How long have you been here?"

He steps up behind me, burying his face in my neck and sliding his arms around my waist. "Not long."

Turning the key, I let us into the dark confines of my home, but I don't turn on the lights. There's enough of dusk's light coming through the open curtains. I lean against the door, turning the lock in the handle as I drop my bag and keys on the floor beside me. Oliver steps in front of me. Only the bottom half of his face is visible, but his eyes are burning hot on my face.

His voice is husky in the darkness. "You've been in my head all day."

"Oh yeah?"

"Yeah." He leans closer, more of his face becoming visible in the soft light from outside. His hand is on my face, finger tracing the line of my jaw, my lips, my neck. Warmth pools in my belly, opening like a spring bud, spreading out to meet his fingertips as they trail along the collar of my shirt. His lips graze mine sending shocks over the flesh of my face that follow his trail across my jaw and down to my neck. "Did you think of me at all?"

Every second. "Yes." My ability to think of words abandons me as his mouth covers mine, his tongue sliding through parted lips to mingle with my own.

"Is this okay?" he asks, sliding his hand up my shirt to cup breasts eager to feel the roughness of his skin.

"Yes." My voice comes out as a breath.

He pulls my shirt up and over my head and discards it, his mouth capturing my hardened nipple as he tosses the shirt to the side. A moan escapes me as he nibbles, his free hand sliding down to the valley between my thighs to stroke me through the thin cotton of my briefs. Longing and need wet the seat of my pants, make me thrust into his hand harder and harder, the motion of it begging him to plunder the treasure beneath. Covering my mouth with his once more, he answers the frantic request of my hips, sliding his hand against the wetness my desire has created, a low grumble escaping his mouth.

"Are you sure?" he asks.

Thrusting my hand down his pants, I wrap my fingers around him and squeeze, moving my hand up and down, swirling my finger around the top of him to spread the wetness his own need has created. I crush my mouth to his and feel him lift me from the floor. Before my thoughts can catch up, my pants have been discarded and I'm seated on my kitchen counter.

I close my eyes as he presses his face between my thighs, riding the waves of ecstasy his movements create. Everything empties from my mind, and I revel in the quietness. There is nothing now but pleasure. My climax is forceful, making my body quake and quiver. He stands, eyes full of desire fully visible in the glow from the awakened streetlamp outside. Picking me up he situates me on his hips, and I wrap my legs around him, taking every bit of him into me. We're against the counter now, my back pressing into the cold vinyl as he pushes into me over and over again. I'm trying to hold on, trying to pull him closer, but there's no more space to fill. He's as close as he can be. As his mouth closes over my nipple once more and his thrusts quicken, I pull him to me, holding him in place as he reaches his pinnacle, the pleasure escaping his mouth in a satisfied moan.

"I won't hurt you, Zed," he says as he kisses my belly, my breasts and my shoulder. "I promise."

I really hope he means it.

Twenty-Two

My call to the therapist didn't go as expected. When I began my story, my excuses, explaining why I can no longer live with my mother, I believed she would hang up and call for transport to come for me, but she remained silent. Then, when I told her about Oliver, how we've decided to have a relationship with zero expectations for greatness, I anticipated she would chide me. Surprisingly, she asked how I was doing with all this change. Have I had anything to drink, anything to swallow. My answers pleased her. At least I think they did. It's the sound she makes when I say something she agrees with. When I've rallied and made it through something tough without thinking about offing myself. She prescribed two follow-ups a week instead of one and I agreed. What else do you do when a situation works out in your favor?

Now, as I sit at a lonely table in what passes for a nice restaurant one town over from home waiting for my father to show up, I wonder if the therapist was wrong in her cautious congratulations to me. Because right now I feel like I'm failing.

I suppose it's time to at least speak to him, tell him how angry I am that he chose to wear blinders instead of seeing what was going on with his little girl. Then again, I wonder if that's why I'm mad at all. Isn't paying attention exactly what my mother had done, isn't that why I hate her? But she didn't only pay attention, did she? No, she ripped the fruit from my womb. Forced me to. Whatever.

Hattie is on board, of course. Her squeal when I asked her to set up this lunch was enough to clue me on. *It's going to go great, Zeddie. You'll see.* I guess she's right about one thing, I'll see.

The waiter has been to the table three times since my arrival, eager to get me a drink. Each time he's sent away his shoulders slump and his stride slow. I can't tell him I'm meeting my deadbeat dad and don't know if we'll get far enough to drink anything. The lunch rush is on, evidenced by the tables quickly filling with men and women in suits and uniforms. We've been seated at a table in the center of the bustling dining room. Not at all the best place for an estranged father and daughter reunion. Then again, it might be perfect. We're not likely to cause as big a scene with a roomful of witnesses, even if we are fifteen miles from the town we both inhabit.

He isn't difficult to spot. He's the only middle-aged man wearing a fading 1980s band shirt and jeans while rocking an outdated party-in-the-back hairstyle. Spotting me from across the room, he throws a hand up in greeting.

"Baby girl," he says, smile still wide. "Look at you."

Too aware of the eyes on us, I shift. "Hi."

Placing his shades and phone on the table, he sits. "You look good."

"Do I?" Cause I feel like shit.

"Hell yeah. Way better than last time I saw you."

The server comes over, a young man, probably my age, with a polished coif and pearly whites. "What can I get for y'all?"

"Beer," Dad says.

"Water for me."

In a flash he's gone, and we are faced with one another.

"Thanks for meeting me, Grace."

Straightening, I say, "I go by Zed now."

"Oh yeah, Hattie said that. I thought you hated that name."

As much as I hate myself.

"Yeah, well. I like it better than Grace."

He nods. "Okay. Zed it is."

Like you have any say.

His eyes are on the menu again, scanning over the lunch offerings. "What's good?"

"I don't know. I've never been here."

Lowering the menu, he smiles exposing tar-stained teeth, and shakes his head.

"What?" I ask, my hand immediately going to my face despite the fact I haven't eaten anything since breakfast.

"I just can't get over it."

"What?"

"You look like Joan Jett."

Ah, the hair. "Oh."

"You look cool as hell, baby girl."

The waiter returns to the table, and I accept my water, then look at my dad. "You can have this look too. All for the low price of misery and desperation." The waiter smirks and I meet his gaze. He doesn't approve of me. That's okay, I don't need him to.

"Are you folks ready to order?"

I tell him to bring me the house burger with fries. My dad orders the same. I think we've both ordered something simple that will get him away from the table faster, but I don't ask.

"Hattie tells me you're working at Hank's place."

I nod. Makes sense to start this way, I guess. Our family has always been very skilled at beating around the bush, but talking about my job isn't at all how I imagined as I readied myself for this heartfelt reunion, Oliver splayed naked across my bed while I searched through the meager offerings of my wardrobe for something to wear. *What do you think he will say,* Oliver asked to which I shrugged and responded, *"I don't care."* But the truth, I realize now, is that I do care. I want him to apologize. I want him to care that he had a hand in my demise. Well, my almost demise.

"Do you like it?" he asks.

"It's fine. Hank wants to give me a promotion. Shift lead."

Smirking, he leans back against the red leather fabric of the chair. "I bet he does."

What the hell is that supposed to mean? "What does that mean?"

He sits forward and leans over the table, elbows on either side of the plate. "Don't tell me you don't know Hank's story."

I lean back and cross my arms over my chest. "I don't care about Hank's story."

"He was with your mom after we split."

Eye rolling is unbecoming, but in some instances it's necessary. Right now, staring at the smug look on his face it's essential. "You mean after you showed us the door?"

He shrugs. "Semantics." Look at my father using big words. Laughing, he adds, "Chump has it bad for her. If Cami told him to jump off the world's tallest building, he would do it without question."

I cock my head to the side. "You think he offered me this position because he wants to fuck my mother again?"

He cackles. "Again? Do you think they've stopped?"

"Yeah." My tone is sharper than anticipated, even by me. "I do think they've stopped. Hank is a good guy and so is Duke. I'd say she's lucky that at least two good men have loved her in this life."

It hits home and he sobers. "I'm a good man, Zed."

"I wouldn't know."

Our waiter is back, his demeanor cheery and upbeat until the climate of our table registers. It's a visible change, the falter of his smile, the hurried way in which he delivers our plates. "Would you like another beer, sir?" Dad nods. "More water?" I do the same. And then he's gone.

My father is looking at me, his brown eyes almost black. I

don't know what my mother ever saw in him. Stringy hair left a little too long, now thinning at the top, and clothes that make him look like he's trying too hard to be who he was before youth abandoned him. I know the truth is that he just hasn't changed. Some people can't let go. Like father like daughter, I suppose.

He toys with the edge of his napkin. "What did she tell you about me? About why we broke up."

I take a big bite of my burger, chewing slowly to prolong his wait time. How dare he be demanding of me after all these years. After swallowing, I shrug. "She didn't talk about you. She didn't have to. Hattie didn't know why, but I did."

"Oh yeah?" He straightens. "Let's hear it then, smarty."

"You chose to believe a child molester over the girl he was abusing."

He leans forward, teeth bared in warning, "Don't be bringing up those lies."

"You asked."

Picking up his burger, he tears into it. I watch him, suddenly devoid of appetite. He focuses on the head of his beer, not daring to look at me. Maybe coming right out with it wasn't the right thing to do, but I'm sick of doing what everyone else considers appropriate.

"Did you know?" I ask. "What he was doing to me."

"What do you mean, what he was doing to you? I knew Angel and Darla accused him, but you never said—"

"I shouldn't have had to."

Shifting, he takes a gulp of his beer, then stares into it for a long moment before saying, "What are you saying here, Zed?"

Dropping my burger, I wipe the grease from my hands before meeting his eyes. "What does it sound like?"

He shakes his head and looks at me, hurt and disbelief burning in his eyes. "He wouldn't. Not my girls."

Chest tightening, I take a deep breath. "Do you think I would lie? I guess all women and little girls lie, right?" The lump burning in the back of my throat makes it difficult to speak.

"That's not fair, Zed."

"You believed him over Angel. You believed him over what you should have seen in me."

"He's my brother."

Hands buried in my lap, I keep my eyes averted. Looking at him now will break me open. "He's a monster and you served your little girls to him on a silver platter."

"Hattie?"

"No." Shifting on the uncomfortable vinyl-clad seat, I shake my head and look up at him. "I don't think so. Just me. Just Gracie."

Leaning over, he presses a hand to his chest. "It can't be true." His head snaps up, eyes shining with confusion. "Why didn't you tell me? If someone was hurting you why wouldn't you tell me?"

There it is. The doubt.

"Do you think I'm lying?"

Lifting his head, his shimmering eyes meet mine. "I don't know."

The burning has moved from my throat to rest behind my eyes. "Are you fucking kidding me?"

"I'm sorry."

Leaning forward, I speak through clenched teeth. "Don't you take his side again and fucking apologize for it."

"That's not fair, Zed. He's my brother. Wouldn't you give Hattie the benefit of the doubt if someone said something like that about her?"

I move to stand, then sit back down. How does one move when their insides are being ripped apart? "Not if it was coming from my child."

"He's my brother."

"And I'm your daughter!" I smack a hand against my chest. "Your flesh and fucking blood!"

His eyes dart around at our audience. "Keep your voice down. Please."

A bitter chuckle escapes from between my trembling lips. "Since when are you shy about causing a scene?"

"Zed, please."

"I don't care how fucking sorry you are. You're not sorry enough, and you're not sorry about the right fucking thing."

"Calm down. We can talk about this." Now he wants to act like a grown up, someone in control of a situation. You're not in control of me, buddy. Never again.

"What are we going to talk about, *Dad*? The fact that you didn't see the monster living under your own roof, or that you didn't believe the warnings given because they came from a little girl?" My eyes blur from tears I refuse to let fall, making his image shimmer before me.

His head is in his hands. "This is not how I thought this would go." He's looking at me again. Can he see how utterly befuddled I am? How furious.

"How did you think it would go? Did you think I would be happy to see you? Did you think Hattie has somehow managed to make me forget you chose your brother over your children? Did you think I would forget that you let him keep coming at me?"

Head snapping up, he says, "I didn't."

"You knew what he was."

"He said—"

"What?" I lean forward again, curling my hands in the hem of my shirt to keep from striking him. "What did that motherfucker say that you would believe over your own daughter? Over *his* own daughter."

"Girls lie. That's what he said."

My gut seizes and breath escapes me. "And you believed him?"

"Well, you and Hattie weren't scared of him. And that wife of his was always a liar. Always one for the dramatics."

"What about today? I just told you he molested me. What about that? This is your little girl telling you that your brother is everything Angel and Aunt Darla said. What about now?"

Shoulders slumped, mouth downturned, and tears tracing

over his unshaven jaw, he asks, "How am I supposed to know the truth?"

The world won't stay still. Our table is floating, and his smug grin is floating before me, ridiculing me.

His voice is slow, morphing into something demonic. "He's my brother."

I stand, tossing the cloth napkin down on my plate. "He's a sick fuck, and you—"

"Watch it, young lady." He's standing too, all fire and fury, tears shining, finger pointing at me in warning. We're a spectacle. "My brother is a good man. He wouldn't do that. Not to me!"

His words knock me back, another twist of the fist in my gut. My legs are pulsing, fight or flight. How about fight *and* flight? I want to hurt him, wipe that confused, hurt look off his face. He's not the victim and neither is Dan.

A calm floods over me and I straighten. "You're just as bad as he is," I say, all emotion gone from my voice.

His finger stabs the table as he speaks, and his blazing eyes bore into mine. "I'm not going to hear another word against him. Now sit down and stop making a fucking scene."

I grab my bag and jerk it onto my shoulder, then lean forward, keeping my words between the two of us. "When I was ten years old your brother decided I was ready for a lover. Your brother took me into a small shed and shoved his cock into my little girl parts. *Your brother* did that. And you let him." I swipe at the rage running in rivers over my cheeks. "Your lack of belief, your lack of intervention, told him he wasn't doing anything wrong. You broke me as much as he did, and I will never forgive you for that."

His voice rises as I walk across the dining room. "Zed! Come back!" My feet continue forward. "I forgot my wallet! Zed!" *Sounds like a personal problem, asshole.*

———

The Carolina sky looks as angry as I feel; dark, heavy clouds hanging over the landscape, flashes of lightning spreading through the length of them, connecting the fury. Is it possible that I have some supernatural power, that the weather is reacting to my tumultuous feelings, mirroring the storm raging inside me?

The Bronco is parked outside The Wet Spot, windows down. I wish it had an open roof. I don't mind if it rains on me. Pour down, I don't give a shit. On the cracked dash, lined up, are three small bottles of vodka. My drink of choice before beginning this whole path for mental wellness. It's all a crock. It's funny the things you realize after you've humiliated your father in a very public place, after you've said out loud the deepest secret you ever kept. I don't think there is any help for me.

I've shut off my cell. Oliver kept calling. Trying to make sure everything went well with my dad, I'm sure. How can I tell him that nothing ever goes well with me? How do you tell your boyfriend that he's hooked his wagon to the wrong horse, that those few days of happiness are all we will have? What words does one use to tell their lover that everything is over? *I'm a lost cause. Go.*

The bottle of *Grey Goose* is in my hand, its little glass body familiar, welcoming. *"Go ahead,"* it says. *"Drink me. I can make you forget."*

At least GG never lies to me. Twisting the cap off, I toss it in the floorboard and bring the bottle to my nose. Forget. For how long? How painful will it be when I wake up tomorrow, probably in the parking lot of The Wet Spot? I'll need more then. Maybe five bottles, or maybe I'll need to graduate to the bigger bottle. The 750. It always starts out as a little. That night it only started out as a few pills, then more, and then *why not take them all?*

I place the bottle on the dash and grab my phone. My fingers are tingling, too long in cold water or too long under a heavy body. *Be a good girl, Gracie, and I'll let you go.* He'll never let me go. Now is the moment I can let him win or I can save myself. I know there's only one choice, and it's the hardest one I'll ever make.

Turning my cell back on, I dial the only number I can; the only person who can help me now.

After several rings, she answers. "I need you," I say through my sobs.

Her voice is panicked. "Where are you?"

"The Wet Spot." The line goes dead after a promise that she is coming, and I pick up the open bottle. *Please hurry.*

TWENTY-THREE

The rain has held out, but the atmosphere is heavy, charged. Everything is pressing down, taking my breath, making my chest ache. I'm winded and twisted up, a squeezed-out dishrag. The scene from lunch keeps playing on a loop; me telling my father the truth and him calling me a liar, him taking my uncle's side. Again. I should have expected it. After all, Dan told me plenty of times no one would believe me. They didn't believe Angel. I didn't believe Angel. Heated arguments between us would end with me threatening to tell and him explaining ever-so-callously why I wouldn't. *Who's going to believe you, darlin'?* Clearly not my father.

Cami flies into the parking lot sending a plume of dust and gravel in her wake. She's out and beside me before my feet are fully on the ground. Closing the door, I lean my head against the frame. She came. After everything I've put her through, she showed up. It isn't unexpected. After all, she showed up after I swallowed a bottle of pills in record time. After six years and without question, she was there.

Turning, I look at her, my puffy eyes meeting hers, and choke out, "Mom," before crumbling.

Her arms are around me as I fall, guiding me to the ground,

her voice soft and reassuring, "It's okay, baby. I'm here." I knew she would be. This woman who won't get out from under the heaviness of my need, my desperation, not even when I threaten to bring her down with me. That's her story, though, isn't it? Hold all of Zedwynne's shit, no matter how heavy. My very own Atlas.

Her hands are on my face. Checking me for injuries just like when I was a kid. *They're on the inside.* "What happened?"

Pulling in a deep, unsteady breath, I say, "I had lunch with Dad."

"What did he do?" Her tone is an accusation.

"He blamed me." I swipe at my cheeks. "Not directly, but I think he thinks it's my fault. And Angel's. Oh god, I was such an asshole to her."

"It's okay." She's shushing me, her hands smoothing my hair, stroking my face. "It's okay."

I look at her, swiping the tears away from my eyes. "He believed Uncle Dan. Over *me.*"

"You told him?"

Nodding, I look at her, chest aching and eyes leaking. "He kept saying his brother wouldn't do that to him. How could he not believe me?"

Her body slackens against me. "I wish I knew."

"Do you think he knew it all along? Is that why you left him?"

Head shaking furiously, she says, "No. I couldn't look at him if I thought that. Your dad and Dan had a tough upbringing."

"Yeah, but—"

"I'm not making excuses. Especially not for that bastard Dan. It just explains why your dad is so easily manipulated by him. Your grandparents were different people before you were born."

"Did someone hurt them? Dad and Dan?"

Sighing, she shrugs. "He didn't talk about his childhood much. He's a pretty guarded guy. Besides, those are his stories to tell, not mine."

"I'm never speaking to the asshole again."

"I can understand why you wouldn't want to." Giving me a quick squeeze, she adds, "But I hope one day he'll come around."

All fury spent; I sag against her. "He said Hank only offered me shift lead because of you."

"He offered you a promotion? That's great!"

I pull back, looking at her. If she lies, I'll know. "You didn't know?"

She shakes her head. "We don't talk much anymore. I wasn't very kind to him after me and your daddy broke up. I knew how he felt about me, and I used him. It broke his heart when I got married."

"Why did you do it, marry Duke instead of Hank?"

She shrugs. "It's hard to explain. I love Hank, but it's not in a way that could keep us going."

"I don't know what you mean."

"Me either." Another shrug. "All I know is that he didn't give me that feeling. He made me feel safe and cared for, but I didn't *want* him." She falls back a little. "I don't think I'm making sense."

I think of Oliver. "I get it."

Fat drops of rain begin to splat against the roof of the Bronco. We stand and crawl inside just before the bottom drops out.

She scans the bottles lined up on the dash, then turns her eyes on me. "Oh, Zed," she says, grabbing the open bottle and pouring it out the window.

"I didn't drink any." My words are almost muffled by the pounding of the rain around us.

She looks at me, eyes shadowed with suspicion. "Really?"

"I wanted to. I don't think I've wanted many things more than I wanted to feel the burn of that vodka down my throat, but I didn't drink it. I called you."

"Not that I'm not over the moon about it, but why did you call me? I thought you would call your sister."

I shrug. "I guess I just needed my mom."

She is her own personal rainstorm, tears falling with the same ferocity as the drops of rain pounding the old tin can we currently occupy. I can give this to her. She's given me so much.

"Thank you for picking me up from the hospital. And for putting up with my shit."

She nods, unable to form words through her heavy sobs.

"I've been angry with you for a long time." I turn my body toward her. "I thought the baby would save us. Me and him. I thought we belonged together because that's what he told me." I lay my head against the headrest. "I thought you stole it all from me."

Taking a deep breath, she says, "When you told me about it... about the baby..." She leans back, her hand going to her forehead for a moment. "I hated him. I hated *me*." She closes her mouth against the quiver, taking another moment. "How could I not know what was going on with you? How could *we* not know?"

Stamping down the bitter bitch inside agreeing with her, I say, "You couldn't have known."

She smiles. "Thank you for saying that, but I should have sensed something was off. Just like your father should have. We should have noticed you withdrawing, should have noticed the way he looked at you. I should have noticed how often he asked to watch you girls, how often he volunteered to when your dad was working." Pressing her hand to her throat, she adds, "He never wanted your dad to call a babysitter." A sob erupts and she buries her face in her hands. "So stupid."

She presses a shaking hand against my cheek. "I'm sorry I wasn't a better mother." After another deep breath, she adds, "And I'm sorry I made you get an abortion. I shouldn't have done that. I was scared and angry. Too worried about what the rest of the world would think about you and us. I hope one day you will be able to forgive me."

She drops her hands to mine and I curl my fingers with hers. I have to hold tight, desperately needing to stay here with her, in a place where I don't hate her, and I don't blame her for everything she did wrong with the best intentions. A part of me forgives her, the little bit of me who needs a mom, but there is more of me unwilling to forget. I've crossed something with her and we're moving in the right direction, but there are still miles to go before we're okay.

THE SUN HAS ALMOST SET by the time I make it home. Pulling my car to a stop in front of the dingy little trailer I'm coming to love, I pull my phone out and stare at the screen. Twenty-seven missed calls, some from Hattie and some from Oliver. They've been trying to reach me since lunch, though Oliver gave up sometime mid-afternoon, sending me a text saying simply, *call me when you're ready.* It's nice that he's capable of giving me space. Hattie, on the other hand, has been steadily texting and calling since I left our father sitting alone in a packed dining room. I hope he was humiliated.

Dialing her number, I wait for her frantic answer, but her voice is clipped and sharp, "I'm glad you're not dead."

"I'm sorry I didn't answer earlier. I wasn't in the best place."

"Mom just told me."

"She called you?"

"She's on the other line now. Hold on." There's a lengthy pause before she returns. "I'm back."

"Hattie—"

"Why did you call her?" The hurt in her voice is palpable.

"Um." Slumping in my seat, I press a hand to my forehead. "What?"

"Mom. Why did you call Mom? She said you were super upset." Her voice softens. "I thought... after everything..." There's a pause and a sniffle. "I thought you would call me."

There are times when I think the human body grows too tired. I've seen it with the elderly; long lives lived with too many troubles faced. *This old heart is tired*, I heard a friend's grandmother say. A week later she was gone. Exhaustion of that magnitude is heavy. It weighs you down and lulls you to eternal sleep. I felt this way one night not long ago. In response, I swallowed a bottle of pills I'd lifted from somewhere I can't even remember. It's the responsibility, I think. This idea that I have to answer for my shit and everyone else's, that I play some major role in their happiness. I could blame my uncle, the way he got into my head and made me believe things that weren't real. I could, but I was like this before him. Maybe this flaw in me is what made it easy for him to choose me.

"Zed?" She's a kid again, her voice small, the hurt obvious. My arms ache to console her.

"Hattie, I'm sorry."

After a sniffle, she says, "You don't need to be sorry. It's stupid for me to be upset."

"It isn't."

"It is. Stupid hormones. I should be stoked you called Mom." Another sniffle. "She was thrilled you called her. I wanted to be happy too, but..." There's a sputter, and then, "I guess I just wanted it to be me."

Pulling the keys from the ignition, I push the door open and head inside. Dropping my bag by the door, I collapse on the sofa, pressing a hand to my throbbing head. "I didn't want to stress you out. I was trying to be a good sister."

"Thank you." She's quiet again before asking, "Do you want to tell me what happened with Dad?"

Dropping my hand, I fix my eyes on the ceiling above. "He didn't believe me."

"About what?"

There are no tiles to count here. Just me, Hattie's questions, and popcorn. "It doesn't matter. Not anymore."

"It must matter. I mean, you abandoned him because of it."

"Is that what he told you?" I sit up, leaning forward, elbows on my knees. "He's great at playing the fucking victim, isn't he?"

"Zed, please tell me what happened. Why did you leave him sitting there and what happened to make you call Mom?"

"I seriously don't want to talk about it, Hattie. Not tonight. Maybe not ever. I'm so fucking tired of talking about it."

"How? You never talk about it. Whatever *it* is."

I switch ears, flexing my fingers to wake them up. "Did he call you or something?"

"Yes. I had to pay for the lunch you didn't eat."

"You didn't have to pay for it, Hattie. He's not your responsibility any more than he's mine."

"You didn't hear him. He was so embarrassed."

I roll my eyes. "He laid it on thick, sounds like."

There's a shuffling on the other end. "Why do you hate him? God!" The sharpness of her tone is a surprise, especially since she began this conversation sounding like an injured child.

Standing, I go to my bag and dig through for my pack of smokes. Lighting up, I take a long drag and drop down on the floor. What am I supposed to say to this? I don't hate him. Maybe. Hell, I don't know. The one thing I'm sure of is that the sight of him makes my stomach turn and my skin crawl. That doesn't seem like an appropriate response to seeing one's father.

She's insistent. "Well?"

"I don't hate him," I say. "I just don't like him."

"But you won't tell me why."

"Not tonight."

She falls silent again, her breathing the only sign that she's still on the other end. I don't know how this conversation has gone from her being heartbroken over not being my emergency call when I was on the verge of collapse to her being miffed that our father felt a bit uncomfortable in public after my departure. I could blame the pregnancy, but this is deeper than that.

"Hattie, are you okay?"

"Yeah."

"I promise I'll tell you everything when I'm ready. I just...can't right now."

"I understand."

"Do you want to have lunch tomorrow?" I'm grasping, but

the thought that my little sister might turn her back on me now is too much. It isn't fair to her, but she's my life raft.

"Sure. I'll pick you up."

"Can we meet? I have group."

"I'll text you."

"Okay."

With a good night, our call ends. Standing, I crush the remainder of my cigarette out, and head for the bedroom. It's time to put this shitty day to rest.

Twenty-Four

The interior of the trailer is still a bit too warm from the oven. The small window units Hank installed are able to compete with the outside temperature alone, but their strain is evident when they're forced to deal with the outside environment and spiked temperatures inside. Oliver doesn't seem to notice, though. He's been fairly quiet since his arrival. At first, I thought he was angry about my failure to answer his calls two days ago, but he's assured me over and over that he wasn't and isn't. Still, I think he's a little upset that he wasn't included in getting my head back on straight. Maybe he wants to fix me. He should probably work on himself first, though.

He keeps looking at me over the baked chicken and mashed potatoes I've prepared with a smile that I can't quite understand. Still not one hundred percent past the incident with my father, I can't be very good company right now. I especially wasn't last night when Oliver asked to come over and I denied him. Before coming back here, to this town, before my hospital stay, I wouldn't have. I've always been desperate to make men happy. In the past, I would've said yes and would've done whatever he wanted last night just to make sure he stayed happy, to make sure he wouldn't leave me. I guess it's kind of cool that I chose me for once.

I shift, uncomfortable under his gaze, "What?"

He smiles, the grease from the chicken glistening on his lips. "I didn't know you could cook."

"It's baked chicken and instant mashed potatoes."

His laugh is sweet, dreamy. "I appreciate you cooking is what I mean."

"Oh."

He takes a bite of the chicken, washing it down with the generic soda I picked up on the way home. "I'm glad you let me come over. I've been worried."

"Why?"

"I don't know. We just haven't spent much time together since you met with your dad."

I avert my gaze. He's right, I've been distant, avoiding him. Not him, exactly, but contact with anyone beyond my work shift. Even Deidre has noticed. If her numerous text messages are any indication, that is.

"How're you feeling?" he asks.

"Fine. My dad has called me zero times, but he's ringing Hattie's phone off the hook. Apparently, he's very angry with me." I take a sip from my glass. "It's laughable."

"Did he get stuck washing dishes?"

"I wish. He called Hattie and she paid the bill over the phone."

"Man."

"Yeah."

"She should've made him suffer."

"That's not Hattie." The chicken is good, if I do say so myself. Only slightly dry. Exactly what I would expect from a beginner. I definitely fit that profile.

I haven't told him about me and my mom. I don't know the rules here. Am I supposed to share everything? Is that what couples do? Of course, telling him will only open the door for more questions. I don't know if I'm ready for them.

I take another sip of soda. The chicken is a little drier than I thought. "Did you talk to Ada?"

He looks confused for a moment and then nods. "Oh yeah. Poor kid. She's sweet, though."

"I guess Ada is the reason Jessica was being such an ass."

"Not at all. She doesn't like Ada either. We have...history."

I place my fork on the plate, looking up at him. "No way. Jessica?" My hackles are up. He's made his hookups with women no secret. At the time I didn't care, but that was before I'd given myself to him, before he'd promised not to hurt me.

"Yeah. When I first came back here."

"Was she working at Jubilee's?" He nods and my throat tightens. Taking another sip of my drink, I half-laugh. "I think I've been had."

He laughs.

My words may sound as though this isn't bothering me, but the uncomfortable rock settling firmly in my stomach says otherwise. *This shouldn't be a big deal. He's a grown man, he's been with other women before.* Even as my logic tries to talk me down, I feel myself gearing up for a fight.

"Seriously," I say. "Do you conquer every girl who works there?"

"Not anymore."

His smiling indicates he's being funny, but this admission, no matter how flippant, is coming across like I'm a conquest. Another meal served to the hungry wolves. Maybe it's the week I've had, but I'm not nearly as amused as he is.

"Do you and Dante have a little bedpost hidden in the back for each of you? Do you tick the girls off as you bed them?"

He sputters, eyes wide. "What are you talking about?"

"You just said *not anymore,* which makes me think that you fuck every girl who works at Jubilee's, which makes me think that I'm just another notch."

"You got all that from me saying two words?"

"How many women working at Jubilee's right now have you fucked?"

He holds up his fingers. "Two."

I shift in my chair, bouncing my legs to quiet the busy currents coursing through them. "And before that?"

He drops his fork and leans back. "I was a newly single guy, Zed. I partied a lot. I fucked a lot of girls."

"How many from Jubilee's?"

"Why does it matter who I was with before we got together?" *Why does it matter at all?*

"It doesn't," I say, but it most certainly does. I told him not to hurt me. He promised he wouldn't, but how can I be sure he won't if his habit is to bed every woman who works at Jubilee's and leaves them, why should I think he'll do me any different? How do I know that he doesn't befriend every woman Hank hires with the intention of fucking them? *What are you doing? Why are you picking a fight? Stop it!*

We finish dinner in silence, and I wash the dishes afterward. He seems to think the tremor has passed, that his *not anymore* has been received as some sort of declaration of love. His arms around me while I'm washing dishes makes it appear that way. I close my eyes, hands remaining in the water as his slide under my shirt and up to my breasts, toying with me until I forget the nagging and turn to him, helping him free me from my pants, my mouth covering his as he lifts me and pushes inside of me.

As we lay on my bed, bodies gleaming from the sweat of our endeavors, I remember his words and the glimmer of pride in his eyes as he admitted to taking every girl at Jubilee's to bed. I remember his soft smile as he claimed, while sliding into me for the second time tonight, to have retired his bedpost. No more notches. *Only you, baby.* How many times have I heard that before? I'm sick of being the girl who gets fucked.

Straddling him, I begin moving back and forth until he

hardens beneath me. He's smiling. The cat that ate the rat. "I don't think this will last long," I say.

He smiles, his eyes only half open. "Probably not. I'm barely conscious."

"I mean us." I take him inside of me and lace my fingers with his.

He's alarmed and intoxicated by my sex at the same time, eyes wide and brows knitted together. "What do you mean?" A small groan escapes him as I pick up the pace.

"I think you're going to hurt me. That you're going to..." I close my eyes, reveling in the feel of him. "That you're going to fuck me until you're tired of me." *Just like everyone else.*

"Stop talking." His eyes are closed.

"No." His eyes snap open. "I'm tired of men telling me what to do." I cover his mouth with mine and quicken my pace. "I'm tired of assholes expecting me to be happy with what they want to give. I'm done with that. When you finish, I want you to leave."

"What?"

He's grasping my hips, trying to push me away, but I clench tighter, riding him until the waves of his reluctant passion give way and he is thrusting with me. He digs his hands into my hips as he crests.

I stare down at him.

He's slack-jawed and confused. "What the hell just happened, Zed?"

"I won't let you hurt me, Oliver. I've been hurt enough." I move off of him to sit on the edge of the bed. "Leave."

Scrambling, he's on the floor in front of me. "I'm not going to hurt you. How could I?" His hands are pulling at me, trying to get me to look at him, but I can't. Not right now. "Please listen."

"I was stupid to give in to you. Especially after finding out that you went to an underage girl after I wouldn't have sex with you."

"I didn't go to her. I didn't *fuck her*. She's..."

"What? Not old enough? Don't worry, she will be soon enough."

His hands are on my face, cupping my hardened jawline. "I won't let you do this."

"Kick you out? It's my house, buddy. If you don't get out, I'm sure Hank will put you out. In more ways than one."

He stands up, pacing the room. "Goddammit!" He's back on the floor in front of me. "You don't want me to hurt you but you're going to rip my fucking heart out right here?" He stands. "I shared everything with you. Gave you everything. I thought..." he drops on the bed beside me, head in his hands, "I thought if anyone could understand the pain of this life it would be you."

In the kitchen my phone rings, the sound shrill and harsh against the quiet in the house. Without hesitation, I leave Oliver sitting on the bed and go to answer. No one calls with good news at this hour.

Hattie's name glows in the dark.

"What's wrong?"

Her voice is clipped. "Heading to the hospital. Get there."

Rushing into my room, I flip the light on and begin to dress quickly. I hope I don't need a bra.

Oliver stands up. "What's going on?"

"Hattie's in labor." I look at him. "Don't just stand there. Get dressed."

I LEAVE him in the family waiting room and head to Hattie's room with my mom. She's staring at me, eyes full of questions. I know she's worried that I have a man with me, that I'm about to fall down the rabbit hole. I don't have the heart to tell her I've fallen and am lying broken at the bottom.

Hattie is hooked up to machines that fill the room with the fluttering pitter pat of her little darling's heart. She smiles when we enter the room, though her eyes are filled with panic.

"Hey," she breathes.

We're both by her side. Mom holding her hand and me her shoulder.

"How are you?" I ask. "Are you in much pain?"

"How far apart are you?" Mom asks.

"I'm fine. Only when the contractions come. They're at five minutes."

The man on the other side of her bed, the man I vaguely recognize as J.C. Leonard, speaks up, "They said she's at a seven."

"Not bad," Mom says. "Shouldn't be long now."

I look at my little sister and her eyes meet mine. "I'm sorry about the other night."

"Don't you worry about that now," Mom says, patting her hand.

She looks at our mother. "I'm a grown woman about to bring another life into this world. I'll worry about what I want to when I want to."

Cami's cheeks color. "I just don't want you to worry."

Hattie smiles. "I know. I love you for that."

The words slide over her tongue effortlessly. I wonder if that will ever happen for me.

Mom smiles. "I talked to your Aunt Darla. Angel is having contractions too."

"I hope not," I say. "She's too early."

Hattie removes her hand from our mother's grasp and grabs mine. "I'm glad you're here."

"Like I would miss this."

She smiles, but it seems a bit weak.

"Are you okay?"

"Yeah." She touches my face. "Just tired. I got an epidural."

My clenched chest loosens. No wonder she's tired. I smile, pushing her hair back from her face. "Rest then. She'll wake you up when it's show time."

She nods and her grip tightens on my hand, reassuring, loving. "I'm so proud of you."

I look to our mother who is running an anxious hand up and

down the pink sheet covering her youngest child. She smiles at me, her eyes glistening, and I smile in return. Maybe it's the promise of new life that's making me swell just now. I don't care. I'm just over the moon to be feeling something other than anger.

TWENTY-FIVE

It's amazing how a moment so beautiful, so full of hope can turn into something dangerous and terrifying in an instant. Mom and I are seated in the waiting room, she's holding onto me, her palms sweaty and cold. They mimic my insides.

Hattie delivered a beautiful little girl, a delicate little angel that J.C. held, proud tears of love streaming down his face. My heart swelled at the sight of him holding his princess. Mom and I moved to him, each of us gazing down upon the next generation of woman in our family. This girl will be safe, she will be fiercely protected, and she will not become the plaything of grown men until she makes the decision to do so. Us, us three, were so involved with this tiny bundle of perfection we didn't notice the increasing pace of activity behind us, the whirl of nurses as they rushed to the aid of the doctor.

Hemorrhaging. The word registered in my mind like a sucker punch, knocking me out of my euphoria. I turned, the intention being to return to my sister's side, but my legs were locked in place. The deathly figure on the bed was not my sister. Certainly, this woman resembled her, but the ashen tone of her skin was nothing like the vibrant hue of Hattie's. My eyes followed the length of her; her deflated abdomen, her relaxed knees (still open as if to push), and then to the blood pouring out in waves from beneath the coverlet.

The lock released and I jutted forward, stopped by a nurse with more strength than her tiny frame promised. "We're clearing the room," she said.

"Hattie!" I clawed at her, thinking I could make the air become something tangible, something I could climb like a spider to get to my little sister whose eyes were closed, and whose arm was dangling over the side of the bed.

"You have to go," the nurse was saying. It wasn't until the arms of my mother were around me, dragging me from the room, that I relented.

I DON'T KNOW how long we've been sitting here, my mother holding tight to me. Oliver is napping beside us, his chest moving slowly up and down. I wonder what he's dreaming of. Is he dreaming at all?

My voice is low, exhausted. "How long does this take?"

Mom shrugs. "I don't know." She looks to the door. "But I wish they would let us know something." A sob escapes her, and she slaps her free hand over her mouth. *You can't shove fear back in, Mom.* She taps her lips, maybe a warning for them to behave. "I just wish they would tell us *something*."

"Me too."

WE'RE LYING in the grass, crickets and frogs doing their best impression of *West Side Story* in the distance. I've never seen the movie, but I know it's a musical and I know it involves rival gangs singing back and forth at one another. Their chorus compliments the balminess of the evening.

Hattie is laughing, her arms outstretched toward the fireflies above us. "I love how they make the sky light up," she says in her little girl voice. "I wish we could light up like that."

I look over at her, me a jaded adult and she in her child form. "You do." I take her tiny hand in mine, pressing it to my lips. "And you have the brightest light of all."

MOM IS SHAKING ME. I see her in flashes as I pull away from the summer night with Hattie. Her eyes are puffy and raw, but she's smiling. I sit up, disoriented until I see J.C., Mom, and Oliver, and the drab wallpaper surrounding us.

Straightening, I jump up, ignoring the ache in my lower back. "What happened? Is she okay?"

Mom is nodding. "She's stabilized."

"Can we see her?"

J.C. steps forward. "Not right now. They've stopped the bleeding, but she isn't out of the woods yet. They need to run some tests."

I step toward the door, but his hand is up to stop me. "I want to see her. I *need* to see her."

His voice is kind but stern. "Not right now, Zedwynne."

The use of my formal name is sobering. I realize this is the first time I've spoken to J.C. since I was a child. He's more formidable than I remember, but I suspect that has something to do with how much he loves his wife.

I nod. He turns to leave, but I stop him. "J.C." He turns and I embrace him. It's brief and awkward. "Thank you for taking care of her."

He's staring at me as if he thinks I'm high but nods. Without another word, he turns and exits the room.

I turn to my mother and Oliver who are staring at me as if I am a pod person, someone possessed by another. "What?"

They shake their heads, and my mom says, "Nothing," then smiles. "Would you both care for some lunch?"

"Is it that late?" He's digging in his jeans, I presume, for his phone. "I have to be at Jubilee's by one for my shift."

Mom looks at her watch. "You'd better get going then. Zed,

do you work today?" I shake my head. "Do you want some lunch? I can drop you by your house and Oliver..." She looks at him. "It is Oliver, right?"

Heat rushes to my cheeks. "Sorry. Yes. Mom, Oliver. Oliver, Camille."

"Nice to meet you, ma'am."

She wears a playful grin. "And you as well."

Oliver is looking at me. I hand him the keys and he asks, "Can you walk me down?"

I look at Mom and she nods. "I'll wait for you in the main lobby downstairs."

HE'S quiet in the elevator, but his arm is around me. I ease into him, enjoying the feel of this moment. It isn't demanding or possessive, it's soft and genuine. There's a lot we've left unsaid. I'm all twisted up inside, nerves jangling and legs jumping. The climb is slow, like one of those days when the hours crawl past and you're sure there's something you should do but have no inkling what it is. This lift is giving me time, but I have no idea what to do with it. When we walk to the parking garage, he remains quiet, creating a divide between us. Does he want me to speak first? Is he trying to formulate what he'll say when the time is right? *Is he going to break up with me? Do I want him to?*

"She's finicky," I say when we reach the Bronco.

"Like her owner." He's smiling.

"We're just nursing old battle wounds."

He smiles, but there's no joy in it. His gaze shifts toward the hospital. "I don't like what you did, Zed." He looks down and puts his hand on the back of his head for a second before saying, "I don't like the way it made me feel." When his eyes meet mine, my heart breaks. "I didn't deserve it. I *don't* deserve it."

My gut is twisting. "I know."

"I know you do. I know you know because you are the one

who told me I didn't deserve it. Before." He looks down again. "Before I fucked it up."

"How did you fuck it up?"

"I shouldn't have come to your house that night. I shouldn't have come onto you. I should've dealt with my shit like you said, but I made it worse. I knew you didn't want to be with me or anyone else. I should have respected that."

"We both made the decision to do this, Oliver. You don't get to take all the blame."

"You were putting it on me last night."

My heart has stopped beating, I'm sure it has. "You're right," I say, dropping my head. "I was."

He pulls the door open. "I close tonight. I'll bring your truck straight home and I'll leave the keys under your door." Even as he's devastating me, he's being kind. Any other asshole would just leave the keys in the ignition. If he brought the damn car back at all.

I drag him away from the door, wrapping my arms around his waist and burying my face in his chest. "I'm sorry. Please don't leave me."

He tosses the keys on the seat and grabs my face. His cheeks are saturated by the rivers flowing over them. *He's breaking up with me.* "I'll be here when you're ready. When we're both ready."

"You're dumping me."

"I'm waiting."

No, he's dumping me. Just like everyone else. Just like Dan when I got knocked up. Just like Barry Overman, and Montana, and all the others. Rage boils inside me, heating me up as it rushes through my veins.

I jerk away from him. "Fuck you."

He's stunned. "What?"

"This is what I wanted, right?" I lean past him and grab the keys.

"Zed, let's talk about this." He's trying to pull me back to him, but I'm too far away, standing now at the back of the truck.

"You got what you wanted. Another notch in that bedpost. Now you and Dante can sit out back and you can tell him how I smell, how I taste."

"Dammit, Zed, it's not like that. Why won't you ever fucking listen!"

I put my hand up to stop his forward movement. "It's always been like that, Oliver. Why should you be any different?" I shove the keys into my pocket. "No hard feelings."

"You're so fucking hot and cold."

"You have no idea what I'm like."

He slams the door. "I know what you did last night was to hurt me before I had the chance to hurt you."

I rush toward him and jab my finger into his chest. "Fuck you!"

He's unaffected, undeterred. "And now, because you've had time to think it over and decide that maybe I'm not the fucking asshole you thought I was last night, that maybe, just maybe, you overreacted, you're angry that I think we should slow down?"

We're close now, noses almost touching. "I didn't want to start this in the first place. I wanted you to leave me alone, but you kept at me. You kissed me at Jubilee's, in front of Dante, and then you showed up at my house! I asked you not to hurt me, but you did it anyway."

His arms shoot out wild and I take a step back. "I said I'm sorry!" Hands on his head, he looks at me. "I shouldn't have gone after you. I should have left you alone." His brow creases and his shoulders drop. "But I didn't hurt you, Zed. I wouldn't. But you can't hear that because all you know is that I fucked people before we were together and one or two of them worked at Jubilee's, so now I must just fuck everybody who works there regardless of whether I've ever looked at them twice." He's shaking his head, looking down at the concrete of the parking deck as if its surface holds some sort of answer. "You've got a skewed sense of reality."

"Really? You didn't admit to fucking every girl at Jubilee's?"

He's looking at me again. He's giving up and I can't blame

him. "I have had relationships with several women who work, or have worked, at the diner, but that's none of your business, *and* it has nothing to do with us!"

I step away and then return, seething. "It has everything to do with us, Oliver. I told you what happened to me. You said you wouldn't do me like that."

His hands dart out to the heavens. "I didn't!" His hands are on my shoulders. "I'm sorry, Zed. I'm sorry I pushed when you asked me not to. I'm sorry I care for you and that terrifies you. But you did this. You wrecked this. I shouldn't have started it, but you damn sure shouldn't have tried to finish it like you did."

I shove him back. "Asshole!"

He's shaking his head, swiping at the tears that have escaped their glassy prison. "No, Zed, you're the asshole. You did to me exactly what you assumed I would do to you. You think all men are bastards because a handful have taken advantage of you and treated you like shit? I've got news for you; women can be bastards too." He claps his hand to the back of his neck. "I may never be okay with how you made me feel last night." His tortured glare pushes me back. "I just need some time."

"Away from me."

"Yes."

"Oliver." I want to reach out, but I always beg them to stay. I shouldn't have to beg. He knew I was messed up. I warned him.

He's already started his descent into the darkness of the garage. "I have to go."

I jump behind the wheel and shove my keys into the ignition. This can't keep happening to me. They can't keep doing this to me. As he disappears into the depths of the deck, I lay my head against the steering wheel, all anger and fire replaced with emptiness. Images of last night play in the darkness he's left behind, his pleas for me to stop serving as the soundtrack. All this time the therapist has been trying to get me to see that I am the victim, but I'm just like them. I take what I want from who I want without a thought, not giving two shits how it might affect other people.

MOM IS WAITING for me by the sliding glass doors that lead into the lobby when I finally return from the parking garage, her brow furrowed with worry. "That took a while," she says. "Did he get off okay?"

I take a deep breath. "Yeah. I won't need that ride after all. He's getting another way to work."

"Are you all right?"

"Yeah," I say averting my gaze.

I can tell by the way she says, *okay* she doesn't believe me. I'm glad she knows not to ask. Maybe one day I'll tell her, but the loss of yet another man from my life hardly seems worth mentioning anymore.

Twenty-Six

Hank has given me time off from the diner so I can be with Hattie at the hospital since Mom and J.C. can't miss work. It's the least I can do for my little sister. She's coming along, but after two days is still weak from the amount of blood lost during delivery. She's sitting up when I arrive, poking at her scrambled eggs with curiosity.

"How do they even look like eggs?" She asks as I pull my chair close to the bed.

"No idea. I guess the same way those meals in Japan come out resembling food."

She scrunches her nose. "Those things are gross."

"Eh. They're probably not that bad." I round the bed, looking down at the plastic walled bassinet positioned for Hattie to see inside. "She looks happy today." I hook my pinky finger in the infant's tiny hand, happy when she closes her fingers around it. I know it's just reflexes, the sully nurse told me that, but I like to think she knows me already.

"Did you decide on a name yet?"

Hattie is smiling at me. "I love the way you look at her."

I can't hide my delight. "Don't try to change the subject. Did you come up with a name?"

She lays back, groaning. "No! We thought we had it all figured out, but when she got here it just didn't fit. I don't know what her name is yet. And the insolent little thing won't tell me." She crosses her arms over her swollen breasts. "I think she hates me."

I laugh. "What?"

"Let's look at the evidence. She tried to kill me, and she refuses to tell me her name. Hates me."

Retracting my finger from the infant, I move over to my chair and sit down, grabbing Hattie's hand. "She doesn't hate you. She's a baby. They don't hate anyone." She expels a putter of laughter. "Have you held her much?"

She shakes her head, her eyes going glassy. "I'm afraid to."

"Why?"

"What if she *does* hate me? I've seen what a daughter hating her mother can do. I don't want that."

"Hattie, stop." I stand and return to the baby's side. Lifting her, I nuzzle the soft pink skin, whispering, "Auntie Zed loves you," before going around the bed with her. My stomach only tightens a little as I place her into her mother's arms. I linger, my eyes meeting Hattie's. "She is a blank slate. The only thing she knows in this life is you. Your voice surrounded her for nine months. You provided her food and comfort. The only thing she knows is the goodness of her mother. I don't know how scared you are right now because I've never been a mom." My heart pinches. *Almost.* "But I don't think you have anything to be afraid of."

Hattie looks at her daughter and then to me. "What if I hurt her? What if I let someone hurt her?"

My throat burns. "Never," is all I can manage.

HATTIE IS NAPPING when I slip down to the cafe off the main lobby for lunch. A chicken salad sandwich and Coke never tasted so good. I'm contemplating answering Oliver's most recent message when I hear a familiar voice behind me.

"That was a rotten thing you did to me, kid."

I turn to meet the angry eyes of my father. *Angry, imagine that.* "Yeah. Well, we seem to be very good at doing rotten things to one another in this family." I grab my trash and walk past him to the bin, aware that he's following me. "Are you here to see Hattie?"

"Yeah. I just left Dan's room. I figure two birds, one stone."

"*Uncle* Dan?"

"Yeah. They've got him in the cancer unit here." Suddenly my chicken sandwich threatens return. "I told you he was here."

"I've had more pressing things to worry about. You know, like my sister almost dying while giving birth to my niece, your granddaughter."

"I know. When J.C. called me, I was all to pieces."

"Is that why it took you three days to get here?"

He spits out a laugh. "I came the day after because J.C. told me she couldn't have visitors on the day of. Just so happens you and Cami were gone."

"Right."

"Are you heading back up? We can ride the elevator together."

My fingers ache from the grip I have on my phone. "No. I was just heading out to make a phone call." I hold up my hand to show him the evidence. "How long will you be up there, you think?"

"Not long. I have to work in a couple of hours."

I nod, then turn and leave him standing by the bin. Outside, I dig out a cigarette and plop it between my lips, lighting it and taking a deep drag. Eyes closed, I will my heart to calm, my gut to untwist. Why is it I always want to vomit when my father is in a room?

My phone pings and I'm not at all surprised to see Oliver's name again. For someone who wanted to end it, he's very communicative.

Stop texting me. You wanted it to end. It did.

Where are you?

I'm looking at his words. How did this become so absolutely fucked up? I never wanted to become involved with anyone. Not after my last relationship, the proverbial straw that landed me near death. I damn sure didn't want to become involved with him. But here I am, staring at my phone, wishing I could ask him to come and talk. Wishing we could fix what I never wanted to create in the first place.

Going into settings I select the option to block his number. I may have to see him at work, but I don't have to talk to him outside of the place. Not anymore.

Another ping comes through, and I see it is Lucinda. She's settling in as well as can be expected for a woman who will be fighting against herself for some time to come.

How's it going?

This means that she isn't doing well. I know this from the last several communications I've had from her. She's thinking about him again, considering coming back or at least telling him where she is. She doesn't get along with her sister and feels like a burden, at least that's the excuse she's using.

Hattie is still in the hospital.

Just saw my dad. Total shitshow.

LOL.

Everything okay?

Tough day, but I have an interview this afternoon, so...

That's great. Where?

Sister's company. Housekeeping.

She'll be great at that.

You're a shoo-in.

I kind of hope so. Been thinking about coming back a lot.

I toss my smoke on the ground.

That's the way these things go. I'll be here for you either way.

Thanks, Zed.

Good luck today.

I want to tell her to put her husband out of her mind, don't sabotage things just to give herself an excuse to return, but I don't want my good intentions to derail her.

You're going to knock it out of the park.

I don't even like baseball.

"SHE'S ALL YOURS, KID," my father says exiting the double doors of the hospital.

I turn, shoving my cell in the front pocket of my jeans. "Thanks."

He lights a cigarette. "I'll see you around." And then, as he's walking away, he adds, "Dan is on the third floor."

His name hits me hard in the chest, taking my breath. I don't respond to my bastard of a father. I head inside and back up to Hattie, trying like hell to regain my composure the entire way.

She's nursing the baby when I enter the room. Her nurse, a

petite woman with shocking pink hair, looks up as if she intends to usher me out, but Hattie assures her I can have entrance. She eyes me as she leaves. For the life of me I don't know why she's judging this hard. I may look heroin-chic, but at least I don't look like bubble gum exploded all over my damn head.

I plop down in the chair beside the bed. "What's her problem?"

"No idea." Hattie's voice is soft, content. "I guess you bring it out in people." She winks, then nuzzles her darling.

"How did the visit with Dad go?"

She shrugs. "Fine. He's pissed at you, though."

I laugh. "Oh yeah? Good."

"Said you practically told him to *eff* off in the lobby."

"He's not wrong."

She chuckles. "I thought as much."

I lean forward, resting my elbows on the mattress by her side. "What did you two talk about? Other than me."

"Nothing much."

I brace myself. "Did he tell you our uncle is here?"

She lays her head back, turning her head toward me. "He didn't have to. I already knew. And before you get angry, I didn't tell you because I didn't want you to stress out."

"It's okay." I smile, though it's false. Their keeping this massive secret from me is certainly not okay. "Our father made it a point to tell me. I guess he doesn't care about my stress levels. Fucking bastard."

"Zed!" She covers the exposed ear of her child. "No *eff* word around the baby."

Her horrified expression has me giggling. "Oh, but you can say pissed?"

She shrugs, "My baby, my rules."

I trace a finger over the baby's closed hand. "Don't worry, Baby Without a Name, Auntie Zed is going to teach you everything."

Hattie laughs, swatting at my hand. "Oh no she isn't."

It feels good to laugh with her. To mean it.

She switches the baby to the other breast, latching her on as if she's been doing it for ages. "Are you okay?" She looks at me. "Knowing he's here, I mean."

"No." I shrug. "But there's nothing I can do about it. And there's no way in..." I look at the baby, "H. E. double hockey sticks he's keeping me away from the two of you."

She reaches out, her hand resting gently on my cheek. "I love you, Zeddie."

My face warms at the nakedness of her declaration. "I love you too. Now," I say, looking back down at the baby, "let's talk baby names. I've always been partial to Eleanor." Her nose scrunches up. "What? We could call her Ellie."

"Absolutely not." She nuzzles the infant. "Don't worry, dumplin', Auntie Zeddie doesn't get to name you."

I lean back in the chair, laughter flowing out into the tiny room, but behind the practiced laugh and the smile, my mind is calculating just when I should pay a visit to the man who made me what I am today. Common sense says I should contact the therapist, tell her that he's in the same hospital as my sister and I'm thinking of finally confronting him, but I don't know if she'll be on board, and I don't want anything to make me second guess myself. This may be my last chance to show him what he's done to me. I can't let it slip away.

IT's good to hear Deidre's voice, strange enough as that is to say. After leaving the hospital I dialed her, hoping she wouldn't answer and I could leave a message, but somewhat delighted when she picked up. It's been such a tough week since I saw her. It might have been beneficial to go to group this week.

"I was about to send out the cavalry," she says.

I chuckle. "I didn't know you were so dramatic, D."

"So, what's going on? How's little sister?"

"Better. The baby is gorgeous."

"And how are you?"

Pausing, I consider her questions. It's easy to talk about Hattie, to report on her progress and talk about how wonderful the baby is. It's even easier to talk about my mother and the softening of my heart toward her, but three subjects I can't broach all, funnily enough, involve men: Oliver, my dad, and Uncle Dan.

"Well? You going to leave me in suspense?"

"I'm coping."

"Coping?"

"Yeah."

There's a pause from her end and then, "Any plans to confront them?"

"I'm using the avoidance method."

She laughs, the richness of it reaches through the phone and wraps around me like a duvet on a cold morning. "And how's that working out for you?"

"I don't want to talk about it."

"That's your problem, Zed. You don't ever want to talk about it. Sometimes talking is better than not."

I sigh. "I just need a little time."

She's quiet, her way of dropping a subject. No one else knows how to walk away from something, to give the space that is needed for someone to process, but Deidre does. She's perceptive, and she's unwilling to prod a dead horse.

"Have you talked to Clay?" I ask.

"Not yet. He has to do so many days before he can talk to anyone."

"That sucks."

"That's the way it is." There's a muffled sound from her end and then, "Zed, I've got to go. Let's meet for coffee once your sister gets home and settled."

"O—okay."

"If you need me before then, just call."

I open my mouth to answer, but the line is already dead. Maybe when we meet, she can tell me what that was about, though I imagine it has everything to do with whoever she's been seeing for the last few weeks. She's still claiming to be single, but it's obvious she's got something going on and I'm willing to bet it's another woman she'll leave in tears. I guess Oliver was right about something, women can be bastards too.

Twenty-Seven

I'm not exactly surprised to find Oliver's truck outside my house upon my return, but I am surprised to find that he isn't in it. *Is he inside my house?* Certainly not. I try the doorknob and it's still locked. Turning, I survey the vehicle again, and then walk across the yard to Hank's back door.

Hanna answers just as I'm considering going back to the house. "Oh. Hey."

"Is your dad home?"

She opens the door wide enough for me to enter. "Living room," she says, attention back on her phone. After a moment she looks back up. It takes a moment for her to process that I need her direction. Throwing her arm up, she points across the kitchen, "Through that door then go down the hallway. It's the door to the right after the stairs."

I nod and leave her standing there, finger already scrolling through the images on her screen. The interior looks nothing like I expected it would. It has all the charm of a Craftsman, that's for sure. I have no idea why I expected it to be cluttered. Isn't that how a widower lives? Keep the reminiscences of the former life while moving on?

Their voices meet me halfway up the hall. Oliver is here. I stop by the stairs, considering that I should probably turn around and go back to my place. Whatever they're talking about isn't my business. I haven't been invited and, considering the status of my relationship with Oliver, I'm probably not welcome, but the conversation seems easy enough, so I step up to the entrance and knock on the open door.

Both men look up simultaneously and instantly I realize my first instinct was right. I am an intruder. "S—sorry," I manage.

Hank smiles. "Zed!" He stands, coming to meet me at the door. "We were just talking about you?"

I look to Oliver, who promptly averts his eyes. "Oh yeah?"

"Yeah. Come in and sit down."

I sit on the sofa next to Oliver, staying as close to the arm as I can to keep distance between us, but I can still feel the pull of him.

Hank sits in the chair across from us. "What brings you over?"

I'm embarrassed to say now. Am I the most narcissistic person on the face of the planet? "I—um—saw Oliver's car in the drive."

He looks at me, this man who managed to wrangle me in only to cast me back out. What's that look in his eyes? Hope?

Hank nods. "I asked him to come by."

"Oh."

"How's your sister?" Hank truly is the most naive man on the face of the planet. Maybe that's why my mother couldn't be with him. One foolish man in a lifetime is more than enough.

"Good." I nod, tugging at the hem of my shirt with anxious hands. "They're keeping her until the end of the week, but things are looking much better."

I shift under Oliver's gaze. "I'm glad she's doing well," he says.

Hank slaps his hand down on his knee. "Yes. Very good news indeed." He smiles. "Well, Oliver, what do you say we let Zed in on the news?"

Oliver nods, fixing his eyes on the heavy oak coffee table before him. "Sounds good, boss man."

Hank is beaming, his chest puffed out and his eyes bright. "I'm going to semi-retire."

"Oh. Wow." I smile. "Congratulations."

"Thank you. I've been thinking about it a lot lately and I think it will be good for Hanna if I'm home more. Especially since she'll be going off to school in a couple of years. Oliver has agreed to assume all managerial duties at the diner." He puts a hand up. "But don't tell anyone yet. I'm going to make the announcement in a couple of days."

I pull an invisible zipper across my lips.

"Now," Hank says, leaning toward me. "I just need to know if you will take the shift lead position I offered you."

Oliver's eyes are on me again. I shake my head. "I—uh—I'm still thinking about it. I've been so caught up with Hattie and the baby." *And breaking up with your new manager.* "Can I let you know in a couple of days?"

Hank nods. "Of course. But don't wait too long. I'd like to get the ball rolling on this."

"Of course." I stand. "I'd better get going. Congrats again." I don't wait for them to say anything more. With urgency, I hustle out of the room and through the house. Hanna is sitting at the kitchen table on her phone.

"So, you and Oliver?" she says without looking up.

"What?" My mind is a whirlwind. I need to go.

She looks up. "I saw you." She motions toward my trailer. "You should keep your kitchen curtains closed.

"Maybe you should look in a different direction."

She shrugs. "Maybe. I didn't tell Dad, though."

"I don't think it matters whether you do or not."

"Probably not." She stands up, tucking her cell into the back pocket of her too-short shorts. "Later."

I pull the door open and head back across the lawn to my place. What the fuck was that about? Tossing my bag on the floor of the porch, I slide into the Adirondack chair and wait. He wants to talk, we'll talk.

It's half an hour later when Oliver exits Hank's house. His pause by the back door lets me know he's seen me, but he walks to his car with his head down. Ridiculous. I wait until his hand is on the handle of his door before speaking. "Hey."

He looks over, feigning surprise. "Hey."

"What's up?"

He leans against the truck, shoulder against the window. "What do you want, Zed?"

"You've been blowing up my phone asking to talk. You're here, let's talk."

He walks over to the porch so quickly I think for a moment he's charging. "You haven't responded to any of my messages, that's a clear indication that you don't want to talk."

I'm standing now, prepared for battle. "I blocked your number."

He throws his hands up.

"You were calling and texting every five minutes, Oliver. I'm trying to deal with shit and can't concentrate because you're blowing up my phone."

He gnaws at his bottom lip, a nervous habit I've come to adore. His eyes are on me. "I can't let you go," he says as if it's painful to voice. "I know I said I didn't know if I could get over that night, but you're all I've been thinking about."

I raise my eyes to the heavens. This is what I've wanted to hear. He wants me. *Needs* me. Yet, this doesn't ease my hurt and anger. My *guilt*. "That sucks for you, then, huh?"

He throws his hands up again, his aggravation bouncing off the still-humid Carolina air. "I don't know what you want, and I don't think I have the energy to find out."

My heart clenches. "Okay then." I grab my bag. "See you around."

"Wait." I turn to look at him. "I *want* to find out." He slumps. "Despite everything, I want to find out."

I cross the porch, descending the stairs to be on equal ground with him. "What I want, Oliver, is to not feel like someone's puppet. I want for someone to want all of me, my body, my heart, my fucked-up brain. I want someone to have the energy to deal with me and even when they think they can't do it anymore I want them to look at me and know I'm worth it. That's what I want."

"You are worth it, Zed."

I nod. "I'm beginning to realize that."

"Where do we go from here?"

I shrug. "I really have no fucking clue. I want you...miss you, but I don't think we're a good idea. I think you were right. We need time?" I lift my eyes to meet his. "Can we do that, though?"

His jaw tightens and releases as he considers my words.

"What I did, the other night... You're right, it was fucked up. I shouldn't have been able to do that to you. I am fucked up."

"Zed—"

I touch his chest. "But I'm getting better. I can see it and feel it. I don't want you to be stuck with the woman I am now. I don't think it will work."

He drops his gaze away from me and my heart cracks. "What do you need, Zed?"

You. "Your friendship," I choke.

He nods. "Then that's what you have."

I smile despite the fact that my heart has ceased to function, and my insides are slowly shutting down. "Thank you."

"Yeah." He steps back, putting needed distance between us. "I guess I'll see you at work then."

I nod, then turn and enter my house, closing the door between us. Leaving him there is one of the hardest things I've ever done. Inside, I turn the lock and slide to the floor, eyes closed. I won't go to him. I won't use my sex as a siren song. I won't destroy him to suit my own selfish needs. It takes everything I have to stay still as his truck fires up and begins backing down the gravel drive. *Please come back. I lied. Come back.* Grabbing my cell, I go to settings and unblock his number. Maybe he will honor my spoken wishes. I really hope he doesn't.

Twenty-Eight

Hattie is sleeping when I arrive, and Mom is reading by the baby's bassinet. Pausing at the door, just before the moment of discovery I watch the older version of myself, finger hooked in the tiny hand of her grandchild, her voice softly filling the room with fairy stories. She might have done the same thing for my child if I'd disobeyed her request and carried to term. I know she would have loved it despite its origin story. No one can blame a child for the circumstances in which they are created. She catches me staring, starts and then smiles. Pushing away from the door, I cross to her.

I motion to Hattie. "How is she?"

Keeping her voice low, she says, "She's just tired. The doctor said she's doing well, and they'll release her tomorrow as long as this afternoon's tests look good."

"Does she know yet?"

Mom nods. "She didn't drift off until after they left."

I look at my little sister, so much smaller now than she has been for months, then gently trace the baby's cheek with my finger. "How is this one?"

"Perfect."

"Can't argue with that," I say, unable to keep the smile from my face. "Anything to worry about with Hattie's tests?"

"No." Her eyes are soft, happy. We're in a good place, I think. At least I am to a point where I can deal with my anger about her past decisions. "I think she's tired because the baby slept in here with her last night." She gives a contented chuckle. "She's just trying to get a little shuteye before this one needs to eat again."

I look at Hattie. "Do you think she'll be okay?"

She grabs my hand, squeezing gently. "Yeah. She's a fighter. Like her sister."

I squeeze back and then pull away. "How's Duke? I bet he's chomping at the bits to see this baby."

Laughing softly, she nods. "He can't wait until they get home."

"I bet." I look to where Hattie is sleeping. Not because I'm worried about her—she's looking well, considering—but because I need to steady myself before I speak again. Today is the last time I'll have a chance to do what Angel suggested. *Let that bastard see what he's done to you.* I won't make a special trip for him. He'll get nothing special from me ever again.

Turning back to my mom, I pat her shoulder. "I'll be back."

"Where are you off to? You just got here."

"I'm going to the cancer ward."

She shudders. "Don't call it that, please."

"That's what it is."

Her gaze is fixed across the room. "Hattie told me your dad mentioned Dan's being here to you."

"Yeah. Probably thinks I owe him an apology."

Grabbing my hand, she squeezes. "I wish you wouldn't put yourself through seeing him again. He'll be gone from your life forever soon enough."

I look down. "She's going home tomorrow, so if I'm going to do this, I have to do it now."

Her eyes are pleading when I meet them. *Don't do this.* She had this look once before when she begged me to *get rid* of my problem.

She shakes her head. "He doesn't deserve to see you."

I pull my hand away, shoving it into the back pocket of my jeans. "He doesn't get to leave this world without seeing what he's done to me."

"Do you want me to go with you?"

"No, I need to do this on my own." My smile is for her benefit only. My entire life I've done things for the benefit of others. This is my time, my moment to take back what he stole, or try to. I'm damn sure not making a special trip to see him. He doesn't deserve any favors. "I'll be okay."

THE CANCER WARD IS QUIET. I imagine that's for the comfort of the patients. It's separated from the rest of the hospital, a wing of its own. I recall this used to be the mental health floor. Otherwise referred to as the nut ward. As a fellow nutter, I'm glad the term is no longer politically correct.

Approaching the nurse's station, I smile at the pretty, young nurse who acknowledges me. "Can I help you?"

"Yes." My fingers are freezing, shaking, and the part of me just beneath the skin is crawling, wiggling as if hooked up to electrodes. "I'm looking for Daniel Skinner." I swallow, hoping the cotton making it difficult to speak will follow the saliva. "I'm his niece." *Former lover here.*

She doesn't believe me.

"My father was just here yesterday. I'm visiting my sister and thought I would come over to see Uncle Dan." I almost choke on the simple syllables of his name.

The little details must be enough to convince her. She nods. "He's down the hall, last room on the left."

How fitting.

The hall of the hospital has become long and warped, taunting me, drawing this out longer than it should be drawn.

With every step, I can feel something pulling me back. *You don't need to go there.* But I do. I need to see him. I need him to see me. I am his monster, and he can't die without knowing it. My stomach turns over and I have to stop, reaching out to steady myself with the wall. Maybe I should turn back. He's probably not even conscious anyway. But I straighten and continue, finally reaching his door after what seems like an eternity.

Inside, a nurse is checking his vitals. I hear his voice, dry and weak. The nurse looks down at him, leans closer to hear, and then gives him a playful swat. He smiles, his yellowed teeth glistening in the soft light above his head. She looks too young to be a nurse (he likes them young), dark hair and petite build. She's exactly his type. I guess not even death can tame the prowler inside him.

I step into the room and the nurse looks up at me. She's pretty. "Hey, hon," she says. "I'll be out of the way in just a sec."

I nod. Steeling my resolve, I step forward, stopping at the end of his bed. He's still looking at the sweet young nurse, no doubt trying to figure out how he can muster the strength to get a little taste. I don't mind. It gives me a moment to look over the man who shaped me. Molded me. It's odd to see him like this, so small. His hair, once thick and chestnut, is thin, his scalp shining in the soft light from behind the bed. His eyes, as expected, remain on the nurse. He's always been hyper-focused. *I get what I want, Gracie.* I steady myself against a wave of nausea. His hands are resting on the coverlet, big and wide, though their appearance has lost some of their strength.

Transported, we're no longer in the hospital room with machines keeping up with his heartbeat and oxygen levels. There's no morphine drip to take away his pain and certainly not one to take mine. We're lying naked on the faux bearskin rug he's situated in the middle of the floor. *It's romantic,* he insists. Who am I to question his knowledge of romance? What do I know at fifteen other than what he teaches me? I giggle as he sits me on top of him, growing quiet as he pushes inside of me. Closing my eyes I begin taking note of everything, the way he fills me, the feel of his hands on breasts that will never be as full as he likes them. We are a moment frozen in time. Ugly, disgusting...wrong.

I pull back to the present with a cry. The nurse looks at me, her eyes questioning if I'm okay. I nod that I am, though I can scarcely see her behind my wall of tears. I look back at him, he who is still oblivious to my presence. *I get what I want.*

The nurse smiles down at her patient, unaware that she's looking the devil in the eye. "All right, Mr. Skinner, I'll be back in a bit. You be good now." She gives me a wink and a smile as she rounds the bed to exit.

His eyes follow her, watching her ass as she rounds the bed, but she's lost when his eyes fall on me. He mouths something but I can't hear him. I want to imagine regret in the watery orbs peering at me over the length of him.

"Hi, honey," I manage after time begins again. My stomach flops as I round the bed, making sure to stay by his feet. I can't be too close. Not yet. "When's the last time we were in a room together?"

He says something else, but I can't hear him.

"Looks like we've both had a hard time of it." I look at the machines and then back to him. "At least one of us may make it out alive."

"Gracie." I heard that one.

"I don't use that name anymore. That poor girl died." My throat is tight, burning. Stomach still twisting, I sit on the bed beside him. "Dad told me I should come by and see you." He's dancing before my eyes, the sick little bastard behind water-drenched glass. "Here I am."

"Glad you came." His hand goes to his throat.

"Does it hurt to talk?"

He nods.

A smirk tugs at the corner of my mouth. "Good. I think that's good."

His eyes are glistening and after a moment I realize he's crying. *Good. I think that's good.*

"Dad says you don't have long left."

He shakes his head.

"I figured I should come by at least once."

"Thank you."

"Don't thank me yet, Uncle Dan. Or should I say *sweetheart?*" I swallow the bile that threatens to spill forth.

He winces.

"Oh, that's right. Not sweetheart. Not for a long time." He motions for me to move closer, but I shake my head. "I'm fine right here." I pat the bed. "I ran into Angel. Did she come and see you? That's why she was in town. At least that's what she said."

He nods. I wonder if he's crying because I'm here or because he needs another hit of morphine. I hope it's the latter. He deserves the pain.

I'm out of polite conversation and I've forgotten why I'm here. This was a bad idea. How did I think this would go? Can I yell at him? Take the pillow from under his head and press it against his face until his breathing quiets?

I stand and he holds a hand up to me. "Don't go."

My anger flares, igniting the flames scorching my throat. "I fucking despise you." He looks away and I lunge forward, grabbing his face to make him look at me, digging what remains of my fingernails into his flesh. "You don't get to look away. Not now."

"Please."

"Please what? Stop?" I am an inferno. *How dare you.* "I remember asking that. So many times, I asked you to stop. But you told me I liked it." My tears merge with those on his cheeks. "You told me I liked it, and I believed you." His eyes are wide, terror-filled. "I believed you. I believed every lie you told me, you fucking bastard." I release him, dropping onto the bed.

After a moment I feel his hand on my shoulder. *Is this when he will apologize? Will he absolve himself before it's too late?* The world quiets, not a sound is audible beyond my beating heart. I turn to look at him. It's only then that I realize he's not trying to comfort me. He's trying to push me. I'm sitting on his drip.

"You're not sorry, are you?"

His eyes are a mixture of fear and something else. *Contempt?*

My voice is a whisper. "Mother fucker." I stand and he tugs the tube toward him. How is it possible that he doesn't regret anything?

"Gracie."

"My name is Zed, you stupid prick."

"Why..." his voice trails off. He closes his eyes. I'm paralyzed. Is he playing the victim? He regains his ability to speak and finishes. "Why are you here?"

Are you fucking kidding me?

"Why don't you tell me, sweetie pie?" Going to the window I look out over the sun-drenched parking deck. "Not much of a view, huh?" I turn back to him. "I guess you won't need one much longer." Another wince. "Do you seriously not know why I'm here? Does the reason for my presence after almost a decade really stump you?" His stare is unnerving. I lean against the wall. "I always thought you were a smart guy, Uncle D. You certainly fooled enough people over the years." I meet his gaze despite every impulse to turn away. "Are you sorry at all?"

His voice seems stronger when he asks, "For what?"

In my life I've felt heartbreak a handful of times. The first time my uncle raped me, the moment the doctor tore the fruit from my womb, and the instant I realized I no longer wanted to live. It hurts. The inside of my chest clinches, a sharp pain radiating from the place my heart should be. It's being torn again, an old wound reopened.

I stumble over to the bed. "Why me? That's all I want to know. Why me?" He tries to look away, but I lunge forward, grabbing his face again, forcing him to look at me. "You don't regret it, fine. You're not sorry, whatever. Just tell me why you chose me. This is your last chance to do something good in your miserable fucking life." I feel the muscles attempting to work beneath my grip, his effort to get away from me, but I increase the pressure of my grasp. "Tell me why."

Our eyes lock. I can see some of who he used to be in there. Spiteful, sadistic. He's angry because now I'm in the position of power. I'm the one calling the shots.

"Because..." He takes a breath while I hold my own. "I knew you wouldn't tell."

His words knock me back. "Bullshit," I sputter.

He shrugs and my instinct is to fly at him, to rip that smug smile right off his goddamn face.

"I don't believe that." *Won't. How did he know I wouldn't tell?*

As if he's heard me, he says, "Remember Angel's doll?" He gasps for breath, a fish out of water. Or maybe he's drowning. God, I hope so. Pulling the face mask up from where it's been resting on his chin, he inhales deeply, closing his eyes.

"I don't know what you're talking about," I say, pulling his focus back. But the truth is, my gut does. Anxiety has it tripping around inside of me.

"Angel's doll." His expression reads as though I should get this from those two words, but I can't. I'm trying, racing backward in my mind to a time I played with dolls. The time before I played with men. But there is nothing.

I straighten. "I don't know what the fuck you're talking about." I move toward him, anger bubbling over in my gut, devouring the anxious tremblings that have me on the verge of discovery. "Look what you've done to me, you fucking asshole. I deserve to know why." My hands are poised to strike. "Stop jerking me around and tell me."

His hands are up in self-defense, though I won't strike him. "You didn't tell." He's whimpering. "You didn't tell."

Backing up, I've suddenly become someone else. Maybe this is what it means when people say they were disconnected from their bodies. I've always thought it was more like being high. Being aware, but only vaguely, that life is still happening, but here I am, witnessing a broken girl begging the man who tore her asunder to tell her why. It's pathetic.

I don't know how long we've been like this; me staring at him, ripping him apart in my mind and mending him back together. The teenage lovesick girl cleaning up after the angry adult version of herself. Pathetic.

Finally, back in my own body, I look at him. "Tell me."

"Angel's doll."

"Stop it! I don't know what the hell you're talking about." Gripped once more by the rage, I lunge at him, and he flinches, holding his arms out. "I'm not playing your games, you twisted motherfucker. You tell me why you chose me out of all the girls in the world or I'll—"

"You wanted her doll. The Ally one."

A flicker of memory. Amazing Ally. Mom and Dad wouldn't buy me one. Not yet. I straighten once more, backing away from the bed slowly. He doesn't need to tell me. Not now. But he will. He has to.

"Angel was such a shit." He chuckles a bit, sending himself into a coughing fit. Recovering, he continues, "She didn't even play with that doll when you weren't around."

The wall stops my retreat, its cool embrace holding me steady as I brace myself for the rest of the story. He has to tell it. I have to hear it.

My stomach lurches. "I remember."

"You were staying overnight with us, and I told you I would get the doll for you to play with, remember?" I nod. "After everyone was asleep, I got it, didn't I?" Another nod as he struggles to take in a breath. I'm on autopilot and there isn't a damn thing I can do to stop this from happening. Not now. "And I woke you up." He smiled. "You were so happy to play with that doll. Do you remember?"

I almost answer. My mouth is open to do it, to play his game, but his eyes are shining too bright. Swallowing the bile reaching toward the back of my throat, I say, "Then what?"

"You sat on the floor in front of my chair and played with her. As I watched you, I got so excited. I just felt this...thing." Another lurch from deep within me sent my hand to cover my mouth. "As I watched you play, I—"

"Masturbated." I can't listen to him describe it. Romanticize it.

His smile is soft. "And you looked up. Watched me. I asked you to sit in my lap and you did. I held you." Eyes narrowed on mine, he adds, "I came harder than I ever had in my life that night, and you didn't make a sound." His eyes are leaking, but I'm not sure if it's from the fondness of memory or disgust because he's now realizing what a monster he is. "I was worried for days that you would tell but you never did." He smiles. "That's how I knew."

My cheeks are soaked, and my chest is breaking open. "I was a *child*."

"You were born for me." I shake my head, hands covering my ears to block out the sound of his voice, but I still hear him say, "You let it all happen. That's the best thing about you, Grace, you just let things happen."

I am reeling and the world is spinning. I slide down, pulling my knees tight to my chest. He chose me for my weakness. Because he knew I could be molded. *Be a good girl.* I crawl across the floor to his trash can, allowing the contents of my breakfast to spill into it. Heaving until everything left in my belly is gone, evidenced only by the bile expelled during my last heaves. Yet still my stomach lurches, pushing up and out nothing. *I am filled with nothing.*

There's a hand on my head, and I know it's his. I pull away, leaning against the wall with my knees to my chest, sobbing until I'm vaguely aware of a dinging. I look up as the young nurse from earlier enters.

"Oh my goodness, sweetie!" She's by my side. "Are you all right?"

"Yes." I swipe at my mouth and eyes. "I threw up in the can. I'm sorry."

"No, no, that's okay. Do you need me to get someone?"

"No. Thank you." I stand up, looking down at my former lover. He's smug.

She follows my gaze. "Mr. Skinner, what's happened to your face?" She looks back at me, all concern has dissipated. "What did you do?"

What did *I* do? My eyes move from her to him. Is he smiling? That smug motherfucker. There's no way I'll let him die thinking he's won.

I point to him. "He raped me."

Scoffing, she points to him. "This man ain't raping anybody, miss." She moves away from me, going to his side. "Did you *grab* him?" She looks at me, her stare scathing. "He's a *dying* man." She straightens. "I'm calling security."

"Not now," I say. "He didn't...not today." His eyes are gleaming. Why didn't I just smother him? I screech as she reaches for the phone. "Stop!" She looks at me and I know this is the only chance I will get to set things right. "When I was ten, he raped me. And he kept raping me until I was sixteen. He told me not to tell and I didn't." I look at him. "I didn't tell anyone."

She steps away from the bed, eyes going from my uncle to me.

I straighten and look at her. "He's not a sweet man and he damn sure doesn't deserve your sympathy. He's a rapist and a child predator."

She looks down at him and then back at me. "You have to leave." She smooths out the front of her uniform. "I have to go and get help. You'd better not be here when we get back."

I look at him, delighting in the fear that's settled in those glassy orbs I once thought held love for me. *Only you, Gracie.* Going to him, I lean over, hoping the smell from my exertions makes his stomach turn here in this last moment that he will ever have with me.

"You're a monster, Uncle D., and I'm going to make sure everyone knows it. As for you, when you finally take your last breath..." My anger licks out at him. "I hope you find there *is* a hell, and I hope in that place you will have a room of your very own, and I hope in your room someone rapes you every day and makes you believe that you love it and that you love them and that they love you. And then I hope at the end of every day you realize it's all a lie."

I press my lips to his damp forehead, then straighten and leave the room. The pretty nurse is standing at the nurse's station, her eyes wet as she speaks to the other nurses surrounding her. Our eyes meet as I walk by, and I nod my thanks. I hope she tells everyone.

Twenty-Nine

My cigarette isn't helping. Maybe nothing will now. Have you ever felt a shame so deep it scoops you out? *You let things happen to you.* Those words. His words. As much as I hate him, he's right. I know it. I've always known it. Tossing the remains of my smoke down into the sand of the hospital's butt-pot, I lean forward on the bench and bury my head in hands that are still shaking despite the time that's passed since my confrontation.

I suppose the therapist will be proud that I stood up to him, that I demanded answers from him. I wonder, though, how she will explain to me what the fuck I'm supposed to do with those answers.

"Zed?" My mother's voice is soft. She's still hesitant around me. I can't blame her. We had a breakthrough outside a strip club. It's not exactly what she imagined, I'm sure. "Are you okay?"

I nod, though I'm not ready to meet her gaze. She'll know if I do. I'm translucent, apparently. Easily controlled, easily read. *You let things happen to you.* The bench groans under the additional load her body adds. I don't flinch when her hand falls on my back. It's nice to feel the weight of it, her concern, her love.

"I'm sorry," she says, voice trembling. "I'm sorry for so many things."

I should say something, but how can I? I'm not even sure my voice works anymore.

"Your sister was asking for you."

I raise my head, meeting her darkened eyes. "Does Hattie know? What he did." *Does she know how easy I am?* "I know she knows about the molestation, but does she know the rest?"

She shakes her head. "Only if you've told her."

"I haven't."

Her mouth turns down, her shoulders falling with it. "Maybe you should."

I throw my body back against the aging wood. "No way. I never want her to know what I am."

"What are you, Zed?" I look at her, ready to take a bite out of her like the old days, but something stops me. "A victim? Someone a bad guy took advantage of?" *Is that what I am?* Her lips are trembling along with my aching heart. "You can't let him keep stealing from you."

"I know." Looking away from her glassy eyes, I focus on the rooftop of the library in the distance. It's new. To me anyway. "I don't want to, but..." She's gathering my hands in her own. Despite the heat outside her skin is cool. "I think I made it easy for him."

"You can't think that way. You were a child." She forces my face up. Maybe she knows my eyes will find hers. "You did nothing wrong; do you hear me?"

The sobs are heavy, pouring out of me with a ferocity that surprises me. It's her, the little girl I was. Gasping for air, I confess, "He said he knew I wouldn't tell."

She's shocked. I know it from the way her eyes widen and the tightening of her grip. I could tell her the rest, could admit that he tested me, and I passed with flying colors, but I won't. Nothing good will come of it.

Her arms are tight around me, her hand holding my head against her shoulder as she rocks. "Shhh, sweetie. It's okay. Oh, baby girl." I cling to her. "I'm so sorry I didn't see it." She pushes me back, holding my face in her hands, pressing her forehead against mine. "The only regret I have in this life is not being there when you needed me. I'm here now, do you hear me? I'm here and I'm not going anywhere. Not ever."

Pulling back, I use my t-shirt to soak up the water from my cheeks, chin, and neck.

"Are you okay?" she asks, and I nod. "Do you want me to leave you alone for a while?" I nod again and she stands up. "I'll go and see about your sister. Will you call me if you need me?" Another nod. "Don't stay down here too long."

She turns to leave but I stop her. "Mom." She turns slowly, unsure. I can't blame her. How often do I address her? She looks as uncertain as her posture indicates. "Thank you for not giving up on me."

Smiling, she opens her mouth to speak, then merely nods, before disappearing inside the hospital.

I'VE SPENT the afternoon silent by Hattie's bed. She knows something is going on, but she's been unsuccessful in getting me to talk. I don't know how to start this conversation. This one thing, this secret, has been mine for so long, I don't know how to open this dialog, as the therapist would say. But he knew this. He knew I would keep my stupid mouth shut. That I wouldn't tell.

Her voice is rusty from lack of talking over the last few hours. "Well?"

My eyes lift to her. The baby is sleeping soundly by the bed, only occasionally jerking in her baby dreams. I wonder what they dream about. Is it the trauma of traveling through the canal? Or maybe she knows what this world holds for girls and women, the shit we have to go through just because we're considered inferior.

Fuck that, Little One. I'm going to make sure you're not looked at as weak.

"Zed?" Her smile is soft. "Talk to me."

I stand, walking over to the baby. Gently, I rest my hand on her swaddled chest to comfort her. Looking back to my sister, I say, "Do you think some girls are born to be misused? Like, branded or something."

She struggles to sit up. "No. No, I don't." Looking at her daughter, I see her eyes flare. "My little girl wasn't."

"I know she wasn't." Tracing the baby's cheek with my finger, I add, "She's going to be a warrior."

"Like her Aunt Zeddie."

Shaking my head, I move to the bed and lower myself to the edge. "No. She won't be anything like me."

Hattie's brow creases. "What's going on in that big head of yours?"

I smile at her endearing insult.

"Seriously." She jabs my arm. "Tell me what's going on. You've been quiet all afternoon. Is it that guy Mom told me about?"

"Oliver?" I shake my head. "No. I mean, we're fucked—"

"Language!" She points to the baby with a smile and a wink.

"Sorry." I smile to appease her. "I shouldn't have gotten involved with him. I don't know how to be a girlfriend."

"You put too much pressure on yourself."

I shake my head. "That's not it." Turning to her, I brace myself. "I don't know how to do it because all I've ever been is someone to..." I look at my niece. "Have sex with." *God, fuck would've worked so much better.*

Her lips purse together the way they always have when she's perplexed. Now she knows this conversation will be difficult. Sisters know.

"I confronted Uncle Dan today."

Her eyes go wide. "What?"

"Yeah. Went over to his room and walked right in." I swipe at a rebellious tear. "He was flirting with the nurse. Flirting. Can you believe it? Dying and he still can't keep it in his pants."

Her hand is covering mine and she pulls me to the bed. "What happened?" She isn't talking about today. I know it because sisters know.

The room is quiet, expectant. The wallpaper seems to come away from the wall a little more, clamoring for the big reveal. Maybe I am the girl who wouldn't tell, the one who would lay quietly as her uncle forced his evil into her. Maybe I was. It's time, I know. Time to let go of what he's done to me. Never forgiveness. He doesn't deserve that, but maybe I do.

"Zed?" her voice is soft.

"He stole everything from me. My sense of security, my trust, my childhood." Swiping at the tears flowing freely now, I grab her hands. "He raped me." I wait for her recoil, but she holds my hand tighter.

"How long?"

"Until I thought I loved him." Her free hand flies to trembling lips, shaking fingers playing over the delicate pink flesh. I know this reaction too. "I was willing for two years." A guffaw escapes from me, lingering in the room before dying away. "I was fourteen and I thought we were a couple." I sniffle. "I thought I loved him because he told me I did. Over and over again." I look at her, heart banging to escape the treacherous cage it's housed in. "He told me I liked it, and I believed him. What kind of person does that make me?"

Her voice is small. "Confused. Manipulated. Traumatized."

I shrug and look away. "Maybe."

"Absolutely." She tugs my hand and I turn back to her. "There's nothing wrong with you. He tried with Angel too, remember? He's just sick."

I shake my head. "Maybe. Or maybe there's something wrong with me. Maybe I have something in me that lets them know I'm easy to use."

"No. You can't think like that. You can't take responsibility for his actions. This is not your fault."

"It is." I nod. "I make it easy for them." I'm back in my uncle's den, Amazing Ally clutched in my arms as he squeezes me to him, his hand pumping, his eyes watching me. I return as the moan escapes his open mouth, my stomach roiling. "I...let things happen to me."

She's found her voice again, and it's strong when she says, "Stop it. This is what they do. They make you think it's some defect in you but it's in them."

"You don't understand, Hattie. You can't and I'm so happy that you can't. This means you haven't had pieces stolen from you."

"But I did." Climbing out from under the bed sheets, she sits close to me and grabs my hand. "He stole *you*."

I drop my head, unable to meet her watery gaze.

Unlacing our fingers, she turns my hand over, tracing the firefly on the back of my wrist. "You have always been the most important person in the world to me, Zed." She smiles as she looks over at the baby. "You have to take a backseat to the bambino now, of course."

A wisp of laughter escapes me. "Of course." Following her gaze, I add, "I wouldn't have it any other way."

She squeezes my hand as she turns back to me. "I'm sorry this happened to you."

"Thanks." Shifting, I lace our fingers again. Taking a deep breath, I say, "I asked him why he chose me. Today. When I went to talk to him." She remains quiet and I think it's to give me time to move forward. "He said it's because he knew I wouldn't tell." Bracing myself, I add, "He also said I let things happen to me."

"Zed."

I wave off the encouragement she's about to try. "He's right."

"He isn't."

I meet her eyes. "He is."

"You can't let him do this to you."

"But that's what I do, Hattie. I let people do things to me." Breaking our connection, I push my trembling hands through hair I haven't washed in two days. "He tested me. Before."

"What do you mean?"

"He...masturbated in front of me." I gasp. "Oh god." I look at her, not surprised to find she's horrified. "I didn't tell, and he knew." My pain escapes in another choking sob. "Was I born for this?"

"No!" Her arm is around me, pulling me close. "No one is born to be a victim." She's already a pro at this mothering thing. "He just needs you to believe that." Releasing me, she moves to the center of the bed and pats the space in front of her for me to follow. When I've settled, she places one hand on each knee, giving me an encouraging squeeze. "If I've learned anything about you over the last few months, it's that you are formidable and you can survive anything."

"I don't think so."

"I do. You have a chance here to let what he said keep you in place, standing still in this spot where he's the victor. Or..." I try to look away, but she catches my chin. "Or you decide that he holds no power over you anymore. You are not the girl he says you are."

Old Zed is gnashing, clawing to get at her. How dare she. But there's something else—someone else—staring at my little sister, feeling her love, and understanding that she's right. She seems to sense this battle going on within me.

"Life is hard to figure out and you've got some catching up to do, but I'm here and Mom is here. We've got you." With that, her arms are around me and the Old Zed is flailing.

Pulling back, I nod. What else can I do? I never expected this, any of it. When I came back home, I was lost, desolate, and now I can see a glimmer in the distance. New Zed is waving to me from there, a genuine smile on her face. I want to get to her. Can I?

"You okay?" Hattie asks.

I nod again. "Yeah. Just numb, I guess."

"I get that." I look at her and she laughs. "I know you don't think I can, but I do. Not in the same way as you, but I get it."

"What do I do now? Where do I go from here?"

Leaning forward, she presses her forehead to mine. "Anywhere you want."

THIRTY

My dad was the only mourner at the funeral. I went to the cemetery, of course, but kept my distance, watching as the preacher gave his final sermon to the man it wouldn't help. I watched as my father laid a rose on the casket, how he wept with his hand pressed against the glistening wood, and then I watched as the coffin was lowered into the ground. I was glad it hadn't rained that day. My uncle didn't deserve the heavens crying for him.

That was months ago. Time, as it has the tendency to do, has moved on and the world has continued to spin.

Now I'm sitting outside of Hattie's house. We're celebrating baby Amelia's four-month mark. Mom and Duke are already here. Duke, no doubt, making googly grandpa eyes at his granddaughter. The man is smitten, and I think it is adorable.

My phone pings as I'm pushing the door of the old Bronco open to head inside. It's Lucinda. She's still in Santa Fe, still working at her sister's company, though she may be making a move to another company soon. She doesn't mention her ex often anymore. I think that's a good sign.

Second interview today!

I pull my coat tight against January's bite.

You've got this! Knock their socks off.

Why I always talk in cliches when trying to be encouraging I'll never know. Maybe one day I can find words to inspire that are my own.

Hattie greets me at the door. She told me once, after coming home from the hospital, that she had a dream when she passed out after the delivery. We were kids, lying in the grass in front of our Gramma's house, staring up at the fireflies dancing above us. *"I told you that I wished I could light up like them and you said—"*

"You do."

She's looking at me now, probably wondering why my eyes are glassy. "You good?"

I nod. "Yeah. Those wind gusts will knock your socks off."

Her hands are on my face. "Good lord, you're freezing! Get in here." Her arm is around my waist and her head is on my shoulder as we walk into the dining room with the rest of our brood.

Mom comes to the door, greeting me with a smile and a quick embrace. "Hey, baby."

"Hey, Mom."

"You okay?"

I chuckle. "You guys don't have to keep asking me that." I look at all of them. "I've honestly never been better."

"All right then," Mom says. "Are you ready to eat? I made your favorite."

AFTER DINNER, Hattie and I are sitting in the living room, a quiet respite from the rest of the group who have decided to play a game of Rook. Amelia is nursing, her little hand pressing against her mother's breast as if to hurry things along. Hattie looks at me. "Are you still going to your counseling group?"

"Yes. In fact, I finally told them everything."

Smiling, she gives me a playful nudge. "It's about time."

I chuckle. "My friend Deidre said the same thing. Said I shouldn't have kept something like that inside for so long and that it's no surprise I'm eaten up with anger."

Hattie laughs. "Wow. She sounds like a peach."

"She tells it like it is," I say with a laugh. "It's refreshing."

"How did they take it?"

"The best way a group of effed-up failed suicides can, I guess."

Her brow crinkles. "What does that mean?"

"It means they understood."

"What about the leader?"

I can't keep the pride from my posture. "She applauded me for my honesty."

Hattie laughs. "Well, that's something at least."

"Yeah."

Switching Amelia to her other breast, she asks, "Did Oliver call?"

"He did." I smile and lean toward her conspiratorially. "We're going on a date."

She smiles, wiping milk from the baby's face. "Yay!" Sometimes I ache to have my own little one. I'm still not even sure I'm capable of it anymore. Hattie is looking at me. "I hope it works out with you two. I really like him."

I smile delighting in the flutter the mention of his name creates in my stomach. "Me too, Little Sister," I say. "Me too."

THE END.

Acknowledgments

There is a slew of people behind every book. Critique partners, beta readers, alpha readers, sometimes family readers, spouses or partners, editors, and many, many more. They all come together at different stages in a book's life to add their touch and make it ready for the world. This one is no different. I've been terrified to write these acknowledgments because I fear I'll miss someone. Just know, if you offered me encouragement, suggestions, or just a shoulder to cry on, I appreciate you.

I would be remiss if I didn't thank the first person to set eyes on this story (after me, of course). Lynn Chandler Willis, you read those first two pages and told me two things: This is going to be good, and it's too in your face, you're going to scare readers away. You were right on the second count. I hope you're right on the first. Thank you for encouraging me to keep telling this story.

Jennifer Lane, you were my first critique partner with this. Your love for this story and your continued support means the world to me. Kristi H., you helped me soften some language and you rooted for this book as hard as I did. Thank you. Debby (Beece) May, I am eternally grateful to you for your work as my WFWA mentor, and for connecting me with Gina. Your belief in this book means the world to me. To my critique gals; Colleen Young, Megan Musgrove, and Dana Armstrong, thank you for having my back and helping me make sense of things when I go off the rails.

Gina Panettieri, you were Zed's champion. I often wonder where she might be if the pandemic hadn't come along. Thank you for seeing the potential in this story, and thank you for taking a chance on both of us.

Kerry Chaput, your (often daily) encouragement and your friendship in this crazy world of publishing keeps me going. Thank you for being here through it all.

To my beta readers: Miranda Hawley, Gevera Bert Piedmont, Micki Morency, Gloria Mattioni, and Tanya E. Williams, you're all amazing and I appreciate you so much. Thank you for reading Zed's story and giving me the feedback I needed to (finally) be ready to send her out into the world.

Last, but certainly not least, to Shane. You have never wavered in your support of this crazy writing dream of mine. I love you, always.

About the Author

Sayword B. Eller writes upmarket fiction about screwed up people just trying to get their lives together. She has published several titles independently, including a collection of short stories, and her short story The Weight of the Words, was featured in the October 2018 issue of The Write Launch. Sayword holds an MFA in Creative Writing from Southern New Hampshire University. She lives in Central Arkansas with her husband and cat.

www.ingramcontent.com/pod-product-compliance
Lightning Source LLC
Chambersburg PA
CBHW022023310726
48972CB00006B/1786